12

NOLON KING
DAVID WRIGHT

Copyright © 2015 by Sterling & Stone

All rights reserved.

No part of this book may be reproduced in any form or by any electronic or mechanical means, including information storage and retrieval systems, without written permission from the author, except for the use of brief quotations in a book review.

The authors greatly appreciate you taking the time to read our work. Please consider leaving a review wherever you bought the book, or telling your friends about it, to help us spread the word.

Thank you for supporting our work.

To YOU, the reader.
Thank you for taking a chance on us.
Thank you for your support.
Thank you for the emails.
Thank you for the reviews.
Thank you for reading and joining us on this road.

12

Prologue

PALM ISLES, Florida
 6:15 p.m.
 A Wednesday in October

AS A POLICE OFFICER, you wake up each day knowing it could be your last.

You get used to it, even if you can never really come to terms with that part of the job. Like the smoker who can't think about cancer. The obese person who still shovels food into his mouth. Death is there, sure, but far away. A someday specter.

But you can't act surprised when Death eventually comes to claim you.

It's your handshake with Fate.

I know my time will come, and I won't complain when it does.

But you're never prepared for Fate claiming the lives of those closest to you.

. . .

OFFICER CLARENCE DUMONT stepped out of the police cruiser to a bank of flashing lights bouncing off the other squad cars and ambulances parked in awkward rows along the shopping center parking lot in front of Goldman's Diner.

The shooting had happened less than fifteen minutes ago, but the media were already setting up camp just outside the barrier of police tape and officers, many off-duty, called in to manage the scene.

The front of the diner looked like a war zone — broken windows, blood everywhere, bodies still littering the floor just inside the doorway. Forensics was photographing corpses, collecting evidence while the paramedics tended to the wounded, both inside the diner and outside in ambulances. A trauma copter was kissing the ground about ninety yards away.

His partner, Patrick Allan, stood beside him, sighing, "Jesus."

Clarence searched the crowd of patrons and staffers gathered outside the diner, being treated by paramedics or interviewed by the police, scanning the scene for Maggie.

Please, be alive. Please, be alive.

Clarence was frozen, unable to will his legs forward for fear that she was among the dead.

"You coming?" Patrick looked back on his way to the diner.

Clarence reluctantly followed, feeling Death's finality anchoring his every move.

So much blood.

He passed a couple of paramedics treating one of the waitresses, Viv, for a gunshot wound to her arm.

She met his eyes and immediately looked away, her sorrow instantly visible.

Oh, God.

Clarence was trained to meet his own end; nothing could

prepare him for what he found on the other side of those shattered doors.

6 a.m. - 7 a.m.
(12 HOURS EARLIER)

ONE

Maggie Kent

Maggie woke to a flashing alarm: *12:00*.

She was certain she'd overslept. Panic swelled inside her, a metallic taste coating her tongue as she reached out to grab her phone. But Maggie's fumbling fingers pushed the phone off the edge and behind the nightstand.

Dammit!

Maggie scrabbled for the lamp then flicked on the light, momentarily blind until her eyes adjusted to the brightness.

She sat up and got out of bed, her bare feet hitting cold carpet. A shiver ran through her. She thought of McKenna, hoping her six-year old had enough blankets to temper the cold snap since they couldn't afford to run the heat all night.

Maggie pulled the nightstand back and leaned over, the corner pushing sharply into her stomach as her fingers blindly searched along the carpet.

She couldn't be late.

Not today of all days, or there was no way on earth Loretta would allow an hour-long break at noon, even for Maggie's life-changing phone call.

She closed her fingertips around the phone's edge and raised it gingerly so as not to drop it again.

The phone's face read: 6:14 a.m.

She was fourteen minutes late. Manageable, but no margin for traffic or other delays if she was going to drop McKenna off at school and make it back across town to Goldman's Diner before Loretta noticed she wasn't there.

I hope Viv and Barbara will cover for me.

Maggie raced from her bedroom and was about to head down the hall to wake McKenna when she saw that her little girl was already awake — sitting in her pink and purple PJs at the tiny kitchen table, staring at the iPad, watching cartoons, a bowl of milk with a few stray Fruit Loops in front of her.

"Hi, Mommy." McKenna looked up with a smile.

Maggie was relieved that she didn't have to wake the girl — ten minutes shaved from the morning routine.

"Good morning. What time did you get up?" Maggie leaned down and kissed her daughter on the head.

"I dunno. Five something?"

"Why didn't you go back to bed, honey?"

"I wasn't tired," she said without moving her eyes from the tablet.

Maggie hated the thought of her daughter waking up an hour early before school and doing nothing but watching cartoons, but it wasn't an argument she was ready to have. And besides, it was one of those educational PBS cartoons, not one of those stupid shows that seemed solely designed to rob children's innocence with crass language, violence, and overly commercialized content.

"Okay, I need you to pause the cartoons, brush your teeth, and get dressed."

"Can I watch them when I'm done?"

"Yes," Maggie said, double checking that her daughter's clothes were in the living room where McKenna laid them out each night before school. They were. Except one of her blue shoes was missing.

"Where's your other shoe?" Maggie looked toward the

front door where they kept their shoes, still not seeing the matching blue.

"I dunno," McKenna said, still glued to the tablet.

"Well, find it, or get another pair of shoes, please. I need to get in the shower."

AFTER MAGGIE SHOWERED, she spent too long blow drying her long brown hair. She wondered if this was why so many moms cut their hair short, because they couldn't afford the luxury of this much time. Maggie would've chopped her hair a long time ago if she thought it wouldn't make her look too much like her childhood pictures, back when she was forced to wear her hair in a low-maintenance cut. She hated the Dutch Boy look and refused to go back, even if it added an extra fifteen to twenty minutes to her morning routine.

After getting dressed, Maggie went to check on McKenna to find her *still* in her pajamas, watching cartoons. The clock read 6:40.

She needed to leave in five minutes.

"McKenna!" she yelled, shriller than intended.

McKenna looked up, blue eyes wide beneath her brown bangs, seemingly surprised as if the few simple tasks she was responsible for had slipped entirely from her mind.

"What?"

"I need you to get dressed! We're running late."

"Okay," McKenna said, running to the living room and grabbing her clothes.

Maggie went to the fridge to grab their lunches. McKenna returned to the kitchen chair, still staring at the iPad as she slowly removed her PJs.

"No, you're not gonna sit here and watch cartoons while you take forever to get dressed!" Maggie grabbed the tablet, snatching it quicker than she'd meant to.

The iPad, like her phone a half hour ago, flew from Maggie's fingers and slapped the kitchen floor.

Shit!

Maggie bent over to grab the tablet, hoping the flimsy silicone case had protected it. She picked it up, turned it over in her hands, and saw the cracks in the glass against the darkened screen. Not only had the front split from a scar at the bottom to a widening web at the top, the ON button refused to bring the iPad back to life.

McKenna saw the broken iPad and cried out, "You broke it!"

Maggie stared at the screen, helpless to rewind time.

"I'm sorry, sweetie. It was an accident."

"No! You threw it!" McKenna's voice cracked, and she folded her arms in front of her chest.

McKenna rarely threw fits. She was a good kid, more often than not. But staring at the broken iPad — the iPad Daddy had given her — McKenna's face flared from pale to full red, tears streaming down her face.

I do not have time for this today!

How was it that crap like this only happened on the one day — of all the days — that she absolutely *had* to be on time, and relatively calm for her big call?

Maggie had to soothe McKenna without bargaining, without scolding her and making things worse, and without delay. Trying to be a perfect parent and do all the "right things" was difficult to do while playing beat the clock. They needed to hit the road.

Maggie sat next to McKenna at the table. She removed the girl's pajama top and replaced it with her school uniform shirt, all while trying to settle her nerves.

"I'm sorry, honey. I didn't mean to break the iPad, but you need to listen when I say it's time to get ready, not just sit there and keep watching cartoons."

"I *was* getting ready! And you just grabbed it and threw it!"

"I didn't *throw it.*" Maggie was about to also explain that McKenna wasn't *really* getting ready. Half her attention was on the cartoons, and she needed to focus on her morning tasks. But Maggie wasn't about to argue semantics with a six-year old in the middle of a meltdown. Especially not this morning.

Part of her wanted to apologize, say she was sorry, and promise to get a new iPad. She *did* break it after all. But a few things prevented her from taking the easier route.

Maggie couldn't afford a new iPad. Hell, Nick couldn't even afford one. She still wasn't sure if he'd come by it illegally. She also didn't want to coddle her daughter or reward a tantrum. It was a tough line to ride, being a single mother — particularly when most of Maggie's foster parents and eventual adoptive mother had been disciplinarian enough to make Catholic school nuns seem like dirty hippies.

Maggie didn't want to be overbearing, but she wasn't about to raise a spoiled kid who walked all over her. She couldn't count the number of mothers she ran into — at school, on play dates, or at the diner — who let their kids boss them around, so concerned with being their children's friends that they were inadvertently making monsters.

Finding the balance was tough. Half the time, Maggie wasn't sure which side she was erring on: too strict or too lenient. There had to be some middle ground where you did right by your kid without terrifying them into a lack of confidence, or an inability to take chances in life.

After slipping on her daughter's dress, Maggie hugged McKenna and stroked her hair, speaking calmly as she explained that breaking the iPad was an accident and that she was sorry. Maggie also said they'd get it fixed, though she wasn't about to promise a time line, especially without knowing if a broken screen *could be* fixed any cheaper than getting a new tablet.

I wonder if Nick's stolen iPad includes an extended warranty?

Maggie finished with a hug. Whenever she yelled at or disciplined McKenna, she made sure she hugged her tight and let her know she was loved. Maggie wasn't sure if it was the "right thing to do" according to the parenting books and magazines, but she did know that *she* was rarely hugged as a child, and there were few things worse than a child wondering if their family loved them.

"I'm sorry for not being ready," McKenna said.

Maggie kissed her head. "Okay, grab your lunch and bag, we've gotta get going."

With everything settled, they left the apartment about twenty minutes behind. As they took the elevator down from the fifth floor, Maggie hoped traffic wasn't a nightmare on their way to school.

She strapped McKenna into the back seat, climbed into the front, and started the car. As she started backing out of her spot, the car made an awful thumping.

Oh no!

She put the car into park, got out, and checked her tires. The rear passenger side was flat.

"Dammit!" she cried out, too loud. Maggie rarely cursed, and almost never in front of McKenna. Today was testing her resolve early.

This can't be happening. I don't have time to change a tire!

Back in the car, Maggie pulled back into the parking spot.

"What's wrong, Mommy?"

"We've got a flat tire."

Maggie grabbed her phone, searched for Red Cab's number, then dialed and waited as the phone rang on the other end for what felt like forever.

Of course.

A woman answered a moment before Maggie was about to hang up. "Red Cab, how can I help you?"

Maggie told her where she was and that she needed a ride.

"Okay, I'll have a driver out to you in about thirty-five minutes."

"Thirty-five minutes?" Maggie hadn't taken a cab in years, but didn't remember having to wait so long the last time.

"Yeah, all our drivers are out on calls right now. If we can get someone to you sooner, we will."

"Okay, thanks." Maggie sighed and hung up the phone.

She sat in the car, staring straight ahead at the apartment building, trying to decide what to do. She could call her work and tell them she was running late, but that would most certainly mean she wouldn't be able to take her break at twelve.

I could just call in sick.

Maggie smiled as the idea floated by.

It had been years since she'd called in sick to a job — even when she was red-eyed and clammy. Calling in sick today would solve all her problems. And it was so easy to do. While Loretta got mad when people were late, she couldn't get mad if Maggie was sick. At least not *as* mad. And Maggie could be home when she got her phone call, not having to worry about dealing with Loretta's mood swings.

Hmm, a day off would be good. We can have a nice mother-daughter day at home.

Truth be told, Maggie needed a day off, especially after all the crap with Nick this week.

Yet some small voice in the back of her mind reprimanded her.

No, I can't just call in sick. Loretta is counting on me. Viv and Barbara are counting on me. Sebastian is counting on me.

Working the diner was hard enough without someone calling in sick. It was so short staffed to begin with. A missing cook or server made the day exponentially harder. And somehow those always seemed to be the days when the diner was most packed. If Maggie called in, she was screwing the staff.

And Maggie didn't want to do that. She genuinely liked her coworkers. Well, most of them. But more than that, Maggie didn't want to be *that person* — the one who called in when they weren't really sick. Part of the problem rather than the solution.

No, she'd go to work, late or not, and figure out a way to take her phone call. If Loretta had a problem with it, well, Maggie would deal with it then.

As much as she hated calling in, Maggie hated conflict more. And Loretta could be either the world's nicest person or its bitchiest, depending on the swing of her mood — and sometimes with just minutes between them. Loretta might really freak out if Maggie had to step out for an hour, especially if they were in the weeds.

Hopefully, Loretta will be in a good mood at lunchtime.

"Mommy, what are we doing?" McKenna asked from the backseat.

Maggie realized that she'd been staring into space for at least a few minutes.

"We have a flat, honey. I called a cab."

"How did we get a flat?"

"I dunno," Maggie said.

But a part of her *did know*.

Or at least she thought she did.

And just like that, Maggie's mood moved from anxious to scared. When she thought about *who* might have flattened her tire, her stomach tightened.

Nick.

Maggie got out of the car and looked at the rear passenger tire, squinting to see if there was broken glass or a nail or something in the parking space. She saw nothing, but that didn't mean that there wasn't anything there. It could've been wedged in the wheel, pushed deeper into the tread when she backed up and pulled back into her spot.

Or maybe Nick knifed the tire to get back at me.

She shook her head. No, Nick wouldn't do that.

Would he?

She looked at her phone and saw the five texts from Nick she'd ignored yesterday and last night. The texts she'd told herself not to read until after her phone call later, to keep them from ruining her mood.

She drew them up on her phone.

THE FIRST: *Call me.*

The second: *Please, we need to talk.*

The third: *I can't believe you're doing this to me. Really? An Order of Protection? PROTECTION FROM ME?!?! What the hell, Maggie?*

The fourth: *This is BULLSHIT, MAGGIE. I NEVER LAID A HAND ON MCKENNA!*

The fifth: *She's my daughter, too. Don't think you can cut me out of her life that easy, BITCH!*

MAGGIE WINCED at the last word, recalling the number of times he'd said the same thing to her face. Each time, looking like he was ready to hit her — again.

Maggie imagined Nick getting drunker as the moon brightened last night, his texts growing increasingly violent the more his brain steeped in fresh liquor. And alcohol wasn't the worst thing he did. There was also the cocaine habit. That scared her most. It changed him from someone she once loved into someone she now feared.

Still, she couldn't imagine he'd flatten her tire.

Would he?

For one, he lived on the other side of town, and if he were drunk as hell, he probably wouldn't risk getting another DUI.

Yeah, but he could've had one of his scumbag friends drive him over. Hell, they were probably all too happy to help him out.

Nick's friends were half the reason she filed the order against him. He'd had visitation rights to McKenna every other weekend. But as McKenna told her some of the things she'd seen, including drug use and one of his friends hitting a woman in the apartment Nick shared with a few of the guys, Maggie knew she had to get her daughter away from that element before something horrible happened — like someone pulling a gun or worse. No, Maggie didn't think Nick would ever *intentionally* hurt their daughter, but drunk or high on cocaine or any of the other stuff he claimed not to do anymore, God only knew what could happen.

Someone was outside Maggie's window.

She jumped, startled, thinking it would be Nick, pissed and ready to hurt her.

But it was Abe, her neighbor.

Maggie rolled down the window, smiling at the awkward tall man with the thick, messy dark hair and thick black-framed glasses. He looked late thirties, though she'd never asked him in the year and a half she'd lived at the apartments, nor in the same amount of time that he'd been coming in for lunch every weekday at the diner.

"Hi, Maggie." He smiled, awkwardly like always, holding his laptop bag, dressed as if for work even though she didn't think he was due to the computer shop near her diner until 8:30 or so. He peered into the backseat. "Hi, McKenna."

"Hi, Mr. Abe," McKenna said in a singsong voice with no trace of her earlier meltdown. "I finally killed the Ender Dragon!"

"Oh, that's great," Abe said. Maggie hoped McKenna wasn't going to go into a big long story about her Minecraft exploits again.

McKenna had first met Abe when he'd come over a few months ago to help Maggie get rid of a nasty virus on her computer. They'd talked Minecraft for the better part of the hour spent killing the virus, then another hour into the pizza dinner Maggie ordered to thank Abe for helping her. Ever since, whenever they ran into one another, she'd go on telling him some Minecraft story or another, leaving Maggie often smiling and whispering, "Sorry."

"Hi." She gave Abe her best waitress smile, despite her sour mood. "Off to work this early?"

"Yes," he said. "We're a bit backed up, so I figured better to go in early than stay late. Something wrong? I noticed you've all been sitting here for a bit."

"A flat," she said, sighing.

"Oh, man, that stinks. Do you need a ride?"

"Oh, you don't need to do that," Maggie said, not wanting to inconvenience him, as he *was* trying to get to work early. "I called a cab."

"Oh." He looked almost dejected, like a wounded schoolboy who just confessed his crush to a girl who wanted nothing to do with him.

A couple of the women at the diner teased Maggie that Abe had a crush on her, why else would he *only* sit at her station? But Maggie thought the idea was ridiculous. Abe was just a nice guy, and had never given her a hint of interest, in her or *any* girls, really. He was painfully shy, and barely managed small talk. But he'd never extended it beyond that. Even sitting in her booth, Abe seemed more focused on his laptop than social interaction.

She felt bad turning down the ride so quickly but wasn't sure what might make things seem less awkward than they were already starting to feel.

"Okay, well, have a good day," he said, turning and heading toward his car.

Maggie looked at the phone. Still another thirty minutes

until the cab's arrival — *if* it was on time. Also, he did work in the same shopping plaza as her. On the other end, but still close.

"Wait," she called out.

Abe turned.

"Could we swing by McKenna's school?"

"Sure," Abe said, smiling.

TWO

Abe Mcdonald

ABE WOKE ANXIOUS, doubts nipping at confidence built slowly over the past few months, second guesses chewing his resolve.

He slid out of bed and slunk off to the shower. Along the way, he caught his reflection and was surprised by what he saw in the mirror. The man in the glass wasn't the usual loser Abe was used to seeing. No, this version of Abe looked confident, ready to face the world and seize his moment — no matter what Fate decided.

He met his stare and repeated his usual affirmations into the mirror.

"I am smart. I am strong. I am willing to do what must be done to get what's mine."

He'd been repeating the mantra for six months, ever since he started going to his confidence coach, Craig Strong. Usually, the words did little to boost his morale. They helped, sure, but Abe rarely believed them.

Today, however, something felt different about the words. Something felt different about *him*.

Today is my day!

Abe was no longer the weak person he'd been for the past three decades and change — that wimp who'd let people stomp all over him. Craig had taught Abe that he was a good person, worthy of respect and love, no matter what others, particularly Abe's mother, would've led you to believe.

Just the thought of Mother caused his confident reflection to waver.

He repeated his mantra.

"I am smart. I am strong. I am willing to do what must be done to get what's mine."

Abe headed into the shower, his last in this apartment.

He wondered what the panhandle would be like. He'd only lived in two places all his life, his mother's house and this apartment. He could hardly believe that he'd be starting a new life in less than twenty-four hours.

Yeah, if I don't chicken out.

He hated that trembling weakness, that voice of doubt that refused to leave his subconscious.

Craig had said this wasn't really Abe's voice. It was the collective voice of everyone who had ever held power over him. It was the voice of his mother, the bullies, the boss who didn't appreciate him, every girl who ever laughed in his face. It was the voice of people who didn't matter without his allowing them to.

He had to stop listening to the voice. Had to substitute it with his own programming until *his* voice became his life's overriding dictator.

"I am smart. I am strong. I am willing to do what must be done to get what's mine."

Abe scrubbed harder.

One of the few regrets he'd have tomorrow would be never seeing his boss, Raj's, face once he realized that Abe was gone. Raj would have to run the shop on his own. *Then* he'd finally see what a valuable, and indispensable, employee Abe had always been. *Abe* had kept the shop afloat the past four years, even though he'd only been given a single raise. Raj would regret not treating him better.

Abe smiled.

He wondered how many people would miss him. Wondered how many people would have suspected he would do what he planned to do. How many whispers from people who had nothing better to do than gossip saying, "Oh, yeah, I always figured he'd go and do that someday."

Judgmental fucks.

Abe stared at himself naked in the mirror and for the first time in a long while felt like he didn't look too bad. He'd been working out, transforming some of his scrawny frame to muscle, not that she'd be likely to care. *She* would love him for who he was, not what he looked like. He could tell that about her. She wasn't like the girls who'd always laughed in his face.

She was different.

And in those moments when he wondered how he could possibly know she'd like him, he had to pull out the biggest of affirmations — the one he still had trouble believing.

You are someone special. You will be loved.

He stared in the mirror and told himself that, but not out loud. That was the one affirmation Abe had trouble voicing anywhere but in his most private thoughts.

Abe's God would say that *no, he was not special. No, he would not be loved.*

Abe's God was the cruel bastard of a God that his mother had drummed into his conscious, as if making him believe would erase her own plentitude of sins.

Abe went to the kitchen, still naked, and made himself a microwave egg, ham, and spinach omelet. He poured himself a glass of orange juice then turned on the tiny TV at his small kitchen table and watched the local news. Today, their biggest concern was some proposed dog park that some citizens were trying to get the city commissioners to vote against because it was too close to their precious gated community.

Tomorrow, nobody would care about the parks. The only

thing on the news would be what Abe did and people wondering where he'd gone.

He finished breakfast and put his dishes in the spotless sink. He thought about washing them but decided to live a little instead. Leave them for the management company that ran the apartments to sort. Abe never much liked them anyway. Bitches that looked at him with phony smiles then laughed behind his back as soon as he left.

There was a time when he would've gone to great lengths to convince these women that he was unworthy of their ridicule. But as Craig said in his seminars, a True Man didn't care what duplicitous women like this thought of him.

A True Man lived the life he wanted, without apology, without seeking permission, true to himself and himself alone.

Abe chuckled, thinking about the dishes in the sink. He thought about taking a shit and leaving the toilet with a steamer. But he didn't have to shit this morning. Maybe his nerves, binding him up more than normal.

He went to his bedroom and dressed.

He looked in his mirror and rather liked the confident man staring back. A man who knew what he wanted and wasn't afraid to go out and get it. The kind of man Abe had always wanted to be — but was only now finding the courage to become.

He looked out the window, down at the parking lot, and saw Maggie and her daughter backing out of their space. For a moment, he wondered if the tire wasn't flat after all. Or maybe Maggie would try to drive to work with the flat. That would ruin everything.

She stopped the car, got out, and saw the flat tire.

Abe's heart raced as part of him thought she would turn and look at his apartment on the third floor, that she would somehow know that he'd slashed her tire.

But she didn't.

12

Maggie got back into her car and eased back into the space.

Exactly as he'd planned.

ABE WAS SHAKING the entire time he approached Maggie's car, wondering if he could go through with it.

He stood outside her car as she stared straight ahead, seemingly lost in thought, not seeing him. For a moment, he saw this as a sign to turn back. Forget everything.

No. I must stay the course.

When Maggie accepted his offer of a ride moments later, he felt like the train was in motion and now there was nothing to do but take the ride and see where it brought them.

As Maggie got out of the car, Abe noticed that her long brown hair was messier than normal. He figured she must've been in a rush.

McKenna climbed out of the backseat, and as she did so, Abe watched as her long, thin legs spread and Abe caught a glimpse of light-colored — *are they white or pink?* — underwear beneath her sky-blue dress.

His heart racing, he turned away quickly, hoping Maggie hadn't spotted him looking.

Fortunately, she seemed too preoccupied to notice.

As he led the girls to his car, doubt churned in his gut.

I can't really do this. Can I?

THREE

Tim Hewitt

TIM WOKE TO SCREAMING — his father standing over him yelling, "What the hell is this?"

Before his blurred eyes could focus, or his hands could find his glasses, his gut twisted at the possibilities of what his father might have found. The hidden porno flash drive from Dima? His diary, in which he'd detailed his father's brutalities against him, even though he kept it locked on his computer? Or maybe the forbidden candy, also from Dima, which he kept hidden in the back of his closet?

He put on his glasses and saw what his father was holding: probably worse than all three fears put together.

Porn, his father might overlook with a "boys will be boys" attitude or an "at least my son's not a fag" comment, given that his father seemed to have an unhealthy fear that his son might be gay. The diary stated truth. Maybe his father wouldn't see things the same way, but the truth was the truth, and that's all there was. The candy was a different story. His father was strict on what Tim was allowed to eat. This despite the fact that Tim was easily the skinniest kid in ninth grade and his father was absurdly obese. The candy, for some reason, would probably be worse than the porn and the diary.

But this might be the worst of all.

It was a progress report, one that Tim thought he had left in his school locker — a report that he'd forged his father's signature on.

He wanted to ask where his father had found it — Tim thought he'd stuffed it in his locker. But staring at the paper in his father's shaking fist, he realized that no, he hadn't put it in his locker. He was running late for his bus, and had shoved it into his algebra book before forgetting to hide it.

"Do you want to explain this?" His father's red, balding face was practically purple, eyes the color of wet brick behind his thick-framed glasses. His hot, sour breath fogged Tim's face as he leaned over the boy's bed.

Tim backed away toward the wall to give himself some more space.

"Don't you back away from me!" His father grabbed Tim by his thick curly hair and yanked him forward — hard.

Tim cried out, and his father let go.

But his father wasn't done.

"What is this?"

"A progress report."

"A progress report, what?"

"A progress report, sir."

"And what is this?" He pointed to the signature. "Is this my signature?"

"No, sir." Tim looked down at his bed.

"That's right. It's not my signature. And yet it says my name, doesn't it?"

"Yes, sir."

"You look at me when I'm talking to you, boy."

"Yes, sir."

Tim looked up and into his father's hateful brown eyes. Tim had often wondered how his own flesh and blood could hate him so much. Was Tim that big of a disappointment? He'd made honor roll every year except one. He slaved away around the house. He had no friends or social life to speak of. And he did everything his father demanded, no matter how difficult or mind numbing the task. Yet his father still glared at him as if Tim had personally wronged him by committing the sin of his own birth.

Tim had spent years with his best friend, or rather his former best friend, Dima, wondering about life's many mysteries. Why did so many superhero movies keep telling the same origin story over and over? Why did George Lucas ruin *Star Wars* with the three prequels? Why did girls only seem to go out with assholes? But perhaps the greatest mystery of all was why didn't their fathers love them?

Except in Dima's case, his father finally came back into the picture last summer. So now it was only Tim's mystery to solve.

It hadn't always been this way. There was a time when Tim's father had been kind, and Tim had felt loved. But those rose-colored memories were so long ago they might have belonged to another child or some imagined life Tim never actually lived. Maybe his father had always been an asshole.

His father's eyes bored into his. He spoke slowly. "How did my name get here?"

"I ... I signed it."

"Why?"

"I dunno."

His father's hand flew out, hitting him hard across the face, knocking his glasses to the bed.

"What did I tell you about 'I dunnos?'"

"Not to say them," Tim said through tears.

It wasn't the pain, though the slap hurt like hell. It was the shame of being smacked across the face that made Tim "cry like a girl" as his father would say whenever Tim cried any longer than seemed right.

"Again. Why did you sign my name?"

"Because I didn't want to get in trouble."

His father laughed. "And how's that working out for ya?"

Tim said nothing. This was, he hoped, one of those rhetorical questions. Answering a rhetorical question would earn him another slap, along with a *don't be a smartass*.

His father started pacing the room as he read the progress report from Tim's algebra teacher. Tim put his glasses back on, as if they would somehow prevent his father from hitting him in the face again.

"While Tim still does his work on time, he often daydreams in class, getting lost in his own world. He'll often be writing stories while I'm teaching the class, even though I've asked him many times to pay attention."

"Is this true?" Tim's father looked down at him. "Are you writing stories during class?"

"Yes, sir. Sometimes. But it's only because I already know the material. I pass all the tests, and I get As in the class."

"Then perhaps the class is too easy for you. We'll see if we can get you into another, more challenging, one."

"No, I like the class!"

Tim immediately wished he could take those words back. Because now he would be expected to explain *why* he liked the class. And the *why* was named Alicia, a girl he'd had a crush on for two years, and had been friends with since elementary school. She was one of the few things that made school worth going to ever since Dima stopped being his friend. She was all he had left, a girl he just happened to be in love with, even if she was clueless about his feelings.

But there was no way Tim could tell his father about a girl he liked. School was for learning, not socializing. If his father knew, he would pull him out of class. Hell, he might even send him to St. Martin's Boys' Academy like he'd threatened to do so many times before when his grades edged away from perfect.

"No," his father said, shaking his head. "You *like* goofing off in class. If you truly *liked* the class, you'd be paying attention, not writing your stupid stories."

"They're not stupid!"

His father stared as if Tim had smacked him.

Tim swallowed.

"What did you say?"

"Nothing ... sir."

His father laughed again. "If you're going to talk back to me at least have the balls to stand like a man when I ask you about it."

His father's logic made no sense. Don't talk back, but *do* stand up for yourself?

Okay, I will stand up for myself.

"They're *not* stupid stories."

"Oh, really? So, what, you're some kind of John Grisham or something."

"I dunno, I never read him ... sir."

"Go get me a story."

"Huh?"

"I want to know how good this writing is that keeps you from paying attention in class. Maybe I'm wrong. Maybe I've got a Pulitzer Prize-winning author under my roof, and I don't even know it. I'd hate to tell you to focus on algebra if you've got a real talent. Now go get me a story."

Tim got out of bed and went into the kitchen where he'd left his backpack hanging from his chair. The bag was still unzipped from when his father must've gone through his books — checking up on him like always. Tim retrieved his algebra spiral and turned, with a stomach full of butterflies, to head back to his room.

As he walked through the living room, he saw his mother peering through the crack of her bedroom door. She quickly turned away, pretending she hadn't seen him as she got ready for work. Acknowledgment might imply intervention — something she knew better than to do, and avoided in all but the most extreme situations.

Tim sighed and headed back into his room. His father was sitting on his bed, hand outstretched and waiting.

Tim thumbed through the spiral to the story he'd been writing last week. A surreal short about a man who wakes up in a town where nobody remembers his name, even though he remembers everyone. Not even his family knows who he is, and he's not sure if he's losing his mind or if something more sinister is happening. Of course, something more sinister was *always* happening in Tim's stories.

But this was the first time his father had asked to read one.

Tim handed him the spiral, stomach churning. He knew his father had read Stephen King, Dean Koontz, and some classic literature, though mostly he read business books — how to make money in the stock market and other stuff. Those books seemed to be working for him as his bank account was fat, even if Tim and his mother were expected to live like clerics who'd taken a vow of poverty. Meanwhile, his father had a nice car, nice jewelry, even if Tim found it gaudy, and occasionally took them to fine restaurants.

Tim sat at his desk, staring at the floor. His father sat on the bed, reading his story.

Tim could hardly believe that his father was reading it. He was quiet, which Tim figured had to be a good sign. He didn't immediately cast it aside as he'd done when Tim came home and showed off his first painting in art class. His father said art wasn't Tim's strength then had him pulled from art and put him into music, insisting that at least music might help develop the other parts of Tim's brain that would be worth a damn in the real world.

Tim continued staring at his carpet as if it had been invaded by tiny Martian colonies and the only way he could see them was to pay very close attention.

His father started laughing. A low chuckle that turned into a phlegmy cough.

Tim couldn't remember any funny parts in the story, especially within the first couple of pages, which was as far as his father had read.

Tim looked up to see his father choking, red-faced, on his laughter. "Oh my God, *this* is what you do in algebra?"

Tim swallowed. He wasn't about to correct him and say not just algebra, but four other classes as well. "Yes, sir."

His father held up the spiral. "Son, this is not writing. This makes your painting look like a Picasso."

Tim swallowed, his eyes welling up. He couldn't let his father's words make him cry.

"This, son, is horseshit. Do you understand me?"

Every fiber in Tim's being told him to nod and say "Yes, sir."

But he didn't.

Instead, he met his father's eyes. "You're wrong."

His father, still holding the spiral tight, stood up. "What?"

"It's not horse ... crap. It's my story. And maybe you don't like it, but that doesn't mean it's horrible. Maybe it's just not your taste."

"No, Son, you just can't see it, can you? No, this isn't my taste. This isn't anyone's taste! This is horrible. You thinking you'll be a writer is fantasy land, not the real world. Don't you want to go to college? Your mother and I bust our asses to give you the *privileges* we never had! Jesus, I would've loved for someone to offer to pay my way to one of the best universities in the country! But no, nobody did that for me. And here we are, with money saved to send you to a real school to give you a decent shot at making something of yourself, and you're gonna piss it all away daydreaming this bullshit?"

His father smacked the spiral across Tim's head.

Tim stayed still, not daring to cry, move, or breathe a word. He'd wait his father out. Let him have his rant, tell Tim what a moron he was and how he never appreciated anything, then Tim would get ready for school and try to put this morning behind him, hoping his father wouldn't pull him out of algebra, let alone the school.

Just keep quiet, and let it blow over.

"I asked you a question."

"Oh, I thought it was rhetorical," Tim said. "No, sir, I appreciate the opportunity you and Mom are giving me. I swear."

"Then why are you writing this shit in class?"

"I dunno," Tim said, flinching when the words left his lips.

"Oh, you *dunno*, eh?" His father's face twisted with contempt. He reached up with his free hand.

Tim winced, thinking he was about to get smacked again, or worse.

Instead, his father reached up and grabbed a bunch of pages in the spiral and ripped them out.

Tim screamed out some incoherent shout that fell between "no" and "stop" but was neither.

His father dropped the spiral, holding the pages in his hands, many ripped in half. Tim cried out and reached for the papers, trying to grab them from his father before he destroyed them.

His father shoved him backward, hard into his desk.

"You sit the fuck down!" he yelled, still tearing the pages and dropping them to the ground like confetti in his nightmare's parade.

Tim slunk back into his seat, staring at the floor, at his story, torn to shreds, tears streaming down his cheeks.

When his father finished tearing the pages, he stepped forward and neatly enunciated. "You will never write another story as long as you are living under my roof, do you understand me?"

"But—"

"Do you hear me?" He grabbed Tim's jaw hard, fingers

digging into his flesh as he turned his face upward, forcing him to meet his eyes.

Tim's tears felt hot, like shame, on his face as he swallowed. "Yes, sir."

His father headed toward the door. "Now pick up this mess, and get ready for school."

As Tim's door closed, he fell to the floor, screaming a silent cry into his carpet, wishing like hell that his father was dead.

7 a.m. - 8 a.m.

FOUR

Sebastian Ruiz

SEBASTIAN SLID the pair of breakfast plates and tickets through the window, smacked the bell with his hand, and called out, "Maggie, order up!"

He briskly whipped around and nearly crashed into Tony, the busboy, his arms stuffed with a tub of breakfast dishes on his way to the dishwasher.

"Watch out, man!" Sebastian yelled as he brushed by, back to the flattop where he was juggling eggs, bacon, sausages, hash browns, pancakes, and Reubens. The diner was slammed for a Wednesday, especially since his help had yet to show and he was the kitchen's only cook.

Loretta waddled in through the back door, where she always parked in the morning to avoid customers before she was ready to be friendly. Sebastian yelled, "I'm alone again, Loretta!"

Loretta whined in her nasally accent. "What? I thought Bob was scheduled."

"He is, but so far he's a no-show. You wanna call him and tell him to get his ass in here?"

"Okay." Loretta walked past Sebastian, squeezing her

temples to ease a headache that seemed proportionate to the diner's chaos at any given moment.

"You need to fire that fool already and get someone reliable in here. If not that, then at least put three on mornings, so no one has to work the kitchen alone."

Sebastian went down the line, flipping shit that needed flipping, one eye on the rail over the prep station to scan for new orders, sighing at the sight of another three added to the four on deck.

"This shit ain't right, Loretta. I can't keep covering for his ass."

"I know, Seb. I'm sorry."

Loretta walked to her office in the back of the kitchen and closed the door.

That's right, bitch. Just keep hiding in the back instead of actually running this fucking diner.

Like he usually did at this time of morning, Sebastian wished he had enough money saved to open a competing diner. He, with a few other staffers, were carrying Goldman's — why not make their own place, where *they* called the shots? He hoped he could take a few servers with him. Maggie, for sure. Jerry, too, and maybe even Viv, if she'd leave. Viv was old, but she was practically a legend behind the diner's front counter, and the old folks all loved her.

Goldman's Diner had been splitting at the seams ever since Loretta's father, Abbott, died last year. Abbott Goldman had been the driving force behind making the diner a city hotspot. Back then, he'd run it with his son, Stan, who handled the books. Loretta handled staffing — something she'd been good at once upon a time. But after the old man passed, Loretta and Stan had a falling out. He took off, leaving her to steer the ship straight into the rocks. Most days were okay, but times like this, when they were short a cook and at least a server (if not two), drained both the bodies and morale of the workers.

God, I'd love to open my own place.

Unfortunately, given his prison record, there was no way a bank would give Sebastian a loan to open a shit shack in Fly County, let alone a diner in a community already packed with them.

But it was nice to imagine. Maybe someday he'd meet someone to partner with, someone more legit, who could get the necessary loans and approvals.

Days like this, Sebastian hated being so damned loyal to this sinking ship. Sure, Loretta paid him decent money, but he could do better.

It was hard to leave a job where he was calling the shots in the kitchen. He was head chef, a title he'd earned through attrition, but earned none the less. It felt good to have people, even if it was maybe only half the crew, respect what he brought to the job. Plus, he had the schedule he wanted, which usually meant weekends off.

He might not even mind staying at Goldman's if the diner wasn't doomed.

But Loretta was running it into the ground. From her failure to manage to scrapping quality fresh ingredients in favor of canned and frozen crap and assuming her customers were too stupid to notice, she was quickly turning her father's once-proud diner into a sad mockery of its former glory. Even though the staff liked Loretta more than her cheapskate brother, at least he knew how to strike the balance required to run a business.

It's a sad realization when the "old days under Stan the Man" are now the "good ol' days."

Maggie shoved her way through the double doors into the kitchen and dropped a plate on the prep area. Her eyes were wet, as if holding back tears.

"What's wrong?" Sebastian asked.

"Table Six."

"*Again?* What is it this time?"

"He said the eggs are *still* too salty."

"I didn't put any fucking salt in them!" Sebastian looked at the plate, and the scrambled eggs sprinkled with liberal doses of salt and pepper. Half the eggs had been eaten. "That fucker put this on himself. What the hell?"

Sebastian wanted to step away from the grill to get a look at the asshole at Table Six but didn't dare move his eyes from the food.

He flipped some pancakes, eggs, and sausages onto a pair of plates then grabbed the order slip from the rail. "These are yours. Table Two."

Maggie stood still, shaking her head, "He asked me to sit here until you've cooked the eggs — to make sure you don't salt them."

"Or maybe to make sure I don't spit in them?"

Maggie grinned. "I won't tell if you don't."

Sebastian laughed, put Table Two's plates in the window, then grabbed three eggs and cracked them on the flattop. Maggie was easy to like. When she returned with a re-fire, she was never a pain in the ass about getting the food remade like some people. Some servers would get pissy, which Sebastian could sort of understand, as their tip was on the line. Maggie was a relative saint.

Sebastian plated another two orders, put them in the window, and rang the bell. "Viv, order up!" He handed Maggie Table Six's eggs. "Here's the king's dish. No salt. No flavor whatsoever."

"Thank you." Maggie smiled, grabbed the other two plates he'd made for Table Two, and left the kitchen.

Sebastian looked from the tickets to Bob as the late chef crashed into the kitchen, punched his card in the time clock, and joined Sebastian at the prep area. Sheepishly, he said, "Oh, man, I'm so sorry. My alarm didn't go off, and I missed the bus, and—"

"Save it. You're here now, so let's get these tickets taken care of."

"Where do you need me?"

"Grill. I'll prep for now."

"Okay," Bob said, getting to work on the grill.

Bob was a slob. An alcoholic in his forties with a raw meat-red face and salt-and-pepper hair like a curtain drawn closed over his eyes. He carried about forty extra pounds that seemed like sixty in his baggy, wrinkled, and rarely washed clothes. He was unreliable as all-fuck, but once at work, he was usually decent enough to keep pace with Sebastian.

As Bob worked the grill, Sebastian peeked out the window into the dining area and saw the fat fucker at Table Six snapping his fingers, calling Maggie back.

Sebastian watched as the man yelled something. It was hard to hear above the kitchen's commotion, but Sebastian read his mouth perfectly. "Are you fucking stupid?"

Maggie apologized and headed back to the kitchen.

Sebastian was waiting. She was even closer to the verge of tears than before but hadn't yet broken.

"What? Not enough salt this time?" Sebastian grinned, hoping for a smile.

"No, he wants more toast. Asked how I can expect him to eat his eggs without fresh toast."

Maggie didn't mention that the man had also yelled at her, asking her if she was fucking stupid. Sebastian wanted to go out there and tell him to kindly get the fuck out of Goldman's before he kicked the teeth from his gums. But he wasn't about to cause Maggie trouble and blow shit up bigger than it needed to be when she never even asked him to stick up for her.

"Bob, get me eight toasts."

"Okay!"

"Eight?" Maggie asked.

12

"I wanna make sure he has enough. I'll have it right out to you."

Maggie laughed.

Sebastian couldn't go out and tell the guy "Fuck you," but he could do it in his own subtle way.

After a couple of minutes, Sebastian grabbed the plate of toast and headed out to the dining room. No putting this plate in the window. He wanted to see this fucker up close and personal. He also loaded another plate with about twenty pats of butter and jelly packets.

The man, even fatter and more obnoxious up close, looked up in surprise when Sebastian appeared with the plates. He looked like the kind of guy who was syrupy sweet when trying to get you to buy from him but treated people he viewed beneath him like shit. Sebastian usually had a good read on people and doubted he was far off.

"You ordered some toast?" Sebastian dropped the plates on top of the guy's newspaper, opened on the table beside his eggs.

Sebastian waited for the man to look him up and down. From Sebastian's six-foot-two frame to his olive skin and dark eyes to his obvious muscles bulging beneath his white tee to the rolled shirt revealing two sleeves of tattoos running up his arms, he'd look like a nightmare to an asshole like this — a Latino with nothing to lose.

"Um ... thanks." The guy moved his plates closer to his eggs with a haughty, frustrated sigh.

Sebastian crossed his arms over his chest, still standing, saying nothing, staring the man down until he nervously looked back up.

"Yes?" the man said, a tinge of righteousness in his voice.

"I just wanted to make sure the toast was to your liking," Sebastian said with no trace of a smile.

"Yes. Thank you."

"And the eggs? Are they to your liking? Hot enough? Not too salty?"

"Um," the guy said, looking down at his eggs, "yes. Thank you."

"Good," Sebastian said, "pleasure to serve you."

He turned and left. He saw Maggie at Table Three, looking over nervously, probably wondering what he just did. He winked and smiled to let her know things were cool. Viv, who was about thirty years older than Maggie, but who took no shit from anyone (ever) was standing behind the counter, trying not to lose her laughter.

Sebastian went into the kitchen, feeling pleased with himself. Cooks didn't usually get to intervene with shitty customers, but he loved those rare moments, especially when they didn't make things worse for the server.

The only thing Sebastian hated more than unreliable staffers were bullies. But bullies were usually chickenshits the moment they met someone who didn't succumb to their supposed power. And they always backed down like the scared little pussies they were.

AFTER TWENTY MINUTES, Sebastian felt like they were back on top. Bob had kicked just enough ass to make up for being late, and the kitchen was under control.

Of course, that's when Loretta finally came out of hiding and made her way to the dining area to mingle with the customers, making regulars feel special, and newcomers welcome. It was one thing she was still good at.

Hell, maybe I'll hire her when my diner eats her diner's lunch.

Sebastian was finishing an order of waffles when Maggie came into the back and thanked him for "whatever you did to Table Six."

"Did he say anything else out of line?"

"No," she said, "but he also stiffed me on the tip."

12

"Sorry about that."

"He would've done it anyway. Jerk. But that's not why I came back here. Someone asked to see you."

"A customer?"

"No, he said his name is Raul."

Sebastian felt his stomach drop.

No, it can't be.

"What's he look like?" Sebastian asked.

"Big, bald, tattoos all over, even on his face." Maggie swallowed, clearly concerned. She might have had the same look the first time she saw Sebastian, but she was *right* about Raul. The man was trouble, and his being at the diner could only mean one thing: shit was about to get ugly.

Sebastian met Maggie's eyes. "Tell him to meet me out back in five minutes, okay? And don't let Loretta hear you."

"Um … okay," Maggie said, looking at Sebastian nervously. He wondered what was running through her mind. Did she think he was dealing drugs out of the diner? He felt like he ought to say something to explain that it wasn't anything like that, but Maggie nodded and went back into the diner before he could say anything else.

Sebastian wasn't sure why he cared so much what Maggie thought of him, but he did. She was a nice girl — a good girl with a shitty ex — but a sweetheart just the same. She tried to be a great mom to her adorable daughter. And he liked that both Maggie and her kid didn't treat him like so many other people — like a piece of shit loser with nothing going on.

But he couldn't spend too much time worrying about Maggie's perceptions. Raul's presence was all that mattered.

There weren't many people Sebastian feared, but Raul Luna sat like a king at the top of that list.

FIVE

Clarence Dumont

Iт wasn't that Clarence hated his wife so much as he wondered why in the hell they were still married after a decade.

They had no children tying them down, and it had been forever since Sheryl had shown the slightest interest in anything beyond the superficial daily bullshit that people talked about.

He couldn't remember their last *deep* conversation, even though he'd try, on occasion, to bring stuff up.

Why are we still together?

He found this an almost constant thought, wading through mornings at the breakfast nook while each of them did their own thing. He read the paper while she stared at her tablet, browsing the web, Facebook, checking the most recent updates to the MLS, and looking at the local news site, half smiling at the opinion forum where everyone dished dirt on politicians and public figures.

"Oh, wow, did you hear about Wes Grant?"

"Commissioner Grant?" Clarence looked up from his op-ed piece about the healthcare crisis and all the dead ends engineered by Congress. He had heard about Grant from another cop on the force but had specifically kept the details from Sheryl.

"Yeah, the cops were responding to a drunk and disorderly call. Grant was out in his yard, wearing nothing but underwear, yelling at his wife two nights ago. You didn't hear about that?"

"Yeah, I think so. No big deal, really."

"No big deal? He was outside yelling at his wife, drunk, in his underwear! That's a pretty big deal."

"First off, they were in their *back yard*, behind a privacy fence, I might add. He'd been swimming, and yes, he was drunk, but it's his house. And it's not like he was running buck wild in the streets with his dick out."

Sheryl looked at him like *he'd* whipped his dick out at the table.

"You're defending the guy?"

"What site are you reading that on?"

"Palm Isles Local Online."

"Yeah, I thought so."

"What? It's a news forum."

"No, it's a rag, owned by your developer buddy, Victor Kozlov, who wants Grant out of office so he can get his puppet, Jerry Mitchell elected in November."

"It's still news," Sheryl said. "He was drunk, fighting with his wife outside. Is that the kind of guy you want in office?"

"We don't know the whole story. And the police came out, made sure everything was okay. It was, and they left. The end."

"Yeah, anyone else would've been arrested. Don't act like your boy isn't getting some preferential treatment."

"First off, he's not *my boy*. Second, it was a personal matter between a couple. This isn't fodder for some forum of anonymous assholes hiding behind *clever* screen names who have nothing better to do than stir up shit."

"Hey, *I'm* on that forum."

43

"I didn't say *you* are an asshole, but we both know you've stirred your fair share of shit."

Sheryl smiled. "Only for the people who deserve it."

"Okay, Ponygirl71," Clarence smiled back.

While she was a bit too schadenfreude-istic with the forum, Sheryl wasn't like most of its resident trolls. The few times she'd stirred shit, it was to go after the assholes in defense of someone getting the shaft. But with Grant, she couldn't see things objectively. The commissioner, who tended to vote on the basis of environmental concerns, had been instrumental in denying too many projects involving her developer friends.

Sheryl was quiet for a few minutes, returning to her tablet while Clarence went back to his op-ed. He bit into his toast with strawberry jam. It had gone cold a while ago. Not caring, he washed it down with a swallow of lukewarm coffee.

"So," Sheryl said, looking at him, "why didn't *you* tell me about Grant?"

"I dunno. I didn't think twice about it. It wasn't on my shift, and I heard about it yesterday, in passing."

"In passing? You sure seemed to know a lot about it for 'in passing.'"

"It's none of our business. Why would I bring up another couple's marital problems? I'm not a gossip."

"Oh, you gossip."

"No, I don't."

"Oh, really? You and Patrick don't talk shit about people? What about all that stuff you told me about Franco and his little problem?"

She had him there. He'd talked a lot of shit about Franco's troubles. But Clarence hated that obnoxious asshole. There was a difference.

"First off," Clarence said.

Sheryl smiled as he prepared to mount his defense.

"First off, I know Franco."

"I know Commissioner Grant," she said, taking a sip of hot coffee.

"No, you don't see him every day, or work with him. Franco is a whole other story. Plus, that dude started shit with me! So, yeah, I took some pleasure in his downfall, but *I* am not a gossip."

"So, what, you're saying *I* am?"

"No, that's not what I'm saying! How the hell did you turn this around to *me* calling *you* a gossip?" Clarence sighed, exasperated by Sheryl's ability to put him on the defensive. Times like this, he could hardly remember how the argument started or who said what. He always seemed to be playing defense, and later, apologizing for God only knew what.

"Okay, so if you're not calling me a gossip, why didn't you tell me about Grant? Were you afraid I'd tell my *evil* developer friends?"

"So, you admit they're evil?" Clarence grinned.

"No, I'm paraphrasing you, sweetheart. Seriously, did you think I'd go around telling people?"

"I dunno," Clarence said. No filter on his thoughts before they rolled off his tongue.

"What? You *don't know?*"

Shit.

"What do you mean you *don't know?* You *really* think I'd go around telling people something like that?"

The first bit of their argument — if you could call it that — had been playful, a typical exchange between them. Now he felt like they'd brushed something raw at the core, something lying just under the surface of their marriage. Something having to do with trust.

And to be honest, Clarence wasn't sure if he could trust her *not* to tell someone. Sheryl thrived on knowing what others didn't and used her knowledge like chips in a game. She was great at emotional poker — and likely mined many a solid lead because of her value to others. But sometimes, she said too much.

"I'm not saying you would *intentionally* go around telling other people stuff, but there have been times in the past when you've let the wrong things slip."

"One time, and I'm never gonna hear the end of it?"

Clarence leaned forward, feeling a burning in his neck, moving from defensive to angry. Sheryl had no right to turn this shit back on him. She had fucked up a few times in the past, saying shit she shouldn't have said, plain and simple. She should at least accept responsibility for those times without trying to write them off as one isolated incident.

"I don't think you understand the sensitive nature of my job. There have been a few times when you've said things that could've cost me my career. Hell, you could've jeopardized ongoing cases!"

"Well, maybe it's time you moved on anyway."

For a moment, Clarence wasn't sure what she meant. Move on from their marriage, or from his job?

"How many times has Lloyd offered you a job?"

Clarence sighed. "Not this again."

"What?"

"I don't need you to keep throwing this in my face. I don't want to work for your ex-boyfriend."

"First off, stop calling him that. We've been friends for twenty years. He's a friend; that's it. And second, why not work for him? Do you realize how much money you can make as an insurance investigator?"

"I *like* my job."

"No, you don't. You complain about it all the time."

"No, I don't."

"Yes, you do. And even if you didn't, your bosses treat you like crap and pay you chump change. You can make twice what you make, or more, working for Lloyd!"

"I don't wanna work for an ambulance chaser."

12

"It's a nine-to-five job. Aren't you sick of working all hours of the day, and on weekends? Don't you want a normal job with normal hours?"

Clarence shook his head and glanced at the clock. It was 7:30; he had to leave in ten minutes. He didn't have time for another ancient argument.

"Listen, I know you make more than me. Your father reminds me every time we're together, and you'd love to make Daddy proud by having me get a 'real job,' but money isn't everything. Despite what you think, and my occasional bitching, I *like* my job. I *like* making a difference in people's lives."

"First off, this has nothing to do with my father—"

"No? Are you sure? Because it seems like, other than this time, you always bring this up a couple days after we visit your folks. Listen, it doesn't matter how much money I make. I'll *never* be right with your father."

"What does that mean?"

As if she didn't know.

"You gonna make me say it?"

"Yeah, what?"

"I'll never be white enough for your father."

"What?" Sheryl slammed her cup on the table. Coffee splashed over the lip. "What the hell are you talking about?"

"Oh, come on, we both know your dad wanted you to marry some white guy."

"My father *is* black," Sheryl said, as if the fact had somehow sailed over Clarence's head.

"Yeah, but his wife is white, and the way he talks about ... oh, come on, you have to realize?"

"Are you saying my father's a racist? Against his own people?"

Clarence did believe that but wasn't quite sure how to say it. Sheryl's father was a retired doctor who had made a fortune and played golf with some of her asshole developer friends. He might not have started off as a racist, but he'd

47

become one over time, often bitching over dinner about "the poor" and the "welfare class" along with minorities of every color. For ten years, Clarence had thought that he and Sheryl both understood this about her father, even if they'd never discussed it. She'd said plenty in the past, hinting at it, how he'd encouraged her to go out with white guys, and how he always seemed to treat her — with her lighter skin and long curly hair — better than Barry, her darker brother with an afro. Could she really be this deep in denial?

"I'm just saying that your father looks at me in that way, like he wishes I was white. Like Lloyd."

Sheryl laughed, though her eyes were tearing up.

"No, he looks at you like that because he wishes his son-in-law had the gumption to do something with his life other than waste it as a small-town cop who's never gonna go anywhere."

And there it was.

Silence stretched the moment. They exchanged a stare, Sheryl too angry for retreat or apology and Clarence stunned from her words.

Finally, he spoke. "Is that what you think?"

"I said it's what my father thinks."

"Yeah, but is that what *you* think?"

Sheryl wiped tears from her eyes. "I think you're just comfortable, maybe afraid to do something else. To try something different."

"No, I'm not afraid." Clarence stood. "Like I said before, I'm happy with my job. Sorry if I won't go work for your ex-boyfriend's ambulance-chasing law firm, but that isn't what I want to do."

"You said you want to help people, you can do that *and* make money working for Lloyd. But you won't even consider it. That's just crazy!"

"Like I said, there's more to life than money."

"You know, instead of laying this all on my dad, why don't we put the blame where it really belongs?"

12

"What?" Clarence said, fists curled at his side.

"This whole *cop thing* isn't about you helping people, it's about you somehow going back in time and saving your mom from *your* father. You've built up this hero complex like you need to save the world or something because you couldn't save your mom from *your dad*. But you can't go back in time, Clarence. And you can't keep living your life in service to a lie."

Clarence felt raw, vulnerable, and cold as his coffee.

"What lie?"

"That you can change the past."

How could she bring up his father? The one thing he'd kept to himself for so long, and had only recently shared with her.

"I'm not trying to 'change the past.' I'm just trying to do the right thing."

"The right thing by whom?"

Sheryl stood, brought her plate and cup to the sink, then left Clarence standing alone.

He curled his fist tighter and decided: their marriage was officially over.

SIX

Joe Harcourt

SOME MORNINGS, Joe wished he'd followed his wife to the grave. Mornings like this: cold, gray, and infinitely lonely.

At least he had his German shepherd, Hoss.

"Come on, boy." Hoss was taking forever to find a spot for his business.

The dog whined, turning in a circle, teasing Joe as if he might do something before tugging his leash in a different direction. Joe sighed and followed Hoss toward the street. The ground was cold and wet, but you'd think it was snowing in Florida judging by his picky dog.

Across the street, Nancy's garage door opened, and her SUV rolled out, probably taking the kids to school. Joe waited to see if they'd stop and say hi. He liked seeing the kids, and they liked to stop and pet the dog, though that was usually in the afternoon when they came home, not before school, when Nancy was usually in a rush.

Hoss looked at the truck, his tail wagging.

But the garage closed, and the truck pulled out of the driveway, heading down the street without so much as a wave.

"Oh, well, maybe later, boy." Hoss sniffed along the road, maybe smelling one of the block's other dogs.

12

Joe looked up and down the street. There were around thirty houses from one stop sign to the other, and he might know three of his neighbors, including Nancy. There was a time, not so long ago, when he knew almost everyone. Or at least half of his neighbors. But that was back when Grace was still alive.

How long had it been? Nearly fifteen years? Twenty? Joe tried to remember when she died. Was it in '95?

He looked up as if the gray sky might have the answer.

A bad sign: in the long list of things he'd been forgetful of as of late, the date of Grace's death wasn't among them.

Until now.

"Dammit, come on, Joe."

Hoss looked up and whined.

"No, not you, boy. I'm trying to remember when Grace died."

Even if Hoss could talk, he'd be no help. She'd died long before Joe adopted him from a neighbor moving into an apartment with no allowance for pets. Hell, Joe couldn't even remember the dog's original owner. She was a nice woman who worked at the bowling alley, but hell if he could find her name in his head.

Hoss finally found a spot he liked and lifted a leg to piss along the road.

A blue Honda approached from a half block up — one of the neighbors he kinda sorta knew from occasional waves. Joe wasn't sure of the guy's name, or what he did for a living. But he dressed nicely and seemed polite enough whenever they'd pass along the street.

Joe lifted his hand and waved. The guy either didn't see or ignored him, talking on his cell phone as he passed.

Joe let his hand fall and tried not to think too much about being ignored by two neighbors in one morning. The guy he didn't care much about. He was obviously on his cell. But

Nancy and the kids, there was no way they didn't see him as they left.

Sometimes, Joe wondered if people only waved or said hi out of pity. "Be nice to the old man, everybody."

Once upon a time, neighbors stopped to chat. They'd ask you over for dinner or drinks. People would have barbecues and invite everyone to the grill. Now, people just smiled and waved for the most part, too wrapped up in their own lives to pay much attention to anyone else.

While Joe supposed he should've felt some consolation that it wasn't just him being ignored, it didn't change how lonely he felt.

"That it for now?" Joe looked down at his dog. "Just one little whiz?"

Hoss wagged his tail and started toward the house.

At home, Joe checked Hoss's food and water dishes to make sure they were full then consulted his medicine box and checked the date against the TV channel guide, just to make sure. His memory hadn't decayed so much that he couldn't remember the days, but you could never be too careful. He certainly couldn't recall taking his pills this morning, but the box marked Wednesday morning was empty, so he must have.

He looked at the calendar hanging over the telephone, at the date circled in red. In the date's box, he'd written: *Dr. Wilson: 8:30 A.M.*

A chill ran through him.

Today was the day he'd get the test results back on his MRI to determine whether his forgetfulness, sleeplessness, and irritability were signs of something serious.

While he sometimes wished he'd followed Grace to the grave, the part of Joe that wondered if it was Heaven or an endless quiet that would follow his final breath wasn't ready to die. The years had robbed him of what little faith he may have once had, and the likelihood that this was all you get —

one lifetime on this rock hurtling through space — grew more crushing with every passing day.

He poured himself a cup of nice, cold orange juice and sat at his kitchen nook table. The dog's leash rattled, circling Joe before Hoss collapsed beside his feet. The kitchen was silent, save for the clock's ticking — a wooden yellow circle with a rather ugly red rooster on its face, marring the wall since Grace made him nail it above the telephone. Though it didn't match the kitchen's mostly beige color scheme, he couldn't get rid of the eyesore, as it was one of the last things she'd bought for the house before falling ill.

He sat staring at the empty chair across from him, where he used to sit with Grace every morning, longing to see her again. He thought of her beautiful blue eyes, her auburn hair. She'd been his childhood sweetheart, best friend, and only true love. Not many people could say they found their one true love, let alone spent most of their life with them. But he'd been lucky.

No, if I were lucky, I would've died with her.

Grace should never have died first. It wasn't fair. She'd always been the healthy one, watching her diet, taking vitamins, and exercising every day. Joe had only taken care of himself while she was watching. He'd never been especially out of shape, but he'd never really minded his diet or exercised all that much either. He'd also smoked for three decades, only quitting the day Grace died — in honor of her, who had always asked, cajoled, and even begged him to.

Despite her healthy habits, cancer had found her and done what it wanted — destroying her vitality, spirit, and then her life across a single cruel winter.

He often wondered how different things would've been if they'd kept their daughter — not just for Grace and him, but for their girl, and *her* family. He hated *what-if's*, but as his remaining days thinned, he found himself wishing he could have them back — so he'd have a chance to make the right choices.

Joe finished the orange juice, stood, and stared at the red circle on the calendar.

SEVEN

Corrine Walker

CORRINE WOKE up late and had to shove her stubborn body out the door for a lethargic morning jog.

Her legs were burning fifteen minutes later, her back breaking. Corrine cursed herself for not staying inside. She returned to her apartment in a defeated stroll, feeling fat, bloated, and like a complete failure. She undressed, refusing to make eyes with the bathroom mirror, then took a shower and got ready for school.

Corrine grabbed a protein shake and headed out the door with barely enough time to park before her first-period students showed up. She climbed into her car, telling herself that she really needed to start waking up earlier. For a month and a half, she'd failed herself by turning her promised morning run into a lie.

Of course, getting up early would mean going to bed earlier, and that was something Corrine couldn't do. She'd been a night owl through her teens and twenties, still managing to rise and shine for classes or work. But now, at thirty-four, working as a high school algebra teacher, she was burning the candle at both ends and feeling it more often than not.

But going to bed earlier had been key to losing her last twenty pounds. She'd slimmed down to 145 — a hell of a lot better than the 260 she suffered through nearly two years ago. But if she didn't find a way to reach her target weight soon, Corrine would settle back into old habits and gain the weight back. She'd never forgive herself, having fought too hard to toss her goals in the garbage.

As she sat in traffic and drank her chalky shake, Corrine wondered why she kept doing this to herself. Why did she stay up until one and two in the morning when she knew she had to get up early? Hell, two was late even if she wasn't going to jog!

It wasn't like she was being productive late into the night or whispering into a lover's waiting ear. She hadn't dated since Julie broke her heart last year. She spent her evenings watching TV, reading, or wasting time on Pinterest or Facebook, living a life's fading echo. Every now and then she'd meet up with a friend for drinks after work, but beyond that, Corrine had a spinster's social life.

Her sister, Dez — the one who could do no wrong in their mother's eyes — would say that Corrine stayed up at night because she was secretly trying to sabotage herself. She didn't *really* want to be skinny because being "too fat" gave her an excuse to avoid another relationship. But that theory was nonsense. Hell, Corrine had been fat *and* happy with Julie! It wasn't that she was afraid to get into a relationship so much as she didn't really want one. She'd needed Julie too much, and needing someone that much left you empty once they were gone.

Far better to focus on herself, her students, and her fledgling photography business. Falling for someone else could derail her successes, few that they were.

So, why am I staying up so late?

Her only answers: boredom or loneliness.

But Corrine believed that boredom was for boring people.

12

There was always something interesting if you took the time to look.

So, that leaves loneliness.

But she didn't buy that either. Corrine had a few close friends, and they were always asking her to go out. Her social calendar could be full every night of the week if she wanted. But she didn't. She liked spending time alone — getting her shit together. It was the first time in a long while that she had been so focused on *her* needs instead of someone else's.

The first twenty years of Corrine's life were wasted trying to win her mother's love. Her twenties were frittered away trying to hold onto one relationship or another. First with men, while still in denial, then with women who were all wrong for who she was and who she wanted to be.

But Julie had been right. Not just right — *perfect*.

Julie was just enough of an extrovert to draw Corrine from her shell and just enough of an introvert to appreciate the little things about their relationship: the quiet moments alone, the romantic getaways, even the time well spent hanging out and cuddling to TV on the couch. They could've been best friends, even if Julie had been straight. But they'd been so much more.

No psychobabble required: Corrine stayed up because staying up was easier than running.

She suffered through the final swallow of shake, pulled into the teacher's parking lot, and found a spot mercifully close to the front.

She was about to get out of the car, grateful for the short walk, then stopped herself, trying not succumb to the growing anxiety.

This is so pathetic.

She took a few deep breaths, exhaled slowly, and focused instead on the day ahead. She needed to get her shit together. Her principal had told Corrine that she'd be observed at some point during the week. This had never been an issue with the old principal, Mr. Lawrence. But his replacement, Mrs. Kern, was another story altogether.

While Kern had never said anything directly, Corrine couldn't shake the feeling that the woman hated her. She wasn't sure why the principal would have any reason to dislike her. Kern was new to the school system, and they had no shared history. But every time she exchanged a word with Kern, Corinne couldn't ignore the woman's icy air — as if her every move was being judged.

Initially, Corrine thought it was because the principal didn't care for gays, but there were two other openly gay teachers in the school, her coworker, Phil Chase, and another a woman, Claudia Wilson. Both seemed to get along *fine* with Kern.

This would be her first observation under Kern, and she had to have everything perfect. Better than perfect. When someone had it out for you, you had to rise above and beyond to prove yourself.

Corrine looked in the rearview mirror and put on her best fake smile.

You can do this.

CORRINE SAT AT HER DESK, waiting for her first-period students. Sometimes, they came in as early as ten minutes before class started. Her phone buzzed with a text from Phil, one of the two openly gay teachers, from his class two rooms down.

You coming to the meeting tonight?

She wrote back, *Yeah, but ugh, I soooo do not want to weigh in!*

Phil, who'd been going to the weekly weight loss meetings with her for six months, wrote back: *Can't be any worse than me. I'm pretty sure I'm pregnant.*

12

She laughed out loud as one of her students, Lu Chin, walked in.

"Hi, Ms. Walker."

Corrine smiled. "Hi, Lu."

Lu sat and dived into her backpack. She pulled out her tablet and started to read.

Corrine looked back down at her phone and wrote back:

Gotta go. Kids are coming in. See you tonight. By the way, if you have a girl, will you name her after me?

LOL. See ya tonight.

Corrine spent the next ten minutes preparing for today's lesson, hoping that if Kern *was* going to evaluate her, she'd pick a later class — maybe fifth or sixth period, those were Corrine's strongest students. Her first period, with the exception of a few kids, was among her worst ever. It was filled with kids who just didn't get it and needed way more help than Corrine could offer: class clowns and the dozers — kids who were also up all night and used her class to catch up on sleep.

The first bell rang and pushed more kids through her door. She went over the day's plans once more, perfecting the planner that Kern would check with what other teachers had referred to as a drill sergeant's attention to detail.

The second bell rang, and the ninth graders settled, save for the cluster of jocks in the back who spent most mornings giggling and screwing around, making jokes at Corrine's expense, which she pretended not to hear. While a lot had changed since she was in high school, some things stayed the same — like asshole jocks with too much testosterone.

After the bell rang, Corrine stood and headed to the back of the class to close the door. Mrs. Kern appeared with a cold smile, three feet away in the hallway.

"Hello, Ms. Walker. I'm here for your observation."

"Great," Corrine said through her most artificial smile.

8 a.m. - 9 a.m.

EIGHT

Sebastian Ruiz

SEBASTIAN SLIPPED the box cutter into his back pocket and ducked out the diner's back door carrying two half-full garbage bags.

He headed across the rear lot toward one of three fenced-off dumpsters serving the shopping plaza. He opened the wooden gate and hurled the bags into the open dumpster.

On his return trip, he spotted Raul, sitting in his shiny-black Mustang.

Raul pulled up to Sebastian, rolled down the passenger side window, and said, "Get in."

Raul was wearing a black tank top and long black shorts, like he'd just finished playing basketball, rolled out of bed, or left Bare Essentials down the street.

"I can't get in, man, I'm on shift."

"Trust me, Seb, you *want* to get in. What I've got to say won't take long."

His heart racing, Sebastian peered into the back seat to make sure Raul wasn't with one of his goons then opened the passenger side door and climbed into the car. The red leather interior reeked of weed. A blue skull glass pipe sat in the center console, probably still hot.

12

Sebastian thought about leaving the door partially open so Raul wouldn't lock him in and take off, but he wasn't about to show the wolf any fear.

He closed the door.

Raul started driving, slowly. Never one for small talk or greetings, he said, "You know why I'm here?"

"Not a clue." Sebastian said.

While Raul was a couple of inches shorter than Sebastian, he was equally wide and maybe more muscular. He was also more committed to tattoos, with nary an un-inked spot on his bod. While Sebastian had never had a beef with the man he once worked for, he had no doubt what Raul could do if provoked.

"Really? Your sister didn't call you?"

"Ana? No. Why?"

Sebastian's nerves were seeking new heights. He'd thought maybe Raul had returned to draw him back into the fold. While Sebastian had broken things off as cleanly as you can with someone like Raul, you weren't really ever done until the big boss said so. And even after a few years of not hearing from the man, Raul was an ever-present shadow lurking in Sebastian's memory. Still, his sister's name was the last thing he expected to hear.

Sebastian tried to mask his fear but was surely doing a piss-poor job.

"Oh, man." Raul laughed hard enough to cough. His face turned crimson through the tattoos. "Really? Your sister didn't call you?"

"I said no, man, what's going on?"

"Oh, shit, bro, she's into me for some big money."

"What the hell are you talking about?"

"Oh, wow, you really don't know, do you?"

"No, I don't fucking know. Now tell me." Sebastian hadn't realized that he'd poised his body for an offensive attack until Raul turned toward him with a look that said he'd better not fucking try.

Sebastian breathed in and out, apologizing even though he didn't mean it. "Sorry, Raul, but no, I don't know anything about this. Please, tell me."

"I think your sister ought to tell you."

Fuck. He's gonna make me beg.

"I haven't talked to Ana in a long time, and I doubt she'd even want to hear from me. Please, Raul, what's she into you for?"

"I'll tell you the *how much*, but not the *why*. That's between you and her, *if* she wants to tell you."

"Okay, how much?"

"Fifteen large."

Sebastian felt as if someone had walloped his chest with a shovel.

"Fifteen thousand dollars? What the fuck? How the—"

"Nah, nah, nah." Raul waved his right index finger back and forth as he turned left and slowly circled the plaza. "That's for you to ask her."

On the list of reasons someone might owe Raul Luna fifteen large, there were only a couple of things that likely applied to Ana. She'd either borrowed a shit ton of money, or she'd been dealing and got snagged by the cops with his product.

"Fine, you don't wanna tell me why she owes you. Then why *are* you here?"

"Well, I was hoping you could tell me where the bitch is. She's been in the wind for more than a week now."

"Fuck." Sebastian shook his head.

"Listen, Seb, I like you. You and me go way back, right?"

"Yeah, way the fuck back," Sebastian said, trying to play friendly while waiting for the other shoe to drop.

"What time does your shift end?"

"Six. Why?"

Raul looked at his clock. "Okay, you got until then."

12

"Until then for what?"

"To get me my money."

Sebastian felt like the fucker who hit him with the first shovel had just returned to slap him on the head.

"I don't have that kinda money! And besides, I'm at fucking work. What am I supposed to do? Go home sick and find a way to shit fifteen Gs?"

Raul turned to him and smiled. "I'm sure you'll find a way. You were always the *resourceful* one, right, Seb?"

Sebastian wasn't sure if that was a compliment to Sebastian's skills as a thief or suspicion that Sebastian had done something, like snitching on others in jail, to lessen his sentence.

Raul's phone rang, the theme to *The Sopranos* filling the car.

Can this clown be any more obvious?

Raul answered. "Yeah, where? ... Ah. Okay, yeah, yeah. No, don't do anything yet. I'm gonna give her brother time to make good."

Raul killed the call and turned to Sebastian. "Looks like we have some good news. Well, good for you and me. Not so good for Ana."

"What's that?"

"My boys have found her, hiding out like the hood rat she is. They're taking her somewhere more secure. So, here's the deal, Seb. Because I like you, I'm gonna give you to the end of day to get me my money. But if, like you say, you can't come up with it, my boys are gonna kill your sister."

Sebastian was about to reach for the razor when Raul's left hand dropped from the steering wheel to the pistol beside him. He had it aimed at Sebastian before he'd twitched a finger toward the blade.

Raul smiled. "Come on, don't make this any uglier than it needs to be, Seb."

Sebastian's body went hot with anger, fear, and shame for the begging to come.

"Please, don't hurt her. I'll find a way to get you your money, but you've gotta give me more time."

"Sorry, Seb. Today is the deadline. You know how these things are, reputations to maintain. I can't let this slide another day, or it looks bad on me. Suddenly, you got people thinkin' I'm off my game."

Sebastian nodded, eyes hot with tears. He wondered what the hell Ana had managed to get herself into, and how much was his fault for not being there for so long. He'd been there for Ana once out of prison, but clearly it was too little, too late. She'd changed for the worse.

Raul pulled back up at the dumpster. "Six o 'clock. Here, take this."

He handed Sebastian a cell phone, likely a cheap burner.

"My number is programmed in. Call me the minute you have any news."

"Yeah." Sebastian climbed out of the car, unable to think, much less say anything else.

Raul drove off. Sebastian slipped the burner in his pocket then pulled out his phone and dialed Ana's number.

He hoped that Raul was bluffing, that his boys didn't have her. Then he could tell her to get the hell out of town. He'd join her, and they'd run — at least until they could figure a way out of this jam.

But there was no answer, and her mailbox was full.

"Fuck!" Sebastian shouted, louder than he'd meant.

He looked around to make sure that Loretta hadn't popped her fat ass out back for one of her day's hundred smoke breaks, but the door was still closed.

Sebastian didn't know what to do.

He didn't have fifteen grand. He'd managed to save almost eight grand, but that was every dime he had to his name. He

12

didn't think Raul would take that, even if Sebastian could get it all in cash by six.

And it wasn't like Sebastian could call the cops and get *them* to help. Raul had sources everywhere, even at the federal level, some suspected. If he talked to the wrong officer, his sister was dead. Sebastian might be next.

He didn't have any friends he could ask for that kind of cash. The few people he was tight with were even bigger losers than him, more likely to be sinking in debt than sitting on savings.

Sebastian sighed, returning to the diner with every fiber screaming that he ought to leave now. He *could* call some friends, maybe someone somewhere would help him come up with *something*.

He went inside and passed Loretta's office. Something occurred to him.

Sebastian stopped, knocked on her door, and waited.

No answer.

He opened the door and peeked inside, pretending to look for her. But he wasn't looking for Loretta at all. He was looking at the floor-mounted safe.

Sebastian had an idea — an ugly, awful idea that might save his sister.

NINE

Tim Hewitt

THE PERSON who'd decided PE should be in the morning was a masochist. Tim scowled, slipping from his school clothes into his gym shorts and tee before anyone in the locker room remarked on his scrawny, bird-chested, pale body.

Getting sweaty left you only two options: you could spend the rest of the day smelling funky, or shower with the Neanderthals — guys with more testosterone than brain cells.

Showering with Neanderthals wouldn't be so bad if they minded their own business. But no. Every shower came with a show in which Tim, or some other unfortunate soul who braved the water, became the target of mockery. Sometimes, they'd call you a fag, pussy, or some other homophobic slur that sounded like it came straight from a YouTube comment. Other times, they'd laugh at you for wearing shorts in the shower rather than going naked because you obviously had a tiny penis. Sometimes, they'd even get physical. Tim had been shoved into a locker twice this year, but at least he'd not been beaten up in the shower or locker room. Yet.

Few things were more humiliating than being beaten up and left crying naked on the locker room floor. A fellow freshman, Glen Herbst, was still a laughingstock following his beat-down. Some of the guys had even recorded it with their phones and put the video on YouTube, adding to Glen's shame.

Sometimes, it seemed like the inmates were running the asylum. Not just at school, but generally, in life. Assholes were assholes, did what they wanted, and almost never suffered the consequences.

Gym's only saving grace was that he got to spend more time with Alicia.

While she was beautiful, with long dark hair, bright-blue eyes, and braces that were an addition to her cuteness rather than a subtraction, Alicia was the sort of girl who seemed clueless to her beauty. Tim supposed if she did know, she'd probably never talk to someone as geeky as him.

Fortunately, Alicia was also smart, witty, and artistic. Since lunch followed algebra, they often sat at a table together, talking about all matters of geekery — *A Song of Ice and Fire*, Brandon Sanderson books, Marvel vs. DC, and video games. Alicia was in many ways Tim's portal to cool things since his father refused to let him play video games or read "garbage" and monitored his free time like a prison camp guard.

Dima had once been his portal to awesome stuff, passing Tim books and comics like contraband. Dima had also let him play games at his house on the rare occasions when Tim was allowed out. But Dima had recently found cooler friends, making Alicia his only link to these other worlds, allowing him to keep some semblance of a tether to his interests. Now *she* sneaked books and comics to Tim between classes. Unfortunately, he couldn't go to her house and hang out and play video games, because God forbid he have a girlfriend — or a friend that was a girl. His father made it clear: girls were a distraction, baby traps that would derail his plans for college — and thus destroy his entire life.

After getting dressed, the boys were led to the gym, since it was raining, to play volleyball. Immediately, Tim regretted getting dressed for gym. Because there, in the bleachers along the wall, sat a few people who hadn't dressed out for whatever reason. Among them, Alicia dragged a pencil across a page in her sketchbook.

She looked up from her drawing, smiled, and waved.

Tim waved back, annoyed that he couldn't be sitting there with her. The other kids, two popular girls and a boy, were sitting at the bottom of the bleachers. She was at the top, as far from them as she could be. They could have shared an entire period alone.

It was perfect time for Tim to ask Alicia to the upcoming Student Luau. The dance wasn't for another month, but in a rare moment of kindness, his father had already given him permission to attend. Tim figured his mother must've pressured him to allow Tim to do something normal for a change. *Sometimes*, she managed a win on his behalf.

Of course, his father had said yes prior to the little forgery incident.

The dance was probably off the table. But Tim figured a month away, with permission previously granted, might be enough to get him there so long as he didn't bring it up until a few days prior.

But going alone would be lame. Tim wouldn't attend unless Alicia would go with him.

He'd planned to ask her at lunch sometime soon. But figuring out when was difficult. Sometimes, one of Alicia's other friends — Greg, Parker, or Kara — would sit with them. They were all nice enough, but Tim never felt truly comfortable around them. Nor did they really have conversations with him like Alicia did. Their exchanges were the bare minimum kind you have with someone in your social circles that you don't really like, or an annoying sibling you talk to only because they're there. It wasn't genuine. They were artsy cool kids with weird hair and weirder clothes. They probably looked at him and wondered why Alicia was wasting her time with a nerd.

Coach Thompson, a fireplug of a man with a baked red face and flaming hair, picked two leaders at "random" (everyone knew he had his favorites) and instructed them to pick teams. As Kip and Jenny went through the class, picking based on friendships first, athleticism second (the two often went hand-in-hand), rosters quickly filled, leaving all the dorky, unathletic kids standing around staring at one another in yet another contest of Who Will Get Picked Dead Last?

After a few more selections, it was down to three, including Tim.

The other candidates were Beth, a fat cross-eyed girl who could barely walk without tripping, and Stinky Pete, a zit-faced spaz who rarely bathed and blurted weird noises at random.

Jenny looked over the three of them. Tim felt insulted.

Oh, come on. There's even a question? I may be scrawny, but I have some muscles. I can play!

"Um ... Beth."

What the hell?

Kip, a preppy lacrosse player who resembled Zac Efron enough to swell his ego, looked at Stinky Pete and Tim as if weighing cancer with Ebola.

"Tim," he said with a sigh.

Well, at least I wasn't picked last. I guess that's something.

A few minutes into the match, both sides were tied. Tim had managed to smack the ball a half-dozen times and keep himself from embarrassment.

Then it was Tim's turn to serve.

The last time he'd played volleyball, he'd tried an underhanded serve and punched the ball out of bounds. This time, he'd serve overhand like most of the other kids were doing.

He held the volleyball straight out in front of him, resting in his palm. His pulse pounded.

Tim squared his shoulders toward the net, feeling the gym's every eye on him. He made the mistake of glancing at Kip, who was standing in front of the net, looking back as if to say, "Don't fuck this up."

Tim looked at the other team, all waiting to knock back his serve.

He pulled back his right arm, palm flat, ready to smack the ball.

Tim tossed it in the air, but was so nervous, the ball went too high. Too forward.

Everything felt like a movie.

But not the kind where time seems to slow for the athlete entering the zone, as muscles in his arms and legs move in perfect, graceful coordination like a well-oiled machine to deliver a laser-precise strike.

No, this movie was the kind where things only seemed to speed up at an almost comical rate, where arms, legs, and even Tim's eyes seemed to conspire against him, all equally out of sync in a display of awkwardness usually reserved for blooper videos.

Tim leaped forward, arms sprawling forward, trying to hit the ball from the bottom and send it sailing over the net.

Instead, his hand found the side — and smacked the ball straight at Kip's head.

Somehow, Tim managed to keep moving forward, uncontrollably, running smack into Avery Carter, Kip's girlfriend, a hot blonde with a large chest that most guys wouldn't mind bumping into. But not like this.

He tried to stop himself from falling. Tried to stop her, too. But they both fell in a tangle of embarrassment and pain as laughter erupted around them.

Time froze. But not in the moment Tim needed to position himself. No, time decided to wait for the worst possible moment, as he was lying atop Avery, straddling her, and she was looking up horrified, maybe dazed.

12

He tried to stand, and in doing so, his hands pressed against her breasts — purely on accident. Time unspooled even slower. Not to foster enjoyment for his life's first touch of breasts — and maybe his last. No, it slowed to make the scene even more awkward and painful, so everyone in the gym could see him standing there with his hands on Avery's tits.

She shoved him away, yelling, "Get off, you freak!"

More laughter echoed off the walls.

Tim's skin sizzled across every inch of his body.

He wanted to get up and off Avery, flee from the court.

He stumbled back, managing to stand as the two girls closest to Avery came to help her, looking at Tim as if he were a pervert.

Kip ran over to Tim and shoved him backward.

"What the fuck's your problem?"

Tim wasn't sure if it was because he'd hit him with the ball, knocked his girlfriend to the ground, or accidentally felt her up as he tried to stand.

"I'm sorry," Tim sputtered.

Kip shoved him backward again, so hard that Tim felt the jolt of his tailbone when he landed hard on his ass.

The moment moved from comedy to horror, with Tim as the victim.

He stared up helplessly, his mind stuck on what to do next. Would Kip really fight him? Or was he blowing off steam and Tim should stay on the floor until Kip had a chance to cool down?

Kip was one of the jocks turned Dima's friend. While Kip hadn't been one of the kids who bullied Tim in the past, he was friends with enough who had that he must've shared their disdain.

Tim heard the last thing he wanted to hear: a girl's voice yelling, "Back off, Kip!"

He turned to see Alicia off the benches, running toward them as if she were about to step in and kick Kip's ass.

"Oh, gonna have your girlfriend stick up for you?" Kip laughed. "Pussy!"

Suddenly, Avery was in the mix, telling Alicia to mind her own damned business. A crowd of kids huddled closer, and for a moment, it felt like a riot might erupt — all because of an errant serve.

Mercifully, a shrill whistle from Coach Thompson disrupted the moment from spiraling further out of control.

"Break it up, break it up," he bellowed, coming over and looking down at Tim, still sprawled on the floor.

Tim felt even more emasculated beneath the coach's glare. Coach hated weak kids like Tim. You could hear it in his barked orders and muttered jokes.

"What's going on?"

Tim stood. Kip said, "Nothing, Coach. Nothing."

"Good, get back to the game."

Coach Thompson looked at Tim. "Why don't you sit the rest of the game out, eh, kid?"

On the one hand, Tim felt insulted that the coach didn't even remember his name. But on the other, at least now he'd have a chance to spend the rest of class with Alicia — even if he was doing so after one of the more embarrassing moments of his ninth-grade career.

"Okay, Coach." Tim followed Alicia to the bench.

He looked back at Avery to see if she was still glaring at Alicia. The last thing Tim wanted was to cause her to become persona non grata like him.

But Avery was busy being consoled by Kip, as if she'd been grievously injured.

Such drama!

Which was why he loved Alicia so much. She was drama free. An easy person to be friends with.

Unlike Dima!

Alicia was geeky but managed to have lots of friends across several groups of kids — the artsy kids, the rich kids, the jocks, and even some of the tough kids. Tim often wondered how she'd managed to be friends, or at least friendly, with so many different types of people while not being an empty-headed, vacuous person like most of the popular kids. Probably because she was a gem.

Again, Tim wondered why she ever bothered to talk with a loser like him. Maybe she wouldn't under normal circumstances. But they'd known one another since first grade, long before most kids split into cliques and made you feel like an outsider if you didn't fit into their little group's narrow set of criteria.

They sat, and Alicia said, "You okay?"

"Yeah," Tim said, reasonably sure that his lack of grace, and the fact that he needed a girl to rescue him, probably didn't bode well for his getting a yes to the dance.

But she's here. Talking to me. That's not something she'd do out of pity.

Alicia bent over and moved the book bag beside her and slipped the black hardcover sketchbook inside it. Tim caught a whiff of her scent — kind of sweet like strawberries, a blend of light perfume and something else, maybe laundry detergent or fabric softener — and deeply inhaled. He loved her scent. He'd never thought much or noticed other people's — just Alicia's.

"Whatchya drawing?"

"Oh, nothing special." She pulled the sketchbook back out of her bag and showed Tim an intricate ink drawing of a young girl entangled in tree branches. Alicia was modest about her talent, but there was no denying her line work or attention to detail. Her drawings were usually somewhere between comic and photo realism. This one leaned more toward comic, with enough varying strokes and line widths to give the drawing a heartbeat.

The trees were alive, branches like tendrils snaking the girl's limbs. But she wasn't scared. Judging by her long wild hair and the way her oversized white pupil-less eyes seemed to glow, the girl was controlling the trees. Or perhaps she was possessed by them.

"Cool. What is it?"

"I dunno. A dream I had. I don't remember much of it, except that I was running through the woods, getting chased by these huge wolves with glowing red eyes. I tripped and fell down a hill into a landing, and I heard, and felt, movement closing in — the ground moving and trees slithering, getting tighter around me, protecting me from the wolves. And suddenly, a path opened in front of me, like a cave made of branches. I'm not sure how I could see in total darkness, dream logic, I guess. Then I came to the end of the path where there was this large, thick tangle of branches. I could see something inside them, like they were protecting something. Then the branches pulled back, and this girl was inside them."

"Wow, that would make an awesome story!"

"Want to write it?"

"Really? It's your dream. You don't want to write it?"

"I'm not much of a writer. Believe me. I'll stick to drawing."

"Maybe we can collaborate?"

"That'd be cool. How would it work?"

"I dunno. I never collaborated with anyone. But it'll be fun to figure out. I'm already getting a few ideas just from your dream. We can write a fantasy story about a girl lost in the woods, being chased by wolves."

"I dunno, now that I think about it, it feels very 'Little Red Riding Hood.'"

"That's okay. Lots of great stories are based on fairy tales and old myths. That's just the seed. We can add our own experiences and ideas to turn it into something totally different."

Alicia smiled and nodded. "Cool beans."

12

As they explored the idea, Tim managed to close out the world around them. The assholes who'd laughed at him. Kip and Avery wanting to start a fight. The coach who didn't even know his name. Everyone ceased to matter.

All that mattered were he and Alicia, the conversation about their story, and a new world full of possibilities.

Tim had never felt more alive.

Or more certain that he was in love with a girl.

He had no clue if the feeling was mutual. How could a girl so pretty, smart, and kind like someone so socially awkward?

Maybe that didn't matter to her. She wasn't like the other kids. She valued friendship, conversation, a sense of humor, and creativity above stupid things like clothes, cars, or muscles.

Alicia was the one.

TEN

Maggie Kent

Just when Maggie thought her day couldn't get any worse — a flat tire then the world's worst customer — her cell phone buzzed with a string of texts.

She asked Viv to cover her tables then ducked into the bathroom to see what was so urgent.

Something at school?

Or ...

Nick!

She sat in the stall, peeing and reading his messages.

The first text read: *We need to talk.*

Then: *You can't ignore me forever.*

Finally: *If you won't return my calls or texts, I'm coming to see you.*

A chill ran through her.

The last thing Maggie needed was for Nick to show up at the diner. He'd cause a scene like he did six months ago, after Loretta fired him.

Loretta had only given Nick a job as a favor to Maggie

after he lost his bartending gig. In typical Nick fashion, he managed to burn through his goodwill within a few weeks. Loretta had to let him go after a month. And then, having nowhere else to go, he started hanging around at the end of Maggie's shift, ostensibly to pick her up at first, but then just to loiter. When he started showing up wasted, Loretta told him not to come back like that again, or she'd have to let Maggie go, too. She couldn't have Nick scaring away her customers.

Maggie looked at the phone, breathing heavily through her nose. Knowing she shouldn't engage him but at the same time knowing she couldn't have him show up at the diner, she texted, *Don't.*

Maggie tucked the phone back into her front pocket, washed her hands, and returned to work.

A minute later, the phone buzzed.

She wanted to see if he agreed not to come but had to ignore the call.

Maggie had tables to tend and couldn't let customers see her checking her phone. She'd have to wait for a lull then sneak back to the bathroom or to the prep area in the kitchen, so long as Loretta wasn't lurking about. Sebastian wouldn't care if she was checking her phone; he knew she was a good worker.

While Maggie scribbled an order for a group of four college-aged kids, a sudden light entered her otherwise dark day — Officer Dumont, or Clarence, as he insisted she call him.

She spotted him at the hostess station. He looked up and met her eyes with a smile. He was with his partner, Patrick, a stocky Irishman in his forties with curly red hair. The guys usually came in for coffee before starting their shift. Sometimes they — or even Clarence alone — would return for lunch or dinner.

Regulars made days like this tolerable. Or — if Maggie

were feeling especially hard on herself — kept her from leaving and finding a better paying, more solid job.

She led the officers to a booth in her section, poured them coffees like always, then brought over a dish of creamer in case they wanted more. "Good morning. How's it going, guys?"

"All right," Patrick said, "what's shakin'?"

"Same ol', same ol'." Even if that wasn't close to the truth, Maggie wasn't sure if she wanted to involve the officers in her morning drama. At least not yet.

"How's that thing we were talking about last week?" Clarence asked.

Well, so much for not mentioning Nick. Clarence had come in for dinner at the end of his shift one day last week and was the one who insisted she file the order against him.

"Not so good." Maggie didn't have time to sit and explain the whole thing. The college kids were getting antsy, waiting on an order that was already sitting in the window.

"Let me just grab some food for that table there, and I'll come right back. You guys eating anything?" Maggie stole a glance at the window.

"I dunno," Patrick said. "I'm thinking about it."

Clarence laughed. "Yeah, that means he'll have two of everything."

"Yeah, screw you, buddy."

"Okay, I'll come back and check on you in a minute."

Maggie stopped at the table of college kids and let them know that their food would be up in a minute.

The blonde with way too much makeup and long fake nails said, "Can I get another Diet Coke?"

"Sure." Maggie grabbed her nearly empty glass and headed to the window.

After dropping off their orders, and the blonde's drink, the heavyset Asian next to the blonde asked for a refill on his Sprite.

12

"Sure," Maggie said, annoyed that he didn't ask when she was there before. Then again, maybe his glass was empty, and she'd been too preoccupied with getting back to Clarence to notice. She grabbed his glass. "Can I get anybody anything else?"

After some head shaking and no's, she refilled Asian Dude's Sprite, checked on her other two tables, topped off their drinks, then headed back to the officers.

"So, did you two decide on anything?"

Patrick was one of those diners who looked at the menu whenever he ate, even though he likely had the menu memorized. He almost always ordered the same thing. She could guess his order while it was still in his mouth but didn't want to embarrass him.

She joked with the guys but always stayed on her side of the line, even if they were merciless with one another. Some of the servers, like Viv, gave it as good as they got it from the cops, but Maggie never felt entirely comfortable being too much of a smartass with the officers. It was one thing for your coworker to joke about your spare tire, but guys could be sensitive when a waitress said the same thing. She never wanted one of her customers to feel uncomfortable.

Patrick opened his mouth.

I think I'll have the French toast, scrambled eggs, and four pieces of bacon.

"Um, I think I'll have the French toast, scrambled eggs, and four pieces of bacon."

Clarence laughed. "Didn't you say you already ate?"

"It was a *light* breakfast."

"You're on a diet?" Maggie asked.

"Yeah, apparently I gained some weight since my last physical."

Clarence said, "No shit, Sherlock. They oughta promote you to head detective."

Maggie laughed then asked Clarence if he was having anything.

"No thanks." He handed her the menu. "So, you gonna update me on that thing?"

Going against his nature, Patrick refrained from jokes or feigned offense at being left in the dark. Maggie figured that Clarence had probably told his partner what was happening.

She told Clarence about the texts and the flat tire.

"You don't think he would've flattened my tire, do you?"

"Can I see the messages?" Clarence asked.

Maggie reached into her pocket then looked at a pair of unread texts.

One said: *No. You don't get to tell me what to do. I'm a grown-ass man, and if I wanna come eat at your diner, I'll fucking come eat at your diner.*

The other said: *See you at lunchtime.*

Her stomach churned at the last message. She handed Clarence the phone then excused herself to go wait on her other tables.

After making the rounds, and having to do a few re-fires, Maggie returned to the officers with Patrick's food in hand and fresh coffee to top off their mugs.

Clarence handed her the phone. Sternly, he said, "Don't respond to him again. I've seen too many of these things escalate way too quickly."

"Yeah, but if I ignore him, he'll only get angrier. And I don't need him coming here, getting me fired."

Maggie felt suddenly exposed, as if her entire section could hear their conversation and were silently judging her. The college kids, who had been talking ever since their arrival, fell silent, as if trying to eavesdrop. Maggie wanted to tell them to mind their own business, but at the same time, she was airing *her business* for all in earshot.

Maggie wished she could leave and take care of this thing with Nick before it got out of hand. But it was just her and

12

Viv in front and Kandi at the hostess stand, and Kandi didn't do tables, as she was pretty busy with to-go orders and seating, which meant Maggie was stuck. There were typically three servers scheduled for a weekday morning. However, the third, Barbara, had called in earlier saying she had a doctor's appointment she forgot about, and she'd be late. *How* late was anyone's guess.

"Tell you what," Clarence said, "I'll run by his place and ask about the tire. Maybe put a scare into him to keep him from showing up later."

"I dunno. I don't think he'd respond well to that."

Patrick shoved a fork full of French toast soaked in maple syrup into his mouth. Chewing, he said, "We can be *very* persuasive."

He smiled as if joking. But at the same time, Maggie felt his sincerity.

"I dunno. I don't need other people fighting my battles. Nick is a jerk, but I don't think he'd ever do anything to hurt me. Well, I mean, intentionally."

Clarence met her eyes. "Listen, Maggie. I don't want to do anything you're not comfortable with. But just last week you said he's been violent in the past, and you think he might be using drugs again, which make him more violent."

"Yeah, but I don't think he'd come here and hurt me. He only hit me when we were still together, and we had a huge fight. He usually just storms off and goes to get messed up with his friends."

Maggie felt like one of those battered women on TV, making excuses for their shitty husbands, with their faces and arms purple and welted. It wasn't like that. Sometimes Nick got drunk. The protective order was more of a preventative measure than anything, to keep McKenna from accidentally being a victim of one of his drunken or drug-induced tirades. Sober, Nick would never set out to hurt either of them.

Who said he's sober now?

Still, Maggie didn't see him as the type to flatten her tire. If Nick was mad at you, he wanted you to know. He didn't do sneaky things. He was too impulsive. And that's why she figured it was best to leave things as they were. Let him get pissed, blow off steam at home, whatever. Maggie didn't want to give him more reasons to be angry at her. That only increased the odds that he'd show up, yelling at her, likely getting her fired.

Maggie struggled to think of a logical explanation why the officers shouldn't pay him a visit — in a way that she didn't come off like a weak woman protecting her abuser — when one of the college kids, the blonde, said, "Excuse me, waitress."

Maggie felt like she'd been caught ignoring her customers and quickly turned to the table. Blonde Girl gave her a dirty look, snapping her fingers for their checks.

Maggie would usually try and soothe a customer's annoyance, especially when triggered by her actions. But at the moment, she was more concerned with returning to Clarence, clarifying her position on Nick, and figuring out what to do next.

She didn't want the cops harassing her ex. Yes, he might deserve it based on the history of shitty things he'd done to her, and McKenna. But Maggie didn't want to make things worse. Maybe that tiger had left its cage the moment she filed the protective order. Now Maggie was trapped in a car without brakes, racing downhill. It was all her fault. Maybe she should've let things stay as they were instead of filing the order.

McKenna hadn't ever truly been in danger.

Had she?

Maggie brought the college kids their checks then stopped at the fountain machine to refill someone's Coke, scolding herself.

Stop.

12

You're making excuses for Nick.

You know it's only a matter of time before something tragic happens because of him and his druggie friends.

Stop being a wimp, and stick to your guns.

He deserved the order, and after those threatening texts — clearly in violation of his order — he deserves a talking to from the cops!

Maggie returned to the officers' booth.

"Okay. If you think it's the right thing to do, then yes, please talk to him."

"It *is* the right thing to do," Clarence said, finishing his coffee. "We'll go talk to him. See what's up and take it from there."

"Thank you." Maggie nodded, hoping she hadn't added fuel to an already combustible situation.

Because if Nick *had* slashed her tires, he might be capable of *anything*.

ELEVEN

Abe Mcdonald

HALFWAY TO WORK, Abe decided to say *hell with it* and call in sick. Why bother going to work one last day just to go through the motions?

No, if he was going to become this new, bold person, why not start now and say fuck you to the man, sit home in his underwear until it was time to get McKenna?

When he'd dropped Maggie and McKenna off at school, he'd pulled off a very important part of his plan — getting Maggie to list Abe as a contact who could pick the girl up later since Maggie didn't have use of her car.

"Are you sure you can pick her up?" Maggie had asked, thanking him so profusely for his kindness that he almost felt bad for lying to her.

"Yeah, no problem at all. I have to run an errand for my boss on that side of town anyway. I can swing by and bring her to the diner after school."

Of course, Abe had no intentions of bringing her back to Maggie.

He was hard just thinking about it.

He went into his bedroom, picked up his cell phone, and stared at Raj's name in the contact field.

12

Even as his finger hovered over the *Call* box onscreen, his heart raced with apprehension and guilt for calling in sick when he wasn't really ill. He thought of his confidence coach, Craig. What would *he* say to calling in sick to work?

He'd probably say I ought to have called in any of the four or so times I was too sick to work but didn't because I was so damned scared Raj would fire me, or because I was so needy of his approval that I worked, sick or not.

Well, not anymore. Raj can go fuck himself. It's time I do what I *want to do.*

"I am smart. I am strong. I am willing to do what must be done to get what's mine."

Abe hit the call button and waited for Raj to answer. He was probably sleeping in late, like most mornings. On the days he did show up to the shop, it often wasn't until noon. Why show up to work early when you can get your poorly paid underlings to do everything for you?

"Hello?" Raj said in his thick Indian accent, sounding sleepy.

"Hey, Raj," Abe calmly said. Not at all nervous like on the few occasions he'd had to deliver bad news to Raj. "It's Abe. I won't be coming in today."

"What?" Raj said, instantly awake and annoyed. "What do you mean you're not coming in?"

"Yeah, I'm not feeling well." Abe tried not to laugh. Part of him would have loved to tell Raj to go fuck himself, but he didn't need to burn his bridge before leaving town. He had to stay as far under the radar as possible, lest some part of his plan — maybe something not yet considered — fell apart. Best to keep up pretenses that this was just another day and this was the same old meek Abe McDonald that Raj had been walking all over for years.

"I won't be able to make it in. Sorry."

Abe considered hanging up. Let Raj stew in confusion and

anger, wondering when the hell Abe McDonald had sprouted hair on his balls.

Instead, Abe listened as Raj tried to work him. First, the guilt. "But Abe, I don't have anyone to cover your shift. I need you to at least open the shop. I'll come in later to relieve you, okay?"

Abe hated the way that Raj always slipped an "okay?" into requests, never giving Abe a chance to say no. Always assuming he'd say yes. Sometimes Raj would call and ask Abe to stay late, then ask "okay?" and hang up before Abe could answer.

Not this time.

"Sorry," Abe said quickly, before Raj could hang up. He fake coughed for good measure. "I can barely get out of bed. Something awful, Raj. You know I never call in, so it has to be bad. I think I'll go to the doctor."

Raj sighed. Next would come a threat. Not a direct one. Something vague: If you don't do *this*, then *that thing you want* won't happen. Raj was great at vague threats. A king.

Surprisingly, no threat came.

"Okay, Abe. I'll cover for you. Just call me later to let me know what's going on, if I can count on you tomorrow, or if I need to make other arrangements."

Abe wasn't sure if "other arrangements" was a veiled threat of his replacement, or if it simply meant that Raj would call in his brother, Sammy, who sometimes worked the shop's busiest shifts. Sammy was a shit employee, but a warm body was better than none. He could at least sell some things, take repair orders, and postpone work until someone more experienced — Abe — showed up to fix things.

"Okay, I'll call you when I get back from the doctor."

For a moment, Raj said nothing.

Uncertainty creeped in, as if Raj had somehow figured him out, or uncovered his plans. Maybe he'd grown suspicious?

12

Suspicious enough to do what?

There was nothing Raj could do, short of come to Abe's house, break in, and discover his plans before their execution.

Abe tried to shake the fear from his mind.

I am smart. I am strong. I am willing to do what must be done to get what's mine.

After the long pause, Raj said, "Make sure you bring a doctor's note. So I have it for the records."

"Yes, sir," Abe said, shaking his head. There were no "records." But Raj was too damned afraid to come out and say he required proof of the doctor's visit, so he mentioned some bullshit records. Raj had a hoarder's organization. If he had any records, they weren't anything Abe had ever seen, and he practically ran the shop.

"Bye, Abe."

Raj hung up, and Abe felt a rush of power. It felt good to finally assert himself.

For too long, he'd been kissing Raj's ass, bending over backwards for the man, even though Raj was unappreciative and only treated Abe for the worse. He wished he'd found leverage sooner. He could've probably forced Raj to pay him considerably more. Maybe he could've demanded specific days off rather than being forced to work every holiday. What computer shop needed to be open on Thanksgiving? Sammy could've easily worked the holidays since they were the slowest days of the year. Sometimes, Abe felt like Raj opened the shop on holidays just to show Abe who was boss, to prove that he still made the schedule and controlled forty-plus hours of Abe's life, whether Abe liked it or not.

That was just the kind of thing guys like Raj did to beta guys like Abe.

But not anymore.

Now Abe was an alpha.

Or on the road to becoming one anyway. And with that came a freedom to never answer to men like Raj again.

He flipped open his laptop , feeling a rush as he went to the directory where he kept recordings from the spyware he'd installed on Maggie's computer after she'd asked him to "look at it."

The software recorded video, audio, and Maggie's every keystroke. Over the past few months, he'd captured login credentials for everything from her bank to her Facebook to email. He had access to everything. Even though she'd been smart enough to make her Facebook account private, he could still peek at her updates, check out the latest pictures and video that were meant for friends.

He loved the updates, which almost always featured photo or videos of McKenna. The more he knew about McKenna, the more he loved her. Yes, she was six. And he realized that loving a six-year-old who wasn't your child, or at least related to you in some way, was something most people could never understand.

But Abe had long ago realized he was different than most people. Purer. Only someone so different could understand McKenna the way she deserved to be understood. The few times they'd been around one another were highlights in an otherwise gray existence.

McKenna was vibrant with life, pure and unvarnished by the cynicism that made so many people ugly. She was kind. She was funny. And she was easy to please — unlike nearly every other complicated person in the world. More than all those things, McKenna was sad. And that was what drove Abe to act.

He'd been reading the emails that Maggie sent to her friend, talking about how horrible of a man the girl's father, Nick, was. A drug addict. A loser. Violent. And on the weekends when he had custody of McKenna, she often came home crying, wondering why her daddy was mean. Didn't he love her?

No, he didn't.

12

But Abe would. More than her father was capable of. More than her mother could manage with her schedule at the diner and attempts to launch a singing career.

Maggie wasn't a bad person like Nick. She was just ill prepared for a daughter. Abe could tell from her emails that sometimes McKenna seemed more burden than blessing to her mother. Maybe she hadn't used those exact words, but Abe could read between the lines.

Everyone's life, but most importantly, McKenna's, would be better in twenty-four hours.

Abe's heart raced as he flicked through the videos captured and downloaded to his computer — footage from Maggie's webcam that she had no idea was being recorded, much less sent to Abe. The spyware's beauty was in its disabling of the tiny red light that indicated the webcam was on. There was no way Maggie could ever know she was being recorded. Well, not unless she was smart enough to figure these things out. Of course she wasn't, not if she needed Abe's help getting rid of basic adware. The first time he fixed her computer, it was so slow and filled with junk, he figured she never saw a button she didn't click yes and grant permissions to.

He hovered his mouse over the latest video thumbnails, all of which he'd already watched, and found his favorite. It was from two weeks ago, taken in Maggie's bedroom just after McKenna got out of the shower.

She was sitting on her mom's bed in a pink robe, open just a bit revealing her chest, but not yet her nipples. Abe pressed play, listening as the girl told Maggie offscreen about her Minecraft game.

"Do you wanna see the house I built for us?" McKenna asked, looking offscreen. From the distance, Abe could hear Maggie say, *Maybe later* in that disinterested, "I have better things to do" tone of voice that must've cut like a blade into her daughter's psyche after hearing it so often.

He watched as McKenna stared at the screen, typing, running her fingers over the mouse, playing the game. If he wanted, he could call the video captured from the game since everything that happened on the screen was also saved and uploaded to a private, anonymous server set up by Abe. While neither her mother nor father probably cared about the house she was making in the game, Abe would show interest.

It was your job as a parent to care about the things your child cared about. Not ignore them. Abe thought of his mother, who had been similarly neglectful of his interests. She cared more about pleasing the number of unstable men who came through their lives in constant whirlwinds of disruption.

Abe leaned forward as the video started to approach the six minute mark, where the girl's robe would fall to reveal more. His hand slowly crept down to his underwear.

ONCE DONE and bathed in the euphoria of a powerful orgasm made all the more potent for the proximity to his goal, Abe killed the computer in disgust.

Abe was *not* a pedophile.

At least not one who acted on his impulses. He thought that men who raped girls, or boys for that matter, ought to be castrated. Anyone that would harm a sweet, innocent child and destroy that innocence should be thrown to the wolves.

While he planned to run off with McKenna, he wouldn't force himself upon her. Ever.

He wasn't proud of being attracted to young girls. He'd tried to be with women his own age, and some even older. But those women wanted nothing to do with him. The few who had, well, they'd done nothing for him.

Abe often wondered why he was the way he was. Was it some malfunction in his brain, the way some people saw homosexuality? It made sense in a lot of ways. Or was it Kurt?

He tried not to think about his mom's scumbag biker

boyfriend, and the things he'd made Abe do as a child. The things his mother pretended didn't happen, even when Abe had tried to tell her.

Did those incidents change Abe early on? Did they prevent him from ever liking anyone but children?

And if so, why didn't he like little boys? That would make more sense if his condition *was* cause and effect. But if it were genetic, whom could he blame? Abe never knew his real father, or if it were passed down from him. And if it was faulty wiring, then only fate was to blame.

While he'd given much thought about the matter, it never led him to anything other than frustration. It wasn't like he could fix himself. He couldn't exactly stare at an adult woman long enough to change his orientation. Whatever made most men like women was barely there inside him.

There were times when he'd watched the videos of Maggie undressing in front of her computer and managed to both get aroused *and* finish off. Little moments like that made him feel less like a monster. Though there was also a part of him that wondered if he was only turned on by Maggie because she was McKenna's mother.

Abe had stopped trying to change what he couldn't. Stopped hating himself because of it. Yes, there was still shame, but not the self-loathing he'd felt before finding Coach Craig.

Now he would embrace that part of himself. He'd take an unloved little girl and give her everything she deserved. He'd give her the love inside him that so many would consider so wrong, so horrible. She would come to appreciate it.

Someday, he hoped, she'd return that love.

Yeah, but what if she doesn't love me? What if she's afraid and wants to go back to her mother? I can't just let her go back, can I? She'd tell the police — though surely they would've put two and two together by then ...

Abe reopened his laptop, this time watching a more

innocuous video, one where she was telling a story to her mom's friend on Skype. A story she made up about her stuffed cat, whom she called Mr. Whiskers.

Mr. Whiskers, it seemed, was stuck in a world full of dogs and didn't know how to find Momma Cat.

It was a sweet story, full of raspy giggles that made her all the more endearing. Tears of love welled in Abe's eyes.

He might be a monster, but could love ever really be wrong?

TWELVE

Joe Harcourt

J<small>OE SAT</small> in Dr. Wilson's office, staring at the plastic plants that filled the air with a feeling of death.

He often wondered why his doctor's staff, with its nice spacious suite and oversized windows along the wall, wouldn't put *real* plants — living, breathing things — in the office to provide some actual life. Most days, the office felt like Death's waiting room.

Joe thumbed through a copy of some golf magazine even though he'd never held so much as a passing interest in the sport — it was that or some awful gossip magazine, or worse, some "health" magazine aimed to scare the hell out of old folks.

He remembered countless doctors' appointments with Grace as she was undergoing cancer treatment in vain. Back then, the offices hadn't seemed quite so morbid, even though, technically speaking, those convalescents were probably closer to death than Dr. Wilson's average patient.

But miracles had been for others, not for Grace.

Joe remembered once when they were courting in their teens, after he'd taken her to see some romantic movie whose name escaped him. He *did* remember their conversation —

Grace had asked why he never danced with her. Back then, couples danced. If you couldn't dance fast, you danced slow. If you couldn't dance slow, you went to Arthur Murray and learned to dance like a man. And Joe *had* gone to dance classes, and had conquered some of his shyness while learning enough basic moves to get him by. Yet whenever they went somewhere where guys and gals would be dancing, he could never work up the nerve.

After the movie, he admitted his fear.

"Scared of what?" she asked him. It had been the first time Joe had ever confessed to being scared of anything. To her anyway.

"That you'll see what a klutz you're with, and you won't love me anymore."

Not long after, Joe was drafted. And while the war scared him plenty, he spent most of his time in the jungle, drenched but unscathed. There were too many things he could no longer remember, but Joe didn't think he could ever forget the mutilated POWs dumped like cattle in ditches, the stench of death and despair that smothered his senses and chewed through his skin to burrow deep into his soul, or the atrocities at seeing the death and destruction wrought by his own men.

In Vietnam, Joe promised himself that if he somehow made it home to Grace, he'd dance with her.

He kept his promise in the spring of '75, coming home, sweeping her into his arms, and dancing in her parents' living room.

That night held two other firsts with Grace. The first time they made love. Then, after, he'd cried in her arms as he told her of the horrors he'd seen. Not his most masculine moment, but it was the closest they'd ever been. That moment forged the rest of their lives in an unbreakable bond, strong enough to survive a rough economy, an unwanted pregnancy, and the losses of both sets of parents. A bond that would've still been as unbending as steel if not for cancer.

The receptionist's voice brought him back to the present.

"Mr. Harcourt? Mr. Harcourt? The doctor will see you now."

Joe set the magazine down and stood slowly so as not to agitate his back, which had started aching when he bent to pour water for Hoss before leaving.

He exchanged pleasantries with the doctor's assistant as she checked vitals and ran down the lengthy list of his prescribed medicines, asking if he was still taking each one. He said yes to them all, though half the names he couldn't remember, assuming he was still swallowing them so long as the pharmacist was filling the order.

As he waited for the doctor, Joe felt a painfully deep, creeping nostalgia. Why had God been so unkind as to make one part of life — the part where you're struggling to get by — so long and arduous while the part where you get to settle down and enjoy what you have — family, friends, and nature's quietest moments — so fleeting. It seemed like sometimes he'd spent his youth preparing for a test that he did everything in his power to ace. But the test flew by in a flash, and none of the things he thought would matter could ever change the results.

In the end, there was nothing but a ticking clock and the mourning of memories lost. And now — depending on Dr. Wilson's prognosis — even those might be fading.

He'd seen how cancer had eaten at Grace in those final weeks. She'd been reduced to a shell of the woman he'd spent his life loving. The person who passed wasn't her. Just a shadow of her life and love.

Would he go the same way?

Dr. Wilson entered, holding a large white envelope.

"Good afternoon, Mr. Harcourt," he said, shaking Joe's hand.

"Hello."

His heart galloped, trying to pry something from the

doctor's expression or from the large faded-blue eyes hiding behind his thick lenses.

"I'd like to show you the MRI scans." The doctor killed the overhead lights then pulled the large black images from the envelope and held them in front of a light board.

"This, Mr. Harcourt is a normal, healthy brain of a man around your age."

Joe wasn't sure what he was looking for, so he said, "Okay."

Dr. Wilson put up a second image with large dark areas missing from the first slide.

"And this is your brain, Mr. Harcourt."

Joe swallowed.

"What are you saying, Doc?"

"Well, this, along with the other tests, indicate that you're in much worse shape than I thought."

"Are you saying I have Alzheimer's? How bad is it?"

Dr. Wilson turned to Joe. "Do you have family you can stay with?"

"What? When?"

"You may have a month or two left where you can still function normally. After that, maybe sooner, you'll need to have someone looking after you full time. Do you have anyone who can do that?"

"No." The doctor should've known he had no family. Didn't he pay attention to the things Joe had told him? Didn't he read his file?

Joe shook his head. "I don't have anyone."

"Okay, well we can help you find a place to help make the transition more comfortable."

Even though the doctor had shown Joe the image and shared the results, he still couldn't believe the verdict. How could his body betray him like this? Of course this treachery was nothing compared to Grace's cancer, but still, it seemed so hard to believe that his brain was slowly — for lack of a better word — vanishing.

Staring at the screen, Joe said, "So, am I going to forget ... everything?"

"Most things, yes."

He closed his eyes, picturing the night he danced with Grace in her parent's living room. The memory had smudged — he couldn't remember the song — but he could remember her pink dress and the bows in her hair. He could see the way she looked at him — the eyes of a woman who loved him without condition or end.

Joe sat in the doctor's office, clinging tight to the memory as if he could somehow save it in a box forever.

Dear God, if I remember only one thing, let it be the way she looked at me that night.

9 a.m. - 10 a.m.

THIRTEEN

Loretta Goldman

MOST DAYS, Loretta felt cursed.

She sat in her office, door closed, staring at the stack of bills on her desk, wondering which to pay and which to postpone. She was two months behind on the diner's rent, past ninety days with two of her biggest vendors, and struggling to pay the utilities each month. But at least she'd met payroll, though she wasn't sure how long she could maintain that either.

She'd already lost most of her best employees to CityZen when it opened up down the street, with a hipper menu to capture a cooler clientele.

If it weren't for her son, Dima, pitching in for free four nights a week, and his friend, Jeff, working nights and some weekends for next to nothing, things would be even worse.

CityZen had taken her best employees, and about 40 percent of her customers.

And Loretta couldn't understand why so many people had left. People loved Goldman's, an institution that had survived — no, thrived — for three decades against all comers: fancy donut shops, chain diners, and buffets. They'd all come and gone while Goldman's stood like an oak against time.

12

Hell, she'd changed her name after her divorce from Kosta back to Goldman because the name was such an institution.

Now some fucking overpriced hipster coffee shop was about to sink a local treasure?

The diner was showing its age. Staff morale had sunk to an all-time low. Customers were crossing the street rather than passing in front of her glass.

She'd missed her father every day for two years, but as she sat in his former office, sinking deeper into a bottomless abyss, Loretta was glad he wasn't here to see what she'd let the place turn into.

Ironically, she'd stepped in to help him when he first fell sick four years ago. Loretta convinced him to take more time off and step away from the diner. Despite being the owner, her father loved the kitchen, and prior to his illness, hadn't missed a day of work in twenty-eight years. He typically shared cooking duties, and when not at the stove, he was out in the dining room, schmoozing with the regulars.

Her father was the son of a second-generation Greek mother and Jewish father. His personality was even louder than his voice, and he always brought the best of both cultures to his cooking. He was loud but never obnoxious, the kind of guy who wanted to trade words no matter where you came from. Abbott was everyone's friend.

The customers — and employees — stuck with the diner during its transition period following Abbott Goldman's death.

Loretta promoted Sebastian to head chef and took over the schmoozing, even though she was nowhere near as good as her father. But she was capable, and enough people knew her, especially long timers who'd watched her grow through weekends and summers. Stan handled the business end — vendors, bookkeeping, staffing, as he'd done for a decade.

But something happened in the aftermath of his death.

Her brother, Stan, started taking risks that their father would have never allowed. He bought expensive TV ads, frittered away their capital on failed social media experiments, and started messing with the menu, trying to "class the place up" and "bring it into the twenty-first century."

He'd burned through their reserves. Worse, he'd burned through decades of goodwill with customers and employees who didn't appreciate the changes. Even now, six months after he left in a blowout with Loretta, she still didn't know what the hell he'd been thinking.

He'd screwed everything up but somehow managed to blame her. He argued that the restaurant was failing long before she came along, and that it was her father holding the diner back by refusing to upgrade or advertise in anything other than the free newspapers. Shaking his fist against the times instead of moving forward to join them. His tactics, Stan insisted, were triage.

The final straw snapped after Stan spent an ungodly sum — well beyond their advertising budget — on a "social media guru" who started posting trivial crap on the various social media sites. It did nothing for their bottom line and cost a ton of money they couldn't afford. Now Loretta was saddled with maintaining these social media profiles on the off chance that they might somehow prove their worth down the road.

When he couldn't throttle her fury, Stan said that if Loretta thought she could do better, he'd sell his share of the diner. It cost her every cent she'd saved over the years and the little left by her father. But it was well worth it to buy Stan out of the picture.

They hadn't spoken in the six months since.

But now, as she sat in their father's old office, Loretta missed her brother.

As bad as things were with Stan's boneheaded decisions, their bills *had been* paid. Stan understood business in a way that she didn't. The ink on his master's degree in business administration was drying while Loretta had found herself knocked up in her first semester at university, forced to leave and raise Dima.

She reached across the desk to her cell phone, tapped her contacts, and hovered above her brother's number.

Am I calling because I miss him, or because I need help?

While Loretta could confess to the former with little shame, she couldn't quite admit the latter. Not to him anyway. Stan was brash and bold like their father but harbored none of his charm. When right, he had a bull's subtlety in letting you know.

She remembered his smug face after they signed the paperwork. He was getting into his BMW outside their lawyer's office. She thought he'd simply leave without a word. Instead, he turned to Loretta and said, "Dad was right about you."

"What do you mean?" she'd asked.

"He asked me to watch over the diner, to make sure that you didn't botch things up."

"Me? I'm not the one who wasted a ton of money on tacky TV commercials and social media bullshit. Dad would've hated that stuff, and you know it!"

"I hate to break it to you, but Dad was stubborn. Just like you. And he was wrong, just like you. Watch. By the time you see I'm right, it'll be too late. And you'll screw this up, just like you do everything else. School. Your first business. Your marriage."

His sideways sneer, and his eyes full of glee as he mentioned Loretta's failed marriage, were punches to her gut. She'd exploded, smacked him in the face, and told him to fuck off.

He stared at Loretta as if considering a return strike then widened his shit-eating grin, climbed in his car, and peeled away from the curb.

That was the last time she'd seen him.

As Loretta's finger hovered over the phone's screen, her

pain felt like a freshly made cut. Her stomach churned, and she put her phone down.

Fuck him.

Loretta grabbed her keys, opened her desk's bottom drawer, reached into her purse, and fished out the pain pills her doctor had prescribed for her frequent back pain.

She opened the bottle, startled to see a lone pill rattling against the plastic.

Did I take them all already?

She looked at the refill date: ninety pills in two weeks. She was supposed to take no more than three a day; the pills were strong, and taking too many could screw up her liver.

Did I already blow through eighty-nine pills?

The more Loretta thought about it, the more sense it made. Her back *had* been hurting a lot. And she'd been having awful migraines. Both she attributed to stress.

Loretta popped the final pill into her palm, slapped it into her mouth, then leaned back in her chair, waiting for the pain to ebb and the opiates to kick in.

Soon she'd feel better, sociable enough to head into the dining room and chat with the guests.

After a few minutes, she called her doctor and spoke to Betsy, the receptionist — a mousy woman who always peered over her lenses at Loretta in a judgmental manner whenever her credit card got declined or when she'd ask for copies of her blood work to track her cholesterol, or make any request that might inconvenience the woman for more than a moment. Of all the jobs in the world, Loretta wondered why anyone would want to be a receptionist.

"Hi, Betsy, this is Loretta Goldman."

"Hi, Loretta. How are you today?"

Loretta said she was doing well, thank you, then told Betsy that she needed a refill on her pain medication.

"Hold on a moment, let me check your file."

Loretta waited, listening to horrible on-hold music

assaulting her ear. After a moment, the music stopped. Loretta thought Betsy was back. But she wasn't. It was a recording stating office hours and whom to contact after hours in case of emergency. As much as Loretta hated on-hold music, she hated the recordings more. They raised your hopes then forced you into three minutes of paying attention in case the person you were waiting for happened to return during the message. The recording gave way to Jimmy Buffet's "Margaritaville," the only song she liked less than "We Built This City."

After the second verse, Betsy returned and asked Loretta to repeat her requested medication.

She did, and Betsy said, "We won't be able to refill that until the eighteenth."

Loretta sighed. "Is there any way you can refill it earlier? I'm all out."

"You're all out? How many are you taking a day? It says here that you shouldn't take more than three. It says take one as needed, up to three times per day."

"I *know* what it says," Loretta said, unable to mask her snippiness. "Sorry. My back is killing me something awful today. I *have* been taking three, it's just that I dropped the bottle last week, and spilled some down my sink. I didn't really think much of it at the time, but then today I realized I was out and, well, I figured I'd call you to see if you can help."

Betsy was silent on the other end.

Probably judging me.

Finally, she said, "I don't think we can call these in. Not without the doctor's approval. I'll talk to the doctor tomorrow and see what she says."

"Tomorrow? You can't ask today?"

"I'm sorry. She left early today and won't be back in the office until tomorrow."

"It's 9:30! You guys just opened, and she left already?"

"Yes, the doctor had a family emergency. We had to cancel the day's appointments."

Loretta wanted to ask why in the hell Betsy was there if the doctor was already gone. She wondered if the receptionist was lying. Maybe the doctor was there, but Betsy didn't want to ask.

Let the addict wait.

But then again, maybe Betsy was there because she had to phone the day's appointments and let them know that the doctor left, and catch up on the billing and stuff she struggled to get through on busy days. She probably had to stick around and answer phone calls — a lot of good that did if the receptionist wasn't willing to call in a fucking prescription.

Loretta wished she'd thought of a better lie. One that Betsy couldn't refuse. Maybe that she'd been on a trip and left her pills in a hotel. Certainly, that would have earned a refill. It wasn't like Loretta made a habit of requesting extra pills. This was a first.

Loretta found her kindest voice. "Are you sure there's nothing you can do before tomorrow? Maybe just call in enough for one day?"

"I'm sorry. I can't," Betsy said in a voice that seemed anything but sorry. Like she was mining some sort of power trip from denying Loretta.

"Thank you anyway," she said then hung up. "Fuck!"

Some nerve to treat me, ME, like a drug addict! I am soooo changing doctors.

She stared at her phone, sitting on the desk's edge, her fingers fidgeting as she tried to figure out how to manage the rest of her day.

She couldn't socialize without the pills. Her back, and now her head, were throbbing too hard. She was a mess when the pain was in such a tight knot — barely able to focus, and on her last nerve. Irritable. The pills helped Loretta be the

12

version of her that people loved. They helped her cope with the stress and eke through her day.

Now what am I gonna to do?

A knock at the door sent her hand flying to cover the bottle. She squeezed it into her hand, swept it into her purse, and closed the desk drawer.

"Who is it?"

"It's me, Sebastian."

"Come in."

The cook, her second-in-charge since Stan left, stepped into her office, looking out of sorts, almost as frazzled as she felt, though she might have been projecting.

"What's up?" Loretta tried to be friendly until the opiates from her single pill — if it was even enough — dented her mood.

"Hey, boss, I just wanted to say sorry about earlier."

"About what?" Loretta had no clue what he was talking about.

"About Bob."

Oh yeah, he'd been bitching about Bob being late. Loretta barely remembered — Sebastian always got worked up about his kitchen staff. The guy was a great worker but at times too intense, freaking out when people showed up a few minutes late. It was a diner, not surgery. She was lucky she could get the handful of people she had to work for so little. How the hell could she expect them all to be on the dot too? Bob wasn't great, but he was good enough for now. Sebastian wanted Loretta to fire Bob's ass yesterday, but she wasn't about to can Bob without a damned good reason. A lack of punctuality wasn't enough. She paid Sebastian well. He could suck it up and make things work until Bob arrived.

"Oh, Bob," she said. "He's here now, right?"

"Yeah, yeah. I just wanted to say sorry, and that you could ignore me. I didn't mean to get on your ass in the kitchen, where other people might hear, ya know?"

While Sebastian was out of line, it's not like he hadn't raised his voice — in front of other people — before about Bob and anyone else he didn't think was doing their job. Loretta wondered why he was suddenly feeling bad about it now, apologizing when it wasn't necessary.

"You all right?" she asked, genuinely concerned that something really was wrong, and he was about to deliver terrible news.

She tried to keep her fingers from fidgeting, lifting them from the desk and folding them over one another.

"No, nothing's wrong." Sebastian shook his head. "I just wanted to say sorry. That's all."

He turned and ducked out of her office.

Loretta had an idea.

"Sebastian?"

"Yeah?" His face appeared back in the doorway.

"Do you happen to know where I could get some pills?"

Sebastian stared back at her blankly.

Loretta was afraid she'd crossed the line — bringing up Sebastian's past, something the two of them had never discussed. She knew her father had helped him after he got out of jail. The former drug dealer had turned his life around thanks, in large part, to Abbott Goldman's faith that he could. He'd treated Sebastian like a son. *Better than his own*, Stan might whine.

As the cook looked at her intensely, Loretta was afraid she'd offended him. Maybe her father wasn't supposed to have shared Sebastian's past.

"What kind of pills?"

Loretta told him.

He looked at her as if trying to decide if he should trust her. Like maybe he *did* have connections. Or maybe he still sold drugs and was trying to decide if his boss was trying to feel him out before she let him go or called the cops.

No. He turned his life around. No way he's selling again.

"No, ma'am." Sebastian shook his head. "I don't hang with that crowd no more. Maybe someone else could hook you up."

The way he was looking at her, Loretta couldn't help but feeling like she'd definitely offended him. He said "someone else" as if hinting that someone else at the diner, someone she didn't look down on, might be a drug dealer and that she was too blind to see it.

Loretta tried not to infer too much; she was on edge and liable to take most things the wrong way.

"It's my back. It went out again. And I'm all out of pills. I dropped the bottle and lost a bunch down the drain. My doctor is out today, so I'm screwed."

"That sucks. Want me to ask around, see if anyone has any?"

She thought about saying yes. It wasn't like he was asking around for illegal drugs. The pills were perfectly legal. Hell, half the women she knew were addicted to one pill or another. There was a good chance half her staff was taking something she could use to dull the edge.

But Loretta thought of her father and how ashamed he would be, both by her need and her employee request.

She shook her head. "Thanks. But no. I don't want people to think I'm trying to find out if they're popping pills. I should probably head home. Maybe try and come back later. We have anything I need to be here for?"

"No," Sebastian shook his head. "Well, wait. Yeah, the fish guy is coming. If you want discounts for cash, then you need to be here."

"Can you wait for him? He usually shows up before five, right?"

"Yeah, usually," Sebastian said. "Want me to pay him?"

"Yeah, just get the money from the safe."

"Sure thing. You go ahead and get some rest. I got you

covered." Sebastian's voice had shed its annoyance. Now it seemed eager.

She was so thankful that he hadn't jumped ship. Despite Sebastian's past, he was one of the few people Loretta could trust with the deposits, paying vendors, and checking them in. Her other maybes weren't every day, most of the day, like Sebastian. The other servers had too many commitments, like Maggie needing to leave toward the end of her shift to pick up her daughter from school.

But Sebastian had no commitments and was always there when she needed him. He deserved a raise the moment the diner could afford it. She'd hate to think what things would be like if he weren't around to keep things in order.

"Thank you, Sebastian. I appreciate it."

"No problem," he said, leaving her office.

The opiates kicked in. Loretta grabbed her purse with a smile. She couldn't wait to get home and rest, knowing the diner was in excellent hands.

FOURTEEN

Sheryl Dumont

Sheryl had a showing at eleven, but she couldn't think about anything other than Clarence's asinine behavior.

She sat in her living room for an hour, livid, staring out the window until her anger rolled to a boil and she finally phoned Chloe. Calling her best friend was the only way she knew to vent the negative vibes before work.

Showing properties required more than skills and knowledge. She had to read and please her clients. That meant putting aside her personal crap and making people feel good about the house or property they were considering. It was a tough job, but damned rewarding when done well.

"I'm gonna need to meet for drinks today," Sheryl said after unloading the morning's events. "You got time for me? Wanna meet at the High Dive?"

Chloe, a pretty blonde stay-at-home mom with twin three-year-old boys, was the best person for times like this. They'd known one another since high school, and Sheryl trusted her to keep things quiet — unlike most of her *friends*. Chloe also had a live-in nanny/housekeeper and loads of free time, making her the perfect person to do last-minute stuff whenever Sheryl's schedule had an unexpected opening.

"Yeah, I need to get out of the house. The nanny was off yesterday, so I had the boys all day. And by all day, I mean *allll-lllll* day. So, yeah, I need a stiff drink or three!"

Sheryl laughed. Chloe was only partially kidding. She bitched about her kids, but knew she'd struck the husband lottery. Life was easy when you were married to one of Florida's most successful plastic surgeons. Though Chloe had always had money, she wasn't like a lot of Sheryl's stuck-up clients, women who never earned anything on their own, who didn't know the value of the dollars they burned through paying someone else to raise their kids.

Old money meant connections, lots of them, and Chloe had dirt on everyone in town. She was always fun to dish with and had fed Sheryl tons of useful info over the years. As a realtor, it paid to know who was sleeping with whom, who was fighting with whom, and who was negotiating with whom — anything to earn an insider's edge.

Even after Sheryl had spilled everything to Chloe, she wasn't done venting. There was something cathartic about bitching, in person, to your best friend that made the day easier to handle.

Sheryl wasn't sure when her marriage to Clarence had begun to decay. It was one of those gradual things that started small. Their relationship was in trouble before either saw it coming. It wasn't even the kind of trouble that a lot of people have — constant nagging or fights. A growing gulf of silence simply stretched by the day.

Once, they'd been happy and in love, telling each other everything about their days without fail.

Now, they woke in the morning to sit in silence, went to bed at different hours, and made love maybe once a month, if that.

They were more like roommates than a married couple. Over the years, Sheryl had tried to tell herself it was his job, her job, or both, always getting in the way. There wasn't much to do. But after a while, she realized it was them, not their jobs. And saying there *wasn't* anything they could do was a lie. They simply *weren't* doing anything to save their slowly sinking ship.

The worst part was that Clarence didn't seem to recognize the problem. He seemed perfectly content to go on this way forever.

She didn't remember him always being so distant. Something had changed, but she couldn't figure out what it was, or worse, when it started to happen. Perhaps it was partly her fault. Shouldn't a good, attentive wife recognize a problem *before* it hatched?

When something as damaging as apathy crept up on your relationship, then you were both to blame, at least a little bit.

There was no sense in bringing that up to Chloe, though. Chloe was her best friend, but that didn't mean Sheryl could share *these* sorts of doubts with her, or anyone, really. These were the deep, dark things you kept to yourself — especially from a gossip like Chloe. Better to focus on today's argument than surface every fear and concern about the state of her marriage.

"How the hell could he think I'd go and tell people about Commissioner Grant? It wasn't like the whole town didn't already know. Is Clarence really naive enough to think that secrets stayed buried in a town like Palm Isles?"

"Now you know I don't ever say anything bad about Clarence, right? But you know the problem?"

"What?" Sheryl felt nervous about the conversation's direction.

"You married an idealist."

Sheryl laughed. "That's a *bad* thing?"

"Oh, honey, how many times do I need to tell you that you fuck idealists, but you marry money?"

Chloe was riffing on an inside joke between them — making fun of Sheryl's father's advice — there were times when she wondered if Chloe really believed it. Her friend *had* married a wealthy plastic surgeon and was living the life of Riley. Yet she rarely talked about her husband like she had about affairs gone by.

Had Chloe settled into a life of Unhappily Ever After?

Sheryl wouldn't ask something so impolite unless Chloe broached the subject. Besides, if she asked Chloe about regrets, Chloe might ask Sheryl if she wished she'd stayed with Lloyd. And *that* was a conversation she never wanted to have again.

Sheryl sighed. "I dunno. Maybe Dad had it right. Marry someone you don't really care about. Then they can never disappoint you."

"So, you're *disappointed* in Clarence?"

"I don't know if that's the right word. I mean, he works hard. But … " she didn't want to trash her husband, even to her best friend.

"But what?"

"I just feel like he doesn't care anymore."

Shit. Are we really having this conversation?

"Care about what? You?"

"I don't know. He's always working, or watching TV, or practicing that damned piano he got last year."

"He's *still* on that? What's he going to do? Start working weekends in the clubs?"

"I don't know what he's thinking. He doesn't tell me anything. I told you that Lloyd offered him a job, right?"

"Yeah."

"And it would pay way more than he's making now. And it's a hell of a lot safer."

"But he said no?"

"Yeah. I don't know if he's too proud, or if he thinks there's something going on between me and Lloyd, or what the hell he's stuck on."

"Well, I can't say I blame him. I mean, I don't know too

many men who *would* take a job with their woman's ex. That's a bit emasculating, don't you think?"

"Clarence has nothing to be jealous of. There's nothing happening between me and Lloyd. We're just friends."

"Yeah, but come on. Most married people aren't friends with exes for a reason. There's always that thought in the back of your mind, that little *what-if*. And it doesn't help that Lloyd *is* damned fine and rich as hell."

"Nothing will ever happen between me and Lloyd again. Trust me. And besides, Lloyd is dating that skinny-ass Asian model chick who can't even buy beer yet, I bet."

"Oh, look who's jealous!"

"I am *not* jealous. We've been over a long time. We're friends; that's it."

"Yeah, but friends don't call their friends' girlfriends 'skinny-ass Asian model chicks.'"

"Please, don't *even* go there. I'm just calling it like I see it. I bet that girl still has her baby teeth!"

"You are too much!" Chloe laughed. "Don't worry. I'm just playing. I'll stop."

"Thank you."

"Okay, so we know *you're* not cheating. Is there any chance that Clarence is?"

"*Clarence?*"

"Well, you said he doesn't pay attention to you anymore. And he's always coming home late. Hanging out at that diner. Who the hell hangs out at a diner after work? Don't cops hang out at sports bars or donut shops or something?"

"I dunno. I mean I'm usually running late anyway, so it's not a big deal." Even as she said it, Sheryl's mind circled a recent, recurring thought. One she'd dismissed at first, but now that Chloe had dragged it out into the day's bright light, she couldn't help but wonder if there *were* something more.

There was a waitress he talked about: an aspiring singer

and single mother named Maggie. She'd made a CD for Clarence, and he listened to it — *a lot.*

Was he falling for her? They'd grown apart, but Sheryl didn't think that Clarence would cheat. He was a nice guy. A *safe* guy, who was glad to be with someone as strong, independent, and pretty as Sheryl and wasn't about to go looking outside the marriage for something else. It was a big part of why she married him, though she'd never tell him that and had only recently admitted it to herself.

She told Chloe about the waitress, and the CD.

"That bitch made him a mix tape?"

"No, it's *her* CD. She's a singer. Or wants to be a singer. I dunno. I only listened to a few minutes. Too slow and depressing for my taste."

"Have you met this singing waitress yet?"

"Um, no. Cops don't bring their wives to hang out with them after their shifts."

"Where does she work?"

"Goldman's."

"That dump? Wow, I didn't know your boy was into trashy girls. Though I can't say I'm surprised; cops do have groupies."

"What are you talking about?"

"You don't know about cop groupies?"

"Um, no. What the hell are you talking about?"

"Oh, girl. There's a whole world you don't know about. These girls that work at places that cops frequent — gas stations, diners, bars, and stuff like that. These women love a man in uniform. They throw themselves at cops all the time."

"You're lying."

"No, I swear. It's a thing!"

"It is *not* a thing."

"Yes, it is. I swear. They call them badge bunnies."

Sheryl laughed. "What? No way. You are *sooo* making this shit up."

"I swear. Look it up!"

"I am not looking up *badge bunnies!* How do you even know about this?"

"I saw it on some daytime talk show."

"Oh, a daytime talk show! So it must be real!"

"It is. And they're usually desperate, unstable women. Fucked-up bitches, and crazy in the sack. They have some weird thing for a man in authority. I don't know if their daddies didn't give them attention or what, but yeah, if you have a badge, you have women throwing themselves at you. You better watch out, or that badge bunny *will* steal your man!"

"There's no *badge bunny* trying to get Clarence!"

"Okay, Sheryl. Plot change. We're not meeting at the High Dive. We're going to Goldman's for lunch. We're gonna check out this badge bunny so we can tell the hoochie momma to back the hell off."

FIFTEEN

Nick Kent

NICK WAS NURSING his hangover with some herb in the living room when the cops arrived at his door.

"Nick Kent?" A voice boomed. "Open the fucking door."

"What the hell is going on?" Gary asked, crawling out of his pitch-black bedroom where Nick glimpsed the set of strippers his roommate had brought home, passed out in his waterbed.

"Hell if I know." Nick stashed his pipe and scrambled to hide his paraphernalia. "Probably my bitch ex called the cops on me for texting her shit."

"Fucking bitch." Gary waved his hand in the air on his way back to the bedroom. He closed the door behind him.

Nick ran into the bathroom, doused his wiry frame in body spray, then changed from his sweats and tee into some fresh jeans and a collared shirt, hoping to mask the skunky scent of weed.

After a third knock, he opened the door slightly, leaving the security chain in place.

Nick saw two cops. One a tall black man and the other a heavyset older redheaded cop with a scruffy beard. He recognized them immediately from when he worked at the diner for a few weeks. They were friendly with Maggie and the other servers — *too friendly*, if you asked Nick.

"Yes, Officers?"

"Can we talk to you?" the black cop asked.

"Sure. How can I help you?"

The redhead said, "Not through the door, asshole."

The black cop looked back at his partner, annoyed, then turned to Nick. "We just want to ask you some questions."

"Yeah, well I don't need you waking my roommates."

"Then we can talk out here," the black cop said.

Nick hesitated, his mind cycling through the many ways the cops could jam him up. If they smelled his weed, they could search the apartment. He'd be fucked with a capital F and never see his daughter again. His roommates would definitely see some time for all the shit in their apartment — shit way harder than weed, including Gary's little gun collection, which may or may not have been legal.

"Okay." Nick unchained the door, slipped through, then closed it behind him.

He met the cops' eyes, hoping that the scent of his Axe body spray was stronger than the weed. "How can I help you?"

"Where were you last night?" the black cop asked.

"Here. Why?"

"Can anyone vouch for you?" said the redhead.

"Do they *need* to? What's this about, Officers?"

"It's about Maggie Kent," said the black cop. "And the messages you sent her."

"Oh, Jesus, really? Is it against the law to text while drunk?"

"It is when your messages are threatening," the redhead said. "Especially after you've received an order of protection."

"It didn't say shit about texting her!"

The redhead looked like he wanted to take a swing. The black cop stared at Nick like he was sizing him up.

He wondered if the nigger cop was fucking Maggie now that he was out of the picture. He'd never known Maggie to go for dark meat, but who knew these days? The bitch was crazy, getting all moody whenever he saw her, always yelling at him about his friends. Maybe she was projecting her own mental illness, which is why she filed the order — so she could twist McKenna against her daddy.

Nick kept a lid on his suspicions, deciding to play it cool and gauge the cops' reactions.

The black cop, whose badge read, *Dumont*, which sounded to Nick like an uppity nigger name if ever he heard one, asked, "Where were you this morning?"

"Still in bed." Nick smiled. "How about you, Officer Dumont? Where were you?"

"Watch your fucking tone," said the redhead, whose badge read, *Allan*.

Nick ignored him. "Why you asking where I was? I was here last night. And here this morning. I haven't left my house in two days."

"So you didn't slash Maggie's tires?"

"What? No, I didn't slash her fucking tires. Is that what she's saying now? Bitch is a liar! I didn't do half the crap she claims I did in that shit she filed, and I didn't slash her fucking tires. Check my cell phone records if you like. I know the NSA is all up on that shit. Triangulate or whatever the fuck it is you all do, and you'll see I was here."

Allan stepped closer to Nick, breathing in his face like a tough guy. "Listen, Nick. This bullshit is over."

"What bullshit?"

"All of it," Allan said. "The texts. The tire slashing. Everything. Do you understand?"

"I didn't slash her fucking tires! That cunt is lying!"

Finally, life lit Dumont's eyes. He shoved Nick back against the door, glaring as if seconds from a swing.

"It's over!"

"Fine, whatever," Nick said, just wanting the cops gone before things got uglier. But he'd remember their fucking names. This shit was *far* from over.

"No more texts," said Dumont, his hand still tight around Nick's neck. "Do you understand?"

"Yeah, I understand," he said staring right into the man's beady, brown eyes.

Dumont let go of Nick and turned as if disgusted by having to touch him. But Allan wasn't finished. He stepped even closer, his hot breath even hotter, using his size to intimidate Nick.

"We're not fucking around, Nick. If you text her, if you go anywhere near her, we'll be back. And next time, we won't be so nice. Got it?"

"Yeah," Nick answered Allan while meeting Dumont's eyes. "I got it."

"Good," Allan said. "And why don't you try taking a shower? You smell like a bag of dirty dicks."

Nick ignored the comment then slipped back into his apartment.

He stared through the peephole until the pigs disappeared into the stairwell then turned, screamed, and punched a hole through the drywall.

Gary's door flew open, though Vinnie's stayed shut. Maybe the fag wasn't home.

"What the fuck, man?" Gary shouted. "You *trying* to make sure we don't get our security deposit back?"

"Sorry." Nick stared at the wall's new hole then down at his red knuckles. "That fucking cunt."

"What happened, man?"

"She got her nigger cop lover to come over and harass me. That's what fucking happened!"

"Yo, ease up with the N word." Gary nodded toward the open bedroom door, and Nick remembered that one of his strippers was black.

"You know I don't mean nothin' by it. I'm just pissed that she's sending some cop to try and scare me away from my little girl."

"That's some bullshit," Gary said. "So, what do you wanna do about it?"

"I dunno." Nick shook his head. "But I'm not gonna let some fucking ni— some fucking *cop* — chase me away from my family."

Nick went into his bedroom, ripped open the nightstand, and grabbed the last of the meth he'd ground up two days ago. He'd been trying to go a few days without using, just to prove to himself that he could. It wasn't even the quitting part so much as not feeling like total fuck-all when he was coming down.

He'd done a ton of coke while dealing from behind the bar, and more or less managed his habit without it fucking up his life, but meth was different.

If cocaine was like tapping into a sun's pure energy, meth was like tapping into a fucking supernova.

And the comedown was ten times worse. Headaches, sweats, shitting toxic-looking, dark-black liquid, and feeling like he'd been hit by a truck were starting to take their toll on him.

Plus, he was starting to look like a meth head — bad skin, scratch marks, and his teeth were starting to gray. He figured if he could somehow slow his usage, maybe he wouldn't lose everything to the drug.

But then today happened.

There was no way Nick could deal with this shit feeling subpar as fuck.

He inhaled a bump and closed his eyes, feeling meth's familiar kiss.

Yes!

In the space of seconds, he'd gone from feeling the walls

closing in around him, weak, and vulnerable, to an untouchable motherfucking rock star.

A god among men, and gods didn't let bitches tell them what to do.

Maggie was going to regret her little order of protection.

He laughed at the title.

As if any *order* could *protect* her from his wrath.

SIXTEEN

Corrine Walker

THE LAST TWO hours had been the most nervous of Corrine's life. And to make matters worse, she had zero clue how she'd done on her observation. Mrs. Kern had shown no expression or emotion, sitting in the back of class, staring ahead, watching — *observing*.

During the five-minute break between classes, Corrine headed two rooms down and met Phil outside his classroom where he usually stood until the students had taken their seats.

"*Soooo*, how did it go?"

"I have no idea," she said trying not to show passing students her inner freak show. "Is she always so ... *cold?*"

"What do you mean?"

"She hardly blinked, let alone gave any indication of how I was doing. The woman is a robot! She didn't even say anything afterward. She just got up and left. It was soooo weird."

"She didn't say anything?"

"No. Nothing. What does that mean? Did she say anything during your observation?"

Phil looked nervous, like he was afraid to give her bad news.

"What?"

"Well, she was nothing like that with me. She was talking to me and the class the whole time. She was a regular Chatty Cathy when she left."

"She hates me."

"No, she doesn't."

"She does! I can tell when people don't like me."

"Who wouldn't like you? You're nice, smart, a great and caring teacher. Any student would be lucky to have you and any principal blessed to have you in their school."

"I dunno. I think she's looking to get rid of me. You heard the same rumor, right? That they need to trim class sizes because they overhired for the year."

"They'd never fire you. You have seniority over at least ten other teachers."

"Doesn't matter. I heard the board told all the principals to try and get rid of teachers with tenure so they can pay the new ones less."

"That's a rumor. Don't worry, Corrine, you're not going anywhere. Especially as long as *she's* here."

Phil glanced across the hall with an eye toward Sarah Tanner standing outside her classroom, talking with Mr. Frank, the computer science teacher in the next hall.

Sarah was fat and surly, the sort of teacher that gave them all a bad name. She was a gossip, with only bad things to say. Unless she was trying to curry favor. She and Corrine had been friends during Corrine's first year teaching, before she realized that Sarah was a backstabbing bitch. The teachers despised her, only slightly more than most of the students and a fair share of moms and dads. She'd been reprimanded several times for her negative attitude toward parents.

"As long as *she* has a job," Phil whispered, "all our jobs are safe."

"No. She's always kissing up to Mrs. Kern. She'll probably get a promotion!"

"How were your kids today?"

"Oh God, a few were so awful. Like they saved their worst behavior for today."

"What happened?"

"Well, let's see, Joey Giglioni spent half the class asking the dumbest questions. I swear, he was trolling to make me look bad — or lose my cool."

"Did you?"

"Nope," she said proudly.

"What else?"

"Mary Aldrich fell asleep. I tried to wake her up subtly before Kern noticed, but the gig was up when she started snoring."

"Snoring? Oh wow."

"Yeah. And there was some other stuff that I'll tell you about later. These kids are so unbelievable sometimes!"

Phil laughed then stepped in front of Corrine so he was facing her rather than standing side-by-side. He met her eyes. "Seriously, don't worry. Other teachers have said the same thing about Mrs. Kern, and none of them had bad reports. You did fine."

"Thanks," she said. The bell rang, and they each made their way back into their classrooms.

Even as Corrine sat at her desk, waiting for the kids to get situated, she couldn't help but worry about her observation.

She couldn't afford to lose her job. There were only a handful of other schools, and none were hiring. If she lost her job, she'd have to either hop on I-95 and drive an hour or move. And she couldn't move easily. She'd made the mistake of buying a house right before the real estate market started raking the bottom. There was no way she'd get anything close to what she'd paid for the house, and an embarrassingly high tab on her student loans made the whole thing a no-go.

She wished her photography business was making more than pocket change. It would be great to teach because she wanted to, or do something she loved where people valued her accomplishments. For too long, teaching had lost its reward.

Sure, there were a few good kids every year, but most were apathetic and doing the minimum to skate by. Her excuses would be easier to make if it were only the kids — they'd been apathetic since she was one herself, and probably long before then. But now parents were, too.

Barely half showed up to parent-teacher conferences. Few helped their kids with their homework or had more than a passing interest in their children's school day. Yet when report cards came and their precious snowflake earned a bad grade, it was somehow the *teacher's* fault.

Corrine could *almost* deal with the students' and parents' apathy. If that was the only problem, she could've sucked it up and plowed forward with her best.

But every year, the politics surrounding the job grew worse. You had bureaucrats dictating what would happen in the schools based on the electorate's every passing whim, regardless of whether the new rules helped or harmed kids.

It was almost like every year the politicians spun a giant Wheel of Ideas and went wherever the needle landed, figuring enough approaches might accidentally lead to doing something right, pleasing voters, and clinging to their easy paychecks for one more term.

I'm thirty-four. I'm too young to be this jaded!

Corrine found it odd that despite the many hated elements of her job, she did still love teaching. There was something about reaching those kids who needed it most that filled something inside her.

Corrine's fifth-grade teacher had changed her life. Prior to Mrs. Fletcher, she couldn't stand school. She didn't fit in. She was overweight. She barely had any friends. Mrs. Fletcher assigned the class a short story to write and opened Corrine's world. She'd never written anything before. Back then, she barely read. But when Mrs. Fletcher, along with Corrine's classmates, fawned over her story, Corrine felt as if she were inhaling the first breaths of a brand-new life.

Mrs. Fletcher had given Corrine the self-confidence to buoy her through the tough middle and high school years, and a lifelong love of reading and writing. If Corrine could be that kind of teacher to even one student a year, then all the crap would be worth it.

Unfortunately, it was difficult to get kids excited about algebra. Corrine wished she could've been an English teacher instead, but those jobs were among the hardest to get.

Corrine didn't feel like she'd made a difference in a single student's life this year. The closest was a kid in her fourth period class, Tim Hewitt. He was smart but wasn't fitting in. He was also a writer. Unfortunately, he wrote during class, forcing her to send a note home to his parents on his progress report.

Judging from a few things she'd overheard him saying to Alicia, Tim's father terrified him.

She'd thought about reaching out to a guidance counselor but had no evidence of abuse. And you had to be very careful about accusations these days, lest you lose your job and get sued by someone's overly litigious parents.

Corrine waited for her students to settle then stood and started the day's lesson. But hell if she could focus on anything other than the observation results that would remain a mystery for another few days.

10 a.m. - 11 a.m.

SEVENTEEN

Joe Harcourt

SOMETHING WAS off when Joe arrived at Goldman's.

It wasn't just that the doctor's visit had put him at the diner later than usual. The place *felt* different.

While the hostess, Kandi, gave him the usual friendly greeting — *Hey, Blue Eyes, how's it going?* — none of the other regulars he'd become friends with over his years coming to Goldman's were sitting in the restaurant's rear. Instead, there were new faces, people he'd never seen, sitting in all of his usual spots.

It was like arriving to a family dinner where someone rotated your relatives with fresh faces. For a moment, Joe was afraid that Maggie wasn't there, even though she usually worked every weekday.

He needed to see her. It might be the only thing that could salvage his death sentence, now just one hour old. A familiar face to make everything okay — or at least palatable.

Well, more than a familiar face, really.

However, when Kandi seated him at a different table toward the diner's front, she said, "Maggie will be with you in a minute" and managed to soften his edges.

Still, something felt *off* about Goldman's, and it wasn't just his table.

Joe unfolded his morning paper and looked around the diner, at all the unfamiliar faces, thinking it odd how a place he felt like he knew as well as his own home could become almost foreign in the space of a few hours and a different seat.

He wondered how the diner would feel to his friends, Maude, Gerry, Stan, and the others, when *he* stopped coming in.

Part of him was upset that his friends hadn't waited. They usually ate at 9:30 and stayed at least an hour. Waiting a little longer for him to come in wouldn't have been much to ask — weren't any of them curious about his doctor's appointment? Not that he'd revealed its true nature.

Joe watched the strangers around him and suffered a painful epiphany: the world would continue to spin without him just fine, thank you.

The diner doors would stay open.

The hostess would harmlessly flirt with some other customer.

Maggie would serve someone else with her warm smile and brighten *their* day.

The world would go on even as Joe's mind and body crumbled to nothingness. He would be a footnote, if that, to these people's lives. To anyone's life, really.

Time marched on, with or without you.

Joe wondered how lonely his last days would be. Would anyone visit him in whatever home he wound up in? And if so, would he be able to pair name to face?

Or would he be truly alone, not remembering a soul, mistrustful, maybe scared of those whose names he once knew?

He'd seen it happen to too many people. Even friends he'd once shared tables with at Goldman's. One minute, they were there discussing their grandchildren. The next, they were in some home, muttering about things no one understood, yelling that the nurses were trying to poison them. He'd visited too many people he considered friends only to have them greet him like a stranger.

The mind went, and things got scary fast.

"Hey, Joe!"

He looked up to see Maggie's smile, her bright-blue eyes beneath brown, slightly auburn, hair that reminded him so much of a younger Grace. The resemblance was uncanny.

"Hi, Maggie," he said, feeling a warmth butter the chill that had spread through his soul.

"How's it going? Late today, eh?"

"Yeah, I had a doctor's appointment."

"Ah. Everything okay?"

He wanted to tell her that no, everything was *not* okay, and never would be again.

But that was a lot to throw at poor Maggie. And, to her, he was just a regular customer. She had no clue she was serving a man who had given her up for adoption when she was still a baby.

Joe wondered if Maggie would still be so kind if she knew who he was. Or would she blame him for the cracks in her life's foundation? From what he knew, Maggie had bounced around with foster parents before landing with an adopted mom who was an overbearing drug addict, her dad a drunk who'd been verbally abusive to them both. Her legal parents were dead and buried, but Joe had little doubt that their parenting had left the sort of lingering scars that were impossible to ever fully recover from.

Yet despite it all, and despite whatever difficulty she had raising McKenna on her own, Maggie had somehow managed to hold her smile, ever present even when dealing with the crankiest customers. Just like Grace had been able to keep her smile no matter what was happening around her.

12

While Joe had been a choppy sea of temper in his younger years, Grace was a glassy lake. It wasn't until their cancer ordeal that he'd mellowed, when he'd finally learned what she'd been telling him for years — *to never let the little things get him.*

Especially when the Big Things could be so devastating.

He remembered a conversation after a particularly upsetting setback at work. While he couldn't remember the details of the hiccup, Joe could recall her words like they were carved in his forehead.

"This only has the power *you* give it. *You* can choose to be upset, or *you* can move on and focus on the things you *can* control."

Of course he'd been dismissive of Grace at the time. Told her she didn't have a clue or any idea of the pressures he was under at work. She was a secretary at a place where her boss loved her work. She couldn't know what it was like to live under the thumbs of bosses who were constantly on their workers, demanding more while finding new ways to give less in return.

Joe had spent most of his adult life working as a machinist at ARC Engineering, until his promotion to manager, which was its own level of mundane hell. He could barely stand it, but the job was stable with decent pay. His parents were raised in the Great Depression and had drilled in him the importance of holding a job *because you never knew when things might get bad, or go from bad to worse.*

Yet following the cancer, after Grace was gone, he finally saw that she'd been right all along — he gave things power over him. He could just as easily choose to not care. Of course, it was easier to adopt that kind of attitude now that he was retired and didn't have to worry about losing his job.

Joe wondered if Maggie had that same inner strength and optimism, if it came naturally to her as it had her biological mother.

"Is everything okay?" Maggie repeated, pulling Joe from his trip down memory lane.

"Yeah, yeah, just routine stuff."

"Good. So, what can I get you this morning? The usual?"

He was about to say yes, the usual — two eggs over easy, toast, three pieces of bacon, and orange juice.

But then he said, "No. I'm feeling adventurous."

"Oh." Maggie arched her eyebrows. "What are you in the mood for?"

Joe didn't have a menu. Kandi had stopped giving him one year ago — he knew it by memory and never fussed with his order.

"Hmmm. What's your favorite thing on the menu?"

"Oh, I dunno. I rarely even eat breakfast."

"If you *did* eat breakfast, what would you get?"

Maggie chewed her bottom lip, thinking — like Grace used to do. There were so many ways this young woman reminded him of his wife. He wished he could hug her, and reveal every secret in that embrace.

But he couldn't tell Maggie the ugly truth because then he'd have to tell her the uglier one — *why* they hadn't kept her. He wasn't sure he could do that. He could barely think about it without guilt rising like bile in his stomach.

Maggie smiled. "Okay. You want to know what I'd have?"

"Yes."

"Do you want me to tell you or just surprise you?"

"Ooh, surprise me. I could use a nice surprise."

"Great," she said. "It's something I make for McKenna and myself on Sunday mornings. We both love it, and while it's not on the menu, I think Sebastian can deliver."

Joe smiled. "I can hardly wait."

"Be right back. Would you like coffee or a glass of OJ while you wait?"

"Just an ice water, thank you."

"Okay," Maggie said, disappearing back to the kitchen.

12

Joe flipped through the paper, skimming articles, but nothing could capture his interest while his heart was wrestling confession.

They'd broached the subject a few months ago when he came in for breakfast. It was just Joe and Maude, who herself was adopted. Parents came up in conversation with Maggie. She admitted to her own adoption, and Joe saw his chance to ask questions without giving himself away.

He'd asked if she knew who her parents were. Maggie said no. He asked if it bothered her. She said yes, especially since her adopted parents had passed away. There was some sense of closure she'd never have, a lingering mystery of who her parents really were — and why they'd given her up for adoption. She'd considered hiring a detective but wondered if perhaps they didn't want to be found. Maybe, she said, it was best just to leave things be.

Joe felt awful. Like he'd stolen something that he alone could return. But cowards can rarely summon the strength. And he felt like a coward more and more as he thought about what he'd forced Grace to do.

Waiting for Maggie to bring her specialty breakfast, Joe again tried to summon the strength. Now might be his best opportunity. None of his friends were there, so he could tell her in private.

But the fear was still strong.

What if she got mad?

What if she hated him?

What if she screamed and told him to leave?

There was an excellent chance she might, after he told her why she'd been abandoned. That it was *his* fault she suffered life without knowing her real mother. That her broken life had turned out as it had.

All his fault.

She returned with his water, smiling like a kid.

"Great news! Sebastian said he'd make it for you! Also, in case you're interested, he's making baked spaghetti tonight."

"Oh, really?"

Joe loved Goldman's baked spaghetti. It was one of the few meals he'd actually order two of, one for dinner and one to take home. The diner only made the dish once every two or three months. Why it wasn't always on the menu was beyond him. "I might have to come back for dinner. Will you still be working?"

"I get off at 6, so if you're here by 5:30, I will be."

"Great," Joe said. "I'll be here."

Maggie left Joe with his water. He kept trying to talk himself into confession. Now he had two opportunities. He could tell her now or wait until dinner.

Later was always easier.

But what if the diner is busier then?

Dinner was a crapshoot at Goldman's. Sometimes, it was hectic, you had to wait for a table, and more demanding tables meant chitchat with the staff was rushed. Other times, dinner was slow, and he had even more time to talk with Maggie.

More time would be good.

Also, if he upset her later, at least she wouldn't have to finish her shift.

It was probably better to wait.

She returned to his table, holding a huge blue plate in front of her, smiling. "Ta-da! Stuffed French Toast with strawberries and cream cheese."

She set the plate down in front of him. The scent of eggs, vanilla, strawberry, and bacon made for a wonderful mélange that rumbled his stomach and showed him how hungry he was.

"That *does* look good! Thank you."

"Sebastian said don't get used to it. He's not adding this to the menu."

12

"Tell Sebastian thank you." Joe laughed. "Though I still think he should add the baked spaghetti as a regular item."

"Duly noted," Maggie said then headed off to another table.

He took a bite. The breakfast was more decadent than his usual meal — he was more of an eggs, home fries, and bacon guy — yet no doubt delicious. But certainly not the sort of thing he'd order every day, lest he get fat.

A thought occurred to him.

Who cares if I get fat? I'm going to lose my mind anyway. Do I really want to prolong my life as a vegetable? Why not go out fat and happy?

He slowly chewed, managing to focus on the paper long enough to read some of the local news. There was some ongoing drama with a gated community not wanting a dog park in their back yard, and a story on the rising unemployment rate yet again. But most of the other stories were about violent crimes — a carjacking, a home invasion, a shooting at a nearby high school. There had been a time, not so long ago, when it seemed like reading about a violent crime adjacent to your life was a rarity. Now, it seemed par for the course.

Joe wasn't sure if he was looking at the past through rose-colored glasses. Certainly, violent crimes had always existed. And he'd seen his share of horrifying brutalities in 'Nam, but things like this weren't supposed to happen in small towns in America. Not at the alarming frequency they seemed to be anyway. And the offenders were getting younger. There was a story a few weeks ago about some kids who'd decided, on a whim, to beat a homeless man to death. And when the police questioned them, the boys said they "were bored."

Bored? So you kill someone?

What is the world coming to?

He turned to the comics page for levity. There was a sense of nostalgia and comfort he felt while reading the funnies. Old comics from his youth, like *Blondie*, *Beetle Bailey*, and *Peanuts* remained a constant in life even as everything else in the paper seemed to change.

After he finished eating, Maggie came by to trade his plate for the bill. He fished the debit card from his wallet and set it on top of the bill, not bothering to check the ticket for accuracy. Maggie had never messed up an order, billed him incorrectly, or anything that a lesser waitress might do.

"So, I'll see you later?"

"Like I'm going to turn down baked spaghetti," Joe said. "I just hope I can eat more after this breakfast! I'm stuffed."

She laughed. "Oh, I didn't tell you!"

"Tell me what?"

"I got an email from an agent who wants to talk to me about my videos."

"What videos?"

"Oh, I thought I mentioned it before. I make these little videos of me singing. I put them on YouTube. Anyway, it's not like a lot of people watch them, but somehow, this agent reached out to me, says he liked them, and wants to talk today. I don't know if it means anything for certain, but maybe he can get me a deal."

"That's great! I didn't know you sing."

She looked down, shy. "Yeah, ever since I was a kid, I wanted to be a singer. But I always figured it was a pipe dream. Everyone wants to be famous, right?"

"So you put your videos on YouTube?"

"Well, originally, I didn't. I had sent my friend, Natalie, a video I sang for her for her birthday last year. *She* put it on YouTube because she thought I deserved to be heard by more people. A lot of people liked it, so she set an account up for me. I've been doing it for about six months now. Like I said, they're not hugely popular or anything, but I suppose if the right person sees them, maybe I could realize my dream!"

"That's great. How do I find the videos? I'd like to hear you."

"Here, I'll write down the URL," she said, grabbing a piece of paper from her order pad. She wrote the URL and handed it to Joe. "Just go there, and you can see the videos."

"I will."

"Okay, well let me take this for you." Maggie grabbed his check and card.

Joe stared at the URL. He couldn't believe she was an aspiring singer. Grace had a gorgeous voice, though she'd been too shy to sing in front of anyone but him, or sometimes at church. Similarities between Maggie and her mother continued to stack.

Joe felt like this was some kind of message — someone, or something, giving him a sign.

I have to tell her the truth.

Today.

EIGHTEEN

Mckenna Kent

McKenna wasn't sure why she felt the urge to hurt Aubrey Burgess. She just did.

They were on the playground for morning recess when Aubrey cut in front of her in the line to get on the slide.

Aubrey, who had never done anything mean to McKenna before, didn't even seem to notice that she'd cut. She was talking and laughing with Julia Nestor, who had been in front of McKenna.

"Hey," McKenna said. "You cut."

"No I didn't."

"Yes, you did!"

How can she lie like that?

"No she didn't," Julia said.

Now she is lying too?

"See?" Aubrey crossed her arms in front of her chest. She turned back to Julia, her hair flipping and swatting McKenna's face.

The two girls joked around, and the line moved up. McKenna stared at the back of the girl's head, watching her dark ponytail bounce as she giggled.

Something about her giggle annoyed McKenna.

12

She now *hated* Aubrey's giggle.

Julia's turn came up. She started climbing the ladder.

McKenna got madder, staring at Aubrey's ponytail.

Then it was Aubrey's turn to climb.

As she reached the top of the slide, McKenna raced up the ladder, not even sure why she was climbing so fast after Aubrey.

She couldn't just let the girl take her place in line and not do anything.

Aubrey turned, surprised, "What are you do—?"

Without even realizing what she was going to do, McKenna threw her arms out and shoved Aubrey hard.

All at once, everything went wrong.

Aubrey started to fall backward, off of the slide.

McKenna tried reaching out to grab the girl and stop her from falling.

She couldn't.

Aubrey cried out, falling backward through the air.

She hit the sand and gasped for air.

Suddenly, a bunch of kids beneath the slide were screaming. Their teacher, Mrs. Lundy, ran toward Aubrey.

McKenna stared down, unable to move. She couldn't believe she'd pushed Aubrey off the slide. Cool air whipped at her hair, and she had to shove it from her eyes to see.

Aubrey kept gasping. Mrs. Lundy knelt beside her.

Oh, God, is she going to die?

What did I do?

McKenna stared as Mrs. Lundy looked up and met her eyes.

Oh no.

Mrs. Lundy looked mad. Very mad.

Mrs. Lundy raced up the ladder and grabbed McKenna by the shoulders.

"What did you do?"

Mrs. Lundy was still staring. McKenna stared back but couldn't think of what to say.

"I dunno."

Another teacher, Mr. Ferraro, was helping Aubrey to sit, asking her a bunch of questions like how many fingers he was holding up.

"Come on, young lady."

Mrs. Lundy climbed down the ladder and waited for McKenna to follow.

∼

McKenna sat in a big chair outside the principal's office while Mrs. Lundy was inside, telling her what happened. At least that's what she figured was happening. She couldn't tell with the door shut.

Sitting across from her, behind a desk, was Mrs. Smith, the principal's secretary. She was typing on her computer, though McKenna could occasionally feel the woman's eyes.

Nobody had spoken to McKenna since she sat down more than ten minutes ago. Neither Mrs. Smith nor any of the other people in the principal's office. Everyone knew she was bad, so no one wanted to talk to her.

They all hate me.

McKenna tried her best not to cry, but couldn't stop the tears once they started. She blew her nose in one of the napkins she'd asked Mrs. Smith for. She felt scared, thinking about how "very disappointed" Mom would be later.

There was no way she wouldn't find out.

She'd hurt Aubrey, and her teacher had seen it. Now she probably thought McKenna was mean, and would never like her again.

She didn't want that. McKenna liked her teacher, and her teacher had liked her before she shoved Aubrey. Her teacher had always said nice things.

"McKenna is so helpful in class."

"McKenna is always polite."

"She does all her work without being asked."

But now, the way Mrs. Lundy looked at her, McKenna doubted she would ever say those sorts of things again.

The principal's office door opened.

McKenna could feel her heart beating so fast, and so loud, she was sure the adults could hear it, too.

McKenna is mean, and has a loud heart.

Mrs. Lundy stood in the doorway. "Come on in, McKenna."

She stood and slunk toward the office as slowly as she could go. McKenna didn't mean to, but she whimpered by the door.

If Daddy was there, he would've told her to stop manipulating them and to stop crying because she's not a (bad word) baby.

But McKenna wasn't trying to manipulate anyone. She couldn't help crying because she was in a lot of trouble. The kind of trouble kids like her never ever got in.

McKenna entered the room. The principal, Ms. Adams, looked at her like she was disappointed, too.

McKenna barely even knew Ms. Adams. She'd only seen the large black woman a few times, and had never been to her office. She looked even scarier up close. Like the kind of principal who had no problem spanking kids.

Last year in kindergarten, Eli Larter said that his brother had been spanked by the principal. McKenna hadn't believed him. She didn't think that teachers or principals *could* spank you. But now, standing in front of Ms. Adams, she was afraid that she was about to get a spanking, just like Eli's brother.

"Please, take a seat." Ms. Adams waved her hand at the brown leather chair in front of her giant desk.

McKenna sat, and the chair made a weird noise. In any

other situation, she might have laughed, thinking it sounded like a fart. But she was too sad for laughing.

Mrs. Lundy closed the door then stood beside McKenna. Mrs. Lundy looked a little like McKenna's mom: short and skinny, with brownish-red hair. That had been good before. But now, McKenna could only think about how she had disappointed a woman who was kind of like her mom away from home, and saw her even more.

"So," Ms. Adams said looking over her glasses, "would you like to explain what happened on the playground?"

"I dunno."

McKenna was mumbling, though she didn't mean to.

"Come on, McKenna, we're going to need something better than that. What happened?"

"I pushed Aubrey Burgess."

"Off a slide?"

"Yes, ma'am."

"Can you tell us why you pushed Aubrey Burgess off the slide?"

"She cut in line."

Mrs. Lundy yelled, "So you *pushed her* off a slide? You could've really hurt her, McKenna!"

"I'm sorry!" McKenna cried, unable to stop the tears. "I didn't want to hurt her."

"So," Ms. Adams said, "what happened when she cut in line? Did you two have words?"

"Have words?"

McKenna didn't know what that meant.

"Did you have an argument?"

"Well, I said she cut, and she and Julia said she didn't. And I was mad. But no, we didn't really fight. She just turned around and ignored me. They both did."

Mrs. Lundy asked, "And what were you feeling then? Were you mad that they ignored you?"

"A little bit, but I don't know why I shoved her. I didn't

mean to. I swear. I wasn't *that* mad." McKenna blew her nose again. The tissue was soaking wet and falling apart.

"Here." Ms. Adams reached across the desk and handed McKenna a box of tissue. She took a few pieces, wound them over the wet ones in her hand, and wiped her nose.

"This is the second time you've acted out in the past two weeks, McKenna," Mrs. Lundy said.

"Second?" McKenna didn't remember what else she'd done.

"Last week, Troy said you took his truck and wouldn't give it back. Remember when we talked about that? You didn't know why you did that either. Remember?"

"Yes, ma'am."

Mrs. Lundy put a hand on McKenna's shoulder and lowered her voice. "How are things at home, McKenna?"

McKenna was confused. Why was the teacher asking about home?

"Okay, I guess."

"Is there anything going on at home, or maybe somewhere else, that is upsetting you? You can talk to us. We're here to help you."

McKenna looked up at her teacher then at Ms. Adams. The principal nodded.

"I dunno. I mean, my mom and dad aren't getting along. And I can't see my dad anymore for a while."

"Yes," Mrs. Lundy said, "your mother told me about that. And how is that going? Does that make you sad?"

It felt good to have them not seeming so mad any more. It also felt good to have them listening. Not many adults listened to McKenna these days, or asked her how she felt about stuff. Her mom was always stressed out and sad. And McKenna hadn't seen her dad ever since his friends had done bad stuff in front of her and she told her mom. The only person who seemed to pay any attention to her at all was her neighbor, Mr. Abe. Whenever she ran into him in the building or her mom's diner, he actually talked *with* her, not just *to* her.

Nobody else really listened.

But now, both her principal and teacher were listening like they really wanted to know what McKenna was thinking. It felt good for someone to care.

"I guess it makes me a little sad. And also, this morning, I think my dad might have flattened my mom's tire."

"What?" Mrs. Lundy said.

"I'm not sure. I heard Mom tell our neighbor, Mr. Abe, that she thought Dad might have done it. I guess he's really mad that he can't see me anymore."

"Did your mother tell anyone else?" Ms. Adams asked.

"Like who?"

"Like the police?"

"I dunno. I don't think so. Mr. Abe took her to work after they dropped me off at school. Why? Is my dad going to be in trouble?"

"We don't know," Ms. Adams said.

Mrs. Lundy kneeled down. "Would you like to talk to someone else? Someone who might be able to help you?"

McKenna wasn't sure what to say. She felt weird talking to someone who wasn't already in the room.

"Like who?"

"We have a guidance counselor here, Mrs. Terry. She talks to students and sometimes their parents. That's her job. She might be able to help you process your feelings."

"Process my feelings?"

Mrs. Lundy nodded. "A lot of times when confusing things are happening at home, children act out at school and do things they wouldn't normally do. Until recently, you've been a wonderful student."

Until recently? She doesn't like me anymore?

"And," Mrs. Lundy added, "I know you didn't mean to hurt Aubrey. I think maybe you're having a tough time with what's happening at home. Having someone else to talk to can help you a lot."

"Can't I just talk to you two?" McKenna asked. "I don't know Mrs. Terry."

Ms. Adams said, "Mrs. Terry is very nice. And she's far better equipped to help you than we are. You can certainly still talk to us, whenever you want. But you'll get along great with Mrs. Terry. She's great with kids."

"Okay, I guess so. Can I go back to class now?"

Ms. Adams said, "Well, first we need to call your mom and explain things to her and then talk with Mrs. Terry. Maybe after that."

McKenna started crying again.

"Do you have to tell my mom?"

"Yes," Mrs. Lundy said. "We have to. But we'll explain the situation. I know your mom pretty well, and I'm sure she'll understand."

Through her tears, McKenna felt something odd.

A part of her wanted Mom to know what she'd done.

Then maybe she'd talk *with* her instead of *to* her, too.

NINETEEN

Maggie Kent

Noon was still more than an hour away, but Maggie's anxiety grew as she stood in for Viv behind the counter at the diner's front.

The counter was the best gig in the house. The serving window was right there behind the counter, and you barely had to walk more than a few feet to serve the twelve seats there. But Maggie didn't care much for the gig. For one, you had to talk to your guests a lot more, and guests at the counter were too chatty for Maggie's disposition. Viv was far better suited for chatting the customers up. For two, Maggie always felt like she was being watched when she worked the counter. The customers were a bit too close, and she felt like she was on display. It made her uncomfortable, and she was glad that she only had to work it during Viv's breaks.

Usually, Barbara would cover Maggie's tables, but given that Barbara was running late, Kandi was doing her best to keep up with hosting, phone orders, and Maggie's tables.

She looked at the clock, hoping Barbara would come in soon. Even though Loretta had left Viv in charge of the front end, making it more likely that Maggie could take her break at twelve, Maggie would still feel bad if they were in the weeds then. Times like this, she wished for a normal nine to five where she could take lunch off without feeling like the train would careen off the track without her constant presence.

Of course, if the call went well, she might never need to work another nine to five, or sling food, ever again. It was still hard to believe that she might have a chance to do something she loved for a living.

Maggie had to temper her excitement. She was getting ahead of herself. She still didn't know exactly what the agent would say. And even if she got a deal, the music biz had no guarantees. Trends changed, as did a fickle public's taste. Whatever was selling now might not be by the time her album came out. She could have a decent debut then suffer the sophomore slump.

Still, the agent, Hollis Atwater, was one of the best around. She'd already turned a few YouTubers into movie stars and had launched a long roster of recording artists. She was the real deal, and if anyone could help Maggie achieve her dreams, it was this woman.

Maggie could still hardly believe that Hollis had reached out to her last week. Sure, you saw shows like *American Idol* where some undiscovered waitress hits the big time, but stuff like this didn't happen to people like Maggie.

Maggie wasn't connected. She didn't even have that many fans on YouTube. And she didn't do any of the things most of the YouTubers did to court success.

Yet for some strange reason that Maggie couldn't understand, it was happening. To her.

She felt a rush of nervous excitement and had to force herself to calm down.

Her inner critic chimed in:

Hollis hasn't called yet.

Nobody said anything about what kind of deal you might be offered. She just said she wanted to work together. That could mean anything. Maybe she wants to hire you as her dog walker. Do NOT get excited yet.

Just chill out, or you'll jinx yourself.

Maggie checked on the two diners at the bar: an old man, and a young woman sitting at opposite ends. Neither needed a thing. The old man was reading the paper while nursing his third cup of coffee. The woman was engrossed in her laptop while occasionally picking at her bagel and cream cheese.

Viv returned from break, tying the apron back around her waist as she came from the kitchen and sidled up to Maggie.

"Thanks, Mags."

"No problem. How's Charlie?"

Charlie was her nine-year-old Chihuahua that she'd dropped off at the vet during her break. The dog hadn't been eating and had a history of various ailments that must've burned through a fair chunk of Viv's weekly take-home.

"I dunno. The vet's gonna do some blood work and call me back."

"I hope you get good news."

"Thanks. So, you excited about the agent?"

"If by excited you mean scared, then yes, yes, I am!"

Viv smiled. "Scared? Why? She must already like your stuff or she wouldn't have reached out, right?"

"I know, but still, what if I screw things up? What if she realizes that I'm not a musician at all? Maybe she thinks I'm younger than I am. Do twenty-nine-year-olds even get signed to record deals?"

"What are you talking about, girl? You are a great singer!"

"Okay, supposing for a moment that I'm a *decent* singer, that doesn't make me a star. I mean, you see those people who fail on *American Idol* all the time. The shy girl who sings great but has zero stage presence. That's me, Viv! I don't know how to sing in front of an audience."

"No, ma'am. I'm not buying it. You know what you're doing?"

"What?"

"You're doing what I did back when I was your age."

"What do you mean?"

"Any idea what I wanted to be when I was younger?"

Maggie didn't think she'd ever talked to Viv about her aspirations. The woman, now in her early sixties, was upbeat, effervescent, and not one to lament the past, so the usual server exchange of *what I wish I could be doing* had never come up. "No, I don't think you did."

"I wanted to be a dancer."

Viv wasn't completely out of shape, but she was about thirty pounds overweight, and not someone Maggie would've pictured as a dancer. She seemed more like someone's spunky grandma or slightly eccentric and outgoing aunt. Viv was into New Age spiritual stuff and seemed too flaky for the discipline, hard work, and dedication required to professionally dance.

"So, why didn't you become a dancer?"

"Because I scared myself out of trying. You know how life gives you all these sliding door moments? Where you have this choice you can make and things will either align perfectly, or you'll regret your decision forever? Well, I had one of those moments. I was an aspiring dancer ever since I was three. When I was seventeen, I had a chance to audition for the Nameless Spectacle Dance Company, which was pretty big in New York. If I got accepted, soooo many doors would've opened for me."

"So, what happened?"

"Tony Bruno."

"*Who?*"

"Tony Bruno was the hottest guy in my school. Oh, Maggie, we're talking Brad Pitt but hotter."

"Oh?"

"Yeah, he was Italian, with jet-black hair and piercing blue eyes. He could've been a male model or a movie star. I was a bit of a late bloomer, and he was the first guy to pay attention to me. And believe me, any girl would've melted for him. So, we started dating, and I got knocked up."

"You have a kid?"

"*Had.* She died when she was nineteen. Heroin overdose."

"Oh, God. I'm sorry."

"Yeah, that's another story for another day. But back to Tony Bruno. So, he knocked me up, and then — big surprise — wanted nothing to do with me. He was on to the next floozy in a line of many. So I gave up on my dream of dancing and settled for this other guy, a "safe guy," Stan Weston, who was sweet and a good dad to a daughter who wasn't even his. Long story short, I let a stupid relationship with a stupid guy derail my entire life. Don't let your moment go. You never know if you'll get it again."

Maggie wasn't sure how relevant Viv's story was to her situation. Maggie had already screwed up and had Nick's baby, but she didn't feel like it had ruined her life. Maybe Nick had swallowed too many of her years, but she was still relatively young and didn't regret having McKenna at all. McKenna wasn't a mistake so much as a blessing. If not for her, Maggie might have never matured and learned to take care of herself.

She grew up *because* she had to support them both when Nick lost his job. Maggie wouldn't let her chances pass by. But at the same time, she knew the odds of becoming a star were slim, and that expectations were dangerous.

"Thank you," she said to Viv. "I won't let this moment pass."

"I know you won't. And you have a strong head on your shoulders. Just don't let anyone, and I'm not just talking about Nick the Dick, but I mean *anyone* tell you that you can't do something. You hear me?"

"Yes," Maggie said, laughing at a sixty-something-year-old woman use the same term for Nick that the other, younger, servers had for her ex: Nick the Dick.

12

It felt good to have someone believe in her so strongly, even if maybe some of that belief was colored by personal regrets.

A couple of guys came in and sat at the counter. Viv took their orders.

Maggie was about to let Kandi know she was back when her phone buzzed in her pocket.

Nick, about to yell at her for sending the cops to his house. Or Clarence to tell her how the meeting had gone.

But it wasn't either of them.

It was the school's number.

Maggie answered, but not in time.

Mrs. Lundy, McKenna's teacher, left a voicemail: "Hi, Mrs. Kent. It's Mrs. Lundy from school. Something's happened with your daughter, and we need to talk."

11 a.m. - 12 p.m.

TWENTY

Tim Hewitt

TIM HAD NEVER BEEN SO excited for algebra.

He practically raced from art class on the other side of the school and threw himself into his third-row seat with two minutes still left before the bell.

He reached into his book bag and grabbed the spiral notebook where he'd written a bunch of stuff for *Project Riding Hood*, which was what he was calling his collaboration with Alicia.

He was anxious to hand her his spiral full of outlined ideas. He'd somehow managed to write seven pages of story gems in the two hours since gym. He thought about setting the spiral on her desk, next to his. But he decided no, he'd rather deliver it like a present.

She'll be as surprised as Dad would be furious.

Tim smiled, drumming his fingers on the desk, waiting. Looking up, he noticed Ms. Walker looking at him and remembered his forged note. He suddenly realized that his father had never given it back, and he was supposed to return it today.

Shit.

He looked down at his desk and notebook, pretending to

be busy, hoping she failed to notice that he hadn't handed in his progress report like all the other kids as they entered the room. He wasn't sure what to say if she asked him where his was. He couldn't return a forged paper — not when his father knew about it.

His joy fell behind the shadows of fear.

Would he have to ask his father for the report? What then? There was no way his father would let him return a forged paper. No, he'd want to make an example. Hell, maybe he'd already called the school and spoken to Ms. Walker.

He didn't dare meet Ms. Walker's gaze.

He listened as more kids came into class, glancing to his left to see if Alicia was there yet.

"Hey, fag," Jeff Soren said as he passed, his arm brushing against Tim's shoulder hard before taking his seat behind him.

Jeff was one of his bullies and also, inexplicably, among one of Dima's new cadre of friends, specifically bred and trained to be assholes in life. He was also good friends with Kip and had probably already heard about the volleyball incident.

Why does Dima like these assholes?

On some level, Tim could understand Dima's sudden rise in popularity. He'd gone from short and pudgy in middle school to tall, slim, and good looking over the course of the summer before high school. He was starting anew. He'd transformed from Dimitri the geeky caterpillar into Dima, the social butterfly, shedding his old life, and Tim with it, like an unnecessary cocoon. Tim didn't like it but could understand it. He just didn't get why Dima chose to befriend some of the same people who had once picked on them both — like Jeff Soren.

If Tim had become suddenly popular, he'd never be friends with the fuckers who made fun of him. He certainly wouldn't be friends with people who had made fun of his best friend. Then again, Tim also wouldn't stop being friends with his old friends just to fit in.

Alicia beat the bell by a second, slipping into class, giggling with Dima.

Ugh.

Tim tried not to let his jealousy show. Alicia had been friends with Dima, too. And it wasn't like Tim could ask her not to be friends with him just because Dima no longer liked him. But he still hated that the two chummed around like Dima hadn't become a major douche bag. Tim wondered if Alicia had even noticed how much he'd changed. She'd asked Tim why they never all hung out together, but Tim brushed it off, saying they just grew apart. He didn't want to admit how much it hurt him that Dima had spurned him for other friends. Though Tim wasn't exactly sure what girls liked, he did know they hated needy guys. He could never show how much it hurt that Dima was no longer his friend.

"Hey, Tim." Alicia sat at the desk beside him.

Dima, behind her, said nothing, as if Tim wasn't even there.

Fucking asshole.

Tim felt his stomach sour, but he had to try not to let Dima ruin his good feelings about the story he was going to write with Alicia.

Everyone settled into their seats and pulled out their algebra books. Ms. Walker stood from her desk and closed the door.

"Good morning, class," she said to an uninspired smattering of "Good morning" returned.

Tim said "Good morning" softly enough to ignore notice from the kids in Asshole Rows, the two back rows of the class where all the assholes — including Dima, Jeff, and five others — sat.

"If you've not yet turned in your progress reports, please

leave them on my desk after class. Today we're going to solve some of the quadratic equations we discussed yesterday."

The class groaned in unison as Ms. Walker turned to the whiteboard and wrote out a problem. While it was simple enough — Tim had never had problems with math, even if he found it dull — he didn't want to be called on.

Ms. Walker laughed. "Oh, come on, they're not *that* difficult. So, who'd like to go first? How about you, Mr. Soren? I think I heard you say you wanted to come up."

The room laughed, knowing Jeff, who was every bit the dumb jock that his appearance suggested, hated solving problems in front of the class. Hell, he probably couldn't solve basic multiplication if *it* was on the board.

As he passed, Tim made sure not to let Jeff see him laughing.

One of the guys in Asshole Rows whistled and said, "Go, Jeffy!"

Jeff, still not at the front of the class, put his arm behind his back and flipped off whoever had whistled.

The class erupted in laughter.

Tim reluctantly laughed, too. Even if Jeff was always an asshole, he knew how to be funny.

Tim turned to Alicia. She met his eyes and was laughing too. She didn't care for Jeff, though he seemed oblivious to her disdain since he was always hitting on her. Then again, he hit on pretty much any girl, and was rumored to have slept with more than twenty since seventh grade.

As Jeff stood in front of the class, attempting to solve the problem, Tim took advantage of Ms. Walker's back being to the class.

He handed Alicia the spiral.

"What's this?" she whispered.

"Some ideas for our story," Tim whispered back.

She opened the spiral and thumbed through the pages. He

watched, dying for a response. Her eyebrows arched, seeing how much he'd written in two hours.

"Wow," she said, her mouth wide open. "Did you skip class?"

Tim laughed and shook his head. He was usually done with his classwork long before anyone else, and used the time to write. According to his father, he should ask the teacher for more work or get placed in more challenging classes, despite four of his classes being AP already. He would've been in AP Algebra, too, if he hadn't tanked the placement test at the end of eighth grade. He did it partly in hopes of landing in the same class as Dima, because Dima wasn't nearly as good at math. But also, he hoped he might be with Alicia, who was smart, just not AP smart. Probably because she was a daydreamer, like Tim wished he could be.

He watched as she read through some of what he'd written, nodding, eyes widening, mouth whispering "oohs" and "ahs" in all the right places.

The class laughed again when Ms. Walker thanked Jeff for his "attempt." She erased his work, but left the problem on the board.

On his way back to his seat, Jeff approached Tim, glaring and jutting out his jaw as if about to hit him, or worse.

Tim looked down.

Jeff bumped him again.

Asshole.

"Now, who else would like to try?"

No one raised their hand. Tim knew the answer but wasn't about to go up and correct Jeff. That was asking for a foot in his ass.

Jeff Soren was for Tim, at the moment, a verbal bully. He'd given Tim shit for a couple of years, but had never actually tried to fight him. He probably saw Tim as a nothing, not worth fighting. Tim was fine with that and certainly didn't want to give reason to elevate his status on the People's Asses to Kick List that was likely knocking around in his half-empty head.

Ms. Walker looked around the class. Tim kept his eyes down, staring at his desk as if the wood's grain held the secrets of life and required the sort of white-hot study previously reserved for Westeros speculation threads on *A Song of Ice and Fire* message boards and reddit.

"Mr. Hewitt, we haven't seen you up here in a while."

No. No. No. No. Why not call one of the other Neanderthals up here to clean Jeff's mess?

Tim's gut did a summersault.

He glanced over at Alicia. She laughed and winked.

He rolled his eyes then forced himself to stand.

While the class had erupted in laughter and jokes when Jeff had gone up, Tim earned no such fanfare. There was barely a sound as he walked toward the board.

He couldn't even look at Ms. Walker as he passed, for fear that doing so would trigger her memory.

Where's your progress report, Tim?

He grabbed the blue dry erase marker on the ledge beneath the white board and stared at the problem.

Tim had two options: he could either race through the equation, quickly solve it, and return to his seat with admirable speed, or pretend to struggle and hopefully avoid Jeff's ire. Or a third option — get it all wrong and possibly remind Ms. Walker of his progress report.

He stared at the board, pretending to work out the problem in his head. He felt the class watching. Time had frozen, as it had on the volleyball court.

His heart raced.

He could feel Ms. Walker staring, probably wondering why he was so slow with the problem.

Thankfully, she said nothing.

Solve it or get it wrong?

If he got it wrong, Ms. Walker would probably know he

did it on purpose. Worse, Jeff might know, and as crazy as it sounded, he might take offense that Tim got it wrong so as not to show him up. Jocks like Jeff had tiny fuses, like Tim's father. The oddest things could set them off.

Tim decided it was better to get the answer right than wrong, so he pretended to struggle with the solution.

He slowly wrote his work on the board. Jeff coughed loud, with a not-so-cleverly disguised *fag-got.*

The class laughed.

Ms. Walker turned to Jeff, "That's enough."

Acting offended, he hacked again. "What? I've got a cough!"

"Maybe Dean Keller can help you clear it up?"

"No, ma'am, I think it's good now."

More laughter from the class.

Tim decided to stop pretending to be dumber than he was. He raced through the solution, set the marker down, and returned to his desk without bothering to see if Ms. Walker acknowledged that he was right.

He knew he was.

As Tim reached his desk, he glanced down at Jeff and smiled. Without meaning to, he winked.

Who's a faggot now?

Jeff's eyes widened in surprise.

Wait! What the fuck did I just do?

Alicia, who had been watching Tim, burst out laughing. Dima, to Tim's surprise, laughed too.

Tim quickly looked down then sat.

His heart was racing.

His breaths were short.

He'd just been cocky to Jeff Fucking Soren. He was a dead man walking.

He couldn't even look back to see Jeff's reaction.

Ms. Walker thanked Tim for his correct answer then went to the board and erased both problem and solution.

Tim wished he could erase the last minute.

Ms. Walker started writing another problem.

Behind him, Tim heard Jeff's desk scoot up an inch.

Oh shit.

Tim pretended not to notice.

Ms. Walker said, "How about you, Ms. Bailey?"

Alicia's eyes went wide.

She looked at Tim, and he managed a half-sick smile. Behind her, Dima patted her on the shoulder. "You're up, Alicia."

She stood and said, "Ha, ha."

Alicia approached the front of the classroom. Again, Jeff's desk squeaked behind him — inching forward.

Why is he moving up?

Tim's heart raced faster.

He didn't dare turn around. He kept his head down, flipping through pages of the algebra book as if it now held the secrets of life.

Jeff's desk creeped up again.

"Faaaagggggooootttt," he whispered.

Tim pretended not to hear.

Kept his head down.

"Faaaagggggooootttt."

Tim wondered if Dima noticed what Jeff was doing. There was no way he couldn't have; they sat next to one another.

If he did notice, is he also encouraging Jeff?

Before now, there had never been a situation to truly test Dima's loyalty. Would Dima join the others in making fun of Tim, or stick up for his former best friend?

The few times Tim had run into Jeff or others in their group and they had shit to say, Dima hadn't been around, was just out of earshot, or pretended not to notice.

And it wasn't as if Tim and Dima had ever had an out-and-out argument where they said they hated one another.

Dima had just kept blowing him off, ignoring Tim until he finally got the picture. Which in many ways was worse than a fight. At least in a fight, there was a reason you stopped talking to someone — a reason other than the other guy no longer liked you.

Jeff's desk squeaked closer.

Tim heard giggling from Asshole Rows, though it didn't sound like Dima was among the gigglers.

Tim's heart was pounding so loud he was surprised it wasn't reverberating off the walls. He braced for whatever was about to happen.

Would Jeff fuck with his book bag on the ground?

Tim wanted to reach down and pull it forward, pushing it in front of him. But to do so, he felt, might only cause Jeff to do something to him.

Squeaaak.

Closer.

"Faaaaggggoooottt," now a whisper right behind him.

Tim pretended not to hear.

"I know you can hear me, you chickenshit faggot. Think you're so funny, laughing at me?"

Tim swallowed. His knees were shaking.

"Sorry, I was j … just kidding," he whispered back.

"Yeah, well, we'll see how funny you are after school when I kill you. See who's laughing then, faggot."

And then, like a crack of thunder, Jeff flicked Tim in the back of the head so hard it felt like someone had thrown a rock at his skull.

Tim yelped and reached for the back of his head.

Jeff's desk scraped back against the floor.

The entire class turned, including Ms. Walker and Alicia up front.

"Is something wrong?" Ms. Walker asked.

The pain was blinding. Tim might be bleeding. He wouldn't know until he looked down at his fingers.

12

His eyes were brimming with tears, but he couldn't allow them to fall.

Crying would invite the sort of laughter and ridicule that would haunt him until graduation, if not longer.

Tim blinked the tears away and spoke, his voice cracking.

"Sorry, just banged my funny bone on the desk."

He grabbed his elbow, trying to sell the story.

Ms. Walker looked from him to Asshole Rows as if she were about to interrogate the lot of them.

Instead, she turned to Alicia. "Okay, you may continue."

Tim lowered his head, ashamed, and certain he'd die before the end of the day.

TWENTY-ONE

Maggie Kent

MAGGIE'S HEART RACED, waiting for the front office to patch her through to Mrs. Lundy, and dying to hear what McKenna's teacher would say.

Had something happened to her daughter?

Was McKenna in trouble?

She was a good kid. Something must've happened *to her*.

Maggie's mind raced through possibilities, from McKenna getting bullied to being in some sort of accident. Maybe she slipped and fell. Maggie had read stories about children dying from innocuous things like slipping and falling and hitting their head in *just* the right way so they died.

She tried to calm herself. Tried to tell herself that if something *truly awful* had happened, Mrs. Lundy would've left a different message or broadcast more urgency in her voice. Maybe the police would've come to deliver the terrible news.

The teacher wouldn't just leave a voicemail that said, "Something's happened with your daughter, and we need to talk."

Maggie felt helpless, stranded at Goldman's, unable to rush to the school without a car. Her only lifeline to the school — to McKenna — was the phone in her hand.

12

She had to know what happened, and the on-hold music, the slow and almost lazily unfolding *Sailing* by Christopher Cross, mocked her urgency — as if she hadn't heard it enough at the diner.

Come on!

Finally, Mrs. Lundy's voice came through on the other line.

"Mrs. Kent?"

"Yes," Maggie said, trying not to voice any of the thousand panicked thoughts that had swollen inside her.

Just be calm, and let her talk.

Maggie listened to Mrs. Lundy tell her everything that had happened on the playground. McKenna had been upset that a girl had cut in front of her on the line to the slide. McKenna had pushed the girl off the slide. Not just down the slide, but *off* the side. She could've been — but thankfully was not — badly hurt.

After the teacher told her everything, Maggie breathed a nearly silent sigh. She wasn't happy but was glad that McKenna — and the other girl, whose name Mrs. Lundy had yet to mention — were both okay.

"Is she in trouble?"

"Nothing too serious, no."

"Are you sure the other girl didn't do something else? This seems so unlike McKenna."

"We spoke to both girls. And while the girl did cut in front of McKenna in line and there were some words exchanged, that doesn't excuse her behavior."

"I'm not saying it does. I just can't believe she would hurt someone like that without provocation."

McKenna had always been a good student. Usually, the teacher's favorite since preschool. She'd never hurt someone, physically or verbally.

There *had* to be more to this.

"Well, we talked to her a bit."

"We? Who's we?"

"The principal, Ms. Adams, and I because — you're right, this *is* unusual behavior from McKenna — and she indicated some issues at home, with her father."

"Her father?"

"Yes. I know he's not allowed to see her at the moment, but McKenna expressed some fear that he flattened your tires this morning?"

"I don't know for sure if it was him. I spoke to the police, and they're going to talk to him."

The teacher was quiet for a moment as if processing details, or finding her next words.

Finally, she said, "We think it would be helpful for McKenna to have someone she could talk to about her feelings, and what's going on with her father."

"She *does* have someone to talk to. She has me," Maggie said, feeling as though Mrs. Lundy was denigrating her job as a mother.

"Yes, but sometimes when there's a situation like this, children need someone else to talk to. This is in no way a reflection on you, but sometimes kids feel stuck in the middle between their parents and don't feel like they can talk to either one without choosing sides. It helps to have a neutral third party. McKenna may feel freer to tell us things she might not tell you or Nick."

"*Choose sides?* I'm not asking my daughter to choose sides. Nick is a danger to her. *She* is afraid of him. *She* told me that she doesn't want to go to his house anymore. Because *she's* scared. This isn't a matter of me wanting sole custody of my child as some way to get back at Nick. This is me protecting my child from him. This isn't about choosing sides."

"I'm sorry, I didn't mean — "

Maggie, already full of steam, barreled forward, cutting the teacher off.

"And one more thing: She can tell me anything she's

thinking. *Anything* at all. I don't know what happened today, but this is the first time McKenna has ever been in any sort of fight with another child. Ever. So I don't think we need to call in the shrinks to diagnose and medicate her because, believe me, that is not the right way to handle a minor discipline problem."

Mrs. Lundy was quiet for a moment. Only then did Maggie realize she'd gone too hard. She'd dragged her own childhood into this, how she'd been treated by her foster parents, and the shrinks who answered everything with medication. While Maggie would never apologize for protecting her daughter, Mrs. Lundy had always been kind. She wasn't one of the crappy teachers like Maggie had grown up with. She was one of the good ones, always spending extra time and going the extra mile to help her students. McKenna had struggled with reading until Mrs. Lundy gave her a stack of books and ignited a love for reading.

Maggie took a deep breath, and did the hard thing.

"I'm sorry. I didn't mean to go off."

"It's okay," Mrs. Lundy said.

"Who do you want her to talk to?"

"Mrs. Terry, the guidance counselor. She's a nice person, Mrs. Kent. And believe me, she's not the kind of person who would suggest you medicate a child that didn't truly need it."

"When?"

"Ideally, we'd like her to see Mrs. Terry today. We could wait for a time when you can come in, or we can arrange a second meeting if we feel it's necessary, when both you and McKenna can meet with her together. Whatever you want. It's up to you."

Maggie sighed, looking at the diner's back door and wondering how the hell she could take off the rest of the day. They were already down a server — two, really. It had been a stretch to leave for this phone call. She might even need to postpone her call with the agent to make up for the time she was talking to Mrs. Lundy. There was no way to leave without heaping grief on everyone else.

"What do you think, Mrs. Lundy? Does McKenna need me there now? Is she upset?"

"She was a bit shaken up, but I think she'll be okay. I think she was a bit worried that she'd be in trouble with you, but no, I don't think you need to rush down here right now. In fact, it might make things bigger than they need to be. Perhaps after talking to Mrs. Terry, things will be fine."

"Okay, she can talk to Mrs. Terry. And then we'll take it from there."

"Okay, Mrs. Kent."

"Thank you for calling. And again — I'm sorry."

"It's fine. I understand."

"Can you have Mrs. Terry call me after the meeting?"

"Sure thing."

Maggie thanked her again then said goodbye.

She paced behind the diner for a bit, hoping that McKenna was okay and not freaking out in the guidance counselor's office. She was a good girl but didn't handle stress especially well. Maggie could picture her crying.

She swallowed, trying not to let her emotions overwhelm her. Maggie couldn't always be there to protect McKenna, and perhaps this was the sort of thing that would help her daughter grow. Not pushing a girl off the slide but an adult conversation about her actions — and their consequences.

She took a moment to prepare herself for customers then opened the back door and entered the kitchen.

She saw Bob manning the grill and figured Sebastian was taking his morning break before the lunch rush.

She headed into the diner, surprised to see that Barbara was now working.

"Hey, I'm sorry I was late," Barbara said, launching into a whole story about her morning, her trip to the doctor's, and a bunch of other details — too many details — which made Maggie wonder if she was lying.

Barbara was an overweight woman in her late forties with long dark hair that she kept in a ponytail. She wasn't exactly server material, as she was chronically tired and complained more than anyone Maggie had ever met. Though she complained, she was a sweet woman who had a crap hand dealt to her in life, so it was hard to hold it against her. Not everyone had Maggie's ability to bounce back from hardships. Hell, Maggie supposed if she had too many more days like today, she might be as sour as Barbara.

Maggie said, "Don't worry" like she usually did. It's not like she had proof that Barbara wasn't really at the doctor's office. Plus, Barbara was a hypochondriac, so it's just as likely she was there, even if only for some phantom ailment.

Now that Barbara was *here*, Maggie felt bad that she couldn't be *there* for McKenna's meeting.

No, no, this is fine. It's better if I'm not there. It helps her grow.

Maggie was almost glad she didn't have her car. She wasn't sure she could be so strong if it were out there in the parking lot. She was definitely glad that Barbara was here. She glanced up at the clock: 11:59 a.m. She may as well just ask Viv if she could take her lunch break now. She could even shave off ten or fifteen minutes to make up for the call with Mrs. Lundy.

She was about to approach Viv, but the front door opened. Maggie turned to see Nick glaring right at her.

Oh, shit.

TWENTY-TWO

Sebastian Ruiz

SEBASTIAN FIGURED he had two shots at taking money from the safe. Once before lunch and maybe another before dinner, when everyone was preparing for the rushes.

But first he had to hit the bank and withdraw his savings.

If he'd taken the money from the safe first, and then Loretta or someone else noticed that he and the money were both missing, there'd be an immediate APB out for him — in which case, he could probably forget withdrawing that much money from the bank.

He asked Bob to cover him during his errand. "If any of the food vendors come, hit me on my cell, and I'll rush right back," he said.

His bank was just a few blocks away, so Sebastian wasn't too worried about not being there to check in the vendors. But as he stood in line with his withdrawal slip, his stomach turned like the summer carnival's Tilt-a-Whirl.

He couldn't believe what he was about to do — rob one of the few people who didn't treat him like a fucking criminal.

But it wasn't like he had a choice. He could either steal money that Loretta probably had insured or let Raul kill his sister.

12

He'd withdraw eight grand and hope like hell that Loretta had another seven in the safe.

Given her lax bookkeeping, deposits, and general managing habits, she might not have made a deposit in more than a week, meaning she could have as much as twenty grand in the safe.

But what if she doesn't? What then?

Fuck if I know.

Everything about this whole thing made Sebastian sick — from his sister falling into debt with Raul to him fucking his future to pay the asshole off.

He could never return to the diner after today.

Or his apartment.

He'd have to go on the run.

And what then?

Fuck if I know.

Sebastian hated his sister in that moment. He'd finally turned his life around. He no longer worked for Raul. He had a steady honest job, and was good at it. He was respected by those who knew him. He had plans to do something decent with his life. To make something of himself.

Now it was all burned to nothing; ashes of hope he never really had.

He hated Ana for putting him in this position. She was six years his junior, only eleven when he went away for ten years to pay for his part in a robbery that led to murder. When he got out, she was already a young woman, squirming under the boot of a too-cruel life.

She left home and their drunk excuse of a mother at fifteen, ran with an awful crowd — anything to get the attention she never had at home. Got knocked up by a piece of shit gangbanger at sixteen and lost the kid four months in. Ever since, she'd bounced from boyfriend to rehab and back so many times he'd lost count.

After he was out of prison, Sebastian had helped, at first,

giving Ana a place to crash and lending her money whenever he could. But every effort to help always bit him on the ass. She stole, lied, or, when shit went bad, ran away, vanishing for months at a time. Then she'd show up, saying she'd kicked the drugs, pleading for a fresh start.

Again, he'd take her in.

Until the last time — six months ago.

He'd finally lost patience, deciding that she'd never get her shit together as long as he was there to break her fall. As his own Narcotics Anonymous sponsor had said, "You have to hit rock bottom before you can crawl up from your hole."

Sebastian decided to let Ana hit bottom.

He told her no, she couldn't stay at his place — at least not unless she abided by his rules. That meant a curfew. It meant she had to hold down a job. It meant that she had to submit to drug testing.

She said okay, at first.

Her good behavior lasted a week. Then Ana came home wasted, fucked up on heroin. He told her to leave.

She cried, begged to stay.

He opened the door and told her to get the hell out.

She did. And that was the last he'd seen her. His final words: *Get the hell out.*

Now his *tough love* might kill her.

Tough love wasn't meant to be vicious.

It felt like no matter what he did, everything turned to shit.

The line moved up a person. There were only three others in front of Sebastian. In minutes, he'd withdraw his money and leave the bank with the only security he had. It had taken forever to save eight thousand dollars. Forever to put himself in a position where he had some sense of safety. If the boss pissed him off, he could walk. Sebastian was beholden to no one. He finally had freedom.

Had freedom.

Now he was about to flush it all to save his sister.

He should tell Raul to do whatever the hell he wanted to do. Ana sowed her seeds, let her reap their harvest. Sebastian had done what he could. Could anyone really expect him to do more? To give away everything he'd worked for just to save Ana from a bed she'd made? And what happened once Raul let her go? Who's to say she wouldn't just fuck up again?

Once an addict, always an addict.

Except that wasn't always the case.

Sebastian had once been an addict himself.

And while he was still — in recovery terms — an addict, he'd turned *his* life around. Drugs no longer controlled him. Maybe his sister had a shot.

But I've given her so many chances. And she's wasted every one.

True. But whenever he thought of letting Raul do what he was gonna do, Sebastian flashed back to when he and his sister were children, to the eight-year-old version of Ana, whom he had loved fiercely. The girl he'd protected from bullies. The girl who looked up to him and thought he could do no wrong. The first person to ever have any faith in Sebastian. Their mother sure as hell didn't think much of him.

But Ana had believed in him.

And he'd let her down.

He couldn't help but feel that her life would be dramatically different if he'd never gone to prison. There was no way in hell she would've fell in with the crowd she had if he'd been around to stop it. No way she would've found herself knocked up and having to flee home. Every shitty thing in her life had happened because she chased love in all the wrong places. Because she had no love at home.

And it was all his fault.

He *owed* her.

Sebastian wiped tears from his eyes and approached the teller window, digging deep into his resolve to do whatever it took to save Ana.

Sebastian made his way back to Goldman's and parked in the rear, his pants pocket bulging with an envelope of hundred-dollar bills.

He checked in with Bob, asking if any vendors had come in, and the grill to make sure Bob wasn't in the weeds. He seemed to be doing fine.

"Nope," Bob said. "You back?"

"In a minute. I need to do something for Loretta."

"K," Bob said, flipping a couple of burgers.

As Sebastian drew closer to what fate was making him do, every person, noise, and movement felt amplified, causing a sensory overload that fueled his anxiety. There were too many variables out of his control.

Would the safe have enough money?

Could he get it to Raul?

Would Raul honor "the deal" and surrender his sister?

How long before Loretta realized her money was missing?

How long until she called the cops?

He'd considered staging a robbery: his first thought. But too much could go wrong. He would've needed an accomplice to hold him up, and the minute you add an accomplice is the moment you surrendered control. Even in a fake robbery, someone could get shot. Then he'd be responsible for another death.

In a best-case scenario, he'd still have to worry if whoever he enlisted could keep his mouth shut. And in all honesty, the only people Sebastian trusted enough to seal their lips were the sort of people who would never involve themselves in such a dumbass scheme.

No, he'd have to take the money and disappear. Take Ana with him, try and start over.

It would be tough, if not impossible. There was a damned good chance he'd wind up right back behind bars. An odd

12

part of Sebastian found comfort in that idea. He'd done okay in prison. Few people fucked with him, and he'd thrived under order with few opportunities to shit the bed. No one to disappoint. No temperamental boss bitching at you for shit someone did to her. You did what you had to do and made it through the day.

But if he went away again, Ana would have no one. And this would all be for nothing.

He had to get it over and done with.

Sebastian slipped into Loretta's office and locked the door behind him, hoping no one would knock. Or worse, Loretta would return, having forgotten something or for some other lame reason.

He went to the safe and clicked the button to start a five-minute countdown that he'd have to wait through before he could turn the combo and unlock the safe.

The timer seemed to slow as if in response to his nerves.

Come on, come on.

Sebastian stared at the red numbers on the digital count down. Minutes ticked, anxiety nibbled his resolve.

I'm gonna get caught.

How the hell will I even be able to get a decent job?

The minute they run my Social, I'm fucked.

He thought of an old friend from back in the day, Elvis Lorenzo, perhaps the only black dude named Elvis in history. He'd seen Elvis at an NA meeting not too long ago. Though clean and sober, Elvis was still working the black market — helping other criminals get shit they needed.

I could ask Elvis to get fake IDs for me and Ana.

Maybe that could work.

He wondered how much fake IDs would cost. He'd have to take more than seven grand, assuming Loretta had the cash in her safe. He'd have to take enough to start over. In time, he'd find a way to pay Loretta back. To make things right.

But even if everything worked out and Elvis could get him

docs and he could find a job, Ana was a huge variable. How long before she started calling old friends to score drugs?

Can't think about that now. One step at a time.

The timer reached zero.

Sebastian took a deep breath, dialed the memorized combination.

It clicked open, and he looked inside at seven green bags zipped shut. Nightly cash deposits for seven days.

There had to be ten grand, or more.

He chewed his upper lip as he unzipped the bags and sorted through the bills, all wrapped neatly in bands and ready for the bank. In each bag was a written receipt for how much was inside.

More than twenty grand in the safe.

Shit.

He swallowed, wondering how much to take. How much would be enough to get fake IDs and a fresh start?

He could take $10,000, but if short what he needed to escape, he wouldn't get another chance to come back for more.

Sebastian took fifteen grand.

He pulled the bags out, set them on the ground, and closed the safe.

He looked around, realizing he'd not thought about where to put the money. Because a lot of the money was in small bills, the bags were too large to stuff in his pocket. He spotted a box of plastic bags with the diner's name and logo.

He tore it open, pulled out two bags, and double bagged the deposits.

He tied the bags up in a tight ball and slipped them into another bag.

There we go.

I'll just tell Bob I'll be right back. I'll head out to the car, call Raul, and get this shit done and over.

He paused at Loretta's office door, staring at the doorknob, suddenly flooded with guilt. He wasn't just betraying his boss and one of the few people who trusted him, he was betraying good people at the diner — robbing from them like a common thug.

His hands were shaking.

No. No. Fuck this sentimental bullshit. I've gotta be tough. I can't think about Loretta. She'll write this shit off. She'll be fine. The diner will be fine.

I've gotta do this for Ana.

He tucked the bag under his arm, reached for the doorknob, then heard the dining room ringing with screams.

12 p.m. - 1 p.m.

TWENTY-THREE

Maggie Kent

"You fucking cunt!" Nick screamed at the top of his lungs, storming into the diner like it was some dive bar stuffed with his scumbag friends rather than her place of employment.

Maggie's heart froze, about to shatter.

His breath was hot on her face, reeking of alcohol. Eyes bloodshot. Fists balled at his side, itching to strike her.

"You sent a cop to my fucking house?"

Maggie slowly retreated until her back was brushing the hostess station.

"I didn't *send* anyone. I told him about my flat tire and about the text messages. He *offered*."

"I didn't flatten your tire."

"No? I just happened to get my first-ever flat tire the day you got notice to stay away from us?"

If she was bold — especially in a public place — Nick might back down.

Instead, he came closer, making Maggie press her back harder against the station.

"Don't think I don't know what you're doing. You and that nigger cop lover of yours. Y'all are trying to take my daughter away from me!"

12

"What?"

Maggie would have laughed if it wouldn't further provoke him. He was already looking for an excuse to hurt someone.

Barbara approached. "Hey, Nick, you need to get out of here."

"This is between me and her." He pointed at Barbara. "So back the fuck off, Tubby!"

"This is a place of business. You can't be coming in here like this."

"Fine." Nick grabbed Maggie by the elbow. "Let's take this outside."

"Ow," she cried out, pulling away. "I'm not going anywhere with you."

Nick reached out again, but Maggie slipped away.

Barbara stepped between them, threw her hands up, and pushed Nick back.

"I said back the fuck off, bitch!" Nick shoved Barbara back hard against the hostess stand.

It sounded like her skull cracked then she collapsed to the floor, knocking the station down as she fell.

Maggie screamed, "What the hell did you do?"

She dropped beside Barbara and brushed her thumbs against Barbara's closed eyes.

She saw a smear of blood on the stand where Barbara had hit her head. A pit formed in her gut; she hoped that Barbara wasn't dead.

Maggie reached out to feel for a pulse, but Nick grabbed her by the hair and dragged her backward.

She screamed, her feet seeking purchase on the floor, flailing beneath her.

He's going to drag me outside and murder me.

A shout from behind: "Let go of her!"

Maggie looked up to see Sebastian rushing from the diner's rear. Viv was right behind him, phone in hand, hopefully calling the police.

Nick must've realized he'd need both his hands. He let go of Maggie and growled.

Sebastian raced forward. He was on Nick before Maggie, or Nick, realized what was happening.

Sebastian hit Nick with a martial artist's precision — a punch in the neck, a blow to the back, and a kick in the ribs once the asshole was down.

One of their customers, a pudgy guy wearing cargo shorts and a porkpie hat, stood from his booth and held up his phone. "I called the cops."

Sebastian stopped his assault, looked at the guy, and said, "Thank you," then joined Maggie to examine Barbara.

"I did too," Viv said. "I'm on with a dispatcher now. They want to know if she's got a pulse. Is she conscious?"

Maggie's fingers had felt a pulse, but Barbara's eyes were closed, and she was still nonresponsive. "A pulse, yes. I don't think she's conscious."

Sebastian kneeled beside her, also feeling for a pulse. He moved to get a better look at her head.

Sebastian looked up at Viv. "She's not bleeding too bad, but she could have some nasty internal bleeding."

A bell clanged, grabbing their attention and fixing it to the closing door.

Outside, Nick jumped into a car, a red Camaro, that someone else was driving, and it tore out of the parking lot.

Sebastian ran to the door. For a moment, it looked like he might engage in a foot chase. Maggie wouldn't have bet against him catching the Camaro.

He turned back to her instead. "I better call Loretta and let her know what's going on."

Sebastian headed into the back to make the call.

Porkpie Hat and a few other customers hovered nearby, offering help.

"Did they say how long the ambulance will be?" Maggie asked Viv.

12

"It's on the way," Viv said as she took a spot next to Barbara and started answering questions the dispatcher was asking on the other end of the phone.

Maggie stared at Viv and Barbara, doing her best to keep her shit together even though every bit of her wanted to shut down, flee the scene, and process what had just happened. Nick had raged into the diner and attacked her. He may have hurt, or killed, Barbara.

He'd lost his damned mind.

But Maggie couldn't think about that now. She had to be there for Barbara.

Barbara's eyes opened, looked up at Maggie and Viv, unable to focus. "What happened?"

"It's okay, an ambulance is on the way," Maggie said.

Barbara reached up to feel the back of her head and pulled away a handful of blood.

"Oh God," she said, staring at her hand, horrified.

"It'll be fine." Maggie put her hand on the woman's shoulder, wishing the cops or ambulance were already there.

Maggie looked around, realizing nobody was serving the patrons, but her hands were shaking so uncontrollably that she couldn't serve a table if she tried. And Viv was still on with the dispatchers.

She thought about telling the guests that it would be a few minutes, to please hold tight, but she couldn't say a word. She was too horrified by events to try and restore normality to Goldman's.

As she looked at Barbara, Maggie still couldn't believe what Nick had done. Her tire was one thing. The text messages another. This was beyond the pale. She never would've thought him capable of such violence.

That's not true, or you wouldn't have filed the court order against him.

You knew this day was coming, you just didn't want to admit it.

Yeah, he may have hit me once ...

No, three times. Why do you keep lying to yourself with this one-time bullshit? It was three times!

Okay, three times. He may have hit me. And no, I didn't want McKenna around that. I didn't ever want him to lay a hand on her. But this ... this is insane.

This is the kind of shit stalkers do. The kind of thing you see on the news when an estranged husband blows his wife and kid away before putting the gun in his mouth.

If he went this far, how much further would he go? Could he kill her? Could he kill McKenna?

The thought filled Maggie with disgust. How could she have trusted and loved this man, capable of such evil?

It's the drugs. He's not the man you used to know!

Her phone rang, scaring her so abruptly that she let out a yelp.

Barbara looked at her then back down, closing her eyes, unable to pay attention.

Embarrassed by her outburst, Maggie fished the phone from her pocket and looked at the screen: *Hollis Atwater Talent Agency.*

Dammit.

She stared at the phone, letting the call she'd been waiting all morning for, if not a lifetime, ring with no answer. The phone call could change her life, but Maggie could only stare at the screen.

There was no way she could talk to the agent now. She had to sit with Viv and Barbara until the ambulance came. Then she'd have to deliver her statement to the cops. And then, well, then she'd have to work. There was nobody else but Viv, and while Viv was her direct boss and a whiz behind the counter, she couldn't handle a full house on her own.

She let the call go to voicemail, hoping she wasn't making the biggest mistake of her life.

Second if you counted Nick.

TWENTY-FOUR

Dima Kosta

DIMA STOOD in the lunch line with Kip, Roger, and the girls, trying to figure out the best way to break from the others to sit with Alicia, and probably Tim, if he was with her like usual — without the guys giving him shit.

It would be tough, especially after Tim pissed Jeff off in algebra and put a target on his back. Now everyone in their crew had seemingly set their sights on Tim, too.

Dima felt bad for Tim: Once Jeff set his sights on someone, he was *going* to hurt them. But hell if Tim hadn't brought it on himself. Maybe getting his ass kicked would help him to finally man up.

In many ways, Tim reminded Dima of everything he once hated about himself — everything he'd fought hard to change before high school.

He was too needy and thoroughly blind to his faults — blaming the world instead of himself for things that happened to him. Yes, he had a shitty home life. His father was a monster, and living there was like squirming under a dictator who monitored your every waking moment. Tim was dealt a shit hand, and Dima had tried to do everything possible to help him.

But you could only lead a horse to the creek and watch it snub the water so many times.

Dima had tried to subtly suggest that Tim change some of the weirder shit that made him such bully bait. Top among the list was his arrogance. Though he didn't intend to, Tim came off as a cocky know-it-all to a lot of people. He'd get into stupid arguments and always had to be right. Dima understood why, but other kids didn't know Tim's history or how his father had shaped him into someone who always felt a need to prove himself.

Then there was Tim's lack of social graces. He was painfully awkward but also too loud, drawing attention to his geeky, overenthusiastic behavior, and his weird, horse-like laugh. He needed to chill if he ever expected to hang with normal people.

But worst of all was the way Tim used guilt. Like Dima's mom. He was a fucking ninja with that shit. But unlike Dima's mom, Tim wasn't an older Jewish woman, so it only made him look needy and controlling.

In an ideal world, Dima would've brought Tim into the new cliques where he found himself suddenly welcome. But there was no way Tim would ever fit in with the cool kids. In addition to all the other stuff, Tim was painfully black and white. Like one of those little kids who obsessed over whether something was right or wrong, fair or unfair, who couldn't ever see the middle or keep his mouth shut long enough to let a little shit slide. He had an opinion on everything and had to make sure he hung that opinion in neon for all the world to see.

He'd never just hang with kids like Roger, Jeff, Kip, or anyone else he thought of as dumb jock assholes. When it came to discriminating against someone based on what they *seemed* like, Tim was just as guilty as the people he hated.

Yeah, Jeff was an asshole and a bully. No doubt. But Kip, Roger, and a bunch of the others that hung out with Jeff were regular guys who liked to joke around. Fun, once you knew them.

But the moment Dima started hanging out with them, Tim started acting like a jealous bitch — always complaining. "How can you hang out with them? They're such assholes!"

At first, Dima felt bad for leaving his friend behind. He hadn't planned to and had tried, for a while, to make time for Tim in his schedule. But there were only so many times someone could make you feel like shit before it became easier to cut them from your life.

Tim was the problem, not Dima, though there was no way he'd ever see it.

Dima paid for his lunch — burger, fries, and a milk — then turned back to Kip, right behind him.

"Hey, I'm gonna take care of something. I'll catch up with you all, K?"

"Yeah," Kip said, half-distracted by a giggling Avery.

Dima walked fast before the others would notice where he was going, hoping to avoid them seeing him crossing the cafeteria to Tim and Alicia.

He didn't give a shit whether they saw him talking to Tim — although he certainly didn't want to be associated with him anymore — so much as he didn't want to give Jeff, who'd be joining Roger soon enough, further reason to fuck with his old friend.

Fortunately, his new friends sat toward the front of the cafeteria while Tim and the other dorks sat about as far back as you could go, as if in hiding.

Dima passed people he'd been friends with back in middle school, greeted with a mixture of scorn and something approaching awe by the dorks. Some, like Tim, were pissed at his *betrayal*. Others wore envy like loud, tacky shirts. But Dima couldn't be responsible for how others felt about him.

He approached the farthest table, where Tim and Alicia sat with a couple of other people Dima didn't know. He wondered why Alicia still sat with Tim and the dorks. Didn't she know people were judging her? That she could do so much better than this crowd? If anything, Alicia should be sitting with the drama or art kids, who shared a few circles. She had enough friends on campus, she could legitimately fit in with almost any of the groups — a rare feat.

Yet she *chose* to sit with the dorks.

Dima wondered if it was out of guilt. No doubt Tim was working the same kind of guilt on her that he had on Dima. He didn't *want* to hate his old friend, but hell if Tim didn't make it so easy.

Dima drew closer to the table, both Alicia and Tim looked up. Tim was holding a spiral notebook full of writing, another of his stupid stories he was probably boring Alicia with. It looked like she'd drawn something in the notebook — a girl and a tree or something?

Tim looked at Dima, confused, maybe wondering why he was at their table.

But Dima wasn't there to see Tim.

He met Alicia's eyes, and she looked down, blushing.

She *had* read the note he passed her at the end of class. He could tell by looking at her; Alicia rarely blushed.

"So, have you thought about it?" he asked.

"Thought about what?" Tim was either asking a question that wasn't his damned business or thinking that Dima was talking to him.

Alicia answered, "Yeah, I'll go with you."

"Yeah?" Dima said, unable to hide his surprise. He'd done so well to cultivate a cooler response when talking with girls, but something about Alicia made him lose his cool — and not in a bad way. "Awesome."

"What are you two talking about?" Tim asked.

"Dima asked me to go to the dance with him."

The color left Tim's face and took his words with it. He stood up, with a look in his eyes that startled Dima.

12

"*You* asked *her* to the dance?"

"Yeah," Dima said, exchanging confused glances with Alicia. "What's the big deal?"

"The big deal?" Tim screeched, his face turning red as he stared at Dima like a lunatic. "*The big deal?*"

"Yeah," Dima said, getting annoyed. How dare Tim talk to him like this, so loud, in front of everyone? Like Dima was his bitch. Didn't Tim know his place in the pecking order?

"You knew!" Tim shouted, his body shaking as if he were on the verge of tears.

"Yo, dude, slow your roll. I have no idea what you're talking about, and you're drawing attention to yourself."

"Fuck you, Dima!" Tim shouted, way too loud.

Dima didn't look around, but he was sure there was a decent-sized audience already watching — maybe even Roger, Kip, and Jeff.

"Dude, what the hell are you talking about?"

Alicia looked at Tim like she was scared for him. She asked, "What's wrong?"

Tim ignored Alicia, like he couldn't even look at her.

"You knew how I felt about Alicia! *I* was going to ask her to the dance!"

Alicia's eyes widened, as surprised as Dima.

Laughter erupted around them. This wouldn't end well for Tim.

Dima leaned closer, lowering his voice, "Let's talk this out somewhere else."

"No!" Tim yelled. "You fucking knew, and you asked her anyway!"

Tim did the last thing in the world that anyone expected: he got up and launched himself at Dima.

Tim had moved so fast, and unexpectedly, that Dima didn't have time to dodge. One second, Tim was standing, and the next, he was throwing punches on top of Dima.

Alicia screamed, "Tim! Stop it, Tim!"

Despite his speed and surprise, Tim's punches were weak. Still, Dima was pissed. Not only was Tim making an ass of himself, he was making Dima look like a pussy.

Dima had allowed this wimpy dork to jump him *and* throw punches. Dima had never had to prove his toughness to get in with the jocks. Hell, he'd never been in a fight. But Dima looked like he could kick ass, so his ability to brawl had never been called into question. The guys had accepted him as one of their own.

But to allow Tim Fucking Hewitt to jump you? No fucking way Dima could let that stand.

Dima laughed, looking up and grabbing Tim's hands in his. "Really? You think you're gonna hurt me?"

He let go of one of Tim's hands so he could slap him hard across the face.

Tim fell back with a yelp.

Dima jumped to his knees then rose, putting his fists out in front of him in his best approximation of a fighter's stance. He might not look like a badass, but he looked a hell of a lot better than Tim, who was already crying like a bitch.

Alicia ran up and thrust herself between their bodies.

"Stop it, you two!" She looked at them both.

Dima held up his hands as if to say, *Hey, he started it.*

Kids chanted around them. "Fight! Fight! Fight! Fight!"

The crowd was too thick and hectic to make out who was who, or whether Kip and the gang were watching. But they had to be close.

Tim, still crying, said to Alicia, "Why are you going to the dance with *him?*"

Alicia, obviously not wanting to have this conversation in the middle of the cafeteria, whispered something to Tim that Dima couldn't hear.

It must've hurt. Tim closed his eyes and made some pained sound as if shot in the gut.

Dima just wanted this all to go away.

12

Still, people were chanting for a fight.

Dima felt as if he and Tim were two trains on the same track, barreling toward a collision. Neither could brake. The crowd demanded a spectacle.

"Come on, Tim, please," Alicia said.

He shook her off, stepped toward Dima, and threw a punch.

He missed, badly, and went flying past Dima and onto the floor behind them.

Laughter erupted.

Jeff moved in from nowhere, fast and savage, kicking Tim hard, twice in the ribs.

"Who's laughing now, little faggot?"

Tim should've lain there, balled up, and let things die down. Jeff was standing over him, calling him a faggot, but at least no longer kicking.

But Tim had clearly lost his shit.

He got up, screaming and crying, and grabbed hold of one of the plastic chairs, lifted it, swinging, metal legs out, straight at Jeff's face.

The crowd lost a collective gasp.

Jeff stumbled back and fell on his ass as the chair slipped from Tim's grip and landed in front of a group of kids. He was lucky — or they were — that the chair hadn't hit them.

Time seemed to slow. Dima felt himself stuck in the instant when the hero saw the bad thing — or many bad things at once — about to happen.

Jeff was getting up.

Tim was staring, frozen and wide eyed.

The crowd smelled blood.

Most people, if not all, were already on Dima and Jeff's side. There might have been a few who felt sorry for Tim. But that sorry went out the window when he swung a fucking chair. He could've killed someone.

Now they wanted to see him pay.

If Dima did nothing, Jeff would likely kill Tim. And not in the figurative sense.

Jeff was a psycho. He'd once put a kid in the hospital for cracking a joke about Jeff's already receding hairline.

Dima's instincts kicked in before his head could tell him no.

He leaped onto Tim, wrestling him to the ground.

Dima managed to get him in a headlock, leaned in close to his ear and whispered, "Stay down."

"Fuck you," Tim cried, trying to break free of Dima's grip.

Dima squeezed tighter, staying on top of Tim. If he were actually wrestling Tim, he might flip him over, try to get a better position. But he couldn't risk Jeff seeing that as an invitation to further hurt Tim. He had to keep himself between Tim and Jeff, put on a show until some teachers came to break shit up.

Come on, where the hell are they?

Chants continued.

Dima didn't dare look back to see where Jeff was. Or Kip. Or any of the others who might wanna tag in and take some shots at Tim.

"Stay down," Dima whispered again, trying to get the message through Tim's thick skull without announcing what he was doing to the entire fucking world.

I'm trying to fucking save you.

Tim continued to squirm, elbowing Dima but not hurting him.

"Stay fucking down," Dima said, a bit louder.

Finally, Dima saw movement in the corner of his eyes — the sea of spectators parting in a teacher's wake.

Ms. Walker.

About time!

She grabbed Dima by the ear, "Get off of him!"

Mr. Oliva was with her, one of the school's deans, a big

stocky dude in his forties. He grabbed Tim from behind and yanked him to his feet.

"I'm gonna fucking kill you!" Tim shouted.

Dima wasn't sure who Tim was talking to. He was looking all around, at everyone, like a caged animal.

The crowd laughed at his impotent threats.

Alicia was frozen, crying as Dima and Tim were taken away, headed to the dean's office.

Alicia followed behind, carrying Tim's backpack.

TWENTY-FIVE

Corrine Walker

CORRINE HAD NEVER BEEN MORE scared than when she'd seen Tim Hewitt pick up a chair and swing it at Jeff.

She was sitting at lunch with Phil, eating a salad while craving a burger. They were discussing the still-unknown results of her review, with her certain she'd done poorly despite Phil's insistence that her worries were for nothing.

Then they'd heard the chanting: "Fight! Fight! Fight! Fight!"

A crowd had gathered, inserting itself in the aisles and rows between tables, fogging their view. Several teachers rushed toward the kids, but as with most fights, the violence was too quick for anyone to stop it.

Corrine and Phil managed to push their way to a vantage point where they could finally see who was fighting and were startled to see Jeff kicking Tim like a dog.

She cried out Jeff's name. He either didn't hear or was ignoring her.

She tried to push her way through the kids, but they were so fixed on the fight that they didn't realize she was a teacher trying to get through. Times like this, Corrine wondered why she hadn't chosen to teach elementary. At least then, she would feel like she had *some* power to intimidate the kids. When most students were taller than she was, and particularly while breaking up fights, it was easy to feel insignificant, almost like a kid herself.

Tim picked up the chair.

He took a swing. The crowd parted just enough for her to see. A chill frosted her core. A feral look had lit Tim's eyes — a look you might see in an animal backed against a wall.

The chair went flying, and Dima wrestled Tim to the ground.

The crowd chanted louder, its sounds were scarier. With its dark energy and barbaric egging on of the fighters, it was hard to believe that these were still children by law. The scene had so quickly descended into chaos. And for the first time in her career, Corrine felt Death's specter slink through the crowds, eager to claim a victim.

She had to stop it.

Corrine shoved her way through the crowd, feeling an overwhelming fear that one of two things would happen. Either she wouldn't reach Tim in time, or — as unlikely as it probably was — the fight would spread throughout the cafeteria and she'd be swallowed by the violence.

The closer she came to Dima and Tim, the tighter spectators were packed.

As Dima held Tim down, Corrine's desperation to reach them grew.

She screamed, causing several of the kids to turn around, wide eyed, and she found her way through them.

She grabbed Dima by the ear, pulling him from Tim. Mr. Oliva grabbed Tim.

"I'm gonna fucking kill you," Tim screamed, looking back and forth with that same frightened animal glare she'd noticed before.

Jeff dashed toward the cafeteria doors, probably hoping to escape punishment.

"Stop him, too!" she yelled at Phil, already a step ahead of her, rushing toward the exit to head Jeff off. Phil wasn't a big enough guy to take Jeff down, but Corrine figured the student would bow to the teacher's authority.

Jeff stopped, as she figured he would. He was an angry kid but not entirely stupid.

She returned her attention to Dima and Tim.

"What is wrong with you two? I thought you were friends!" Corrine released Dima's ear and looked them both in the eyes.

Neither breathed a word. But something about the way Alicia was standing there, staring at them both, said volumes. Two boys fighting over a girl.

Though that didn't explain why Jeff was kicking the hell out of Tim.

Corrine flashed back to Jeff's comments when Tim was at the board, calling him a faggot, disguising it as a cough. There was bad blood brewing among all three, or four, of them. Now it had boiled over. She looked at Tim, unable to help feeling like the boy had snapped. He was shaking, crying, and staring at the floor as if suddenly realizing the severity of his actions. Not the fight, which he'd started, but rather the picking up of the chair and threatening to kill whoever it was he said he was going to kill.

There had been too many school shootings for his remarks to be written off as mere anger. An investigation was inevitable. The guidance counselor would want to talk to all involved. The principal might decide to report the incident to the police — *just in case.*

Corrine sighed, considering how much he may have harmed his future with one incident. If only she'd reached him sooner.

Phil brought Jeff over, and together they headed for the dean's office.

12

THE THREE BOYS sat side-by-side on a bench in front of the dean's office. Phil stood over them like a cop on duty.

Corrine was on the phone waiting for someone at Tim's house to answer so she could ask them to come pick up their son. Such violent acts were automatic suspensions for all involved, no matter who started the fight. Though how many days would be up to the dean.

She'd already called Jeff's and Dima's mothers. Jeff's mother couldn't get out of work, so he'd have to sit in the dean's office for the rest of the day. Dima's was on the way.

Tim's father finally answered.

"Hello?"

"Hello, Mr. Hewitt. This is Ms. Walker, Tim's algebra teacher. Is it possible for you to come down to the school?"

"Why? What's he done this time? Forge something else?"

"What?" Corinne asked, confused.

"This isn't about that progress report you sent home? The one he forged my signature on?"

Corinne remembered that Tim's report wasn't among those turned in earlier. She wanted to ask about the forgery, but that conversation would be better in person.

"Your son was in a fight. And school policy states that anyone involved in a fight is suspended from school for a few days."

"Suspended?" Mr. Hewitt yelled into the phone. "What happened?"

"We're in the process of getting to the bottom of that now. I can tell you more when you get here, if you're able to pick him up."

"Jesus Christ, I've got shit to do, you know? Can't you people manage a few children?"

Corrine bit her tongue. What "shit" was more important than his child's welfare? From what she knew of the man, again from things she'd overheard, he was a fat ass who sat at home all day while his wife punched a clock.

"This happened during lunch, Mr. Hewitt. He wasn't in class at the time. Like I said, I can tell you more once we get to the bottom of what happened."

"Sounds like you all are running around like chickens with your heads cut off down there."

She inhaled a deep breath then slowly let it out. "Are you able to pick up your son?"

"Yeah, I'll be right down."

Mr. Hewitt hung up.

Great. Can't wait to chat. Jerk.

TWENTY-SIX

Abe Mcdonald

ABE HAD STARED at the two dresses laid out on the bed for no less than twenty minutes, trying to decide which to give McKenna for their first day together. Girls liked dresses, and the first outfit would set the tone for their day. Maybe their entire relationship.

It wasn't that he thought one dress was an obviously better choice than the other. But at the same time, they were different enough that if Abe chose the wrong one, it may signal to her that he didn't know the first thing about girls.

He needed McKenna to trust him. He needed her to be comfortable. He wanted to make her happy, so happy she'd never miss her parents.

He'd spent a great deal of time and consideration choosing the perfect dress. He'd studied many catalogs, sales fliers, window shopped in the mall, and had even taken note of the kinds of dresses McKenna wore when he saw her. She seemed like a girly girl, someone who enjoyed dressing up and looking pretty, though she never took it too far with gaudy makeup or excessive jewelry. She'd probably think beauty pageants were gross. He'd never seen her dress provocatively

— refreshing given how so many parents allowed their little girls to dress like whores.

McKenna wasn't like that. She was pure. Innocent. Beautiful without need for such artificiality.

With the right guidance — away from her parents — she could become the perfect young woman.

The first dress was a soft, pastel sundress with pink straps, tied off with a thin red ribbon fixed into a bow. The second was a bright sky-blue, peppered with faint-white polka dots and a simple braided leather belt wrapped above the waist.

Abe was still staring at the dresses when his kitchen timer went off.

He'd have to decide later.

First, he had to get his brownies from the oven. Special brownies for McKenna on the way "home."

In addition to researching dresses, he'd also poured hours of work into finding the best method of sedating McKenna without any harm.

Originally, he'd planned to use chloroform, douse a rag, and knock her out. It seemed simple enough, effective, and probably not too dangerous. But there was something about putting a rag over McKenna's mouth that felt too violent. Abe didn't want to start their relationship with such a forceful, physical act.

Plus, he didn't know if she'd remember. It would take him far longer to earn her trust if she did. He needed to find a way to convince McKenna to stay with him of her own free will — not that she could ever be truly free. Once he took her to their new home, he couldn't return her, no matter how badly things went. It was too risky, and it wasn't like he had enough money saved to find a third location and another fake ID.

Abe chose to lace McKenna's brownie frosting with diphenhydramine. It would take longer for her to fall asleep, and the sleep wouldn't be chloroform deep, but he figured it would be enough to get the job done.

12

He pulled the brownies from the oven and set them on the stovetop for cooling as he mixed a small amount of fudge frosting, enough for one piece, with the diphenhydramine capsule's contents. The scent of chocolate blending with the slightest hint of butter set his stomach rumbling, but he didn't want to eat anything too sugary now that might sap his energy for later.

His plans were perfect, and the brownies smelled delicious, but Abe was still uncertain if he'd used the right amount of pills in the frosting. Too little, and it wouldn't work. Too much, and she could overdose. It wasn't like he could call the pharmacist and ask, "Hey, how many sleeping pills should I put in brownies to knock out a six-year-old girl?" So he erred on the side of caution and put less than he might have put otherwise.

Which is why he also bought chloroform, in case Plan A failed him.

He returned to the bedroom and checked McKenna's suitcase. He'd packed it with a Nintendo 3DS, a handful of games (all with at least 4.5-star reviews), a few books — paid for in cash — that she might want to read, clothes, and some personal grooming supplies.

It felt good to buy things for her.

Abe had never had a girl to buy things for. Women his age didn't give him the time of day, not that he'd ever had much interest in them. And being an only child, he'd never had nieces or nephews to buy things for.

Abe had been alone for too long. Soon, that would be over.

McKenna would grow to love him in time. Sure, she'd miss her mom, and maybe even her scumbag loser father for a while after Abe told her that something had happened to them. That would be hard. But he had to be strong, patient enough to wait for those familial binds to fade away and make room in her heart for him.

He stared at the bag, suddenly realizing a glaring omission.

In many of the videos he'd seen of McKenna, both those her mother posted on Facebook and the surveillance he'd taken with the program he installed on her laptop, she was taking her doll, Rosie, to bed.

He couldn't expect McKenna to believe the story that they were going to meet her mom later without her doll.

Damn. Damn. Damn.

He'd have to break into her house and get the doll. Fortunately, Abe had long ago managed to copy her key, after snagging the one marked spare from a pegboard by the door.

He'd never used the key, so he hoped it was functional and not a spare to something else.

Deciding on the right dress would have to wait.

Soon, it would be too late. People would be coming home from school, lunch dates, and whatever else unemployed people and stay-at-home moms did during the day. Abe had to be in and out of McKenna's apartment before then.

He grabbed both dresses and gently laid them into her suitcase then put it in the closet and closed the door. He grabbed a pair of leather gloves, and Maggie's spare key from a bowl on his kitchen counter.

He headed out his front door, locked it, then walked down the hall to the stairwell and ascended two flights of stairs. The apartment complex was six stories and L-shaped. He lived along the longer stretch, which was fifteen apartments long. Maggie and McKenna lived two floors above him along the shorter end, which was only five apartments long. It was good that he had to pass fewer apartments — and fewer open windows where people may be looking out — on the way there, but the girls lived at the end apartment, which was less than ideal. If someone happened to emerge from one of the other units, it was all the more obvious where he was at. He'd be stuck trying to explain why he was trying to break into Maggie's place.

Abe kept his head down and turned away as he walked past the other units, just shy of a run.

Latin music blared from one of the apartment's open windows, but he didn't dare turn to see if the curtains or blinds were open as well.

Just keep walking.

He arrived at Maggie's door and wasted no time. He didn't look down at the pool below where someone might be looking up, though he had a bit of cover from a few large hanging plants that Maggie had hung outside her place.

He slipped the key in the lock, heart racing. The key felt tight. His heart raced faster.

Please work. Please work.

He slid it in as far as it would go, and twisted the key.

It wouldn't budge.

No!

He panicked.

He thought of his confidence coach, Craig, and repeated his mantra under his breath.

"I am smart. I am strong. I am willing to do what must be done to get what's mine."

He remembered Craig's advice to face adversity with patience. *That* separated winners from losers.

He took a deep breath, withdrew the key, then slid it in again. It went all the way in.

Abe turned the key, unlocked the door, and stepped inside before anyone appeared in the hall.

The door closed, and he sighed with relief.

The curtains were all drawn, shrouding the living room. The apartment was cool and smelled faintly sweet, a scent he both enjoyed and remembered smelling on both Maggie and McKenna earlier in the car, along with the prior three times he'd been in their place.

He flipped a switch beneath the pegboard with keys and sticky notes, plastered with things to do and numbers to remember.

The lights went on.

He looked around the house — sparsely furnished with the basics: a small sofa, a tiny dining room table with three mismatched chairs, a modest TV, an older Nintendo Wii game system. Tidy. A few paintings brightened the walls — cheap things from Target or somewhere. Other than the Wii, the living room showed no signs of a child.

The last time he'd been there, toys had littered the place. Now, the living room and kitchen looked almost sterile.

Poor girl must be so sad here.

Even though she'd always been kind and smiled and laughed at his jokes, he'd also seen an inner sorrow — likely caused by her parents.

While Maggie *seemed* like a good mother to the casual observer, Abe knew the truth. He'd seen her fatigued eyes — the look of a mom who didn't really want a child, who saw her more as a burden than a blessing. He'd seen her occasional annoyance with McKenna. Maggie probably didn't even *want* custody of her daughter. The girl was probably a bargaining chip during a nasty breakup with her white trash loser husband, Nick, to get more money — assuming he had any to give. Or maybe McKenna was simply spoils for the victor.

All the more reason that she belonged with Abe.

He would never take such a precious, beautiful child for granted. He would never be annoyed by a single word from her mouth. He would truly love her in a way that nobody probably ever had.

Abe froze with the realization that *this* was what love felt like.

He'd never known love, only lust. What male hadn't? He'd known unrequited love in his school days. But he'd never felt the kind of love that would drive a man to sacrifice. The kind of love where you put another's needs before your own without even flinching.

This is the kind of risk you take for love. Breaking into a house to get your love's doll.

Someday, McKenna would realize all that he'd done for her. Well, not all. She could never know the truth: that he'd taken her, or that her parents were still alive. But she would know that he'd sacrificed his old life for a new one with her. That he'd given his heart and soul completely to her.

And she would come to love him, in time.

True love required patience, and Abe would gladly give it.

He looked at her bedroom door, painted blue with a large wooden M toward the top along with some *Frozen* posters — another rare sign that a child lived in the house. Something about the posters tore at his heart, but he couldn't figure out *why* he felt sad. Only that a hug from McKenna would make it go away.

He put his hand on her doorknob and twisted, feeling like an interloper about to step into the girl's most sacred of places — a place where he could learn what she treasured most.

Maybe there was a diary in her dresser?

Maybe more toys to make their trip feel like home?

Her room was pink, of course, with plenty of blues. He'd have to keep that in mind for her new room.

He looked around at her dresser where there were little plastic ponies lined with precise care. A few picture books filled a small shelf under her nightstand's single drawer. He ran a gloved hand over the books, looking at the titles. More *Frozen* books, some books about a witch he'd never heard of, and a few with a kitten on the cover.

He wondered if McKenna wanted a cat.

A cat could be a great tool to help the girl mourn her mother. A pet could also be used to get McKenna to do things she didn't want to do, should he have to employ any heavy-handed techniques.

The idea felt so right, he was surprised he hadn't thought of it before. Yes, it was a bit manipulative, but things might not go as smoothly as he hoped.

Abe made a mental note to pick up a kitten once they were settled. Maybe something gray that looked like the kitten on her books and her stuffed Mr. Whiskers doll.

He opened her nightstand drawer, hoping for a diary but seeing only a small photo album instead.

He picked it up and looked inside. There were a few pictures of her when she was a baby and a few a bit older with her parents. But the book was mostly empty pages.

There was nothing sadder than an empty photo album. Maggie would someday come into this very room and look through the album, wishing she'd taken more photos.

Abe chided himself. He was being too hard on Maggie. There was a good chance they just hadn't printed photos, but surely her computer was full, as he'd already seen firsthand.

Of course, he'd have to trigger the software to wipe the computer once he left and remove any traces of his presence.

Then she'll wish she'd backed those photos up.

He felt sad for Maggie but shoved the emotion as low as it would go.

It was her own fault. If she'd been a better mother, McKenna never would've popped up on Abe's radar. He never would've thought twice about the girl if she'd been happy. If she hadn't *needed* him.

He returned the photo album, closed the drawer, then turned to her dresser and caught his reflection.

He hated himself in the mirror. Tall, scrawny, flour white. An old evil troll in a princess's bedroom.

How can she ever love me?

Abe shuddered through a wave of repulsion.

He stared into the mirror. "I am smart. I am strong. I am willing to do what must be done to get what's mine."

You are someone special. You will be loved.

He almost believed it.

He opened the girl's top dresser drawer in hopes of finding her elusive diary. If she had one, he'd take it. He wanted to know everything he could about her, especially the things she'd only write to herself.

No diary in the drawer.

Instead, he saw neatly folded underwear and T-shirts.

He picked up a pair of underwear, pink with purple flowers.

They felt so soft in his fingers. He brought them up to his nose, inhaling the scent of laundry detergent and fabric softener.

He imagined the underwear on her, and felt two things at once: arousal and disgust.

The arousal was a drug, though, impossible to ignore, overshadowing his guilt and inappropriate thoughts.

He shook his head and tried to think of something to banish his thoughts, digging into his mental Rolodex of shameful experiences.

He thought of the time when he was eleven. In the bathroom, sitting on the toilet, touching himself — he didn't even know what masturbation was back then — while looking at the racier pictures in the back of his mother's *Cosmopolitan*. He thought he'd locked the door. But one minute he was holding his hardening penis while trying to find a nipple behind the lace of a brunette's bra, and the next his mother was screaming.

Screaming led to smacking then to her calling him a disgusting monster, which led to punishment, which led to months of her telling him that if he touched himself he'd go to hell.

She locked up the magazines. Or maybe she'd thrown them out and stopped buying them. Abe was never sure.

So he was forced to find other images to look at.

This was before they had cable, a computer, or anything that might promise breasts.

He started looking at tamer periodicals that didn't invite his mother's suspicions. Catalogs, family-centric magazines, and whatever he could find on TV in the rare moments he was left alone.

He found it odd that his mother, who was such a whore, was so damned concerned about him seeing a tit. If she were still alive and knew he liked young girls, she'd probably stab him with a cross.

He wondered if he'd ever get to touch McKenna the way he had dreamed of doing. He wouldn't ever force her. He'd wait until she was ready — however long that took.

I just hope she's not too old by then.

Abe's predilection gave him a specific age range of interest, six to eight, maybe up to nine or ten. He'd never been attracted to a girl once she'd started to mature.

And what are you going to do then? You'll be stuck with her!

No, she's different.

Abe wasn't sure how he knew, but he felt certain that he'd love McKenna no matter her age. It was crazy to try and guess what this girl would be like so many years from now, but Abe couldn't help his feelings that McKenna might be the one girl he could grow old with — even with a thirty-one-year head start.

Abe found her doll and picked it up. He brought it to his nose, inhaling her scent with his eyes closed.

It won't be long now before I can smell the real thing.

He imagined kissing her, on the head, of course. Just a peck, to feel her soft hair on his face.

Tears welled in his eyes.

This is what love feels like.

12

He was about to take the doll and leave.

His cell phone rang.

He dropped McKenna's doll on the bed and reached into his pocket. But it was tough to pull out the phone wearing gloves. After a few fumbles, he held the screen up and saw Maggie's name on his caller ID.

His stomach soured.

Was she calling to tell him she didn't need him to pick McKenna up after all? She got someone else?

Please, please, please, don't be bad news.

He answered, heart racing, hoping she couldn't somehow know he was inside her home.

"Abe?" she said, her voice sounding wet with tears.

Oh no, something's wrong. She's going to cancel and ruin everything.

"Yeah," he said, trying to bar the alarm from his voice. "Are you okay?"

"Yeah, just something's come up. Do you think you can do me another favor?"

"Sure, what is it?"

"Is it possible at all for you to swing by and pick McKenna up early?"

"Yeah, what's wrong?"

"Something happened with Nick, and I want to get her here on the off chance he might try getting her from school."

"Yeah, yeah, I can do that. You think he's going to try and pull her out of school? Why?"

"He's not allowed to see McKenna anymore. I got an order against him, and he's not happy."

"You think he'd try and do what? Kidnap her?" Abe asked, worried that his plan might fall apart.

The word *kidnap* felt strangely odd leaving his lips, as if Maggie might sense his intentions by him voicing the word. That her mother's intuition would go off and sense that he wasn't what he seemed. That he was the monster his mother always said he was.

"I don't know what he'll do. I just figured it'd be better to get McKenna and bring her to the diner now. Can you get off of work?"

"Yeah," he said, not bothering to explain that he'd already called in for the day. "I'll head over in a few minutes and get her."

"Thank you."

"My pleasure." Abe hung up the phone.

His plan had accelerated nearly two hours; maybe a blessing in disguise.

If McKenna went missing, Nick would be the first suspect, giving him more time to get out of town.

Whatever happened, Abe's destiny was a half hour away.

TWENTY-SEVEN

Sebastian Ruiz

SEBASTIAN WOULD'VE BEEN GONE. Would've been on his way to Raul with the money if not for that pain in the ass, Nick, showing up and smashing Barbara's head into the hostess station.

"Fuck!" he yelled in Loretta's office, pacing with the door shut, trying to decide what to do next.

He could leave, but the cops would be there any second, and leaving now, midshift, with so much attention on the diner, could get him busted before his meeting with Raul.

He had to sit tight and wait for the drama to settle.

He grabbed the bag of money and hid it better, beneath the filing cabinet next to the desk where no one would accidentally discover it.

Sebastian picked up the phone and called Loretta to fill her in on the drama. If he told her what had happened and could spin it in a way that made her believe the matter was under control, she wouldn't feel a need to return.

He got her voicemail.

Good. Maybe she's passed out.

He left a vague message, fulfilling his obligation to let her know something happened without ringing alarm bells that would send her racing back to work.

"Call me back when you get a chance, or I'll just let you know more tomorrow."

That should do it.

He looked at the TV monitor on Loretta's desk showing the closed circuit feed: a grid of four locations in the diner. One of the two cameras at the restaurant's front showed two officers entering the diner, followed by a pair of paramedics.

Sebastian left the office, returned to the front, and saw the two officers — regulars, Clarence and Patrick — taking Maggie's statement while the paramedics tended to Barbara.

He asked Viv if she was okay and she said she had things handled. Then Sebastian checked with Bob and filled him in on everything he'd missed from his spot in the kitchen. Then Maggie came back and said the cops wanted to talk to him.

"Can I get a statement from you?" Clarence asked, notepad and pen in hand. Patrick stood beside him, his stare unnerving — as if he could see Sebastian's anxiety, or sense the bag of money.

Sebastian told them everything that had happened, down to the make and model of Nick's car. Unfortunately, he didn't get a tag number — it was missing from the back, which in Sebastian's mind showed intent to do some heinous shit.

The paramedics carried Barbara out on a stretcher to the ambulance. "How's she going to be?" Sebastian asked.

"Not sure. Head wounds can be tricky," Clarence said. "But she's in good hands."

"You gonna get this guy?"

"Oh, yeah." Patrick nodded. "This asshole, and his friend, are going away for this little stunt."

"Good. Never did like that punk-ass bitch."

Silence settled between them while Clarence finished scribbling Sebastian's details. Patrick kept staring; a sheen of sweat licked Sebastian's back.

12

Why you staring at me, man?

He did his best to avoid the officer's eyes, while also not flinching suspiciously. He kept looking around the diner as if still lost in thought about the shit that went down.

The longer Sebastian avoided his gaze, the more he felt Patrick's probing stare.

Clarence and Patrick had been coming to Goldman's forever. Servers fawned all over them at every opportunity, laughing at their jokes, ensuring they got extra food on their plates, and generally treating them like VIPs. Sebastian had only spoken with them a few times when the officers were back in the kitchen chatting with Loretta. They'd been cool to him, not treating him like a thug as so many beat cops had. But he knew better than to ever feel *too relaxed* around any cop. Even if Sebastian had left the life of crime behind, it had colored his interactions with people, and cops in particular — forever.

Now, as Patrick kept staring at him, Sebastian felt like a suspect — even though he had nothing to do with Nick. Barely knew the fucker.

Sebastian finally met Patrick's glare, to prove his innocence.

Patrick spoke. "You okay?"

"Huh?" Sebastian said, having already looked past the cop and toward Viv refilling a customer's coffee.

"You okay? You don't look too good."

Clarence stopped writing and eyed Sebastian, looking the cook up and down.

A voice inside told Sebastian to run, to get the hell out without looking back.

But that voice was insane.

He hadn't done anything.

He wasn't guilty of shit. *Yet.*

Part of Sebastian wanted to confess. The same part that hated what he'd been, and had worked damned hard to earn some respect and atone for his sins. That part saw these two cops as friends, men whom he could confess to, and be forgiven. Men who might be able to help him get his sister back without all the machinations.

Yeah, Raul had snitches in the department, but Clarence and Patrick weren't crooked cops. They were standup guys. They could be trusted.

How the hell do you know that? Crooked cops don't go around wearing signs sayin' they're crooked. Being nice makes you better at being crooked.

He felt their stares, waiting for his answer.

Sebastian sighed, shook his head, and wore his best performance. "Nah, I just can't believe what happened to Barbara. And what Nick might've done to Maggie if I hadn't been here."

Patrick smiled. "Well, good thing you were here, eh?"

Sebastian couldn't tell if he was being patronizing, condescending, or genuine. "So, what's next? You gonna have someone here in case he comes back? What's Maggie supposed to do? I mean, she can't go back to her place with this psycho on the loose, can she?"

Clarence said, "We've got people on it, and we'll assign an officer in an unmarked car outside the diner, and one to her house tonight."

Sebastian swallowed. "Good."

"Thank you for your help. We're going to talk to some of your guests and get their statements." Clarence folded his notebook then slid it into his chest pocket.

Sebastian nodded. "No problem, thank you all for coming."

The cops moved to the customers for additional statements. Maggie approached Sebastian and met his eyes. "Thank you."

"It's okay," he said.

12

She nodded toward the kitchen, indicating that she wanted to talk away from the patrons. He followed her into the back where Bob was too busy cooking to pay them any mind.

Maggie's eyes were red, brimming with tears. "I'm so sorry."

She looked like she needed a hug. He and Maggie were friendly, but they'd never been huggers. She wasn't bubbly and overly enthusiastic like a lot of the other servers who hugged their way through every social setting. Maggie was friendly but reserved — like someone with shadows in her past. He could respect that.

He went ahead and threw his arms around her anyway. "It's not your fault, girl. Nobody's blaming you for shit that clown did."

She hugged him tight, sobbing into Sebastian's chest.

"I'll never forgive myself if Barbara doesn't get better."

"She'll be fine," Sebastian said, still hugging and hoping.

Sebastian thought of Ana, held hostage somewhere for whatever the hell she did, probably crying, wondering if she was about to die, helpless and afraid, praying that her big brother would come through.

Anger bubbled in his gut.

How dare Raul pull this shit on his family? Ana should've been off limits based on Sebastian's past service alone. Raul had lost his honor. Your gang was supposed to be your family; Ana should have been off limits.

But Sebastian didn't know the circumstances of what happened. Perhaps Ana had used her brother's relationship with Raul, or one of the other people in his organization, to get drugs. Maybe she'd done this to herself.

Still, it was hard not to imagine Raul as the spider, waiting for the helpless to stumble into his web.

Fucker.

Maggie pulled away. Maybe their hug had outlasted his intentions. "Okay," she said, "I better get back in there and help Viv."

"Yeah," Sebastian said. "And I better help Bob."

"Okay." Maggie smiled and nodded awkwardly before turning around and heading back into the dining room.

Sebastian stood in the doorway, watching the cops talk to a couple in a booth by the front door. Again he wondered if maybe they could be trusted, if they could help him get Ana out of her situation.

He felt trapped between who he was in the past and a future so full of potential just a few hours ago.

He could return the money. He could talk to Clarence and Patrick and tell them everything. Maybe they could track Ana's cell phone, like in the movies.

But then what?

Even if they got her back, it wasn't like Raul would see jail time. Even if he did, Raul had reach beyond bars. He'd never let Sebastian and Ana get away with involving the cops. They'd be lucky to be breathing by the time jurors were selected for his trial.

They'd be marked for death.

That's the way the real world worked. The world he'd grown up in. There were no cops saving the day. No Happily Ever Afters. If you wanted something done, you had to take care of that shit yourself.

Sebastian thought of Nick storming into the diner and the scene's immediate escalation. Men like Nick and Raul didn't understand half measures. You could only stop men like that if you acted without hesitation.

A new plan came to mind as he thought about jail, and his cellmate, Gino.

Gino owed him.

But going to Gino would mean signing a deal with the Devil. Sure, he might help, but not without strings attached.

12

But if things went well, perhaps he could save Ana and keep their lives somewhat intact.

He hoped.

TWENTY-EIGHT

Sheryl Dumont

SHERYL WAS RUNNING LATE since her showing went long. Bad news, she had to delay lunch with Chloe. Good news, Sheryl was pretty sure she'd sold a property that had been on her list forever, a three-bedroom '70s split-level home just outside a more desirable oceanfront neighborhood. The couple buying it wanted to live right near the beach but didn't have the budget. This, about a half mile from where they wanted to be, was an excellent compromise even if the house needed some love.

After she finished with the showing, Sheryl called Chloe and told her she was ready to meet at Goldman's and check out the badge bunny waitress.

About ten minutes from Goldman's, Sheryl felt a gnawing in her stomach. She was hungry, but the discomfort was guilt.

No matter how she dressed it up, Sheryl was, in essence, spying on her husband. And the way she saw it, when a marriage reached a place like that, things might be beyond salvation.

But Sheryl was also feeling something that had to be fear.

What good could come from seeing this waitress? What if she *were* young and hot, someone any guy with a pulse would check out? Would that make Sheryl feel better? Or would it only make her more certain that Clarence was cheating?

Going to the diner would confirm nothing.

But it had seemed like such a good idea a few hours before at Chloe's suggestion.

Now all Sheryl wanted was to call her friend and suggest another venue for lunch. Maybe the High Dive.

Sheryl's phone rang. She thumbed her steering wheel to answer hands free.

"Hello?"

"I'm almost there," Chloe said.

"I was thinking, maybe we should call this off? Eat somewhere else."

"What? No way you're chickening out."

"I'm not chickening out, I just don't see any good that can come from this. It's not like we're gonna go there and find Clarence fucking her on a table, right? And it's not like we can ask her if she's screwing my husband."

"We could."

"Shut up. We are not asking that!"

"Sometimes, the direct approach is best. It catches people off guard. They don't have time to think of a credible lie, so they tell the truth, either verbally or with body language."

She surprised herself with a confession: "Maybe I don't want to know the truth."

Sheryl came to a red light, two blocks from the diner.

Chloe said, "So, you'd rather live in denial than know the truth?"

"I dunno."

"I could understand that if things were going well at home. Nobody wants to rock the boat when things are fine. But you're not happy. So why would you want to continue laboring under an illusion when you can find out the truth?"

"I don't think we're going to find out anything. I think this visit to the diner will only lead me to be *more* suspicions."

"Okay, I understand what you're saying. But hear me out. I'm your best friend, right? Do you trust me?"

"I guess."

"Screw you, *I guess*." Chloe laughed. "Okay, here's the deal. We're going to go to the diner like we planned. Because A) I am starving and B) it'll be hard to get a table at the High Dive. So either I'm gonna go to Goldman's and eat by myself, and who knows what I might say if left to my own devices, *oooooorrrr* you come with me, as planned. We don't have to say anything, but I wanna see this badge bunny and get a feel for her. I'll know if something's up."

"Just by looking at her?"

"I'm very perceptive. Sniffing out women who go after married men is one of my talents."

"Fine," Sheryl said, not agreeing with Chloe so much as wanting to avoid an argument and tend to her rumbling stomach.

She arrived at the diner, surprised to find two cop cars and an ambulance in the parking lot. Paramedics were carrying one of the waitresses out on a stretcher.

Something was going on. But given that there were only two cop cars, the emergency was likely something minor. Maybe a workplace injury, a heart attack, or some other routine call.

Sheryl navigated the parking lot and got a better view of the cop cars. Numbers on the rear said that one belonged to Clarence.

Shit!

She parked on the lot's far end and called Chloe back.

"Hey, I'm here, but change of plans."

"What?" Chloe sounded annoyed that Sheryl had seemingly chickened out.

"Something's going on here. There are two cop cars, and paramedics are carrying a waitress out on a stretcher. No way we can go in there now. I've made fun of him eating here enough times that it would look downright suspicious if he saw me waltzing through the door."

"Fine." Chloe sighed. "Lemme call the High Dive and see if we can get a table."

"I'll head over there now. Call me if they say no."

"Don't think you escaped anything, girlfriend. We're going back to the diner later."

"Fine," Sheryl said, relieved to delay the discomfort of seeing the waitress who might be screwing her husband.

1 p.m. - 2 p.m.

TWENTY-NINE

Tim Hewitt

TIM STARED at the wall clock like a condemned man awaiting execution. It was quarter past one, and his father was on his way to school for a meeting with the dean.

At the moment, Dima was in the dean's office, telling his side of the story, which no doubt would paint Tim as the instigator. Tim would get a more severe punishment while Dima might skate away with barely a consequence. There was no way that the dean, or probably anybody else, would understand that while Tim had *technically* started the fight, Dima had provoked him.

He'd asked Alicia to the dance, despite knowing that Tim had been in love with her forever. Tim had sought Dima's advice — not that he had any more experience with girls than Tim at the time — on how best to tell Alicia how he felt. Particularly when his father would never let him go out on a date in the first place. How did you "go out" with someone when your father barely let you leave the house?

Dima had always said "Just tell her, man, and let the chips fall where they may. If it's meant to be, it'll find a way. Maybe she'll wait until you graduate."

Such a laissez-faire approach was easy when it was someone else's love life involved.

At the time, Tim had thought Dima was either tired of hearing him yammer on about Alicia all the time, or just didn't understand the complexities of his home life. Dima knew Tim's father never let him go out except during the summer, and occasionally on weekends when he wanted Tim out of the house, so maybe Dima thought Tim was overstating his father's opposition to dating. Or that Tim was using his father as an excuse to never tell Alicia how he felt.

But now, after this, Tim wondered if maybe Dima's motives had always been underhanded.

Perhaps his old friend had been sowing the seeds even then, hoping Tim would make a fool of himself so Dima could sweep in and declare *his* love for Alicia.

It seemed a bit Machiavellian for Dima, who wasn't exactly a genius. Sure, he was into the same geeky things and was a funny guy, but he never seemed smart or calculating enough to purposely sabotage Tim's chances with Alicia.

Tim waited, wondering what fabrications Dima might be spinning. More than that, he wondered what Jeff, who had been the first called into Dean Keller's office, had said. He probably told the man something short and sweet — Jeff left the office five minutes later, on his way to internal detention — probably because his parents weren't around to pick him up.

Tim looked down when Jeff left the office, not daring to meet the bully's eyes. Had he looked up, Tim was certain that Jeff would've glared at him or somehow signaled that Tim would pay dearly.

Jeff couldn't know that whatever punishment he planned would probably pale in comparison to the beating waiting at home.

The clock's second hand continued to tick. Tim turned the

scenario in his mind. It would start when his father arrived. He'd look down at Tim with disappointment bordering disgust. Then they'd go into the dean's office where Tim would sit beside his fat fuck father, feeling small and trapped in the chair beside him. His father would either play it cool or be caustic as he tended to be around those he saw as beneath him. But he wouldn't show his full rage. It would stay buried until they arrived at the car, or worse, behind closed doors at home. Tim wasn't sure when it would come, but when it did, spittle would fly from a snarling mouth on his crimson face, fists balled and voice like thunder.

Tim's stomach lurched. He stood and said, "I think I'm gonna be sick."

The secretary rolled her eyes and pointed to the bathroom.

Tim ran out the double doors, made a right, and raced down the hall into the boy's bathroom.

He was ten feet from the first stall when he lost control.

Vomit raced from his gut to his mouth.

His first horrible instinct was to contain the vomit until he reached the stall by smothering his mouth with his hands.

It didn't work out. Instead, hot puke splashed all over Tim's hands, back into his face, onto his clothes, and all over the floor.

Tears stung his eyes. He stumbled forward on the slippery mess and made his way to the stall where he finished emptying his stomach.

He retched until there was nothing but an ache that screamed from Tim's throat to his balls.

He looked down at himself, at the chunks of whatever the hell he'd had for breakfast creaming the bowl.

He had to clean up quick.

There was no way he could let his father see him like this. It would only disgust him further, and worsen his beating. A few years ago, they'd been on a road trip to their aunt's house when Tim had to piss. Bad went to worse until he finally begged his father to stop. His father had refused to pull over, saying it was Tim's own fault for drinking so much water before they left. He'd just have to wait it out and deal with the consequences of his actions. Tim couldn't wait long. Ten minutes later, he pissed himself. His father swung to the shoulder and yanked Tim out of the car by his hair, screaming at him for ruining his seat. He beat the hell out of Tim on the roadside then threw his pants and underwear on the ground and forced him to sit bare-assed on the seat until they went to a store where Tim's father added to the humiliation by buying Tim the ugliest shorts he could find, tight red ones with white stripes that didn't match his button down blue shirt. Tim had been forced to wear those shorts, without underwear, the rest of the day.

There was no way Tim's father would let him into the car reeking of puke. He'd probably make him strip right there in the school parking lot.

He grabbed a handful of paper towels and started scrubbing his shirt over the sink, knocking chunks of puke into the basin.

Behind him, a laugh.

Tim looked up in the mirror to see Jeff standing in front of the bathroom door.

It swung shut behind him. Tim swallowed a lump of fear.

"Well, well, well, what do we have here?" Jeff looked at the floor then up at Tim. "*Wittle* Timmy have a *bewwy* ache?"

What was Jeff even doing in here? Wasn't he supposed to be in detention? Was he stalking the halls, knowing Tim would come to the bathroom, waiting to corner him? The fucker was a predator in a roid-fueled ninth grader's body.

Tim kept scrubbing at his shirt, saying nothing, hoping Jeff would just go away.

As if that ever worked with guys like him.

"You think you're better than me or something?"

Tim turned, surprised by the question. He shook his head

and said, "No. Why would you ask that?"

"You think I don't see the way you look at me?" Jeff walked over to Tim and stopped on the other side of the puke, roughly six feet away.

Tim was confused. He did everything possible to *avoid* eye contact with people like Jeff. When, before today, had he ever looked at Jeff in an insulting way? Was Jeff's hate for him borne of confusion? If so, was there any way to undo it and maybe talk his way out of a beating?

"I honestly don't know what you're talking about, man. If I did something to offend you, I'm sorry."

Jeff stared at Tim, his expression blank enough to confuse him further. Was he pissed? Was Jeff considering Tim's explanation? Had he come to make amends?

Jeff kept quiet.

"And I'm sorry about what happened in the classroom," Tim continued. "I was just trying to joke around with you. I thought you'd think it was funny."

"You think making me look like a fool in front of the whole class is *funny?*"

He stared at Jeff, unable to believe his ears. Did he really think that *Tim* had made *him* look like a fool? Jeff was the one calling him a faggot when Tim was at the whiteboard.

"I'm sorry," Tim repeated.

Jeff looked down at the puke then back up at Tim. For a moment, Tim felt like the bully felt sorry for him, that he saw how the situation had spiraled out of control. That Tim had puked all over the place, and was obviously in trouble. Maybe, just maybe, Jeff would let shit go.

Jeff turned to leave, giving rise to Tim's hope that yes, the bully might forgive him.

Jeff reached the door. But instead of opening it and leaving, he reached up to the lock, twisted it, and sealed them in the bathroom together.

Oh shit.

12

Jeff turned back to Tim.

"I told you I was gonna kill you, Timmy. You ready to die?"

Tim shook his head, thinking that begging was all he could do. "Please, Jeff, I'm sorry. I didn't mean to piss you off. I swear it—"

Jeff stepped toward the light switch then silenced Tim's pleas with the dark.

Oh God, no.

Tim couldn't see a thing.

He didn't know what to do. Move from the last spot Jeff had seen him and try reaching the door for escape, or move, maybe make sounds which would draw Jeff to him quicker.

His hoarse laugh sawed through Tim's bones.

"Faaaaggggoooootttt," Jeff whispered, moving closer, though how close he was, Tim couldn't tell. Jeff seemed to be moving back and forth, playing with Tim's sense of perception.

The red letters marking EXIT over the door were all Tim could see in the black. But even that red glow wasn't enough to cut the darkness around them.

The pain came — a fist to his chest.

He doubled over, falling to his knees, into his own sickness, gasping for air.

He was down, blind, out of breath.

He'd never felt more vulnerable.

He braced for impact, a hail of fists to his head, kicks to his ribs, something else.

But nothing came but Jeff's giggles in the darkness.

"Timmy, Timmy, are you crying?"

He was but said nothing.

"Are you ready for the next round?" Jeff whispered, his voice seeming to come from behind.

Tim raced forward, hands and knees slipping in vomit as he scrambled forward on all fours toward the exit.

Hands grabbed his hair, hard, pulling him backward, slamming him toward the outer wall of the bathroom stall. His glasses fell from his face.

Jeff punched Tim in the left side of his head then ran away, laughing in the dark.

"Stop it!" Tim cried out, hating his obvious tears. A grown-ass high school student begging a bully to stop.

He felt pathetic.

Powerless.

Then, silence.

A silence so stretched that Tim wondered if Jeff hadn't somehow slipped out of the bathroom, maybe into the shadows like an assassin.

He stared at the EXIT sign again, the red glow promising an end to his torment — if he could reach it.

Did he dare try again?

He couldn't just sit there and wait for Jeff to give up hitting him, could he?

Then again, how long could Jeff continue? It was only a matter of time until someone — another student, or hopefully a teacher — came along and wondered why the hell the bathroom door was closed. What then? Jeff wasn't going to actually kill him. There was no way he'd get away with it. For one, there were cameras all over school. Even though there were none in the bathroom, he couldn't murder Tim.

Jeff just wanted to scare him.

Tim would wait him out and hope he'd give up.

Silence continued. Tim wondered where Jeff was, and what was he doing.

It was too quiet.

Tim could feel his heart racing.

He wanted to reach around in the darkness and feel for his glasses, but was afraid that Jeff somehow possessed infrared vision or something, would see him searching for his glasses, then stomp on his fingers.

12

Maybe I should just go for the EXIT?

He slowly started to stand, unwilling to crawl and risk Jeff stamping on his fingers.

He inched forward in the darkness.

He figured he was about twelve steps from the door.

Eleven.

Ten.

And then the sound of movement behind him.

He jumped, turned around, and threw his arms in front of his face in hopes of deflecting the blows.

But there was nothing.

Tim turned back toward the door.

Nine.

Eight.

Maybe Jeff would let him go.

Seven.

Six.

A whisper in his left ear: "Boo, bitch!"

Jeff shoved him hard against the wall and slammed the back of Tim's head into the tile wall.

Tim screamed.

"Help! Help!"

Jeff laughed in the dark then grabbed Tim by his shirt collar and shoved him up against the wall.

Outside, someone banged on the door, a woman's voice, saying, "What's going on in there? Open up."

Again Tim screamed, "Help!"

Jeff shoved Tim harder against the wall as if to say, *You'll go when I let you go.*

Jeff's hot breath fogged his face.

"I'm not done with you, Timmy. Not even close. You've just become my personal fucking mission this year. You happy about that, faggot funny boy?"

Tim said nothing.

Jeff pushed hard into Tim's chest then let him go.

Jeff turned the light back on then opened the door to find Ms. Walker standing there. She'd been in the dean's office when Tim went to the bathroom, so she must've come to check up on him. Maybe the secretary had told her that Tim was about to puke when he ran out of the dean's office.

"What's going on in here?" She looked at the puke on the floor then at Tim, who must've looked like he'd been hit by a truck.

Tim saw his glasses on the floor, picked them up, surprised they weren't broken, and slipped them onto his face.

Jeff said, "He got sick all over. I was trying to help him get cleaned up."

"Is that true?" Ms. Walker asked.

Jeff, standing behind and towering over their algebra teacher met Tim's eyes as if to say he'd damned well better not disagree.

"Yeah," Tim said.

"Why was the door locked?"

"An accident," Jeff said, his smile full of bullshit.

Tim was pretty sure that Ms. Walker wasn't buying a word, but she seemed to be playing along for some reason — perhaps to spare Tim further embarrassment. Maybe she sensed that Tim would be in even hotter water if he told her what Jeff had done, so she wouldn't press for details.

"Why aren't you in detention?"

"Had to use the little boy's room," Jeff said.

"Well, get back."

"Sure thing, Mrs. W."

Tim wondered if the dumb jock didn't know she wasn't a Mrs. or if he was calling her that as some sort of insult to remind her that she wasn't married, and that there were rumors she was gay.

Jeff smiled at Tim then winked and left.

Ms. Walker looked at Tim as if he was a sorry, wet dog washed up on her doorstep.

12

"Let's get you cleaned up," she said, grabbing a handful of paper towels.

He wanted to sob, thankful for even the slightest kindness.

She brought him to the nurse, who ushered him into the back where there was a shower, and allowed him to wash up. The nurse left him some clothes to put on once finished. He wasn't sure if they were from the lost and found or if the school had clothes for unfortunate times such as this.

He dressed in a black surfer tee and baggy blue sweatpants. It wasn't clothes he'd normally wear, and people would probably wonder why he was wearing sweats, but it didn't matter since he wouldn't be returning to class.

Ms. Walker met him in the front of the nurse's office, wearing the kindest smile — a variety that proved her understanding and promised that things would be okay.

"Feel better?"

"Yes, thank you."

"Okay, let's get back to Dean Keller's office. Do you want to tell me what happened back there?"

"Not really." Tim figured that he'd been hit in places she couldn't see. He saw his bruises while showering, but nowhere that his teacher could see.

"Okay," she said. "I understand."

They walked back in silence. Tim held his tears.

He didn't want to cry because of all the bad shit that had happened today, or even that he was likely to get another beating at home. Tim wanted to cry because of his teacher's kindness. *Someone* understood when Tim thought he had no one.

"Thank you," he said.

They entered Dean Keller's office. Tim's father was waiting, looking at him with the opposite of Ms. Walker's mercy, his eyes filled with the same hate burning in Jeff's.

THE MEETING WENT SURPRISINGLY WELL. His father hadn't blown up. He listened to the facts — that the boys had fought, and that no one was sure what started it. However, school rules mandated that all parties in a fight be suspended from school for five days.

Tim sat quietly while Ms. Walker said she was concerned by his threat: "I'm going to f'ing kill you."

Fortunately, they weren't going to call the police or any of the things a school might do in the aftermath of such a statement. It was the heat of the battle rather than a direct threat. It could be overlooked if Tim got counseling.

Tim's father didn't argue. Didn't say much, which both surprised and scared him.

Tim got in the car, wondering what his father was thinking. Why hadn't he blown up at least a little? He'd never seen his father *this calm*. Why hadn't he said he was going to be punished until the end of time? Maybe he'd finally make good on his threat to send Tim to St. Martin's?

Tim said nothing during the drive home, certain that he'd find out soon enough.

He sat next to his father, trying not to think about the coming punishment and thinking of Alicia.

Maybe a boy's academy would be best for him after all. He'd never have to see her face again.

It wasn't that he didn't *want* to see Alicia, though he didn't if she was suddenly dating Dima.

But Tim wasn't sure he could ever look her in the eyes. Not after she said what she'd said to him right after the fight. While trying to calm him, she asked him why he was doing this.

He said that he loved her, and that Dima knew it.

Then she said something that he'd never forget.

"But, Tim, you're just a friend."

No matter what his father did at home, nothing could hurt more than that.

THIRTY

Joe Harcourt

Joe carefully unfolded the paper with Maggie's link.

He pecked at his keyboard, Hoss sighing at his feet.

"Come here, boy, want a scratch?"

Hoss put his head in Joe's lap and looked up at him, brow furrowed. Joe ran his fingers back and forth over the dog's scalp. Hoss wagged his tail as if a scratch between the ears was better than steak.

The YouTube page loaded and displayed Maggie in front of a keyboard. Beneath that he saw a selection of additional videos. Joe wasn't sure if they were Maggie's original songs or covers of contemporary hits, which he wouldn't recognize.

He scrolled down the page and clicked one at random: *Halfway to Here*.

The video started. The screen showed Maggie wearing a blue T-shirt, her hair pulled back in a tight ponytail. She started playing the keyboard. Twenty seconds passed with nothing but slow, somber notes. Joe wondered if he'd clicked on an instrumental.

Then she opened her mouth and sang.

Joe's jaw dropped; Maggie sounded exactly like Grace.

The similarity in their voices was startling, even if they

shared little in style. Joe closed his eyes. If he didn't know better, Joe would've thought Grace was singing to him. God, how many times he wished he could've gone back in time — to have even a few moments back where he'd chosen his work over spending time with Grace. Even mundane moments. Even the times when they'd fought. Anything to have her for a few more minutes.

In many ways, Joe thought it cruel that people didn't know how long they had on Earth. How much different would people treat one another if they knew the true limits of their time? How much more would people appreciate one another? How much more likely would people seek to cooperate rather than entrench themselves in petty differences?

He listened to Maggie's song about a woman who felt as if she were always halfway to where she needed to be. Halfway good enough to please her love. Halfway to happiness. That if only she could be all that he (whoever *he* was) needed, she'd finally feel whole.

He wondered if the song were autobiographical. He knew she was separated from McKenna's father, though he'd never asked why. And from the information he'd received from the private detective, who found Maggie for Joe, her husband was bad news.

He tried to remember the man's name. He'd read the report enough times to have a distaste for the man. But sitting and listening to Maggie, he couldn't remember his name.

Not that it mattered.

Joe finished the song then started another.

When he hit play on the next song, *This, For You*, the opening music triggered a memory.

What song does this sound like?

Joe couldn't place it, but remembered a moment, back when he'd been really sick. He was in his thirties, with pneumonia, in the hospital. He remembered lying there, surprised

12

that something he'd thought was a routine cold could knock him out for so long.

He must've looked awful because he remembered Grace curled on the chair beside his bed, holding his hand, looking at him with her big sad eyes.

Though she'd never give voice to the possibility of losing him, he could see the fear in her eyes.

She'd held his hands, stared into his gaze, and sang a song that sounded like Maggie's.

He closed his eyes, sinking into the moment. It was a well-caressed memory, even if he'd never told Grace how much her singing had touched him in that moment.

Why didn't I ever tell her?

If Joe had known how long they had, he would've told Grace how much her singing had meant to him that day in the hospital. How much he felt her love, and her fear. How it had reached inside and given him strength to get better.

He didn't believe much in stuff like sudden healing, positive thinking, or miracles crafted by love. But in that moment, at his weakest, Joe *had* believed that her singing had healed him. As had her love.

But once he was better and free of the hospital, real life resumed, and he felt silly confessing to something so ridiculous. The worst part was that he would've only looked silly to himself. Grace did believe in those sorts of things. She believed in the power of the mind. She believed in God, angels, and all sorts of magical things that Joe had always found ridiculous.

But for a moment, just a moment, her singing had made him believe in something more than himself. Something more than the present. Something you didn't understand with logic, though you felt it with your heart.

If I'd only told her.

But he hadn't. Another line in a list of regrets and things unsaid.

Why was I so afraid? Afraid of what? Admitting that Grace might be right? Or afraid of shedding my cynicism at the first blush of death like a deathbed convert?

Joe hated himself for being so weak.

As Maggie's song played, his memory of Grace singing returned in Technicolor. He could remember her clothes — a long navy-blue dress and a white peacoat he'd bought her the prior Christmas. He could see that look in her eyes as if they were still sharing the room. He could see her hands on his, so small by comparison. He could see her mouth moving, her sweet lips bringing music to life in his heart.

But in the memory, he couldn't hear her song.

It was a song he'd thought about a hundred times, if not a thousand whenever he heard it played on a radio or TV show. She'd even sung it to him a few other times after his hospital visit, usually to help him sleep after an especially stressful day at work.

Why can't I remember the song?

He squeezed his eyes tighter as if to bar the present and capture the past.

He could see her beside him, close with no regard to catching his sickness. Holding him close, wiping her hand over his sweaty brow, coaxing him to health.

He was nearing his memory when the song stopped.

He opened his eyes, and hit play again.

But then there was an advertisement, for some stupid household cleaner, which jarred Joe from the moment.

The ad ended, and he played the song again, hoping to recapture the past.

But it wasn't coming and left him only with his frustration. He balled his fist and slammed it onto the table.

Startled, Hoss jumped back, whining.

"Sorry, Hoss. Didn't mean to scare you."

He held out his hand for the dog to resettle in his spot.

12

Hoss came forward, head slightly down, tail between his legs like he was in trouble.

Joe reached out and scratched between the dog's ears, letting him know that things were all right.

Hoss's tail went back to wagging.

Joe clicked on another song and watched as Maggie continued to remind him of Grace.

Joe wished he could remember her song and hoped it wasn't another memory lost to forever. The worst part was he had no idea how many things he'd already forgotten. Would he even remember that he'd lost the song come tomorrow? Or, worse, might he even forget that he'd ever been in the hospital to hear her sing?

If given the choice to die sooner, but keep his memories of Grace, he'd choose to die — even if that meant leaving the world today.

THIRTY-ONE

Loretta Goldman

Loretta wanted to kill Dima.

She drove back from the school meeting, fuming. "What the hell is your problem?"

"I don't have a problem," Dima whined, crouched in the front seat of their minivan as if embarrassed to be driven home by his mother.

She shook her head, letting out a long sigh.

"You know you ruined my day, don't you?"

"So sorry if me getting into a fight that I didn't even start ruined *your* day."

"Enough of the sarcasm." Loretta smacked him on the shoulder.

"Yes, ma'am." He glared out the passenger side window, still refusing to meet her eyes.

"What happened?"

"I already told you, the dean, and Ms. Walker the same thing. The story isn't gonna change. Tim got pissed at me for asking out Alicia, and he came up and attacked me."

"No, I mean what else happened? Come on, there's gotta be something more. You two are best friends."

12

"We haven't been friends since last year. Shows how much you pay attention."

"How much I pay attention? Excuse me, but I ask you what happened at school every time you come home, and all you ever tell me is the same damned thing — 'nothing.'"

She said "nothing" like he did, straight from the mouth of a sulky teen.

"It doesn't matter. Let's just drop it."

"No, I will not 'drop it.' I want you to tell me what happened between you and Tim. You used to be thick as thieves."

"God, Mom, nobody uses that expression."

"Whatever. I want to know what happened between you. Tim's a good kid. He wouldn't just attack you."

"First off, Tim is *not* a good kid. You don't know the first thing about him."

"Excuse me? So you were lying all those years you said he was your best friend?"

"No. I'm just saying, he's got ... problems."

"What kind of problems?"

"His dad is a dick."

"Watch your mouth."

"Okay, his dad is a *penis*."

"Ha, ha. Okay, I knew that," Loretta said, grateful for the opening. "You told me before that he doesn't let him out and stuff."

"Yeah, well his dad also hits him. Like, a lot."

"Really? Wow. That sucks. Does the school know?"

"I don't know, I'm not his social worker."

"So, what kinds of problems does he have? Are you saying he's a bully?"

"Ha!" Dima laughed. "Yeah, right. He couldn't fight his way out of a wet paper bag."

"So, what's his problem?"

"I dunno, why don't you ask him?"

"No, I'm asking you. You were his best friend; clearly, you know something."

"I don't know. He's just all weird and moody and stuff. It's hard to be his friend. He's always so negative and feeling sorry for himself. I tried being his friend and helping him out, but damn, it was like a full-time job, and he was holding me back."

"Holding you back?"

"Yeah, nobody wants to hang out with him. And all these years, I thought people didn't like me. But it wasn't me, it was him. People like me fine. But he's like kryptonite to friends."

"So, what? You just stopped being his friend so other kids would hang out with you?"

"It wasn't like that. I tried to bring him along, introduce him to the other kids, but he was a complete d-jerk about it. He didn't want to be friends with them anymore than they wanted to be with him. He's a geek, Mom, he doesn't fit in."

"So, what's this about Alicia? Tim liked her, and you knew about it? And you still asked her out?"

"First off, he was never gonna ask her out. He's been talking about her for years, Mom. And I tried, for years, to get him to ask her out. But he was too much of a pussy—"

"Dima!"

"Sorry! He was too much of a wuss. He wasn't ever gonna ask her out. What was I supposed to do, wait for him to get up the courage and for her to shoot him down? It's not like he had her on layaway."

"How do you know she would've shot him down?"

He laughed again. "Come on, Mom. It's Tim. Alicia's only friends with him because she feels sorry for him. She doesn't like him like that."

"She told you this?"

"No. But I can tell."

12

"Yeah?"

"Yeah," he said, his voice rising defensively. "Besides, I like her. A lot. Even if Tim and I were still friends, I might have still asked."

"You'd choose some girl over a friend?"

"She's one of my best friends. I've known her since first grade. She's not just 'some girl.'"

"So, you asked her out, and Tim did what?"

"He freaked out like some kind of psychopath! He said he was gonna kill me."

"I'm sure he didn't mean it."

"You didn't see his eyes! I've never seen him so mad. He looked like ... a crazy person."

Loretta thought on what her son had said, her eyes on the road.

"Hey, you passed our turn."

"You're coming with me to work. Something happened, and we're shorthanded. I have to go back."

Loretta expected complaint, but Dima said nothing. While he'd changed a lot since he started visiting his father on weekends again, Loretta was glad to see that his work ethic hadn't changed. Though his better-than-decent tips surely had something to do with it.

After a few minutes of silence, she said, "You're going to call Tim and make this right."

"What? No way."

"He's your friend, Dima. You have to understand that whatever's going on between you now is a phase. You'll be close again. But if you don't try and talk to him now, that might never happen. Trust me, I've let my pride screw up more than a few friendships."

"I don't care if I ever speak to him again. He's a loser."

Loretta smacked him again, this time on the back of the head, hard enough to get his attention.

"Excuse me, young man, we don't use that word in our house."

"We're not in our house. And Tim *is* a loser. A geeky, psychopathic loser. And I don't want to be his friend."

"What happened to you?"

"What do you mean?"

"You didn't used to talk like this. I think this is your father's doing. Ever since he came back into your life, you walk around acting like a big shot. Like you're too good for stuff."

"What? You'd rather I walk around like I'm not good enough for anything?"

"Maybe we need to reconsider your father's visitation rights."

"Bullshit!"

If Loretta weren't driving, she would've smacked her son across the face.

She glared at Dima, letting her eyes do her hands' work.

"This has nothing to do with Dad!"

"You didn't act like this before. You were nice. You were humble."

"No, I wasn't humble. I had no self-confidence. I was afraid to disappoint anyone, afraid people wouldn't like me, afraid of *you.*"

"Me?" she asked, surprised. "What are you talking about?"

"Do you know what it's like since Dad's been gone? What it's like to be your son? No matter what I do, it isn't good enough. If I get Bs, you ask why I didn't get As. Anytime I screw up something at the diner, you're, like, a million times harder on me than your staff. No matter what I do, it isn't good enough. Dad was right. *Nothing* makes you happy. So, why try?"

This wasn't Dima talking. This was her ex, Mark. Dima never would have talked to her like this before his father came back into the picture.

12

Loretta looked over, but Dima was staring out the window, seeming like he was trying not to cry.

He wasn't glaring back or looking for a fight. She wondered if he really felt like he said.

"I'm happy." Loretta tried to keep from crying herself.

"Yeah, right," he said with a shrug and a sniffle.

"Okay, maybe not happy, but I'm happy with you. Not at this moment, but overall, I'm very proud of you, Dima. You're one of the only things I've ever done right in my life."

"Yeah, well why can't you show it more often? Why do you always have to criticize me and lay a guilt trip whenever I do anything that doesn't please you?" He pulled his jacket over his head, body shuddering.

She swallowed. Tears trickled down her cheeks. She hated seeing her son like this and hated it more that she might be the source of his pain.

She thought she was doing the right things. She was being tough but loving, like her father always had been. But as she thought back to her teen years, she remembered feeling the same way — like she could never please him. Was she repeating his sins? Loretta thought she'd erred on the tender side, but maybe she *was* being more tough than loving. Being a single mother was difficult, but being a single mother trying to keep a business afloat, with so many people's lives depending on you, was thankless. A boulder on her shoulder that she never felt able to move.

She wanted to explain this all to Dima, but as Loretta looked over at her son, crying under his jacket, she couldn't find the words.

She put a hand on his shoulder. "I'm sorry. You know I love you, right?"

Dima nodded.

Loretta wanted to stop and talk this all out, but as she pulled into the diner, she saw the two officers standing outside, watching her swing into the nearest spot, waiting to talk to her.

Her conversation with Dima would have to wait. Loretta got out of the minivan, feeling that her world was one loose thread from spiraling out of control.

THIRTY-TWO

Abe Mcdonald

ABE LOOKED in the rearview mirror and wondered when the brownies would kick in and soften the girl's awareness.

McKenna was reading a book she'd borrowed from the school library and looked rather alert even though they'd been driving for nearly fifteen minutes. If she stayed up much longer, there was no way he'd be able to hit the highway unnoticed. Nor did Abe think he could drive much longer without rousing her suspicions and making McKenna wonder why they weren't at her mom's diner yet.

He had to stall.

Abe looked in the rearview. "Hey, McKenna? I need to run by my apartment and pick something up. That okay?"

"Sure," she said, eyes glued to the book.

Good.

Aside from her lack of sleep, everything was going as planned. He'd picked her up from the school without incident. She ate the brownie without noticing the laced sedatives. Soon, they'd be on their way to a new life.

His stomach was doing somersaults: dread and excitement. He couldn't believe how well things were going. Or that by this time tomorrow, McKenna would be his girl.

Abe turned his car onto 17th Street and peeked in the rearview, admiring her beauty. It was one thing to admire McKenna in photos and videos, but neither captured her cuteness or innocence quite like real life. It had been difficult to fully appreciate her without the risk of Maggie noticing his awkward stares, until now.

The way McKenna's long light-brown hair framed her round, angelic face. The way her piercing blue eyes peered out from under her bangs. The way her tiny pink lips moved as she read to herself. He could stare for hours and never tire. And he could never absorb all her beauty, even if he stared for a lifetime.

It won't be long now, though. I'll soon be able to look at her every day without having to worry about accusations that I'm some sort of sicko.

While Abe was definitely attracted to young girls, he was far above the common pedophile. With him, it wasn't sexual. At least not completely.

He appreciated McKenna for the work of art that she was. Countless paintings and photo sets celebrated the beauty of youth. Was he so wrong to admire it, too? If so, he didn't care. He'd stack her beauty against any adult model. She'd come out on top every time. And Abe didn't think he'd be alone in that judgment.

If people were truly honest with themselves, they'd share his admiration. Unfortunately, perverts and child rapists had ruined such appreciation of youth. Nowadays you couldn't say something like "Your daughter is so beautiful" without earning an ugly look from her mother or getting punched by her father. He remembered a little girl who'd come into the shop with her parents a few years ago, a small Spanish girl who looked around five.

She was easily one of the most beautiful girls Abe had ever seen. He could still see her clearly in his mind. Cute pigtails, a pink sweater, and an adorable denim skirt with striped pink-and-blue leggings. She had big, brown eyes accentuated by a bit of pink eye shadow that complemented her outfit. She seemed a bit young for makeup, but Abe tried not to be judgmental.

He could barely stop himself from staring as he talked to her parents about their malfunctioning computer. After he told her parents how much the computer would cost to fix, and how they were better off getting a new one, which they could conveniently buy in his shop, they stepped aside to talk it over out of earshot.

While they debated what to do about their computer, Abe watched the girl pace in front of the counter. She was looking at the shelves, casting her eyes across the products, mostly high-priced accessories that people could buy online for a fraction of the cost. It was the computer shop's equivalent of overpriced king-sized candy bars in a gas station. The girl made her way to his counter, where a few of the latest tablets were on display.

She looked at the tablets then up at him with her big, brown eyes. She said, "Can you get YouTube on those?"

"Yes. You can also play games, read books, watch movies. Pretty much anything you can do on a computer."

She asked him some other questions, and suddenly they were in the middle of a conversation. Abe didn't remember what they were talking about, but couldn't forget what killed the conversation.

"You sure are a pretty little girl."

He'd meant it as a compliment and not at all as pervy as it must've come across to her parents, who were approaching the counter when the words left his lips.

He wasn't sure if it was his tone or the look in his eyes as he stared at the girl, but things went suddenly scary. The father met his eyes, and Abe knew the man could see his naked lust. Abe had been discovered as the monster he was.

Time froze. Abe wondered what would happen next. Would the father punch him out? Would he call the cops? It wasn't as if Abe had done anything, or even said anything all that bad. Yet somehow he felt like they knew *what* he was. For a long moment, the girl's parents stared at Abe the way a mob looked at Frankenstein before the pitchforks came out.

"We'll just take our computer." The father grabbed his unit from the counter, open case and all, in a sudden hurry to flee the shop.

Then they were gone.

Abe had wanted to call in sick the next day, out of fear they'd return to confront him. Maybe they'd even bring a friend to "take care" of him. Or ask to see his boss. That fear in Abe's gut lasted for weeks, entrenching itself into his every waking moment as he kept waiting for someone to accuse him of being a monster.

He'd replayed the scene in his head at least a thousand times, trying to assess what had happened. He didn't think he'd said anything crude. He'd never intentionally say anything inappropriate to a child, but what if he'd *thought something* out loud? His thoughts were worse than his words, and if he'd given voice to one of the more horrible ones, even under his breath, that could've explained the parents' reactions.

Days turned to weeks then months. Nobody came to the shop to arrest him or beat him up. No one posted a review online accusing him of being a kiddy diddler or something horrible.

Nothing happened.

After a while, he wondered if maybe he'd read too much into the moment. Maybe they hadn't realized what he was. Maybe they'd had a fight over the computer or realized they could get a cheaper computer almost anywhere else and simply decided to leave. Maybe he'd looked so freaked out over being caught talking to the girl and thinking he'd said something bad, that he gave off a creepy vibe.

Still, it had made Abe nervous enough that for a while, he avoided talking to any children who came into the shop. He was afraid that they, or their parents, would see what he really was. Maggie and McKenna were the first people whom he allowed himself to relax around. Maggie had her own shit to deal with and wasn't some paranoid helicopter mom worried that every male was a molester. Her child could talk to adults.

This was part of the reason that Abe figured Maggie would be glad to be rid of McKenna.

Sure, at first, she'd be sad. And scared. But after a while, she'd get on with her life, and probably be a lot happier without the girl around.

Abe had read Maggie's older emails to her friend from high school, Jenna. How sometimes, even though she hated admitting it and they weren't thoughts she often had, she sometimes wished she'd never had McKenna. She loved her, of course, but a part of her felt like her life had stopped being hers the moment McKenna entered the picture. It had tied her to Nick and sealed her fate: to be stuck in an unhappy marriage with an addict forever.

"My life was over before it had even really begun," she'd written.

Abe wondered how McKenna would feel to know that her mother felt that way about her. Perhaps, if the girl had trouble adjusting to her new life, Abe would show her the letters he'd saved. *That* would show her that she was better off with him.

He pulled into the apartment complex parking lot and killed the engine. He got out then opened the back door to let her out.

McKenna grabbed her book bag and her book then slid out of the car. With her mother not around, Abe indulged in another peek up her dress as she got out of the car.

Soon, he'd have more than a peek.

His felt a rush of excitement at the prospect that someday she'd show him willingly all that she hid out of modesty now. If she didn't want to show him, he'd find other ways. He already created a hidden camera kit that he could place in their new shared bathroom, so he could watch her change and bathe.

Halfway up the stairs — he didn't want to risk winding up in an elevator with a neighbor who might imagine an odd vibe and blow the whole thing to hell — Abe's phone buzzed. Ahead of McKenna, he discreetly fished the phone from his pocket, glanced at the screen, and saw it was Maggie. No doubt wanting to know where her daughter was. He wasn't late enough to cause her concern, but if he didn't take the call, she might grow suspicious before McKenna felt groggy.

He stopped at his door and answered. "Hello?"

"Hey, Abe, it's Maggie. Just making sure everything went okay at the school?"

"Yes, everything's fine. I had to stop by my apartment to grab something for work so I don't have to make a trip back from the diner before I head back to work."

"Ah, okay." He could sense the nerves creeping into Maggie's voice, maybe at the idea of this grown man taking her daughter to his apartment before bringing her to the diner.

"Want to talk to her?" Abe hoped to kill suspicions before they took root. Without waiting for an answer, he handed the phone to McKenna. "It's your mommy."

"Hi, Mommy!"

After a moment, "Yeah, I'm okay. We just have to pick something up at Mr. Abe's. He gave me a yummy brownie!"

Abe imagined Maggie on the other end of the phone putting the pieces together. *Brought her to his apartment. Gave her a brownie.* He hoped she didn't suss out his intentions or the jig would be up immediately.

He watched McKenna talk to her mom.

"Yes, I know," she said.

He wondered what that was in response to. Had Maggie warned her daughter not to let strange men touch her? He hoped he hadn't come off as *that* kind of creep. He hoped the

12

months of goodwill he'd earned with Maggie would pay off, at least until he left town.

"Okay," McKenna said, "I love you, too. See you soon."

She handed the phone back to Abe, and he nervously took it, half expecting Maggie to be yelling at him on the other end. But she was calm and didn't seem suspicious.

"Thanks again for picking her up."

"No problem. We'll be on our way as soon as I get the stuff I'm looking for."

He figured that "looking for" might buy him a few more minutes, but probably not long enough for McKenna to fall asleep. Maybe that was best. If McKenna did fall asleep at his house, it might be harder to leave the apartment with her. Carrying an unconscious child that wasn't his *might* trigger alarm bells even among the most jaded of neighbors.

He said goodbye to Maggie then unlocked and opened his front door to let McKenna inside. She crossed the threshold into his apartment. He took one last look in the hallway then followed, locking the door behind them.

2 p.m. - 3 p.m.

THIRTY-THREE

Sebastian Ruiz

IT HAD BEEN ABOUT ten minutes since Sebastian returned the money to the safe — and about nine since his second thoughts started.

He was sitting in the restroom stall, trying to call Gino. But Gino wasn't answering his phone.

Without Gino, there was no way he could get his sister back, unless he dared to try and rob the safe again. He realized how ridiculous it was to lock the money in the safe when he hadn't even called to see if Gino was around. They hadn't spoken in nearly a year, and it was stupid to assume that Gino still had the same connections that Sebastian would need. Much could happen in a year.

Fuck.

Sebastian decided he'd better go unlock the safe and pull the money back out in case he needed to put Plan A back into play.

He washed and dried his hands, left the restroom, and was about to head to Loretta's office when he bumped into her son, Dima, clocking in.

"Dima?" he said, surprised. "School out early?"

"No, I got suspended, and my mom said I may as well make myself useful around here."

"Suspended? What happened?" Sebastian didn't care but couldn't afford to reveal the panic rising in his chest.

Dima told him some story about getting into a fight, but Sebastian had a hard time listening. He kept subtly looking around, searching for any sign of Loretta. Was she here, too? Maybe she'd dropped Dima off before going back home, which would mean he could slip into the office and get the money.

But then he heard Loretta's annoying, over-the-top laugh as she entered the kitchen with the cops. Patrick was telling her some story about "some fucking mook" they nabbed last week who tried to dress like a woman to get away.

Shit. She's back.

Just like that, Sebastian's last resort dried up. There was no way she'd leave now, not until later in the evening. Dima usually worked until around eight. She'd take him home after that.

Eight o' clock was two hours past Raul's deadline.

The two cops followed Loretta into her office. She closed the door, her laughter still audible.

Sebastian wondered what they were doing in there. For a moment, a fear gripped his gut that she'd somehow found out about him taking the money — even though he'd already returned it. Maybe she had a hidden camera in the office and was about to show the cops evidence of his attempted thievery.

He watched her office door with a sick certainty that the cops would come out and march right over to him, tell him to put his hands behind his back.

Everything inside him said to leave for Gino's.

"You okay?" Dima asked, staring at Sebastian.

He left the kid's story a while ago. Dima might have asked

him something, but Sebastian was staring at the office without saying a word. No, that didn't seem suspicious at all.

He looked at Dima. "Man, that's some fucked-up shit."

The kid was clearly bitching, and that seemed a decent enough response to feign attention. Even if Dima had asked something, Sebastian could play off his delayed response as an inability to get over just how fucked up said shit was. He sprinkled an, "I've been there, dog" for good measure.

Dima nodded, said thanks, then went to the restroom with his Goldman's black polo to prepare for his shift.

Sebastian looked over to Bob, who was in the weeds with orders backing up on the rail. They were short staffed, and now the diner was filling with customers, many no doubt drawn by morbid curiosity after seeing the paramedics cart someone out. Nosey fucks just *had* to come over and see what was going down at Goldman's. Never mind that the person getting carted out might've suffered from food poisoning for all they knew.

Bob glanced over at Sebastian.

You gonna help or what?

Sebastian would've been on the grill in any other circumstance. He was good at clearing the rail faster than any cook in Goldman's history. Papa Goldman had said so himself. But right now, all he could think about was his sister, and reaching Gino.

He walked up behind Bob, put his hands on the man's shoulders, and squeezed. "You got this, big guy? I'll be right back — just gotta check on something real quick."

Before Bob could respond, Sebastian was racing out the back door, cell phone in hand, calling Gino again. He walked to the other side of the dumpsters for privacy.

He rang Gino — six rings before he picked up.

"Hey, it's Sebastian."

"Hey, roomie. How's it going?"

12

No time for small talk. Sebastian had to cut to the chase and hoped being abrupt didn't turn his former cellmate off.

"I need a favor."

"Hold on. I'll call you right back."

"Okay." Sebastian hung up, hoping that his "I need a favor" hadn't scared Gino away.

He waited, watching a classic black Camaro with blacked-out windows cruise by the lot. Maybe one of Raul's men keeping tabs on him. He stared at the car, refusing to flinch or turn his head like a bitch. If it was one of Raul's men, fuck 'em.

The car kept going.

Sebastian's phone rang. On the screen, *Unknown Caller*.

"Hello?"

"Hey, it's me," Gino said, "had to get to a more secure line. So, what was this about a favor? You finally come around on my uncle's offer?"

Gino's uncle, Petr Romanov, was head of the Romanov crime syndicate. In gratitude for saving Gino's life, he had, through Gino, offered Sebastian a job in his organization. Said he could even pick a less hands-on job if he was retired from heists. But Sebastian hadn't wanted anything to do with the Russian mobster, or his organization. Raul was a schoolyard bully by comparison.

"No, I'm not looking for a job. I'm hoping your uncle can help me with a little problem, though."

"How little a problem we talking about?"

"Raul Luna."

"Wow, that's a big problem. Get specific. It's okay, we're on a safe line."

Sebastian wasn't sure if his own line was safe, especially if Raul had reached out to some dirty cops and put someone on his phone. But ticking time made caution claustrophobic.

"He took my sister, and he's asking for fifteen Gs to get her back."

"So, you need a loan?"

"Could you lend me that much? Like, within a couple of hours?"

"I might could get it. But I'm not sure with no strings attached."

"What kinda strings?" Sebastian asked, figuring it was probably too much to expect a loan like that without a catch, regardless of their history.

"I dunno. Let me reach out to my uncle. I'll call you back."

"Please hurry." Sebastian hated the desperation in his voice. It made him look weak, and most people in Sebastian's old world seized frailty for exploitation. He hoped Gino was different.

"I'll get back to you ASAP, one way or another."

"Thank you," Sebastian said, breathing a sigh of relief, hoping he might be closer to saving Ana.

"Anything for you, brother." Gino sounded sincere.

Sebastian hung up. His life, or his sister's, was again out of his hands and given to Fate.

THIRTY-FOUR

Abe Mcdonald

ABE WATCHED in the rearview as McKenna nodded off in the back seat. She fought it at first, eyes closing, then waking in a start. But that only happened a couple of times before she was out and a smile spread across his face.

This was it.

His plan had worked. He could hardly believe his luck. Abe thought for certain that something would throw a wrench into it. He'd forget something, or the girl would get a ride from someone else. Maybe he would slip and give himself away.

But Abe was about to get away clean.

He navigated traffic, telling himself that he wasn't yet clear of the woods. He still had to make it to the cabin upstate, and plenty could happen between now and then. He still had to pick up the van, waiting at an old nature trail where barely anyone ever went.

Abe found himself wondering if the nature trail was a bad place to park. It had seemed like the perfect location — a secluded spot out of the way of ubiquitous security cameras. The trail itself was used by walkers, runners, and the occasional birder, but it had fallen out of favor in recent months after the city upgraded another trail three miles south. The newer trail had restrooms, water fountains, benches to sit, and even a few pavilions. That killed this trail for everyone but diehard locals, and maybe teens looking for an out of the way place to smoke or fuck after hours.

But at two in the afternoon, Abe figured he'd have all the privacy needed to swap vehicles and ensure that McKenna was contained on the off chance she woke before they reached their new home.

ABE PULLED into the trail's parking lot, pleased to see they were alone. The lot was bare bones government land, secluded along a rarely traveled dirt road. There were eight spaces: four in front of one long cut log, and another four in front of a second. There was a gap, wide enough for a golf cart, between the two logs leading to the trail itself, which branched both east and west.

Abe's van was in the second farthest spot to the west, abutting the forest line. He pulled into the last spot, between the woods and vehicle, which should guarantee his privacy while transferring McKenna to the van, unless someone happened to jog by at that exact moment.

He turned off the car and glanced again in the mirror to see McKenna sleeping. Then he saw his own reflection, and the doubt in his eyes.

I am smart. I am strong. I am willing to do what must be done to get what's mine.

He took his keys from the ignition then softly opened the driver's side door. He left it ajar as he slid from the car, careful not to make too much movement or noise.

He opened the trunk then grabbed the duffels holding everything they'd need — fake IDs, money, clothes, food, toys, games, books, and other supplies which he figured should last them through their first week or so.

12

Abe carried the bags over to the van's passenger side and piled them on the floor behind the bucket seat, which he pulled up to give him more room.

He went to the driver's side, started it, turned on the AC, and slid the rear side door open, glancing into the woods along the trail to make sure no one was coming.

He was all alone.

His luck was holding out.

Abe opened the car door, slid in next to McKenna, and put his hands beneath her legs, hoping like hell he wouldn't wake her. How would he ever explain what was happening? He wondered how many child abductions turned to murder because the child couldn't be controlled or the kidnapper realized that they'd gone too far and they couldn't return the child without getting fingered for the crime. Abe hoped it wouldn't come to that. He'd feel awful if he had to kill McKenna to keep her quiet.

Her eyes remained closed as he pulled her from the car. Her body was limp in his arms on his way to the van. He was surprised by how light, how *tiny*, she felt in his arms.

The realization was jarring. For so long, he'd been obsessing about her, watching McKenna on videos, looking at her photos, and sometimes talking with her in person. All those times, she'd seemed bigger, somehow *older*. Or perhaps it was *he* who felt youthful, like he was able to live some parts of the happy youth he never had.

But now she felt so childlike and fragile, and he felt so old and awkward.

Like Kurt.

His mind flashed for a moment to the man who had taken his innocence, and how he'd been so kind and gentle, at first — letting him ride on the back of the motorcycle, giving him toys, taking him to McDonald's. And then he'd been rough, taking what Abe would not willingly give.

No, I will not be like that!

Waves of revulsion and confusion rolled through him.

Abe placed her into the van, closed the door, then looked back at the woods to make sure nobody had seen him transferring her from his car to the van.

No one there.

His luck was holding out.

He went back to the car, grabbed the rest of his stuff, locked the door, and realized this was the last time he'd ever see his car.

The next person to see it might be a park ranger or whatever they called the city workers who tended the trails. After that, the police would be looking at it, searching for evidence, collecting their samples to link him to the abduction. Then his car would be all over the news, with a sad-looking newscaster asking anyone who had seen the car, or the man and girl, to please call some tip line.

Then there would be the stories about him. People interviewed. Abe wondered what they'd say. Would it be a situation where everyone was surprised? Or would there be interviews with people who said, "Oh, yeah, I always knew he'd do this someday. It's the quiet ones you've gotta watch out for. The quiet, creepy ones, and he was as quiet and creepy as they come."

His stomach churned again as he climbed into the van's front seat. There was a wooden partition with a door between the cabin and bay. He opened the door, barely large enough for him to squeeze through, and made his way into the rear to make sure McKenna was still sleeping, and to get her situated.

Once in the van, he had more privacy, and the riskiest part of the endeavor was over, unless he somehow got pulled over by a cop between now and his arrival at the cabin. He took a moment to calm his nerves before getting back behind the wheel.

He took another moment to savor the sight of the little girl spread out before him, her long hair spilling on the van's

12

carpet. Her legs spread ever so slightly giving him a longer look up her skirt, at her underwear.

His heart raced, accelerated by both his taboo arousal and the danger of being caught leering at this girl in a public place, despite the fact that it was almost impossible for anyone to see him through the tinted windows in front or the thick red curtains in the van's rear. The vehicle looked like a handyman's old beat-up work van to anyone not looking too close.

He stared at McKenna, fighting the urge to touch her. To run his hands along her long legs. To trace his fingers over her chest.

No, I won't touch her — until she invites me.

Yet the worst part of himself, the unquenchable lust that sometimes took over, had other ideas.

Go ahead. It's not like she'll know. Touching isn't a violation if she doesn't even know you touched her, right?

Abe's fingers hovered over her legs. He dared to brush her inner thigh.

His heart raced faster.

His strongest desires were cranked to eleven. He was hard as a rock, and it was all he could do not to relieve himself right there. No, he wouldn't have sex with her. She was still too young, even if she gave him permission. But there were other things he could do.

Abe was sweating. If anyone happened upon the van at that moment, he'd look like the monster he probably was.

He swallowed, shaking his head, trying to shed his lust before it pushed him too far.

His cell phone rang.

He'd forgotten to turn off the ringer, and had to answer it before the ring woke McKenna.

He fumbled into his pants pocket. The ring was louder out of his pocket.

McKenna turned, disturbed by the noise. Abe fumbled with the phone, searching for the silence button.

Instead, he accidentally picked up the call.

It was Maggie.

"Hello?" Maggie said.

Shit!

Abe couldn't hang up. That would be too suspicious.

He also couldn't talk to Maggie in the back of the van. That would certainly wake McKenna.

He hit the mute button, crawled back into the front of the van, hopped out, then unmuted the phone.

"Hello?" he said, certain he sounded odd.

"Hey, it's Maggie. Just checking to make sure things are okay? Is she behaving?"

"Yeah, yeah, she's an angel. Took a bit longer than I thought, but we're on our way back now. Should be there in about ten minutes. Do you mind if I brought her by the shop first so I can drop my stuff off? Boss is on my case, and I feel bad leaving in the middle of the day."

"Yeah, yeah, that's okay. So, how long do you think you'll be?"

Abe tried to think of an appropriate time, a head start without raising suspicions.

Then a horrifying thought: *what if Maggie asked to speak to her daughter?*

"Maybe fifteen, twenty minutes tops. Then I'll drop her off at the diner. That work?"

"Yeah," Maggie said. "Thanks again."

"My pleasure."

Abe hung up then pulled the SIM card from the back and pitched it into the woods. This would be the last place his phone would ever be used.

Now he was a ghost.

Abe got back into the van and noticed, to his surprise, that a black sedan was parked in front of the other log.

How long has it been there?

12

It must've pulled up while he was on the phone with Maggie.

Did they see me throw the SIM card?

It seemed unlikely; he was blocked by the van, and the SIM card was tiny.

Tinted windows kept him from seeing inside the sedan, but in the back of his mind three words kept turning.

Unmarked cop car.

Abe wasn't about to wait around for someone to get out of the car. He started the van and backed out, on his way to a new life with his new love.

THIRTY-FIVE

Tim Hewitt

"Go to your room," Tim's father said before the door closed behind him.

His voice was flat, emotionless ... *odd*.

His father had barely looked at Tim the entire drive home. Now he was ordering him to his room instead of sitting in the living room for his usual berating. Tim wasn't sure what was going on in his father's mind, but it had to be awful.

Tim went to his room without argument, fished the spiral notebook from his backpack — the one with the story he was going to write with Alicia — lifted his bookcase and slid the notebook beneath it. The last thing he wanted his father finding was evidence of him writing on the very day he ordered him not to.

Tim sat on his bed, waiting.

After the day he'd had, part of him wanted to break down and scream into his pillow. But he didn't know when his father would come to the door or call him, and he couldn't allow the man to see tears.

"Tears sicken me," his father had said whenever Tim's emotions claimed him. He'd get another five lashes for crying. And the belt stung for days.

12

His father hated weakness in other people, especially his son. Rather ironic, considering how many crutches the old man leaned on in his own life — figuratively and literally. He was gluttonous to the point of obesity, yet Tim's diet was regimented almost to the calorie. His father was an alcoholic who couldn't function without his drug of choice even though he often railed against "druggies." And though his father espoused the virtue of pulling oneself up by their bootstraps, and denigrated society's so-called "takers" and "entitled parasites," the man was the definition of a parasite at home.

The lazy fuck did nothing around the house except dictate which chores Tim and his mother did, and worse, he held them to a drill sergeant's exacting standards. Perhaps most ironic, before his father started successfully investing money in the stock market a few years ago, he was living off his wife's earnings and a disability check he collected for a condition that didn't prevent the man from doing what he wanted, yet somehow kept him from working a job.

How could someone hate others who were not all that different from himself? Was his father truly that blind to his own flaws?

Tim looked at the clock and wondered how long his father would wait. It was just after two, giving them about three hours before Tim's mom came home.

Would his father wait for her arrival?

Tim hoped not.

Things were always worse when his mother was there to witness the trauma. She rarely intervened, which would only earn her a beating for interference, but there was only so much brutality she could see before saying something. It always cost her dearly when she did.

It was one thing for his father to beat Tim. He could almost accept it as punishment for something he'd done wrong, even if it felt like he couldn't do anything right in his father's eyes. It was another thing altogether for a man to beat his wife. What had she done? Other than give birth to a child he clearly never wanted?

Tim often wondered why his mother didn't leave the monster. After a particularly awful night, two years ago, he thought she finally would. Tim's father had come home drunk, verbally abusive, and took it out on Tim, and then his mother when she tried to stop him.

When he had fallen asleep, or rather, passed out, his mom told Tim to pack a suitcase. They were going somewhere where his father would never touch him again.

For a moment, Tim was hopeful that perhaps they could truly flee the beast. But then his father woke and saw what they were doing. He went to his study, where he spent most of his time, and grabbed a gun. He put it to his mother's head and promised that if she ever tried to leave him, he'd find her and put a bullet through her "stupid bitch skull."

It was the last time she'd displayed any bravery.

Tim had often wondered what would happen if *he* ran away? He figured he could probably get away with it, too, because he doubted the monster would come looking — that would involve getting off his fat ass. Hell, his father would probably be happy to have Tim out of the house. One less disappointment in a world chock full of them.

But Tim couldn't leave. He was afraid if he did, then all of his father's wrath would be channeled onto her.

For now, Tim saw himself as a barrier between himself and his mother's abuse.

And that was fine. Tim could take it. Usually.

But what would happen when he went off to college or moved out? Or hell, went to St. Martin's if his father finally made good on his threat? Tim couldn't be there forever to protect his mother.

What then?

Minutes ticked by. Tim's thoughts returned to Alicia and how badly he'd screwed things up. Not only did he lose any chance he ever had of dating her, he'd probably lost her as a friend. That hurt more than anything.

Now, he officially had nobody left.

It had been one thing to lose Dima to that asshole, Jeff, and the popular kids. Hell, Tim even predicted it when Jeff got a job at Loretta's diner during the summer, and Dima started telling stories about how cool and funny Jeff was. Tim had complained to Dima, asked him why he always wanted to talk about Jeff. He'd made Tim feel stupid, like a jealous lover.

"It's not my fault your dad is an asshole and only lets you go out during the day, when I'm working. Of course I'm gonna talk about Jeff and the other kids because that's who I'm hanging out with. I thought you'd be happy for me, that I finally made friends with the cool kids."

There was a time when Dima would've realized how hurtful that comment was and why it injured Tim. His cluelessness spoke volumes.

That had been the beginning of their end.

But it had been okay because Tim still had Alicia. Someone who made his remaining pain somewhat bearable. Tim didn't need a lot of friends like Dima apparently did. He just needed one really good one, one person who recognized his talents, appreciated his kindness and sense of humor. Just one person to make life worth living.

Now she was gone.

Tears flowed. Tim put his glasses on his nightstand and buried his head in the pillow, trying not to scream. Even a muffled scream might travel outside his bedroom.

He'd been crying for what felt like ten minutes when his bedroom door exploded open. The knob punched a hole in the drywall.

Tim jumped up as if he'd been caught masturbating and saw his father's crimson face a second before the man's hand swung forward and smacked Tim across the face hard enough to send him back into the wall on the other side of his bed.

And just like that, it was on.

His father's fists wailed into Tim's chest, head, and ribs. He threw his arms in front of his face to protect himself.

"Put your arms down, boy!"

"Stop it!" Tim screamed.

He didn't stop. Instead, he grabbed Tim on either side of his head then shoved his skull into the wall.

His father climbed onto the bed, despite his bad left leg, and kept his hands on Tim's head, pressing him into the wall as if he could somehow shove him *through* it.

"Please," Tim cried.

"You think this is all a game?" his father said, making little sense, his voice slurred, his breath hot and reeking of alcohol, spittle flying from his mouth and into Tim's face. "You think I'm a fucking fool?"

"No," Tim cried.

"No, what?" his father yelled, letting go only to slap him hard on the side of his head.

"No, sir," Tim said. Tears and snot streamed down his face.

His father's face was inches away. Hate filled his eyes. The same breed of rancid loathing that Tim had seen in Jeff's. Tim couldn't understand what he'd ever done to earn this sort of hate from anyone, let alone his father. He had tried so hard to be good. Compared to most kids, he was well behaved. Other parents would kill to have a child who did all their chores like Tim; who never got into trouble at school; who didn't lie, cheat, or steal; who didn't hang out with "bad kids"; who made the honor roll nearly every semester.

What did I ever do to deserve this?

"You are done with that school. Do you hear me?"

"Please, don't," Tim cried.

"You think I appreciate being made a fool of? To have

your teacher and dean sit across from me, judging me like I did a bad job raising you?"

Tim wasn't sure if he was supposed to answer. He said, "No, sir."

His father, still holding his head hard against the wall, continued.

"You have it so easy, and yet you don't appreciate it."

Easy? I do everything around here! I work my ass off and don't get to ever go out and do anything. I don't make any money, and I'm not even allowed to have a job. I'm a prisoner!

Tim would've spoken his thoughts if he didn't think they might get him killed. There was no arguing with his father, ever. Especially when the asshole was drunk.

How could he be drunk so quickly? Had he been drunk in the meeting at school and I didn't even notice? Maybe that was why he was so quiet.

But he wasn't being quiet any longer.

No, this was Fully Enraged and Drunk Off His Ass Dad. The very worst version of an already horrible man.

His father's eyes drilled into his as if he were trying to probe Tim's mind, to see what awful things he was thinking. Tim wondered if the man *could* read his thoughts. Sometimes, it felt like it.

His father let go of his head, though Tim could still feel the vise-like grip as if his fingers had left permanent impressions in his skull.

His father stood, getting off the bed gingerly, then finding his walking stick. He looked Tim up and down then around his room as if taking inventory.

"I've already made the calls. You will be going to St. Martin's on Monday. You can pack one bag of essentials. Everything else will be donated."

"What do you mean everything else will be donated?"

Tim looked around at his room, at the books lining his shelves, childhood toys that he held for nostalgia, and his computer. He never felt like he'd had much, but suddenly, as his father threatened to take it all away, he realized how much he truly had. And how hard it would be to part with.

"No," Tim said. "You can't get rid of my stuff. I'm not going away forever."

His father stepped forward, as if considering grabbing Tim by the head again.

Tim flinched.

His father stayed put, a small smile claiming his lips.

"This is not *your stuff*. As long as you live under my roof, this is *my stuff*, which you are borrowing."

"What? That's insane. Grandma bought me most of my books. Not you."

His father's eyes said that Tim should have kept his mouth shut. He turned, looking at the shelf.

"Yeah, maybe this is the problem. This stuff is rotting your brain, turning you into an idiot." He picked up a book from the shelf, a hardcover first edition of Stephen King's *The Talisman*, his favorite book ever, and a gift from his grandma before she passed. His father looked at the book as if were titled *A Teen's Introduction to Communism*.

"This is the problem right here. Everyone says you live in this little imaginary world of your own and you need to grow the fuck up. But how can we expect you to when stuff like this is polluting your mind?"

"It's not a bad book. I thought you used to like Stephen King."

"For a developed mind, perhaps, but yours is still too impressionable, given to flights of fancy. You're not responsible enough to read fiction. They're keeping you from doing your real work."

"I get straight As! I do everything you ask around the house! What work am I not doing?"

"You calling me a liar?" His father flung the heavy book hard at Tim. He barely missed, putting a dent in the drywall behind Tim.

12

The book fell to the bed.

Tim grabbed it and looked at the warped spine, pissed that his father had damaged *The Talisman*.

"This book is a first edition!"

His father reached out and grabbed the book.

Tim refused to let go.

His father glared at him.

"Let go," he said, his voice low and sinister.

Tim didn't want to let go. He wanted to grab the book back and tuck it away somewhere, safe from harm.

But his fingers held no courage.

His father snapped the book away, held it up with both hands, then ripped the cover right off.

"Stop it!"

His father dropped the book then started grabbing more from the shelf, tossing them across the room one by one, calling each book either "filth" or "trash."

All Tim could do was sit on his bed and watch — crying.

Books were scattered all over his room and out into the hallway. His father finished pulling the last one from the bookcase then flipped the shelf over and smashed his walking stick into the back of it as if he could break the shelf with his stick alone.

Tim's heart froze when he saw the notebook lying in plain sight.

Immediately, Tim realized that his reaction revealed that there was something important on the floor. His father looked down at the notebook then bent over and picked it up.

"Hmm, what's this?"

Tim jumped off the bed. There was no way he could let his father rip up another story, especially one he was writing with Alicia, even if she never wanted to speak to him again. This was *their* story. She'd drawn and written in the notebook, complimenting his creativity — something no girl had ever done.

Before Tim could grab the notebook, his father brought his walking stick up fast and thrust the end into Tim's chest, pushing him back onto the bed.

"Sit down!"

Tim stared helplessly as his father opened the notebook. "What's this? Another story? You're writing another fucking story?"

"No, it's an old one! One I was writing with Alicia! Please, don't ... "

"Don't what?"

Tim didn't want to say because his father was a monster who would derive pleasure from doing the one thing that would break Tim's heart most.

"Don't what?" his father repeated, ripping pages out, and letting them flutter to the floor.

"No!" Tim jumped up and grabbed the notebook.

His father wouldn't let go.

They stood there, both gripping the notebook. His father's eyes said that Tim had gone too far.

For a moment, Tim thought perhaps by standing up for himself and not being "such a fucking pussy" that he'd earned his father's respect. That his father would let go of the notebook, and leave the room.

But that didn't happen.

Instead, Tim's father let go of the notebook then used both hands to shove Tim back into the wall. But this time, so fast, and so hard, and with a pain so blinding, Tim felt as if the back of his skull had split in two.

Tim slumped against his bed, wanting to stand, desperate to run from the room, but unable to do anything but watch his vision blur as darkness claimed him.

THIRTY-SIX

Abe Mcdonald

ABE HAD BEEN DRIVING for nearly fifteen minutes when McKenna woke up screaming.

"Help!" She banged on the partition behind the driver's seat, unable to see him as there were no holes or openings which allowed for sight.

Shit. Shit.

He had to pull over and calm her.

"It's okay," he yelled, "It's me, Abe."

"What happened? Where am I?" McKenna cried on the other side of the partition.

"It's okay, we're in my friend's van. My car broke down," he said, hoping his voice was more calm than it sounded.

McKenna fell quiet, as if struggling to believe him.

Abe wondered if some part of her was aware that she'd been drugged. It seemed unlikely, but who knew what kids were taught these days what with stranger danger and everything. Maybe they were taught to know the signs of being drugged?

It was a shame what the world was coming to.

"I want out," she cried. "I want my mommy."

Abe had to find a place to pull over, preferably somewhere

without any witnesses that might hear the girl scream. Then he'd have to silence — and restrain — her for the rest of the trip.

Time to use the chloroform?

"Okay, just give me a minute. I need to find a safe place to pull over."

"Okay," she said, sniffling.

Abe took the next exit and drove a quarter mile until he found a large shopping center where he could park far from the entrance without being bothered. The likely cameras were a negative, but he didn't think anyone could trace this vehicle to him or the abduction; he was good so long as no cops happened to drive by and hear the girl scream or see the van shake from a struggle.

He stopped the van then reached into his jacket pocket, found the chloroform, and doused a small red rag with the liquid.

He palmed the rag, unlocked the partition, and opened the door.

McKenna had started to approach the door, but stopped when he pushed his way through; there was no way they could both fit through at once.

He crawled into the van's rear. McKenna's eyes widened, and she backed away.

"It's okay." He smiled. "I won't bite."

Usually, she would've laughed at a comment like that, not that he'd ever said that particular phrase to her. But she was clearly scared, and probably sensed his intentions no matter how hard he tried to disguise them.

Abe was on his knees, he couldn't get any taller in the back, and she was on all fours, pressed against the rear doors.

He kept the hand with the rag, his right, hidden from view.

He met her eyes. "It's okay," he repeated, "my car broke

down, so I borrowed a friend's van. We're on our way to your mom's diner now."

"Really?" McKenna's lips trembled. Her wide blue eyes met his, and he felt like a bastard for lying.

"Really," he said.

"Why can't I sit up front?"

"Because kids have to sit in the back. That's the law, I think."

He moved closer, near enough to reach out and cover her mouth with the rag. But he didn't want to do it violently and scare her. Abe had to find a way to ease himself over, put his arm around the girl, and gently knock her out. It was important not to terrify her.

Yet he couldn't help but feel she was already there, with quivering lips and shaking hands.

"Are you okay?"

"I want to see my mommy."

McKenna looked near tears, and her tears felt like daggers in his heart. Abe hated how he had made her feel this way. It was a terrible way to start their relationship.

"We *will* see her, in just a few minutes." Abe came closer.

McKenna scooted a few inches to her left, putting distance between them, without wanting to be obvious.

He met her eyes, and she looked down. He reached out with his left hand to touch her cheek, and she flinched.

Her whole body was trembling.

He thought of Kurt in the dark living room while his mom was passed out drunk, reaching out to tousle his hair, some kind of weird foreplay, testing the waters to see how much Abe would allow his touch.

"Are you scared?"

McKenna kept looking down, unwilling to meet his eyes.

She nodded, and tears rolled down her cheeks.

Abe felt like a monster more than ever before. All the

shame he'd ever felt for his attraction to little girls paled in comparison to scaring this innocent child.

A voice of reason shouted in his head: *abort the mission! Bring her back to her mother, and forget it.*

Another voice said no.

Use the rag, and knock her out. We're past the point of no return. She knows what you are. If you bring her back, the police will find you and lock your ass up for life!

He was paralyzed in indecision, the cold rag in his hand begging for use.

"You don't have to be scared of me. I'm a friend. And I'd never hurt you. I love you and your mother far too much to ever hurt either of you."

McKenna met his eyes with the sweetest smile. "Really?"

"Really. I fixed your computer, right? And I dropped your mom off at work, and you at school, and then she had me pick you up. She wouldn't have me pick you up if I was scary, would she?"

"I guess not," McKenna said.

"Here, let me help you up front."

"I thought you said I couldn't ride up front."

"Ah, I'm sure it'll be okay. If anyone says anything I'll just tell them you thought it was scary in the back, all right?"

She smiled. "Really?"

"Really." He opened his arms to hug her. "Here, gimme a big hug!"

Now was his chance to grab her and put the rag on her mouth. If she accepted his hug. But they'd never hugged, and it was probably too bold of a move.

McKenna surprised him with wide open arms.

As he wrapped his arms around her, the chloroform rag in his right hand gained weight.

Do it. Do it now before she realizes what you're up to.

He inched his right hand up her back, toward the back of her head. All he'd have to do was turn her face into his palm.

12

He thought of Kurt again, and the first time. How he'd started by tickling Abe, then climbing on top of him. It seemed like harmless horseplay at first. But then the touches got harsher, in places Abe knew he shouldn't be touched. When Abe got scared and tried to get away, Kurt shoved his facedown into the couch, hard, told him to "Shut the fuck up."

And then Kurt did the unthinkable. Ripped his pants down.

Abe's memory screamed through to his present.

As he continued hugging her, he felt like he was about to burst into tears.

I don't want to be her Kurt.

Yet another part of him continued to demand action.

Do it. Now. She's on to you, and if you don't do it now, you're dead.

I am smart. I am strong. I am willing to do what must be done to get what's mine.

He reached up to tilt her face toward the rag.

"Thank you for letting me sit up front, Mr. Abe."

Something in the way she said his name stopped his hand.

An innocence in her voice reminded him of her frailty in his arms. How much of a child she truly was, and how no matter how much he wished otherwise, he could never be a boy again. His childhood was over, and he could not reclaim it with or through her.

She didn't deserve his perversity, to have her innocence stolen from her as it had been from him.

While he'd often been made to feel like a monster for his desires, he didn't truly think he was one. But if he took McKenna from her mother, he would be a demon no different from Kurt, who took what he wanted when he wanted. He'd pretended to care about Abe, but if you truly cared about someone, you didn't destroy them.

I am not a monster.

Perhaps he'd already gone too far. Abe had drugged and

tried to kidnap her. Maybe he'd pay for this crime even if he didn't follow through with it. Maybe McKenna would tell her mom about the "weird ride" in the van, and the police would come to question him. Maybe they'd investigate him and find his plans before he could destroy them.

Part of Abe was furious. That part that never got what he deserved in life.

Come on. You planned this all out, you may as well go through with it! Don't be a fucking quitter.

I am smart. I am strong. I am willing to do what must be done to get what's mine.

Abe withdrew from the hug and met McKenna's eyes, still uncertain of what he would do. Maybe he *had* come too far. Sometimes, when you've gone this far, the best thing to do was floor the gas and barrel ahead without looking back.

"Are you okay?" she asked. "You look like *you* are crying. Are you scared back here, too?"

Abe laughed, wiping a tear from his eye. "Yeah, maybe just a little."

"Grown-ups get scared?" Her eyebrows arched in disbelief.

He laughed, again.

God, I love this girl.

And that was exactly why he couldn't go through with his plans. Because he loved her. And he refused to allow his desires to corrupt that love.

"Come on," he said, "let's get you back to your mother."

THIRTY-SEVEN

Maggie Kent

MAGGIE COULDN'T SHAKE the feeling that something was wrong. Call it mother's intuition, but the insistence that her baby girl was in trouble wouldn't fall silent inside her.

The feeling had started nagging Maggie shortly after Abe had abruptly hung up almost ten minutes ago. At first, she tried to shrug the feeling away as an unrealistic worry invited by all the horrible things that had happened with Nick. But the more she tried to ignore the sensation, the more it itched, demanding her attention.

A lot of the worry had to do with the way Abe had seemed to be rushing, hanging up before she could say hi to McKenna.

It felt odd to be on the phone with someone caring for McKenna without speaking to her. It would've been one thing if Abe had been a family member or longtime friend, but he was a neighbor and patron of the diner whom she really didn't even know that well. Maggie wondered if McKenna had thought it odd that her mom didn't ask to talk to her when she called back.

At first, Maggie told herself that Abe was just in a hurry to get whatever it was to his boss. And she felt guilty because it was her fault she'd taken him from his job to pick up McKenna. It was too much to expect of Abe because he wasn't family or friend. You didn't ask acquaintances or regular customers for this kind of favor. And she couldn't exactly be pissed that he didn't rush right to the diner, or that he abruptly hung up. He didn't have to do this for her at all.

Yet there was something unshakeable in the back of Maggie's mind — a feeling she couldn't quite suss out.

It wasn't that she thought Abe would *do something* to McKenna. He seemed rather harmless. Geeky and socially awkward, yes, but not someone she'd have to worry about.

But yet there had been something odd in his voice.

Something *wrong*.

Her fifteen minute break was quickly disappearing; Maggie debated whether or not she should try to call back.

She didn't want to pester him, or make Abe any later than he already was. But at the same time, Maggie didn't think she could go back to work with this uncertainty occupying her mind.

She called him back, but there was no answer.

Maggie looked down at the phone to make sure she'd dialed correctly. Perhaps the service had cut out in the diner as it sometimes tended to do no matter how many bars of coverage she had.

She stepped outside, behind Goldman's, and tried again, pressing her ear hard to the phone.

Still, no answer.

Maybe he's in the car and doesn't answer the phone while he's driving. That's admirable, isn't it?

Or maybe he's at the shop right now, talking to his boss, explaining why he was running late and the last thing he needs is me calling.

Or maybe they got in a car accident, and they're both dead, the phone ringing as paramedics are walking over their bloodied, crumpled bodies.

No! Stop thinking of these things!

12

Maggie tried to shake the horrible images, but they wouldn't stop coming.

For the first four years of McKenna's life, Maggie was plagued by terrible visions of things that might have happened to McKenna whenever she was out of sight.

Many nights, Maggie had woken up in the middle of the night, convinced that McKenna had rolled over in her crib and was somehow suffocating on something — a stuffed animal, the corner of the crib, a blanket.

When her daughter was in daycare, Maggie would have horrible, painfully sharp visions of some horrifying accident, ranging from the realistic such as falling off a playground swing to the supremely unlikely like a fire breaking out and somehow trapping McKenna in some small and unreachable corner of the school.

Maggie hadn't had thoughts like these since she started taking the anti-anxiety pills — *maybe the school shrinks were right to medicate me* — meds when McKenna started kindergarten, but now they were back with a ferocious revenge.

Something had happened to McKenna and she needed Maggie to act.

Now!

But what could Maggie do? Her break was over, and the diner was already shorthanded. She couldn't expect Viv to handle the entire diner, even with Loretta and Dima's help.

She looked at her phone's address book and found the number to the computer shop where Abe worked.

Her finger hovered above the shop's name, desperate to dial.

What if Abe had lied to his boss? Told him he had to do something else, or said there was some emergency so he could get time off to pick up McKenna? If I call now and the boss answers, and I ask where Abe and McKenna are, I could get him in trouble, or worse, fired.

Maggie didn't call.

But she couldn't just sit and do nothing.

The more helpless Maggie felt, the more certain she was that her daughter was in danger.

She tried to remember Dr. Rodriguez's advice, to try and separate reality from irrational fears. That advice kept her from calling.

But only barely.

She looked at her phone's address book and saw Clarence Dumont's cell number begging to be dialed.

Call the cops? Really? And what then? Report that Abe is late bringing McKenna to the diner? Late in doing me a favor, even though he already said he'd be late?

Besides, Clarence had to be sick of her today. First, he had to go pay Nick a visit, then he had to appear at Nick's brutal crime scene, and was now, presumably, out tracking him down. Maggie felt like she had her own personal police officer today, and hated the feeling that she was putting him, and his partner, out. They should be out chasing *real criminals*, not dealing with her domestic bullshit.

It was bad enough that Maggie felt responsible for what happened earlier, and that Barbara might not even recover from her injury. She didn't want to compound drama by freaking out over Abe.

Yet Maggie couldn't shake the awful feeling that McKenna needed her. She felt it in her every cell, in her bones, in her heart. Her daughter needed her.

Yeah, but how many times have I felt that before? And nothing was ever wrong.

I can't let fear rule my life.

I was doing better. I'd found the strength to leave Nick, and things were finally looking up. Now I'm freaking the hell out at the first sight of a setback, like someone off her meds and in desperate need of psychiatric help.

Maggie pulled up the computer shop on her phone and was about to dial when the diner's back door opened and Loretta came out.

12

"Hey, Maggie, you almost done? We need you inside."

Maggie looked down at her phone, assuming that Loretta thought she was already on a call. Loretta was a cool enough boss to not give Maggie a hard time if she truly needed a few more minutes. Though, Loretta *would* passive-aggressively bring it up later and make Maggie feel guilty for slacking off on the job.

She could easily say no, but the time said that Abe was still within his window. If she called the shop any sooner and got him in trouble, she'd never forgive herself.

"Yeah," she said, returning the phone to her pocket and heading back into the diner.

AFTER ANOTHER TEN minutes of constantly watching the front door for McKenna, Maggie could barely bottle her fears.

She was waiting on a six top of Canadians running her ragged with one request after another. And she doubted she'd get a tip no matter how much she bent over backward to please them. While Maggie wasn't one to blindly accept stereotypes, such as Canadians being poor tippers, she'd been waiting tables long enough to know the odds were against her. Plus, the way they were treating her, they clearly had no respect for her time or job.

Maggie would often play a mental game with herself when she could see things going south: *Will They or Won't They Tip?* And if they *did* tip, how little would they leave? Usually, such mental exercises were designed to make time fly, but every minute that Abe didn't come through the door with McKenna was another minute that felt stretched to infinity. And no amount of mental distractions could soften the waiting.

Maggie figured Abe was running at least ten minutes past his most generous estimate. She wanted to duck back outside and try calling again. And if she couldn't get a hold of him, screw it, she'd call the shop. If he got in trouble, well, it was his own damned fault.

Maybe he shouldn't have lied to his boss to begin with.

Maggie paused to laugh at herself. Her inner critic scolded:

Who said he even lied to his boss? Wow, you're all over the place with your assumptions and accusations! You need to chill out, girl.

But no, the time for "chilling out" was over. Abe was late and hadn't called.

Something is wrong. I can feel it.

The longer that Maggie ignored her gut, the more she'd hate herself if something truly *was* wrong.

That was the kind of timid action that had allowed Nick to control her life for so long.

Lil' Miss Maggie, afraid to rock the boat, afraid to upset the status quo. Even if the status quo sucked.

Maggie wasn't sure which she hated more, her anxieties or her weakness.

Dr. Rodriguez identified both as products of her upbringing, bouncing around from one foster home to another, never really fitting in anywhere. Often suffering from abuse, mostly verbal. Eventually, Maggie found herself living in constant fear. If she was in a bad house, she was afraid to anger her abusers. In a good house, she was afraid to do anything that might disappoint her foster parents and make them decide they were better off without her.

She'd grown up on a tightrope until Maggie was finally adopted by Francine and Stewart. They hadn't been much better. Both were abusive drunks, but in their own way, they'd meant well. Broken people doing their best, with intentions that were usually more good than bad. Despite everything, they loved her — in their own twisted ways.

Her inner critic chimed in.

12

It doesn't matter what your parents were like. You need to get a grip and control yourself before your fears start infecting McKenna.

Maggie's inner critic made sense. She'd already seen signs of anxiety in McKenna. Little things, nothing too terrible, but still, the seeds had clearly been planted. The only thing Maggie wasn't certain of was who, or what, had put them in the soil. Was it Maggie's fears and anxieties? Was it genetic? Or perhaps it was a product of living with the explosively erratic and abusive Nick? It might have been any or all of them, who knew? Either way, Maggie couldn't stop doing her best to make sure that McKenna was shielded from the worst of life.

Maggie told the Canadians she'd be right back with more drinks then went to the restroom, made her way into one of the two stalls, and pulled out her phone.

She called Abe again, but only got a ringing phone.

Dammit!

She was about to surrender and finally call Clarence when the bathroom door opened. Someone made their way into the stall directly next to hers then sat.

Maggie couldn't tell if the person was a customer, a coworker, maybe Loretta. Regardless, she couldn't risk being overheard on the call.

She returned the phone to her pocket, washed her hands even though she hadn't used the bathroom, then went to get the Canadians' drinks.

Halfway back to their table, the front door opened. Maggie's heart nearly stopped in her throat.

It was McKenna, standing next to Abe! And she looked perfectly fine.

Maggie fought the urge to toss the tray of drinks on the Canadians' table and run to the front door. She delivered drinks to each person, screwed up once, confusing the fat, bald guy's Diet Coke with his wife's Dr. Pepper, apologized, then said she'd be right back, even though it was clear they had yet another immediate errand, or one more "suggestion" for Sebastian.

Maggie raced to McKenna, scooped her up into a giant hug, and held her tight, relieved to see her safe and sound.

She looked McKenna over, not even caring if it was obvious to Abe that she was inspecting her daughter to make sure she was well.

"Hi, Mommy," McKenna said.

"Hi, baby, I was so worried about you." Maggie met Abe's eyes to let him know she wasn't happy.

All the fear and frustration of not being able to reach him on the phone had boiled over to anger, and she didn't feel like hiding it. That's something Old Maggie would've done.

New Maggie was pissed, and didn't care who knew it.

"What happened?" she asked, only slightly aware, but not caring, that half the diner could hear her. "I tried calling you several times!"

Abe's eyes widened. He looked somewhere between shocked and assaulted by her intensity.

"I'm so sorry. My car broke down on 18th street, and I had to wait for my friend, Stephen, to let me borrow his van. He was working on something at the park, and said he'd wait with my car until AAA sent someone out. Meanwhile, this one fell asleep in the car, waiting. I was afraid to wake her, so I put her in the van, and I think she got kinda spooked."

"Fell asleep?" Maggie asked, the hairs on the back of her neck standing.

Something *was* wrong. Something about the way Abe was talking, looking her in the eyes, almost staring, when he usually avoided eye contact, which made him seem shy. His speech was also different, a faster cadence than usual. And McKenna falling asleep? Waking up in a van? This was getting way too creepy for Maggie.

Abe said nothing.

Maggie met McKenna's eyes. "Why did you fall asleep?"

"I dunno." She shrugged. "I remember being really tired then just waking up. Then Mr. Abe brought me here."

Maggie tried to remind herself that it wasn't uncommon for McKenna to fall asleep in the car, especially if they had errands to run. Particularly on days when McKenna woke early as she had today.

"Are you okay?"

McKenna smiled. Something seemed off about her, but she didn't appear to have been through anything traumatic. Maybe it was the playground incident. McKenna was probably worried that she was in trouble, and dreading the conversation that would have to wait until after Maggie's shift.

She turned to Abe, wanting to shove a finger into his chest — hard because she was pissed that he had her so scared — and demand answers.

"Why did you come here first? I thought you had to go to your shop, and then here?"

"Well, we were running so late anyway, and I couldn't call you to tell you why, so I figured I ought to get here before you got freaked out and called the National Guard. Plus, I left the computer — the one my boss is waiting on — in the car, so now I have to find a phone and call Stephen and tell him to get it out of the car before AAA hands it over to a mechanic at Al's Garage. Then I need to have Stephen drive me back to the shop. What a day! Could I borrow your phone to try and call Stephen?"

Abe looked desperate. His eyes were wide, mannerisms fidgety, and body language frightened.

Yeah, kinda how you looked ten minutes ago, her inner critic said.

Suddenly, Maggie felt horrible for her overreaction.

Now that Abe was here, in the flesh, things felt right. Not 100 percent right, but it seemed obvious that he was having a rough day, which explained his fast talking and odd responses.

"I'm sorry," she said. "I ... just ... well, she's my one and only, and ... well ... "

"It's okay," Abe said, smiling. His eyes said he understood, and that Maggie didn't need to explain.

"Here." She handed him her phone.

He took it and was about to call Stephen when his fingers paused over the screen.

"Crap," he said.

"What?"

"I don't remember his number. It's in my phone, and my phone is dead."

"Ah," she said. "Is his number listed? You can call information."

"No, I don't think so," he said, returning her phone. "I better head on over there, or maybe get to the garage and see if I can get the computer before it *mysteriously disappears*. I trust Al, but not necessarily all the guys that work there, ya know?"

"Yeah," Maggie said.

"Excuse me," one of the Canadians shouted loud enough for the entire diner to hear, "can we get some service?"

Maggie turned and held up a finger. "Just a moment." Loretta, working another table behind theirs, looked up at Maggie, her lips pursed in disapproval.

"Crap," she said, echoing his *crap* a moment ago. "I've gotta ... "

"Yeah," he said, smiling. "Me too."

"Thank you. And again, I'm sorry. Let's do dinner sometime next week and let me make it up to you. Okay?"

He looked at her, and for the slightest moment, the odd flutter returned. Something weird going on with Abe that she couldn't decipher.

"Yeah, that would be great."

Maggie could tell he didn't mean it.

Abe said goodbye and left, the bell on the door clanging as it swung shut behind him.

She turned to McKenna and said, "Go have Viv set you

up at a table and give you some crayons and paper, okay? We're gonna be here a while."

Maggie still wasn't sure how she'd get home. Maybe she'd call a cab and keep from inconveniencing anyone else.

"Okay, Mommy."

Maggie returned to the Canadians' table, a few of them giving her stink eye, well, save for Fat Guy's wife, who looked embarrassed that her husband was making a scene.

"I'm sorry," she said, "now how can I help you?"

They rattled off their requests. Maggie stared at her daughter as Viv brought her to a table in the rear.

It had been a long day. From the flat tire to Nick going postal to missing the agent's call to the scare with Abe to the shitty customers, none of that mattered now that she knew McKenna was safe.

Maggie smiled, despite the annoying Canadians. No matter how shitty the world decided to be, Maggie still had her little girl, and that made everything worth it.

THIRTY-EIGHT

Tim Hewitt

TIM WOKE to a thumping in his head that hurt more than any other pain his father had ever inflicted.

He reached up to see if he was bleeding. Touching his head hurt, a lot. Surprisingly, his fingers showed no blood.

He glanced at the clock: 2:51 p.m. He'd only been out for maybe ten minutes. The last thing he remembered was his father fighting him for the notebook then shoving him into the wall. After that, the world went fuzzy. He sort of remembered looking up at his dad, but then nothing.

He slipped on his glasses and looked around his room.

His books were still scattered all over the floor. No doubt his father would make him pick them up later and probably even put them in a box for donation. Hell, the bastard would probably make Tim take them to the Salvation Army himself and hand the books over as some kind of "growing experience."

But Tim didn't see the notebook he'd been fighting his father for. Not even the pages his father had ripped and dropped to the floor without the slightest fuck given.

He felt a new flash of anger.

Not just at taking the notebook. But at leaving Tim lying

on the bed. Is that what you were supposed to do when someone had a concussion or was knocked out? Walk away? Weren't you *supposed* to try and keep the victim from sleeping?

Hell, maybe he'd hoped Tim would die.

Part of Tim wished he *hadn't* woken up from the injury. It would be a lot easier than facing the rest of the night, or the life after that. Tim was certain his father would demand an encore performance for his mother. They'd have the same "discussion." His father would show her the notebook, assuming it wasn't already destroyed. He'd announce that Tim would be going to military school on Monday and no, there would be no arguing, Judith, you baby him enough already.

And just like that, Tim's life would be over.

Sure, military school might offer an escape. But Tim had little doubt that he'd just run into more of the same wherever he went — assholes whose sole mission was to target the weakest person and make their life a living hell. Tim was always that person. He was a bully magnet, and some things you couldn't ever change. Bullies could sense that you were a big steaming pile of pussy no matter how hard you fronted.

It was hard to believe that when he woke this morning, life had seemed almost full of promise.

Tim's biggest concern was whether he could summon the courage to ask Alicia to the dance. Maybe she'd say no, but he probably could've maintained their friendship.

Now his world had gone to shit in less than eight hours. He'd lost his only friend. He'd made a terrifying enemy of Jeff. And his monster father was about to ship him off to military school.

Tim stared at the books on the ground. The torn edition of *The Talisman* broke his heart.

His grandma (on his mother's side) had been sharing books with Tim ever since he could read. One of the advantages of running a used book store. At first, she lent him old hardback *Peanuts* collections. Then she lent him old *Hardy Boys*.

When he got older, she lent him books by Koontz, King, and Piers Anthony, which he devoured as quickly as she could deliver them. His favorite book had been *The Talisman*, though. They'd talked about it a lot, as it was the first King she'd lent him.

On his twelfth birthday, she presented Tim with a first edition of the book in nearly mint condition. One of her regular customers knew she was a huge fan and sold it to her for a decent price. Tim wasn't sure of the book's market value, but it was a prized possession for sentimental reasons that he'd never sell, no matter how much money someone offered. It was a reminder of one of the only other people who'd been nice to him, taken by cancer last year.

To see it on the floor now, its cover torn off, pages pulled out and crumbled, only added fuel to his burning anger.

He stood, his head still hurting and a bit dizzy, then went into the bathroom.

He couldn't see the back room of the house, but Tim could hear the TV blaring, tuned to his father's usual choice, a twenty-four-hour news channel. No doubt his father was lying on the couch, drinking, stoking his anger at the world.

Tim pissed then found his reflection while washing his hands. His face was black and blue, a gash on his forehead, dried blood. He looked like he'd been in an accident.

He stared into the mirror, hating that he'd allowed all this to happen to him. Allowed so many people to fuck him over. Allowed kids like Jeff, and countless others, to bully him over the years. Allowed Dima to treat him like shit, without ever demanding the respect he deserved. Allowed his father to bully him and his mother for so long.

He always tried to please everyone.

Tried not to rock the boat.

Tried not to stand out.

Tried to make people like him.

But all he ever got was shit in return.

He no longer saw the nice kid he usually saw in the reflection. Instead, he saw a coward staring back.

A coward that he loathed for letting all this happen.

Real men didn't *let life happen to them*. They tackled their hardships. They stepped up to bullies and knocked them down. They stood up to their fathers. They didn't let friends take advantage of them.

Suddenly, Tim could see what his father saw when he looked at his son, and why he was always so disappointed.

His father had raised a little bitch.

Tim was tired of being a little bitch.

Tired of turning the other cheek.

He stepped out of the bathroom slowly and headed toward his father's study.

Once inside, he closed the door softly.

Calling the room a "study" was something of a joke considering there weren't any books, or even a desk. The room was more like a pub. It had a bar, four stools, a pool table, a dart board, a card table, and lighting fixtures his father had bought from a restaurant supply store. His father occasionally had friends over, other drunk assholes like him, who also talked down to Tim.

Aside from the rare times when his father was in a drunkenly *good* mood, Tim wasn't allowed in the study, because that's where Father kept his guns.

Tim grabbed the keys to the gun cabinet behind the bar.

His heart raced as an idea formed in his mind, a few steps ahead of his actions.

He opened the cabinet.

There were pistols, a shotgun, and several rifles, all displayed like objets d'art.

So many guns to choose from. While Tim's father had taken him to a shooting range many times, trying to "butch him up a bit," Tim wasn't well versed enough about guns to know their names and model numbers. His father knew every gun's name, of course. As if the guns were his children.

He certainly loves them more than his child.

Tim wanted to take something his father loved, the way his father had taken from him.

He grabbed the shotgun and the ear plugs his father wore to the shooting range.

~

TIM STEPPED INTO THE DEN, aiming the shotgun at his drunken father passed out on the couch despite the TV's blaring volume.

His spiral notebook was on the coffee table, torn to shreds. Beyond salvage.

Gone forever, the story. Gone forever, the drawings and kind words that Alicia had written to Tim.

"How dare you?" Tim asked, gun shaking in his hand.

His father didn't hear him. His father halfway turned away, his face now buried in the cushions, and farted.

Tim raised his voice.

"I said how dare you?"

Still, nothing.

Tim turned and shot the TV, silencing a commercial hawking gold.

The blast had been so loud that Tim was certain his ears would be whistling if not for the earplugs.

His father sat up, startled, and froze in his seat when he saw Tim aiming the shotgun right at him. He held his hands over his ears, mouthing a complaint that Tim couldn't hear.

His father's eyes widened then narrowed when he saw the source of the explosive blast. Surprise turned to anger.

"What the hell did you do to my *TV?*"

He started to stand. If Tim didn't do something, his father

12

would be on him in a moment, calling his bluff, then beating on him again.

Tim shot his father in the left knee.

He fell back screaming, clutching his wound, staring up at Tim incredulously.

Tim's hands were shaking.

His heart was racing.

It was all he could do to keep the vomit inside him.

He stared at his father, barely able to believe he'd just shot him.

So much blood.

"What the fuck?" his father screamed, reaching over to the coffee table toward his phone.

"Don't!" Tim shouted.

His father's hand froze. He looked back at Tim.

"I have to call an ambulance, or I'll bleed out. Do you really want that?"

"When did it ever matter what *I* want?"

"What the hell are you talking about? Stop fucking around, and let me call an ambulance."

"No," Tim said. "First, we talk."

"Talk? What the hell is—"

"Shut up!" Tim aimed the gun at his father's head. "I talk then you answer."

"Okay."

"Okay what?" Tim asked.

"What?"

"This is where you say okay, sir," Tim said, feeling a shit-eating grin push his cheeks up.

His father looked up at him like a petulant child, barely able to make eye contact.

"Say it," Tim said.

"Okay, *sir*."

"Good. I knew you could do it."

His father continued to glare at him as he pressed down on his knee, trying to stop the blood with his fingers.

Tim asked what he'd wondered a million times.

"Why?"

"Why what?" Father's voice cracked in pain.

"Why do you hate me so much? What did I ever do to you?"

Tim began to cry.

He hated himself for crying and letting his father see how much the man had hurt him, but couldn't wipe the tears away while maintaining his aim.

Father looked down, as if searching for answers in the wound, then looked up.

"I don't hate you."

"Bullshit!" Tim said. "You said you wished I'd never been born. You don't say that to someone you love."

"I don't know, Tim. What do you want me to say? What will get you to put the gun down, stop this fucking nonsense, and call an ambulance?"

"No, you don't get to be mad at me. You did this to yourself."

"No, you're the one holding the gun, Son. Not me. Why? Because Daddy didn't show you enough love? Because, unlike most parents, I refuse to coddle you? Because I demand respect and for you to do your very best? Oh, yeah, *I'm* the bad guy now."

"Don't you put this on me."

"Everything you do is on you, Tim. That's your problem, boy. You're always looking for someone else to blame when things don't go right. Oh, my friend doesn't like me. Oh, a bully picked on me. Oh, the girl I like doesn't like me back. Boo-fucking-hoo, grow the fuck up, boy."

Tim couldn't believe his father was being so mean.

Why wasn't he begging for his life?

Why wasn't he saying whatever he needed to say to get his son to put down the gun?

He wasn't that stupid, was he?

Why wasn't he attempting to justify his cruelty?

He could've said anything: his father abused him and didn't know better; he didn't know how to show love; or maybe he was an alcoholic and couldn't help it.

Something. Anything other than turning it back around and attacking Tim.

He was no longer sure what to do.

He hadn't planned this far ahead.

He didn't intend to kill his father. Though he wasn't sure what he planned, other than making his father sorry.

But now he had to do something, or his father would bleed out and die.

That would turn Tim into a murderer.

"I'm going to call an ambulance, and we're going to put this nonsense behind us."

Tim's father reached for the phone again.

"No," Tim said.

"What?"

"No, I need you to tell me why. Why do you do the things you do? Why are you so cruel to me and Mom?"

His father looked down again then started to laugh.

"What do you want me to say, boy? Want me to give you some sob story about how I really love you, but I need to be hard on you? I think that's a given."

"No, it's not. You don't do these things to people you love. How can you look at your child and raise a hand to harm them? *How*?"

His father stared at him, pursed his lips, and said, "Fine. You're right. I *don't* love you. There's not a day in my life that I don't wish you were never born. Want to know why, do you, Son?"

"Yes," Tim said, hot tears streaming down his face.

"Because you trapped me. I never intended to marry your mother. But then she got pregnant with you, and that was it. That was the beginning of every bad thing in my life. You. You and her."

Tim pulled the trigger.

Twice.

Once in his father's chest.

The second shot in his head.

3 p.m. - 4 p.m.

THIRTY-NINE

Abe McDonald

She knows.

It was all Abe could think as he sped from the diner.
Maggie knows.
She didn't know *what* she knew, but she suspected *something*. And that was all it would take for Abe's life to unravel.

She'd tell someone. Maybe that cop she talked to all the time. Then someone would start looking into Abe. If they looked hard enough, who knew what they'd find? He'd never been so stupid as to save the illegal varieties of porn he sometimes indulged in, but he *had* saved several gigs worth of photos and videos of McKenna. Sure, they were on an encrypted drive, but Abe was also smart enough to know that the feds had built in back doors to most of the market's encryption tools. His particular tool might be safe, but in this day and age, he had to figure nothing was foolproof.

Abe's laptop held the keys to his obsession. The right person could piece his plans together, even if he'd never followed through.

There were ways out, of course.

He could shred the hard drive's contents then dump it. But

12

the thought of deleting all the images and videos of McKenna sickened him.

He thought of fictional killers. How the ones who got caught didn't just make a dumb mistake, they also kept trophies. Something belonging to the victim — a lock of hair, photographs, clothing, jewelry, *Dexter's* blood slides, there was always something that these people used to relive the crime. He figured there was probably some sexual element there, too, not that he was an expert on serial killers.

Photos and videos of McKenna didn't serve as a bridge to his crimes, though they were illegally obtained, but rather as a connection to *her*.

Abe drove, not sure where he was going, his mind flashing on McKenna's most private moments captured forever. Photos and videos of her birthday party with her friend, Lucy, of her playing at the park, of her losing her first tooth, of her playing piano, of her drawing one of the characters from *Frozen*. Videos of she and her mom talking, another of McKenna giggling through one of her mother's longer stories. So many moments lived vicariously alongside her — as if they were memories shared — Abe couldn't stand the thought of erasing them, and saying goodbye to McKenna forever.

Wasn't it enough that he'd decided to abort his plans? That he returned the girl to her mother?

Like a judge is going to say, "Oh, you changed your mind. OK, you're free to go, pedophile!"

His planned life was now a pathetic delusion, and Abe was the loser who had lost by believing.

"I am smart. I am strong. I am willing to do what must be done to get what's mine." Abe said, laughing as he cried.

"I am stupid. I am weak. I am *not* willing to do what needs to be done to get what's mine!"

"You are nobody special. You will not be loved!"

Abe was stopped at a red light, yelling at himself when he spotted a cop car in the turn lane beside him.

He glanced over to see the cop, a young black man, staring at him, probably thinking him a lunatic. His partner, at the wheel, had his eyes on the road ahead.

Abe smiled and waved, hoping his nerves weren't obvious.

He looked ahead, his eyes on the light. He thought about pretending to adjust his radio tuner, but didn't most guilty people do that when a cop was around?

He kept his hands at ten and two, staring at oncoming traffic. There was no one in the opposite turning lane; when Abe's light went green, he and the cop would probably go at the same time.

Abe needed that cop car to turn first. If it didn't, the cop might have decided, *Fuck it, let's go straight and follow the nervous man in the rape van.*

The cross-traffic light turned yellow; Abe and the cop's light would turn green any second.

Come on. Someone pull up to the turn lane.

Abe kept staring. The yellow light took forever to turn.

Cross traffic stopped.

A red VW Bug pulled up to the line in the opposite turn lane.

Yes!

But the Bug was too late to trigger the light.

Both lights ahead, for the straight and turn lanes, turned green. Abe drove forward, heart pounding. Traffic moved like molasses.

He risked a glance in his side mirror, but the cop car wasn't turning.

No, no, no.

Abe thought of all the items in his van. The computer, fake IDs, bags of clothing for himself and McKenna, the toys, the books, the ...

Oh shit, I forgot to put her Rosie doll back.

Abe remembered the most incriminating bit of evidence

— the bottle of chloroform and rag buried under his passenger side seat.

Shit! Shit!

If the cops pulled him over and decided to search him, almost everything else was explainable. It wasn't like they'd search his laptop for a routine traffic stop. And the clothes and toys, well, it wasn't as if they were in a big bag marked: *KIDNAPPING GEAR*.

But the chloroform told a much darker story.

That would be enough to take him in.

He prayed that the cop car wouldn't follow. That it would just stay at the light and do whatever it was cops did when they were stopped at green lights for no apparent reason.

He peeked at the side mirror again.

Still there.

Yes!

No sooner had Abe sighed with relief than the lights on top lit up, and the cop car raced up from behind, following him.

No, no, no, no!

Please, be for someone else.

Abe slowed, moving to the right lane so the cop car could pass him.

But it didn't.

It followed right behind him.

"Pull over," a voice said over the car's speakers.

And there it was: the Moment of Decision that his mentor and confidence coach, Craig, had spoken of so many times.

There were these moments in life where we had to make a choice. Do we do the hard (and right) thing, or do we take the easy way out? The Path of Least Resistance?

So many people chose the Path of Least Resistance. But those cowardly moments never paid off. They always led to more of the same, more sadness, more heartbreak.

Abe thought of all the times in his life when he'd chosen

the easy way out, chosen to continue along the same path out of fear. He wondered how his life would be different if he'd told someone about his molester. If he'd forced his mother to do something about Kurt, or had maybe just run away from home. How would his life had been different if he'd sought treatment instead of being afraid to admit his attraction to little girls? Maybe he could've had a normal life.

He didn't know if people like him could ever be cured, but he could've tried harder to change. Or at the very least not fall in love with a damned child!

His life had been filled with one easy decision piled on top of the next. He never took the hard road, or did what he knew he should do.

Moments where you chose the Path of Most Resistance required a bravery possessed by only a few. That's why so many people were miserable. At least that was his mentor's philosophy: *Do the Hard Work to Make the Life You Want.*

Only now, with the police behind him, did Abe see that taking McKenna had not been a bold decision. It had been the cowardly one: indulging a fantasy that could never exist. An insult to reality and the life he should have been trying to make for himself.

But I was bold in giving her back. Doesn't that count for something? I didn't follow through on a wrong decision. I didn't destroy her life in some selfish obsession.

I did the right thing.

He pulled over, tears streaming down his face. There was no way the cops would let him go. Everything was over.

The rest of his life would be lived behind bars or, at best, at home, but what kind of life could he live as a registered sex predator? Who would hire him? People would rush by his apartment. Parents would point at his home, warning their children of the wretched man who lived there.

That was no kind of life.

But neither was the one he was living.

12

Abe's life had been a lie for years. Hiding who he really was out of fear that nobody would like him, nobody *could* love him.

He stopped the van.

The cruiser stopped behind him.

He looked down at the duffel bags on the floor. The bags that had promised a new life, a life of happiness, just he and McKenna, and maybe a kitten. Yeah, a cat would've been nice.

He reached down, unzipping one of the bags he'd prepared for her, and found her Rosie doll.

He sat in the van as the cops presumably ran his plate to find out who they were dealing with before they approached him.

He stared at the Rosie doll, her big painted brown eyes and giant smile staring back and offering comfort.

There was something so simple about the doll that made Abe yearn for a different childhood, a chance to go back before everything had gone bad. Before his innocence had been so violently stolen.

Life had been so good then. Comparatively anyway.

He cried harder, staring into Rosie's eyes and yearning for an impossible life.

He brought the doll to his face and kissed its head, inhaling the scent of its owner.

He shuddered at the thought that he'd almost destroyed her life.

Then, *an idea.*

A bold idea that he didn't dare think through and risk the chance of not acting on.

He slipped the doll under his shirt then reached for the driver's side door handle and opened it.

He stepped out of the van, the harsh afternoon light bright in his eyes.

One of the cops barked over the loudspeaker, "Get back in your car!"

Instead, he stepped forward, one hand under his shirt, holding the doll tight.

His heart raced as he forced himself forward against every instinct of self-preservation.

"I am smart. I am strong. I am willing to do what must be done to get what's mine," he whispered, still stepping forward.

Both cops got out of the car, raised their guns at him.

"Down on the ground!"

He continued forward, tears streaming down his face.

"I am smart. I am strong. I am willing to do what must be done to get what's mine."

He met the officers' eyes, the young black man who had seen him yelling at nothing, and the other man, a young redhead with an awful complexion.

The redhead yelled again, commanding him to get down on the ground.

Abe's hand tightened on the doll, then he moved fast, yanking it from under his shirt, raising it as if it were a gun.

The officers fired.

He wasn't sure how many times. He went down immediately, blinding pain overwhelming his senses.

Abe lay on the ground, blood spilling from his body onto the asphalt, the doll fallen beside him, just out of reach.

He struggled to stretch his fingers to touch the doll's happy face.

Inches away when his body stopped responding.

FORTY

Sebastian Ruiz

SEBASTIAN PUNCHED OUT FOR LUNCH, which he always took a half hour or so before the early bird dinner rush started at 4 p.m.

He usually spent his break sitting in his car, listening to the radio and reading the paper, or at least the sports page to see how the Dolphins and Heat, now without LeBron, were doing. Sometimes, he followed the Marlins.

Today, Sebastian was all about his phone.

He sat in his car, waiting for Gino's call. He'd texted Sebastian a half hour ago, asking if he was willing to do a "small job" in exchange for the money.

Sebastian had texted back *yes* even though he didn't know what the job was or if fulfilling the job was in place of paying back the loan. He'd accept the details, whatever they were. He had less than three hours before Raul would show up to collect.

He'd said yes and told Gino he'd call him back during his break, hoping he'd send someone by with the money.

Sebastian called Gino, waited for a return call on a secure line then said, "Okay, I'm on break. You gonna send someone by?"

"Uncle had another idea," Gino said.

"What do you mean *another idea?*" Was this the knife behind his back? Or was Gino about to exploit Sebastian's desperation and demand more? Not one job, but working for his uncle for six months, or longer?

"Well, I told Uncle the details of your particular situation, and he agreed that while you are in a jam, he wasn't about to hand that, and let me get this quote exact, 'fucking greasy Spic,' a dime of his fucking money."

"Fuck," Sebastian said, balling his fist and punching his steering wheel. "So, what's this mean, Gino? Am I fucked?"

"Not exactly, Brother. Uncle says he'll get your sister back. You won't owe him a dime, though he'd still like your help with a job."

"How's he gonna get her back? Does he know where she is?"

"He has his ways of finding out."

"He knows I need this, like, right away, right? You told him about the deadline?"

"Yes, yes, don't worry. He already has his guys on it."

"Really? Wow."

Sebastian sighed. If Gino's uncle was on it, then maybe it was fine to let hope into his heart. When Gino's uncle wanted something, he generally got it, no matter who stood in the way.

"So, what's the job? Did he say?"

"He didn't say."

"He knows I'm not an assassin, right?"

Gino laughed, though Sebastian wasn't sure if he was laughing because Uncle Petr's reputation was someone who routinely used assassins or that the idea of using Sebastian as a hired killer was absurd.

"Don't worry, he knows your specialties. And he knows you're like a brother to me, so you don't need to worry that you've signed a deal with the Devil. It will be a fair deal, my friend."

"Thank you," Sebastian said. "So, what now?"

"Just sit by your phone. Hopefully, I'll have good news for you soon."

"Tell Uncle I said thank you."

"Anything for a friend, Sebastian. Talk to you later."

Sebastian hung up and tried to resist the urge to indulge his excitement. He'd learned from his Abuelita Rosa early in life that you never tempt el diablo by showing too much joy. The Devil hated joy, and the moment you let it into your heart, he'd always work to undo it.

Sebastian was nowhere near as superstitious, or as Catholic, as his abuelita, but some things weren't worth risking.

So he buried his joy and instead focused on the many things that might go wrong. It wasn't just to keep his hopes in check, but perhaps he'd think of something that he might have overlooked, something he could tell Gino before his uncle's men moved in.

His mind as blank and bothered as his stomach, Sebastian decided to head back inside the diner.

Loretta was holding court in the kitchen, spinning some painfully unfunny story — not that she wasn't laughing — to Dima, that punk-ass bitch, Jeff, and Viv.

Not wanting to hear Loretta drag on, Sebastian removed his apron and went into the dining area where he'd seen Maggie's daughter, thinking that maybe he'd sit and chat with her while waiting out his break.

McKenna was concentrating deeply on a page from a coloring book, the tip of her tongue sticking out of her mouth like Michael Jordan in the zone.

"Whatchya workin' on? Is that for me?"

She looked up, slightly startled. A huge smile claimed her

face. She leaped from her seat, threw her arms wide, and embraced him. "Sebastian!"

He patted her back as he hugged her. She was such a happy kid. Seeing her reminded him a lot of how Ana was before turmoil had sent their lives to Hell.

"It's Elsa," she said, holding up the page. Sebastian wasn't sure how good most six-year-olds were at coloring, but the page looked great to his eye.

"Who is Elsa?" he teased as if he'd not heard her talk about the movie, *Frozen*, on any of the other dozens of times she'd been dropped off at the diner when Maggie had to stay late.

"She's from *Frozen!*"

"Is that the movie about training your dragons?" he teased.

"Noooo!"

"Oh, I know, it's that movie with the giant meatballs falling from the sky!"

"Nooooo!" she said, giggling.

"Um," Sebastian said, trying to think of something else that might make McKenna laugh. "Oh, it's that movie with the talking purple dinosaur!"

"Noooo, that's not a movie, that's a TV show, *Barney!*"

"Ohhhh, sorry, this *Frozen* thing ain't ringing any bells."

"It's the movie about the sisters, Anna and Elsa, and Olaf the snowman, and …"

Maggie walked up, interrupting, "Are you telling him about *Frozen* again?"

McKenna held up her colored page for Maggie. "He thought *this* was Barney!" McKenna's disbelief was priceless. Sebastian loved teasing her — and how serious she looked when she tried to explain why he was wrong.

Maggie played along. "You thought that was Barney? Man, Sebastian, I think you need glasses."

"Yeah!" McKenna said, "you need glasses!"

"Or maybeee," Maggie said, "maybe he needs to see *Frozen!*"

"Yeah!" McKenna said. "Wanna borrow my DVD so you can watch it?"

"No, no, that's okay." Sebastian raised his hands in mock surrender. "I believe you."

Maggie looked him up and down, probably noticing his missing apron. "You on your break?"

"Yeah, I figured I'd pester your daughter."

"Want some of my fries?" McKenna sat back down in her booth.

"Can I?" he asked, sitting on the opposite side.

"Sure! Do you want Mom to get you a drink or maybe a burger?"

"Thanks," Maggie said, "I didn't realize I was now waiting on *both* of you."

Sebastian laughed. "Better watch the 'tude, lady, or I'll stiff you on your tip."

Maggie smacked him with her pad. "Do you want anything?"

"Break will be over in a bit, and I think your chef on duty is on the slow side, so I'll pass. I *will* take a Coke, though, extra ice."

Maggie laughed as she left to get Sebastian's Coke.

McKenna pushed the bowl from her side of the table to the middle then pushed the plate where she'd already poured ketchup. "Here ya go, Sebastian."

"Thanks." He picked a couple of fries from the basket and dipped them in ketchup. She'd ordered the fries maybe fifteen minutes ago, and had barely touched them.

"Why aren't you eating?"

"I had a brownie earlier."

"A brownie, and you didn't bring me one?"

"They weren't mine to bring. It was from my neighbor, Mr. Abe. He picked me up early from school."

"Ah, okay." Sebastian watched her color the page.

Normally, Sebastian would joke around with McKenna, maybe asking how she got so lucky as to get out of school early. But he knew she was here early because of what her father had done, and he certainly didn't want to do anything that made her think about that. He wondered how much she knew, if anything.

Maggie came back and hung out for a few minutes talking since they were between busy periods.

Sebastian enjoyed the distraction. He always liked talking with Maggie and her daughter. They were good people. Guys like Nick didn't deserve to have such a loving wife and a wonderful kid.

He wanted to ask if there'd been any word on Nick, or on Barbara. He hadn't heard a word since Loretta had said goodbye to the cops. But he couldn't bring it up in front of McKenna. He hoped that the cops had found Nick and beat the living shit out of him. You saw clips of police brutality all the time on the news, but rarely to the right people.

Sebastian had no problem with someone catching a beating — if they deserved it. Hell, he'd sign up for the police academy tomorrow if he could help scrub the streets of the right motherfuckers.

But, alas, shit didn't work like that in the real world. Bad cops beat up or shot innocent people or relative innocents who didn't deserve to die while the good cops were too by-the-book to take care of the people who should be taken out. Sebastian wouldn't last a day as a cop, too frustrated by all the red tape and an iron inability to affect *real justice*.

They kept talking. Sebastian marveled at Maggie's ability to wear a mask and keep her shit together even as her world fell apart. He knew from their earlier conversation that she was damned close to snapping, but hell if you could tell by watching her now.

He looked at McKenna, picking at her fries. "Do you know how lucky you are to have such an awesome mom?"

Maggie met Sebastian's eyes. He could tell she might cry if he got too mushy with the compliments. Still, he wanted to say something sweet. People rarely took the time to tell those in their life nice things, and right now, he figured, she could use it.

"I know," McKenna said.

Most kids might have followed that with some sort of sarcastic response like "She tells me all the time" or something. But nope, McKenna said it matter-of-factly. Despite her father, she was still a sweet kid with none of the cynicism of most children he'd seen, or hell, even the teens he worked with, like Dima and Jeff.

"I'm pretty lucky, too," Maggie said, reaching over to give McKenna a hug. Tears welled in the corners of her eyes.

Sebastian lightened the mood. "Well, just 'cuz you're Mom of the Year and stuff doesn't mean I'm gonna tip."

Maggie wiped the tears from her eyes and laughed. "Thanks. Now if you all don't need anything else, tables are calling."

"Yeah, me too," Sebastian said, "after I eat a few more of your daughter's fries."

Maggie headed to a group of diners who had just taken their seats.

He watched as McKenna colored, the tip of her tongue sticking out of her mouth, a wide smile on her tiny face, happy as could be despite everything.

Sebastian hoped he'd see his sister's smile soon.

FORTY-ONE

Sheryl Dumont

AFTER A LIGHT LUNCH WITH CHLOE, they decided to window shop for a while, heading to the mall before returning to the diner to check out the badge bunny.

Sheryl wasn't feeling too hot. She was clammy and out of sorts but figured if she told Chloe she wasn't feeling well, her friend would accuse her of trying to bail on their trip to the diner.

So Sheryl said nothing. Chloe was in the mood to shop, but Sheryl didn't really have a lot of money to blow. It was weird having come from wealth with a rich father and almost taking a vow of poverty by marrying a cop. She earned plenty as a realtor, but was squirreling as much of it away as she could in case the housing market crashed again. Which made shopping with Chloe difficult sometimes, particularly when she was dropping five hundred dollars at Victoria's Secret like pocket change.

After Chloe was shopped out, they hit the food court like teenagers killing time.

"So," Chloe asked, "whatchya gonna do if you find out Clarence *is* sleeping with this bitch?"

"Let's not jump ahead. We don't know anything yet, and

we probably won't even after going to the diner. What do you think? She's gonna be wearing a pin that reads, *Ask Me About the Married Men I'm Screwing?*"

"No, but there are other ways to know. Just follow my lead."

"What, did you also learn how to be a detective watching daytime TV?"

"No, from watching *Sherlock* on BBC America, but I can always tell when someone's lying."

"Yeah, does your husband lie to you a lot?"

"Stan knows better. I'll cut his dick off, or take half his money in the divorce, in which case he might beg me to take his dick instead."

Sheryl laughed.

Chloe leaned closer, took a sip of her bright-pink fruit smoothie, and said, "There was a time that Stan had a little thing on the side going on."

"What? *Stan?*"

Sheryl had wondered why Chloe never seemed particularly passionate about Stan. She'd secretly suspected that her friend had married for money, even if she'd lied to herself, but maybe this little secret was the reason she seemed so nonchalant when discussing her man. He'd broken Chloe's heart and turned their union into a marriage of convenience.

"Yeah, it was a one-time thing, about two years ago, with a woman he met at some conference. He came home, and I could tell right away. I confronted him, demanding to know when he was planning to tell me."

"Oh shit."

"He played dumb, but I could tell. I told him not to bullshit me."

"And?"

"He told me everything. He actually broke down and cried."

"Wow," Sheryl said. "Why didn't you tell me?"

"Honest?"

"Uh, yeah."

"I didn't want you thinking I was an idiot for staying with him."

"Well, I'm surprised you did. What happened to cutting his dick off or taking half his money?"

"Well, yeah, I'd do that *now*, if he did it again! In a heartbeat. But I dunno — there was something so sad about his confession that even though I was angry, I couldn't stay that way."

"What do you mean?"

"Well, and here's where you might think I'm stupid, but hear me out, there were reasons he did what he did."

"I'll bet! Reason one, he's a guy. Reason two, he was horny."

Chloe laughed but not the same hearty laugh she'd normally lose herself in. This was close to the bone, and Sheryl had to be careful not to come off like she was attacking or judging her.

"I'm sorry," Sheryl said, "go ahead."

"Well, we got to talking, and as it turns out, things had changed after the children were born. I stopped paying attention to him. We'd sorta become strangers with our kids being the only thing we had in common."

Sheryl knew exactly how she felt, minus the children.

"And Stan didn't feel loved. So some pretty pharmaceutical rep chatted him up, made him feel special, and well, he had a moment of weakness. I can't blame him. Well, I *did* blame him. Oh, boy, did I blame him. But after a while, I had to decide if I was going to let one mistake destroy our lives. Yes, he'd messed up, but I had the choice whether to forgive or hold it against him forever."

"Wow," Sheryl said, "I don't know what to say."

"Nothing much *to* say, really. In some ways, his little affair probably saved our marriage."

"How?"

"It made me realize that I'd been neglecting him, taking him for granted. He realized how much he loved me when he saw how hurt I was."

Sheryl wanted to call bullshit. Wanted to tell her friend that she sounded like one of those stupid women on daytime talk shows who blames themselves for their husband's inability to keep their dick behind the zipper.

But maybe Sheryl's defensiveness was more to do with her own marriage's shaky ground and just how much culpability she shared for decaying the foundation. Maybe she'd driven Clarence into the arms of that waitress.

Suddenly, her stomach felt as if it were in the midst of a free fall.

Sheryl pushed back her chair and walked toward the restroom, briskly at first then quickly at a full run.

She shoved the stall door open and made it just in time to vomit her salad and drinks.

Oh, God!

Sheryl thought she was done when another violent retching forced up whatever was left in her stomach.

Doubled over the toilet, she heard Chloe behind her. "You okay?"

She turned, thankful that Chloe was already holding a handful of paper towels. She was a good friend like that, always knowing what Sheryl needed before she could ask.

Sheryl grabbed the towels and wiped at her mouth then at the toilet where chunks had hit the seat. Some had fallen on the floor around the porcelain, but she wasn't about to get on her hands and knees in a public restroom. The thought made her want to puke again.

"Are you okay?" Chloe repeated after Sheryl had cleaned at the sink.

"I dunno, I felt a bit sick, but didn't think I'd puke. It's weird because that's, like, the fourth time I've thrown up this month. I didn't think anything was wrong because afterward, I usually feel all right."

"Fourth time you puked this month?" Chloe said, eyebrow raised.

"Yeah, why?"

"*Really*, you're asking me why?"

"Yeah, why?" Sheryl repeated, confused.

"Hello? Maybe you're pregnant?"

"What? Me? Pregnant? No way. We barely have sex, and as far as I know, we can't have kids."

"Why do you think that?"

"I told you, like, six years ago we were trying all the time and couldn't get pregnant."

"So, did you two ever go to a doctor or fertility specialist?"

"No, because at the time there was a lot going on with our careers, and it seemed like if it was meant to be, it would happen. If not, no big deal. It's not as if either one of us really has the time for children anyway. We barely have time for us."

"But you said you threw up four times this month, right?"

"Yeah, but that doesn't mean I'm pregnant! Maybe I have a bug."

Chloe looked her up and down, nodding. "You know, I wasn't gonna say anything because seriously, what friend wants to hear that they look like they've been putting on the pounds, but I think you've gained some weight."

"Shut up."

"No, your tits and your belly look a bit … "

"Shut up," Sheryl said, "don't even joke."

"I'm not joking! Have you taken a pregnancy test?"

"No!"

A couple of women entered the restroom. Chloe nodded toward the door so they could continue the conversation in the hallway.

"We need to get you a pregnancy test."

"No, *we* do not."

"Oh, come on, don't you wanna know? Believe me, you don't wanna wait any longer to find out — especially if you plan to do something about it."

"What do you mean *do something about it?*"

"You know, abort? I mean, if you find out that Clarence is putting his gun in that little badge bunny's holster, you aren't going to actually have his kid, are you?"

"I wouldn't have an abortion!" Sheryl said, surprising herself. She'd always considered herself a pro-choice woman, but had never considered what *she'd* do if she had an unwanted pregnancy. She'd never even had a close call. But thinking about it now, she certainly couldn't kill a child growing in her, even if Clarence was screwing the entire Goldman's staff.

"Ah, I get it," Chloe said, "that's smart."

"What's smart?"

"Keep the kid, you get more money in the divorce! Brilliant. I can hook you up with a great lawyer. He'll take Clarence to the cleaners. Well, for as much as he can. Clarence *is* on a cop's salary, after all. Think it would be too late to convince Clarence to take that job with your ex, before you divorce him?"

"Wow, you are just ... just unbelievable," Sheryl said, surprised by the speed and depth of her friend's scheming.

Sheryl was suddenly overwhelmed with emotion and found herself wanting to go home.

Chloe stopped, likely seeing the tears welling in Sheryl's eyes. "Oh my God, I'm sorry, I didn't mean to make you cry."

And just like that, Sheryl collapsed into her friend's arms, crying.

The women who had entered the restroom after them exited, giving Sheryl and Chloe a wide berth as they passed.

Sheryl, feeling embarrassed, pulled away and wiped her tears with the back of her hands, sure she was ruining her mascara.

She went back into the bathroom to fix herself.

"I'll be right back," Chloe said, likely wanting to give Sheryl and her breakdown some privacy.

Sheryl stared in the mirror and wondered if it was possible. Maybe she *was* pregnant. She *was* feeling particularly emotional in addition to the sickness. And her period was late — a couple of weeks, not that she'd ever been all that regular.

After Sheryl finished crying, she reached into her purse, found her phone, and called Clarence.

She wasn't even sure why she was calling. She just wanted to hear her husband's voice and maybe say she was sorry for how she'd been neglecting him these past few months.

More like years!

She was surprised when he answered. "Hey, what's up?"

There was a time he would've added some term of affection. Maybe, *Hey, baby, what's up?*

"I just wanted to say hi."

"Hi."

Sheryl heard guys talking in the background. It sounded like he was out somewhere with other cops, hanging around in some gas station *or maybe the diner*, shooting the shit. She heard a woman, or a few, giggling in the background.

"Hi," she repeated, suddenly flummoxed for words.

"Um, is everything okay?"

"Yeah," she lied.

"Okay ... um, did you need something? I'm kind of in the middle of something."

Hearing the people in the background chatting, laughing, *maybe even laughing at her calling him*, felt like a blade of dejection straight to her heart.

"No, I'll see you later," she said fast, eager to get off the phone, but also wanting to let Clarence know that her feelings had been hurt.

"I'm sorry," he said. "Did you want to talk?"

"No, clearly you don't have time for me. Why don't you just go back to your buddies?"

Sheryl hung up.

She stared in the mirror, furious: at him for being a jerk, herself for calling, and everything in general.

She returned the phone to her purse, wondering when he'd call back. Usually, he did, right away. But not this time. Which only made her angrier.

Screw him!

She didn't want to talk to him anyway. He was being a jerk and didn't even realize it. Sheryl shouldn't have to tell him when he was being an asshole. Or argue with him until he understood what he'd done wrong. They'd had too many little arguments like this. No huge blowout fights, just little shit where she'd get mad, he'd defensively apologize, then they'd go another round until he eventually realized that he'd hurt her feelings. Half the time, Sheryl wondered if Clarence really meant his apologies or if she'd merely browbeaten him into them.

She was glad he wasn't calling back. Frankly, she didn't feel like having an echo of arguments gone by.

Sheryl was about to head out to find Chloe, but her friend entered the restroom holding a small white Walgreen's bag. She handed it to Sheryl.

"Here."

"What is it?" Sheryl reached out for the bag.

"So you'll know."

She opened the bag and saw the pregnancy test.

FORTY-TWO

Clarence Dumont

CLARENCE STARED at the tiny screen, resisting his urge to hurl the phone onto the ground and stomp it into a hundred tiny pieces.

Why did Sheryl always put him on the defensive? No matter what he said or did, he could never win when it came to his wife. And now she was making him feel bad for doing his job?

He was standing just outside the front door of O'Malley's Neighborhood Pub where someone had spotted Nick earlier. Patrick was inside chatting up the bartender, a fortysomething woman named Mona, whom Patrick knew in some way he wasn't saying. Clarence had been hanging back just inside the entrance when Sheryl had called. Nick wasn't there, and Patrick wanted some space to talk to the woman, so Clarence figured he'd answer. He usually tried to call her during lunch, but because of the bullshit with Nick, he'd worked through his break with no chance to call.

Best to pick up so she's not worried, he had thought.

Boy, what a mistake.

I shouldn't have answered. This *is my reward: her thinking I'm hanging out with my friends or some bullshit?*

12

Sometimes, managing Sheryl's mood swings felt like a full-time gig. The last thing he needed was another ball-busting thankless job.

Standing outside, waiting for Patrick, Clarence considered calling her back but then found his balls.

No, fuck that bitch. Let her *apologize for once.*

He hated thinking of his wife as a "bitch." He'd never called her that, not even when grousing about her bullshit to Patrick. Clarence rarely spoke ill of Sheryl to anyone — a bit old-fashioned in that regard. But it was hard not to think such horrible things after she blew up over nothing.

Clarence slid the phone into his pocket and turned as Patrick exited the bar, shaking his head.

"Nothing?"

Patrick shrugged. "He was here earlier with his douche bag roommate, Gary. They were loud and obnoxious — I know, big surprise — and Nick was bitching about his wife. They got into it with the barback, Lex, and the manager yelled at them to get the hell out before he called the cops. That was about an hour ago, and she has no idea where they went when they left."

"Shit," Clarence said. "And I haven't heard a word from Hatcher."

"*Hatcher's* watching the apartment? Hell, he's probably at the Wendy's drive-through, or napping."

Clarence might have laughed if Hatcher napping wasn't a distinct possibility. The man was notoriously lazy, bouncing around from shift to shift and partner to partner rather than losing his job. Several theories suggested that Hatcher had incriminating photos of the chief and a goat or worse, which prevented him from being fired or getting relegated to desk duty at the very least.

Patrick led the way to their squad car. "So, the wife called?"

"Yeah, how'd you know it was her?"

"The way you slunk out of the bar with your tail tucked between your legs, for one. Wanna hear two?"

"Not particularly." Clarence opened the cruiser door. "Maybe you'd like to tell me about Mona instead — you and her a thing or what?"

"Off and on," Patrick said, getting into the driver's side.

"Really? No shit." Clarence sat in the passenger seat and closed his door.

"Hey, I have a social life, too."

"*Too?* You implying I have a social life? I'm married, man. This is about as 'social' as my life gets, me hanging out with you all damned day in a car. I'm just surprised that anyone would want to date your grumpy ass."

"I happen to be a sparkling conversationalist," Patrick said, backing out of the lot.

"*Sparkling?*" Clarence laughed. "Wow, she said that? She must be desperate. So, what's her deal? No friends? A crippling case of Tourette's? Does she have a tail or twelve toes?"

"She's a lovely woman, thank you very much."

"Oh, wait, I got it, she's trying to marry to get into the country. Is that it?"

"Anyone ever tell you you're an annoying son of a bitch?"

"Oddly, you're the only one. Everyone else thinks I'm a *sparkling conversationalist.*"

Patrick shook his head and sighed but was clearly enjoying the banter. While he *was* a surly prick at least six out of every seven days, Patrick was also the best partner Clarence had ever had. He'd been partnered with green cops, lazy cops, crooked cops, racist cops, and, more often than not, overly aggressive cops, so he appreciated a laid-back officer who did his job without engaging in all the negative bullshit that too often came with the position.

Patrick said they'd swing back by the apartment, just to make sure that Hatcher wasn't slacking.

Halfway there he said, "So, you wanna talk about it?"

"About what?"

"That look on your face after you got off the phone."

Clarence shook his head. "Just some bullshit."

"What kinda bullshit?"

"Nothin', man."

"Dude, you can't just keep that shit inside."

"What are you talking about?"

They stopped at a red light. Clarence looked over to Patrick.

"Keeping all that stuff inside will kill you, or your marriage."

Clarence wanted to ask him what gave him, a guy with three divorces, the right to dole out marital advice, but Patrick sensed the objection.

"Trust me, I've burned through enough relationships to know what I'm talking about."

The light turned green, and the car moved ahead. Clarence said, "Wait, are you saying that you, *HotHead McGee*, kept shit inside?"

"Believe it or not, yes, I did."

"No, I refuse to believe it."

"I swear."

"Is this the same Patrick Allan who shot a toaster in the commissary when it wasn't working?"

"Man, shoot a toaster one time, and suddenly you're a maniac!"

"And what about the Wilson case?"

"*That* wasn't my fault."

"You body slammed a guy in a wheelchair!"

"That asshole had it coming!"

"He was in a fucking wheelchair!"

"Look at you, you prejudiced motherfucker. Some of us treat all people equally, able bodied and otherwise. An asshole in a wheelchair is still an asshole."

"Spare me the sanctimony," Clarence laughed. "I'm just

saying I don't picture you as someone who has ever bottled anything, unless you have a secret microbrewery in your garage. You don't exactly come off as someone with *trouble expressing emotions.*"

"Well, I'm different at home."

"What I wouldn't have paid to see that."

"Oh, you like to watch, do you? I always figured you were a kinky mofo."

"Now you're projecting."

"Stop trying to make everything a joke. I'm serious. I had some real issues until I saw a shrink."

"*You* saw a shrink?" Clarence was shocked, even though his partner's anger could definitely benefit from professional treatment.

"I *see* a shrink, actually."

"Wow. I had no idea."

"She said I should express my feelings in a productive way rather than 'letting them gather like a storm cloud.' She said that's the short road to being destructive."

"Well, I'm not destructive."

"No," Patrick said, "but you do keep shit inside."

"Is this a therapy session?"

"No, just a friend offering space to share your thoughts."

"Wow, I don't know if I like this new side of you, Mr. Sensitive McGee. Kinda creeping me out."

"Fine, hide behind jokes, Chuckles, but you won't be laughing when you're signing divorce papers. Ask me how I know."

Clarence was getting pissed, for real now, at his partner's intrusion into his personal space. A total lack of serious conversations was one of the things he liked most about Patrick. When they weren't solving crimes, they talked sports or bullshitted about the job. They never crossed the thin line between their work and personal lives.

"Listen man, I appreciate what you're trying to do. But it's just normal marriage stuff that everyone goes through. We'll be fine."

Patrick looked like he wanted to say more, but he met Clarence's eyes, pursed his lips, and nodded instead. "Cool."

They drove the rest of the way to Nick's apartment in a heavy, uncomfortable silence. All it would take was opening up for Clarence to sweep the clouds from his own sky, but he didn't feel like discussing Sheryl with anyone other than Sheryl. Only he and his wife could fix their marriage.

They pulled up beside Hatcher's unmarked car.

Clarence said, "Hey, man, I know we bust each other's balls all the time, but I appreciate the offer to talk. It's just I should talk to Sheryl first. If we can't work things out, then maybe I'll cry on your shoulder like a bitch."

"Or we can go out and get drunk." Patrick rolled down his window and turned to Hatcher. "So, anything?"

"Nothing." Hatcher shoved a Funyun into his mouth and licked his fingers.

Clarence looked up at the second-story apartment and saw movement behind the blinds.

"Someone's in there," Clarence said. "The blinds just moved. You haven't seen anyone come in or out of the apartment?"

"No."

"And you've been on the place the whole time? No bathroom breaks or anything?"

"Or maybe a break to get Funyuns?" Patrick added.

"Fuck off," Hatcher said, as if Patrick was kidding.

Patrick popped out of the car. "We're going up."

Clarence followed Patrick toward the stairs.

"I'll go 'round back." Hatcher dragged his fat ass out of the cop car and ran toward the building's rear, just in case whoever was inside the apartment decided to pull a Spiderman.

Clarence caught up to Patrick then took position behind him, gun in hand. Patrick knocked on the door.

No answer.

He knocked again.

"Open up! Police!"

Still nothing.

He banged on the door again, loud enough for everyone on the second floor to hear. "Police. Open up. Don't make us come in there."

A beat then the sound of a deadbolt twisting open followed by a chain being slid from its latch.

The door opened to a skinny Italian-looking guy in his early twenties with long dark hair, an immaculately trimmed thin beard, thick eyebrows, and red silk pajamas.

"Hello?" he asked, his voice effeminate.

"Who the hell are you?" Patrick asked.

"Vinnie, I live here."

Looking over Vinnie's shoulder and into the apartment, Patrick said, "Who else is here?"

"Nobody. Just me."

"Mind if we take a look?"

Vinnie appeared nervous, and afraid to refuse. He shook his head then opened the door.

Patrick stepped in.

Clarence waited at the threshold, eyes on the shifty-looking guy.

"So, where are your roommates?"

"I dunno. I just got up."

"Just got up?" Patrick said. "Must be nice."

"I work nights."

"Where?"

"Anton's Square. Bartender."

Anton's was a popular late-night gay bar.

"When's the last time you saw Nick and Gary?"

12

"I dunno. Yesterday, maybe?"

"And they haven't called in or anything?" Patrick asked.

"I'm not their keeper," Vinnie said, too sassy for Patrick's taste.

Patrick turned and got in his face, "Hey, no need to get bitchy."

Vinnie's eyes widened. He'd be a pushover if Patrick decided to roll on him hard. Meekly, he apologized.

"Lemme see your phone."

"What?"

"Let me see your phone. I just wanna make sure you haven't been in contact with them today."

Vinnie looked at Patrick then Clarence. "Do you two have a warrant?"

Clarence, still standing at the front door behind Vinnie said, "No, but God help you if you make us come back with one. Way I see it, we have enough to lock all three of you up on paraphernalia alone. I'm sure if we look around, we can find the drugs to go with it. Maybe enough for possession with intent to distribute? What do you think, Patrick?"

"Ah, easily. So, what's it gonna be, Twinkletoes?"

Clarence rolled his eyes. Did Patrick really need *another* course on discrimination? Clarence hoped Vinnie decided to play ball because Patrick had just given him ammunition for court, maybe get charges dismissed or bring a suit if things turned ugly.

Vinnie looked down. "I'll get my phone."

Patrick followed him to his bedroom.

"Nice room you have here," Patrick said. "You have taste and money — why are you living with these two dirt bags?"

"Gary's an old friend who fell on tough times. And Nick's a friend of Gary's, so I'm kinda stuck with him. What did they do now?"

Vinnie handed Patrick the phone.

Patrick scrolled through the recent calls list then said, "Well, good news is I don't think Gary did anything, yet. But Nick, now Nick is definitely in some hot water. Went to his ex's job and attacked a waitress."

"Oh, God." Judging from Vinnie's expression, he seemed genuinely concerned.

"So, we're looking for Nick," Clarence said. "We just want to talk."

"Hey, what's this?" Patrick held the phone to Vinnie's face.

"What?" Vinnie said, looking scared.

"Says that Gary called you about ten minutes ago."

Vinnie threw his hands up, "I was sleeping. I swear."

Clarence raised his eyebrows. "So, you didn't get the call?"

"No." Vinnie's body language said he was lying.

"Bullshit," Clarence said.

"What? I told you, I was sleeping."

Clarence turned to Patrick. "Let's call this in. I'll hit the judge and get a warrant."

"What are you doing? I gave you my phone and told you the truth!"

Clarence said, "Then tell me why you were peeping out your blinds about the same time as you got this call. A coincidence?"

Vinnie fumbled for words but felt his back to the corner.

They could approach the situation in a couple of ways: Patrick's, which was usually forceful and involved intimidation, or Clarence's, subtle but likely more effective.

Clarence met the man's nervous eyes. "Here's what I think is going on here. Correct me if I'm wrong, okay?"

Vinnie nodded.

"I think your boy, Gary, is probably not a total asshole. Right? But then Nick comes around, and all of a sudden, Gary's acting different, not quite like the guy you know, and bad things start happening. Sound about right?"

Vinnie nodded again.

"Yeah, I've had friends like that. And I tell you, people like Nick, they're cancer to friendships. You let them hang around because you figure what's the worst that can happen? I mean, Gary's a big boy, right? But Gary's also probably *too* good of a guy and doesn't want to turn his back on Nick in his 'time of need,' so he lets him stay here, 'til Nick gets back on his feet, right?"

Vinnie nodded. Three in a row.

"But let me tell you, Vinnie, you don't ignore cancer. You nip it in the bud. You see where I'm going?"

Vinnie stared at them blankly.

Clarence sighed. Clearly, he'd misjudged Vinnie's intelligence.

Patrick stepped in, "My partner's trying to say you should let us cure your cancer. You'd like that, wouldn't you? To get Nick out of your lives?"

Vinnie nodded, finally getting it.

"So," Patrick asked, "he called, you answered. What did he say?"

"And you're not gonna ... " Vinnie looked around the apartment, " ... come back with a warrant or go after Gary?"

Patrick smiled. "We're here to get rid of your cancer, Vinnie. That's it. We're like proctologists:, great at dealing with assholes."

Vinnie looked down then started his story.

Gary had been at a friend's, a guy named Ronald Dempsey, and needed Vinnie to bring him some cash — two-grand — to get Nick out of town for a bit. Could he do it? Gary said to make sure the cops weren't watching, and if they were, to make sure they didn't follow.

Vinnie had promised that he would but looked out the window and saw them in the parking lot before he could hit the bank.

"Thank you for your cooperation," Patrick said. "Now, we're just gonna need one more thing."

"What's that?"

"For you to come with us. It's time the proctologists paid Nick a visit."

4 p.m. - 5 p.m.

FORTY-THREE

Tim Hewitt

TIM DIDN'T GET why his father loved this shit so much.

He sat in bed and downed another swig of Jack Daniel's, still unsure of whether he was feeling what he was supposed to be feeling.

Isn't alcohol supposed to make you happy? Fun to be around?

Not that Tim's father had ever been accused of being happy *or* fun to be around. But other people seemed to enjoy drinking. Dima had talked about sneaking into his mom's liquor supply a couple of times, getting "good and shit faced" like it was a fun place to be. All Tim had besides an awful taste in his mouth and a burning in his throat was a pounding headache and a dizziness that seemed to be getting worse by the second.

He wasn't even sure why he picked up the bottle, other than a final "fuck you" to the old man now lying dead on the couch. Tim's father had been all "my precious" like Gollum with two things: his booze and his guns. The guns had been used against him, why not pilfer his booze?

Tim was oddly unemotional in the moments following his father's shooting.

But as he stared at the clock and knew his mother would be home around 5:15, the situation's gravity weighed heavier on him.

What would she say when she saw what he'd done? Would she be scared? Angry? Would she think him a monster? Or would she understand? Maybe she'd be glad that the true monster was finally dead? He'd abused her for years, physically and emotionally. Tim had killed his father for her as much as he had for himself.

Would she help him cover up the crime?

No, that shit only happened in movies. In real life, people called the police.

Tim thought of all the stories he'd seen in the news about kids who shot their abusive parents. Sure, some got off or were handed a light sentence, but most went to jail or were locked in an asylum for a long time.

He'd imagined killing his father plenty, but Tim never thought he could do it. But as detailed as those fantasies had been — he had more than once imagined skinning his father alive — he'd always figured the easiest part would be convincing the cops that his dad deserved to die. Somehow, they'd see what a monster he'd been, and that would be enough to set Tim free.

But now he realized that it wouldn't be the cops he'd have to convince. Murder wasn't a traffic ticket that could be ripped up. "You're right, kid. Your dad was a dick. Here, go home, and forget about it. Hey, how about I give you an honorary deputy's badge for a job well done?"

In reality, he'd have to convince a judge for a pretrial — then in all likelihood, a grand jury after that.

What if they try me as an adult? I could get the death penalty!

That was something else he'd never considered, but kids *were* charged as adults, particularly for violent crimes. And this was definitely that.

He took another drink of the fire water and swallowed, trying not to gag.

Still not helping.

He considered going into the living room and calling the police to turn himself in, before his mother came home. He didn't want to put her on the spot or force her to report the crime. It would break her heart, and she'd been through enough already.

He drank more as he imagined the call. Should he cry and act like it just happened? Perhaps that would play well for the jury? Then again, if he fake cried, maybe some voice analyst would be called in to testify revealing Tim's artificial regret.

But I was afraid!
But was I afraid at that moment?
Did I feel like if I didn't shoot him, my life was in danger?

Tim wasn't sure.

And the weird part was the more he drank, the less Tim felt like trying to convince the police, a jury, or even his mother *why* he'd done it. All the *Whys* in the world wouldn't put breath back into the corpse.

Tim's life was over.

Sure, he might get out of jail or a facility of some sort in a few years, but he killed his fucking father. Who would ever hire him? Or love him? He'd never get a chance to live a normal life.

Tim broke down and cried.

He'd hated his father so long, was furious at him for destroying his life that he just wanted to finally end the oppressiveness of being the monster's son. But now, in the ultimate of ironies, Tim had sealed his fate forever.

He'd killed his father, along with any hope for a normal life.

He took another drink, wishing he could go back in time and do everything differently.

Hell, even one thing *done differently today might have resulted in something other than this.*

Tim considered his day and all the many moments that made it and all of his choices. Every thought seemed to circle back to Dima and Jeff.

Dima had stolen his chance at love.

Jeff had stolen his dignity.

Tim wondered what they'd think when they heard that he'd killed his father. He imagined them hanging out together, laughing.

"I told you he was a fucking loser!" Jeff would say.

Would Dima stand up for him and say that Tim's father deserved it? That Tim had snapped, and that they ought to feel bad for him? Or would he laugh along with Jeff, not wanting to rock the boat and risk capsizing status with his cool new friends?

And what about Alicia? He couldn't imagine her taking any pleasure out of this. Even if she only thought of Tim as a friend, that didn't mean she hated him or wanted to see him in jail. She'd probably feel sorry for him, just like his mother.

Tim took another drink, thought of people feeling sorry for him, and felt his anger swelling.

He didn't want people to feel bad for him or to be the butt of a joke ever again. He wanted respect!

He flashed back to Jeff shoving his head into the wall in the dark bathroom, threatening to kill him. It wasn't enough for Jeff to beat him up — he had to prove he was tough, and that Tim was his bitch.

Who's a pussy now, bitch?

Tim smiled at the thought of pulling a gun on Jeff, of seeing his eyes widen with the kind of terror he thrived on.

See how big and brave he was with a fucking gun in his face.

But bullies like Jeff never got what was coming. They skated through life with friends, good jobs, and lots of sex. Then they got married and treated their families like crap.

Maybe terrorized them for shits and giggles or to feel like a man.

Someone oughta stop him before he breeds and ruins someone else's life.

Tim imagined Jeff having a child and that child growing up under Jeff's thumb, desperately wishing for his pain to end. Maybe even considering shooting Jeff. Then he or she would go to jail.

Tim looked at the clock again. There was a good chance that Jeff and Dima were working at the diner, probably laughing about all of Tim's trouble.

Tim wished he could head on over there, put a gun in Jeff's face and watch him piss himself like a scared little bitch.

Tim laughed, imagining the headlines: "Local Kid Snaps and Kills Father, Kills Local Asshole."

Ha! I bet they'd even put "Local Asshole" in the paper, too. I mean, he is an asshole, right? And don't they usually identify people by their job title or notable feature? Well, they're not gonna put "local busboy" or whatever the hell he does at the diner. They'd put asshole. They wouldn't even need to use his name in the article — everyone would know who it was.

Tim took another drink, his headache fading with a warmer buzz.

Why couldn't Dad have been a pill addict instead? At least then I'd feel good for sure.

Tim looked down at the bottle of Jack and decided he'd had enough. He got up from his bed, feeling a heaviness in his head from standing too quickly, then waited a moment before heading into the kitchen.

Tim felt famished.

He ignored his father's body, passing it on his way into the kitchen.

He opened the fridge and found a cake his father had bought for no special occasion. The man just liked cake, particularly the cakes from Shoreside Bakery, a small but popular bakery that put their overpriced cakes (and cupcakes) in thick, pink almost plastic-feeling boxes that probably cost a few bucks each. His father bought cake there every week, it seemed, but Tim had only tasted their sweets a few times, on special occasions.

Tim normally wasn't allowed any sugar, save for fruits, even though he was practically anorexic compared to every other boy his age. Tim's father had determined that Tim, and nobody else in the house, needed to "watch his diet" and eat healthy.

Fat fucking hypocrite.

Tim pulled out the cake, slammed the refrigerator door, dropped the box on the counter, then opened the lid and smiled.

The cake was brand new, not yet cut into, with a creamy chocolate frosting. Tim went to the cupboard and grabbed a plate. Halfway to the drawer for a fork, Tim thought, *Fuck forks,* then reached down and grabbed a squishy handful and shoved the cold cake into his mouth like a pig.

It was great fucking cake.

Tim smiled then brought the box into the living room, staring at the corpse on his way to the couch.

His father's eyes were wide open, staring straight at Tim.

Blood had soaked the leather couch and dripped down into the carpet. The man's pants were soaked with urine and shit.

Boy, would he be pissed at this mess!

Tim sat on the coffee table a foot from the corpse and studied the man who'd fed on Tim's fears for so long, ruling his roost with an iron fist.

"Not so tough now, are ya?" Tim shoved another piece of cake into his mouth. "By the way, thanks for the cake! I'd let you have some, but you've really been letting yourself go. I mean, look at you. Fat gut, fat legs, fat arms. And Jesus, you ate so much you shit your pants. Tsk, tsk. Maybe we should send you to military school, get your fat ass in shape, eh? What do you think about that?"

Tim giggled, shoving more cake into his mouth. Part of him felt wrong for laughing at the horror around him, but that only made it funnier, and harder to throttle the laughs.

"What? You want some cake? Does the little piggy want some cake? Here!"

Tim grabbed a thick wad of cake and threw it at his father's face.

"Is it good? What? I can't hear you!"

He threw more cake at his father, his laughter nearing hysteria.

He wanted to grab his father's cell phone and take a photo, send it to Dima. "Hey, me and Dad are having cake, wanna come over? Maybe we can play pin the tail on the dead man."

Tim burst into heaving laughter.

Or maybe he could send the photo to Jeff. "Hey, Jeff, remember how you said you were gonna kill me? Well, guess what, *faggot*, I'm gonna keeeeel *you*."

He laughed at the thought of calling Jeff a faggot since the guy was such a fucking homophobe. If Tim ever got the chance to get him alone with a gun, he'd make him suck on it first.

Suck it really good. Yeah, who's a faggot now, faggot?

Tim looked at the clock again and thought about Dima and his new buddy, Jeff, yucking it up at the diner.

Fucking traitor.

Tim stared at the cake then up at his father's cake-covered corpse.

The laughter died.

Shit. How am I going to explain that? It was one thing to kill him, but this? To throw cake at his body? There's no way anyone's gonna feel sympathy for me now.

12

"Fuccccck!!" Tim screamed, hurling his cake across the room.

Again, he thought of his mother coming home. She'd look at her husband then at Tim. She'd cry for certain.

She'd think her son had lost his mind.

Maybe I have!

She might even be scared; the thought of his mother being scared of him was too much for Tim to bear.

He started to sob. Rocking back and forth, weeping.

"What have I done? What the *fuuuuuck* have I done?"

After a few minutes, his crying went dry.

Tim was no longer sad.

No longer angry.

No longer afraid.

He felt, and was, nothing, as if someone had smothered his emotions with a blanket. He felt oddly separate from his surroundings, not quite out of body, but not exactly removed.

He felt almost mechanical, knowing he should feel something, *do something*.

But Tim just sat there, feeling and doing nothing.

After what felt like forever, he finally stood, disrobed in the living room, and let his clothes fall to the ground.

Then he went to the shower to wash the cake from his body.

He stared at the chocolate chunks swirling around the drain, bubbling up and down before surrendering to the darkness below.

Still, he felt nothing.

Tim turned the water hotter, as hot as it would go.

Even scalding, he still felt nothing.

Tim left the shower and went to his bedroom. He passed the mirror and caught his reflection. For a moment, he thought there was someone else in the room.

He got dressed then went into his father's study, back to the gun cabinet.

He found a pistol and matching ammo then loaded the gun.

He slipped on a jacket, found some cash in his parents' bedroom, put it in his wallet, then slipped the gun and ammo into his jacket pocket and left the house forever.

It was about twenty blocks to Goldman's Diner.

FORTY-FOUR

Joe Harcourt

JOE FELT like the world's weight was in his jacket pocket as he sat for dinner at Goldman's. In a sense, it was. Not just his world, but maybe Maggie's as well.

Knowing he shouldn't, and probably couldn't, reveal everything to Maggie in person while she was finishing her shift, Joe decided to write everything down in a letter. His scrawled pages had many benefits, chief among them, he'd be spared her possible anger. But also he'd been able to clarify his thoughts and tell her everything he thought she might want to know without the pressure of a face-to-face.

His confession had been hardest to write. It was his fault that Maggie never knew her birth parents because he'd refused to raise another man's child after discovering Grace's infidelity. *He'd* forced her to make a decision: *the child or him.*

She chose him.

Joe always wondered if Grace had regretted her decision. Not in choosing him, but in giving her child away. There were times over the years when they'd be sitting quietly together, and she'd be staring off into space, and he couldn't help but wonder if she was thinking of her child and the life as a mother he'd forced her to surrender. He could never summon the courage to ask. He didn't want to surface the affair, or remind her of his cruelty.

Even on her deathbed, he didn't dare ask, afraid that her dying regret would be the one thing he made her do. Joe wondered if Grace had died hating him just a little.

Maggie might very well hate him after reading his letter.

He was okay with that, so long as she knew that it wasn't Grace's fault, or even her decision, to give Maggie up for adoption. That her mother had loved her very much and had fought to keep her. Joe had been obstinate, and cruel. But Grace had loved the child growing inside her.

Joe figured it was the sort of thing an adopted child ought to know, no matter how bad he looked.

A downside to giving Maggie the letter was that he wouldn't know how she took the news until he saw her again. That would be an uncomfortable moment, enough to consider never returning to Goldman's. Why put her on the spot?

Joe left his number at the bottom of the letter, in case she had questions, promising himself that he'd never see her again without her initiation.

That thought killed something inside him. No, Maggie wasn't his daughter, but she was all he had left of Grace: a single connection to the only woman he ever loved.

Maggie approached the table. "So, you're back for the baked spaghetti, eh?"

"You know it," he said, afraid that his voice would betray his emotions. His hands shook so badly he had to bury them under the table.

"Great. And what would you like to drink?"

"A large glass of milk, please."

"Okay," Maggie said and slipped away.

The diner was far busier than the usual weeknight, though not yet a full house. Maybe it was good that Maggie wouldn't have much time for small talk, especially if Joe couldn't calm his racing heart.

12

A commercial piped through the diner's speakers, reminding him of the song Grace used to sing to him.

Is that it?

The commercial ended before he'd had a chance to figure out if that was the song, let alone its name.

Maggie returned with his milk. "Spaghetti should be here soon. Would you like some hot rolls and butter before you eat, or with the spaghetti?"

"Now would be good," he said, if only to bring Maggie back to his table.

She returned with the basket of rolls and a few pats of foil-wrapped butter. Joe said, "I watched your music videos earlier."

"Oh, you did?" Maggie smiled. "And?"

"I loved them. You have a beautiful voice."

"Aw, thank you." Maggie blushed and turned shyly away.

"You should be on the radio."

"Fingers crossed. Though I might've blown my one shot."

"What do you mean?"

"Remember earlier I said an agent had emailed me? Well, I was supposed to be on a call with her at noon, but then my ex, Nick, came in, and things got ugly."

"What happened?"

"Oh, it's too much to go into now. Let's just say he hurt one of our waitresses, Barbara, and now the police are looking for him."

"Oh, my God. Is she okay? Are *you?*"

"A bit shaken up, but otherwise yeah, I'm fine. I missed the call with the agent, and I'm kind of afraid to call her back now with an excuse."

"I'm sure she'll understand."

"Yeah, but I'm not sure it won't give the wrong impression. Who wants to sign a singer with a nut job stalker of an ex? YouTube has a ton of talented singers without the baggage."

"None as talented as you."

She laughed. "Okay, now you're just lying."

"No, I'm not. You remind me a lot of my wife, Grace."

"She sang? You never told me that."

"Well, until this morning you never told me that *you* sang."

"Fair enough," Maggie said, still smiling.

"She was far too shy to sing in front of anyone but me, but God, she had the voice of an angel. So do you."

"Aw, that's so sweet! Hold on, I'll be back in a few." Maggie left to check on a couple of women who'd just been seated.

Joe stared at the women. One looked familiar, a pretty black woman in her thirties, with shoulder length curly hair.

Where have I seen her before?

Joe thought she might have been on the news. She looked pretty, and her makeup and hair were done well enough for TV, but he didn't think that was it. He stared, hard enough to hopefully jar his memory.

Joe hoped she wasn't a neighbor. He ran into people who said hi to him all the time whose faces looked familiar, but he was unable to place them. He wasn't sure if it was his condition or if he just had a bad memory for faces. But he felt certain he knew this woman. Almost felt like he should get up and go say hi. But if he did, and couldn't remember her name, he'd feel like a fool.

At one point, her blonde friend, equally attractive, but with a lot more jewelry and makeup, caught Joe looking. He quickly turned before she thought he was a dirty old man.

He reached into the bread basket, grabbed a warm roll, spread some butter on it, and took a bite. He could eat a meal of rolls and butter alone, though he didn't dare eat more than one while still slightly full from his heavy breakfast.

Have to save room for the baked spaghetti, especially since this might be the last time I have it.

The finality of lost time felt like an anchor on Joe's heart, tearing through his guts and ripping him apart from the inside. To think that everything he'd ever thought, said, did, and been would soon be nothing — not even a memory — frosted him in an icy depression.

Times like this, Joe wished he had a faith to lean on.

Yeah, a lot of good faith did Grace.

Joe tried not to feel bitter about God taking one of the kindest people he'd ever known, but it was difficult. There were times he wondered if there were a God then what would that mean for Grace? Aside from her affair, he doubted she'd committed any serious sins. And the affair had been his fault, as much if not more than hers. Surely, God would forgive her, and she was secured a place in Heaven. At least he liked to believe that.

But if she were in Heaven and there were an afterlife, they'd still never meet again. Joe considered himself a decent man, but that didn't buy you a ticket, at least according to his understanding of the *Bible*. He wasn't sure which was worse — that there was no Heaven or afterlife and this was it, or that there was, and he was wrong, and Grace was somewhere praying to see him again with no chance that she could.

Maybe I'll convert when I lose my mind and forget my lingering doubts about God. I wonder if that would count?

Joe was considering another roll when he heard a tiny voice behind him.

"Hello, Mr. Joe."

He turned and saw Maggie's daughter, McKenna, beaming up at him with her adorable cheeks and contagious smile.

"Hey, honey, what are you doing here?"

"My mom had our neighbor, Mr. Abe, pick me up from school and bring me here because her car broke down."

"Oh," he said. "Wow, you've really grown since the last time I saw you."

"I know," she said matter-of-factly and pulled out the chair opposite Joe and sat down.

He laughed at her boldness, or lack of understanding that you didn't sit yourself down at someone else's table. Kids were so adorably naive. At least they seemed that way from the few he'd been around. He looked at McKenna's smiling face, wishing again that he and Grace had started a family. Even if they hadn't kept Maggie, they could've — should've — tried harder, seen a fertility specialist, something other than giving up.

"What are you having for dinner, Mr. Joe?"

"Baked spaghetti. And you, young lady?"

"I dunno. I had some fries before, but I'm not sure if that was dinner. I like baked *pasketti*."

"Me too," he said, smiling.

Maggie appeared a moment later, "I'm sorry, is she bugging you?"

"Oh, not at all. I enjoy her company."

Maggie said, "You should go back to your table and color."

"But he said he enjoys my company," McKenna said. "And I'm bored of sitting by myself."

"It's okay. Really, I *could* use the company. I eat enough meals alone, so this is a nice change of pace."

"Can I sit with Mr. Joe?" McKenna asked, folding her hands together. "Pleeeease, Mommy?"

"Wow, she's good," Joe said.

"Tell me about it." Maggie turned to McKenna. "Okay, but go get your coloring stuff and your drink and bring it over here so someone else can have your table."

"Okay!" McKenna hopped out of her chair and ran back to her table.

"Thank you," Maggie said. "Just let me know if she bothers you."

12

"Not a bother at all," Joe said, pleased to spend time with the granddaughter he might have had.

McKenna came back carrying a bunch of coloring books and a pink plastic box full of crayons. She dropped them on the table and sat back down across from him.

"Whatchya got there?" he asked.

"I've got two *Frozens*, I've got a *Doc McStuffins*, and I've got a *Despicable Me* coloring book."

"Wow," Joe said, not familiar with any of her books.

She opened one of the two *Frozen* coloring books and showed him her already colored pages.

"Good job," he said.

"Want me to color something for you?"

"Sure."

"Okay, what would you like me to color?" she asked, holding up each book again.

"How about the one with those little yellow things on the cover. Are those Twinkies?"

"No, those are minions." McKenna giggled.

"OK, that's what I'd like. Minions."

"Okay." McKenna opened her book, searching for just the right page to color. He wasn't sure what her criteria was, but it was adorable to see her carefully consider each page. She finally found one she liked, opened her little pink box, grabbed a yellow crayon, and started to color.

The page was filling with yellow when Maggie returned with Joe's baked spaghetti. He inhaled the hot steam, savoring the scent of tomato sauce and cheeses cooked into the pasta.

"Here ya go," Maggie said.

"Thank you."

"Are you coloring something for Mr. Joe?"

"Uh-huh. He chose *Despicable Me*."

"Ah," Maggie said. "Big fan?"

"Never seen it," he said. "You?"

"I've seen them both, roughly a hundred times each. The minions are cute. Can I get you anything else?"

"Nope, I'm good."

Maggie left, and Joe dug into his pasta. McKenna was going to town in her coloring book.

In the space between them, Joe realized how little he and a six-year-old had in common. He stared at his plate, feeling awkward, searching for something to say.

"So, how was school today?"

"It was *OK*." The way she said it, with a slight purse to her lips, suggested that it had been anything but.

Joe considered probing but then thought maybe it wasn't okay because of whatever had been happening between her parents. He didn't want to bring up something that might make her feel bad.

"So, are those coloring books all from movies?"

"Not Doc McStuffins, she's a TV show."

"And did you see all these movies and TV shows?"

"Yup."

"Which do you like the most?"

"*Frozen.*"

"Ah." He took a bite of pasta, thinking of the next thing to say.

"How's your *pasketti?*" McKenna looked up from her coloring.

"It's good. Have you had it?"

"No."

"You should ask your mom to try it. It's really good. What sorts of foods do you like?"

"Um ... pasketti, salad, burgers, cucumbers, salad, macaroni and cheese, grapes, oranges, mangos, pizza, cookies, cake, ice cream, um ... tacos, I dunno, a bunch of stuff. What about you?"

"I like a lot of stuff, too. My favorite is probably a nice steak, baked potatoes, and diced carrots with butter."

"I do *not* like carrots." McKenna made a disgusted face and stuck out her tongue. "They're yucky."

Joe laughed. "Have you even tried them?"

"Yes, and I *don't* like them."

"Fair enough. What about your mother, what does she like?"

"Hmm, I dunno. The same stuff, I guess. Except that she *does* like carrots."

"What sorts of things does she like to do? When she's not working? What do you two do together?"

"Um ... we go to the park, we go to some of my friends' houses and play, and sometimes we go to the movies, but not so much since my dad left. A lot of times, she's too tired to do anything, so we'll just sit at home and we'll watch TV or play with my toys."

"Does she sing to you?"

"Yeah, how did you know?"

"Well, she told me she sings, so I figured she probably sang to you. How about you? Do you sing?"

"Yeah, do you want to hear?"

Joe smiled at her eagerness to perform.

"I'd love to."

"Any requests?"

To see her taking requests like a seasoned lounge singer made him laugh, though he was careful not to laugh too much; he didn't want her to think he was laughing at her.

"Hmm, I don't know if we'd know the same songs. Why don't you sing me your favorite."

"Okay," she said and started to sing. At first, she sang softly, but then, once she really got into it, McKenna was singing loud enough to draw looks from the diners — including the familiar-looking woman's friend. The black woman was gone from the booth.

Maggie, who had been at another table, rushed over, mortified, "What are you doing, McKenna?"

"Mr. Joe asked me to sing my favorite song, so I was singing *Let it Go*."

"OK, well you can't sing that loud in here. You'll get me in trouble."

Loretta, the diner's owner, came over with a big smile, "It's okay, Maggie. I happen to think Goldman's could use some live music." She turned to the rest of the diner, "Doesn't everyone agree that McKenna did a lovely job on her song?"

The diners broke into applause. McKenna looked down, her face flushed red behind a giant smile.

Maggie laughed then made a lowering motion with her hands, "Okay, okay, thank you all. You're too kind."

Maggie returned to her service while Loretta stood next to Joe's table. "Hey, kid, we should get you a hat, and you could clean up on tips!"

McKenna smiled.

Loretta asked, "So, Joe, I see you're back for the baked spaghetti."

"You know it. You really should add this to your menu."

"But then it won't be special," Loretta said.

"Yeah, well I'm not getting any younger, Loretta. Not sure how many *special* days I have left in my calendar."

"Oh, Joe, don't be so morbid. You're not that damned old. Hell, half the morning regulars have you beat by two decades!"

Joe considered telling her that he wasn't kidding, and that he wasn't sure how long he had left before he stopped remembering his own name. Not that it mattered. It wasn't like he was coming back to the diner — unless things went a lot better with Maggie than he had any right to hope.

"What's *morbid*?" McKenna asked.

"Don't you worry about it, Little Miss *Thang*," Loretta said, tousling the girl's hair. "It's just old people talk."

"You're not old," McKenna said to Loretta.

12

"Aw, bless your little heart! Hey, Dima, get this girl a cookie."

Loretta's son, Dima, came over with a couple of chocolate chip cookies on a plate and handed them to his mother. It seemed like the boy had grown at least two inches since the last time Joe had seen him at the diner. His hair had also grown: long, dark, and hanging over his eyes in what Joe figured was the trend among high school kids.

"You hear what she said?" Loretta looked at her son. "She said I'm not old."

"Aw, I didn't know McKenna was losing her sight," Dima said, laughing.

"Hey, McKenna, maybe you can give my son some lessons on how to be polite?"

McKenna looked up at Dima then eyed him up and down, nodding. "Yeah, I think I can work with him."

They all laughed.

"All right, honey, I need to get back to work. I'm gonna leave these cookies right here on this little plate. One is for you, and one is for Joe, but only if he finishes all of his baked spaghetti, okay?"

"Okay. And thank you, Mrs. Loretta!" McKenna smiled and grabbed one of the cookies.

Loretta and Dima left the table.

Joe stared at McKenna, delighting in her happy demeanor. "What about me? Am I old?"

"Yes, *very*," she said matter-of-factly.

Joe pretended to clutch at a knife in his heart. "Oh, ouch."

"What?" She giggled. "You *are* old."

"It's okay. You're right."

As if realizing he might have taken offense to her words she said, "It just means you know lots of stuff."

Joe nodded.

"I mean, *looooots* of stuff." McKenna rolled her eyes.

"I used to," he said.

"What do you mean *used to?*"

"Well, when you get *really* old, like me, you start to forget stuff."

"Really?" Her eyes were wide, as if hearing a secret.

He laughed again at her animated expressions. "Yes, really."

"What kinds of stuff do you forget?"

Joe wished he hadn't stumbled into the subject, not wanting to unload his burdens on a child.

"Just stuff," he said, trying to switch topics.

Before he could redirect, she continued, "Like what kinds of stuff? Do you forget your name?"

"Some people do, yeah. I haven't forgotten my name, though."

"Do you forget your mommy and daddy?"

"Some people might, yeah."

"And do you forget your children?"

"Um … I don't know. I don't have any kids. I would hope not."

McKenna's eyes welled with tears. Her face turned red.

"What is it?"

"I don't want my mommy to get old and forget me."

"Oh, honey, you don't have to worry about that. Your mom is very young."

"No, she's not. She's older than me!"

"Yeah, but I'm talking *really* old people. And when she's that old, well, you'll be old, too."

McKenna burst into fresh tears and fled from the table. "I don't wanna get old and die."

Joe got up to follow her, feeling as though everyone in the diner was watching him, probably wondering what on earth he'd said to upset the sweet little girl who had been so happy and singing just minutes ago.

McKenna ran straight into Maggie and hugged her waist. If it hadn't been for Dima, Maggie would've dropped the tray of drinks she was taking to a booth. Dima grabbed the tray before disaster struck. "Which table?" he asked.

She told him then he took the drinks so she could comfort her daughter.

Maggie looked down at McKenna. "What's wrong, sweetie?"

"I don't want you to get old and forget me. And I don't wanna get old and die."

"What?" Maggie looked up at Joe confused.

"I'm sorry, we were talking, and I said something about people forgetting stuff when they get old, and all of a sudden she got really upset."

"It's okay," she said to Joe.

Maggie hugged McKenna and started talking to her in a calming voice. Joe felt like an interloper standing there, so he headed back to his table, feeling like everyone was watching him.

He sat down and stared at his food, his appetite gone, feeling awful for upsetting McKenna so much. Maybe it was good that he didn't have kids if he was this terrible at reading them or knowing what not to say.

He looked up and saw Maggie leading McKenna to the diner's rear for a private discussion.

He felt the letter in his jacket, the letter that might break Maggie's heart in much the same way. Maybe he was better off saying nothing, taking the secret to his grave without destroying her life.

After a few minutes, Maggie returned and collected McKenna's coloring books and crayons. "I'm so sorry. She's overtired and had a rough day at school. She's going to sit in the back and calm down."

"No, don't apologize to me," Joe said. "I'm so sorry I upset her."

Watching Maggie take the girl's coloring book and crayons, Joe felt like either he, or the girl, was being punished, and she wouldn't return. He hated to think that his last interaction with the girl that could have been his granddaughter in a life gone by would be upsetting her so.

"She'll be fine. She just needs some time to calm down. Do you need anything else?"

Joe looked at his glass of milk, half empty but no longer ice-cold like he liked it. "I'll take a Diet Coke. Wait, no, make it a regular Coke."

"Okay," Maggie said then left to get his drink.

Joe stared at his plate. The spaghetti was likely still warm enough to be good, but his heart raced with the ticking clock. If he didn't work up the courage to give her the letter soon, he wasn't sure he ever could.

Joe pulled the envelope out of his pocket and set it on the table. In his scrawled hand it read: *Maggie Kent.*

FORTY-FIVE

Sheryl Dumont

SHERYL TOOK her seat in Maggie's booth. "I can't believe you dragged me here."

Chloe had asked the hostess if Megan — a name she pulled out of thin air — was working when they arrived. The hostess said no, Goldman's didn't have a Megan. Chloe looked around and said, "I'm trying to remember who it was that gave us such great service last time we were here. I thought her name was Megan. Maybe it was, umm ... Mmm—?"

"We have a Maggie," the hostess offered.

"That's her! Maggie! Is she working?"

Chloe winked at Sheryl: *that's how it's done, Sister.*

"Yes." The hostess smiled then grabbed a pair of long, laminated menus and led them through a diner that looked at least two decades behind the times. The location was good, but Sheryl couldn't imagine selling this place to anyone without a massive renovation. She'd be far better off selling the space itself.

Taking their seats, Sheryl was certain that the hostess had figured out that she and Chloe were full of shit. In a minute she'd say something to Maggie, tip her off about the two suspicious women asking for her.

When Maggie approached their table, pad in hand and a warm — but surely artificial — greeting, Sheryl couldn't help but look away, as if the waitress could see right through her.

"I'll have a Sprite," Chloe said.

"And you?" Maggie turned to Sheryl.

She looked up to see Maggie smiling her phony smile.

"Do you have sweet tea?"

"Yes, we do."

"I'll have that, no lemon."

"Okay." she smiled. "I'll be right back."

Sheryl watched Maggie walk away, disgust bubbling in her stomach. She was young and pretty, with perky tits and a nice ass, for a white girl. She also had long brown hair and blue eyes. Clarence had a thing for white girls back in the day, blue-eyed ones in particular. Sheryl was the first black girl he'd dated, which he didn't confess until two years into their marriage. Given his obsession with her father somehow being a self-hating black man who wanted his daughter to "marry white," maybe Clarence was projecting.

"Well?" Chloe said.

"I hate her."

Chloe laughed. "Wow, and here I was thinking I'd have to talk you into hating her, that you'd be all soft and thinking, *Oh, no, she isn't a badge bunny.* But wow, you've out *Chloed* me."

"Well, I'm still not convinced she's screwing Clarence, but I can't stand that perky little smile. You know who smiles like that? Bitches."

"Bitches who steal your man," Chloe added.

Maggie returned with their drinks; Sheryl felt a surprising revulsion.

She took a sip of tea then handed it back. "This is too sweet."

"I'm sorry," Maggie said. "Do you want me to bring you an unsweetened tea and you can add your own sweetener?

We've got sugar, we've got the pink packets, the yellow, and the blue ones."

"No, I don't want *unsweetened* tea, I want sweet tea, just not *that sweet.*"

"I'm sorry." Maggie gave her another fake smile then left with her tea.

Chloe looked at Sheryl. "Oh, me-ow, girl."

Sheryl laughed but felt a pang of guilt for being so petty to a girl she didn't know, who could very well be perfectly innocent. Still, that feeling was outweighed by the sensation that this little bitch was playing her for a fool, making moves on her husband as if Sheryl was clueless enough to let some badge bunny move in on what belonged to her. She imagined Clarence sitting at a booth with a big dumb grin while Little Miss Maggie shook her ass, batted her lashes, and flashed him that big perky smile.

Bitch!

Chloe laughed at Sheryl, "Wow, you look pissed."

"Well, it's your fault. You're the one who convinced me to come here, so deal with it."

Chloe raised her hands. "Okay, okay."

Maggie returned, tea in hand. "Here ya go, ma'am. They made a fresh batch. Let me know if this works for you."

Oh no, she did not just ma'am me!

Sheryl took a sip. Now it wasn't sweet enough, but she wouldn't admit it. She could add sweetener. Sheryl didn't want to give the waitress a reason to suspect her intentions. She'd wait until Maggie left to add sweetener.

"Have you all decided what you'd like?"

"No, we'd like a few more minutes, please," Sheryl said coldly.

"Okay, I'll be back."

Sheryl was looking at her menu rather than the waitress but assumed Maggie was still giving them her phony smile.

She skimmed the menu, disgusted by the offerings. Fried this, fried that, everything loaded with carbs, fat, or calories.

"I can't believe Clarence eats this crap. No wonder he's gained twenty pounds in two years."

Chloe laughed. "It looks good on him."

"Oh, so now *you're* eyeballing my man?" Sheryl joked.

"Sorry, he's too young and not in my income bracket," Chloe joked.

If anyone else had said that, Sheryl might've slapped them. But she knew Chloe was playing into her reputation as a gold digger. Chloe happened to be one of the few people in Sheryl's life who hadn't wondered why she was marrying a cop a decade ago. While she did acknowledge that Lloyd had been a damned good catch, too good to throw away, Clarence was a decent, loyal, man, the kind you could start a family with.

Not that that was going to happen.

Sheryl thought of the pregnancy test in her purse, and her promise to Chloe that she'd take the test in the diner's restroom. Maybe she'd do it after they ordered, but Sheryl wasn't ready yet.

Chloe was suddenly full of giggles.

"What?" Sheryl asked, still pissed.

"That old man, I think he's checking us out."

Sheryl looked over, but the old man quickly looked down at his plate. Yeah, he'd been busted, though he didn't seem like a creeper.

"Come on, he's someone's grandpa," Sheryl said.

"So, he's still a man. You think grandpas don't get boners?"

"Ew, I am *not* having this conversation. Maybe he recognizes me from the fliers or signs on the bus shelters? Or maybe he recognizes you from the Golddigger's Club?" Sheryl gave Chloe a snarky smile then grabbed her purse.

May as well get this over with.

12

"I'll be back. If the badge bunny returns, get me a salad."

"Should I give her a hard time, too?"

Sheryl smiled then made her way to the restroom, went into the stall. She unwrapped the test and held the stick carefully, so she'd get urine on *it* rather than her hands. But Sheryl couldn't go.

Dammit. Come on.

Her nerves were working against her. Outside the restroom she heard applause.

Why are people applauding? Did Maggie fall on her ass?

As much as that idea made her smile, Sheryl figured it was probably someone's birthday. Or maybe someone had proposed.

Pity the woman whose man would propose here. Now that's a marriage that won't last!

Finally, Sheryl managed to pee on the stick.

Now came the waiting.

She sat in the stall, staring at the test's tiny window, wondering if she'd see two lines for pregnant or one for not. In three to five minutes, she'd know.

Sheryl heard two other people enter the restroom. Given that there was only one other stall, waiting for her results while sitting on an unused toilet would inconvenience someone else. The last thing she needed was someone stalking outside, waiting for her to leave the stall.

She stood, slipped the test kit into the plastic wrap, and then the box. She shoved both, along with the instructions, back into her purse, exited the stall, washed her hands, and left the restroom behind her.

Maggie was at the table, talking to Chloe.

Oh, God, Chloe better not have said anything!

Chloe was the sort of person who would be direct, especially when acting on behalf of a friend. She wouldn't think twice before asking, "So, are you a badge bunny?"

Sheryl sat. They were talking about what came on a

Reuben, and neither woman looked like hell had broken loose. Things were likely cool — for now.

"Okay, I'll have that," Chloe said.

Maggie turned to Sheryl, "And you, ma'am?"

Again with fucking ma'am? Fuck you very much, bitch.

Sheryl smiled back, equally phony.

Fuck the salad.

"I'll have a burger, medium, with Swiss Cheese, nothing else. No lettuce, no tomato, no mayo or ketchup, nothing. You got that?"

"Yes," Maggie said, her smile cracking.

Good, I'm getting under her skin.

"And what would you like as your side?"

Sheryl looked down at the menu, taking her sweet time, feeling Maggie's impatience, even if the girl buried it relatively well.

"I'll have fries."

"Okay, ladies," Maggie said, taking their menus and leaving.

Chloe looked at Sheryl. "What happened to your salad?"

"When in Rome."

"So ... what are the results?"

"Of what?" Sheryl played dumb.

"You know!"

"I don't know. I don't want to look yet."

"Oh, come on, the suspense is killing me."

"What was all the applause about?"

"The little girl, over there with Bad Grandpa, was singing that damned *Frozen* song. I'm so glad I don't have girls! Now let me see the test!"

"No! You'll have to wait."

"You're such a tease."

Sheryl smiled, enjoying Chloe's frustration. She *hated* not knowing something, and this was eating her alive. It was delicious to watch.

12

Suddenly, the little girl at the other table started crying.

Sheryl looked up to see the old man trying to console her. But she got up and ran — right over to Maggie.

Oh shit, that's her daughter?

Maggie handed her tray to another waiter then bent to console her daughter. Sheryl felt tears welling up in her eyes.

Even though it had nothing to do with whether or not Maggie was after her husband, Sheryl couldn't help but feel moved by seeing the woman comfort her little girl. Sheryl felt like a monster for her treatment of Maggie.

"You okay?" Chloe noticed the tears in her eyes.

"Yeah, yeah." Sheryl reached into her purse and pulled out the pregnancy test to distract Chloe from pressing her; Sheryl wasn't even sure why she was crying. It wasn't like she had a child and felt some empathetic sadness over weeping offspring.

Before she could look at the test, Chloe grabbed the box.

"Hey!"

Too late: Chloe was already pulling out the test.

Chloe's eyebrows arched. "Oh, my God."

"What?"

She handed Sheryl the test.

Two lines.

Of course.

FORTY-SIX

Nick Kent

NICK PACED HIS FRIEND, Ron's, apartment, agitated, scratching his arms, wondering when the hell Vinnie would show.

"Where the fuck is he?"

"Relax," Gary said from the couch where he was smoking a joint with Ron, both of them playing *Call of Duty* on the Xbox. "And would you sit the fuck down? You're fucking up my high."

"How can you relax?"

"Because I'm not the one who fucked up. And you pacing like an idiot ain't doing shit for no one. So sit down, and chill the fuck out, Bro. He'll get here when he gets here, and then we'll get you out of town."

But Nick couldn't "chill" when a million volts of nerves were alive inside him. Sure, the bumps of meth he'd been doing for the last half hour didn't help, but the whole diner thing had been a disaster.

He'd lost control, and now that waitress might be dead.

He could be facing a murder charge, and surely he'd lost whatever chance he ever had of fighting for custody of McKenna.

And it was all Maggie's fucking fault.

Nick's dad was a legendary asshole, but he was right about one thing: women were *waaaay* more trouble than they were worth. He should've known that Maggie would pull a stunt like this — trying to steal his daughter.

He should've seen it coming with the constant criticisms. Was it his fault that he lost his job and everything went to shit around the same time? Sure, he drank and did some recreational drugs, but he wasn't an addict. Booze and coke helped him cope with the depression that came from not being able to find a job that paid more than dick. He was a far worse person to be around *without* something to dull his pain's edges. He'd lost his temper a few times and couldn't get a job, that didn't make him a monster — or give Maggie the right to take his child away.

He'd been stupid to think she was different from the other bitches in his life. She'd been sweet and naive when they met. Old Maggie would never have done something like this.

But maybe she didn't change. Maybe she'd always been like this, and *he'd* been the naive one, stupid enough to miss it.

Was she always *playing me?*

Maggie never complained back when he was making bank at his bartending job, easily bringing in four or five times what she pulled in from her shit diner job. But the bitch was out the door a few months after he got fired. Or, more accurately, *he* was out the door.

Had she always been a gold digger like the rest of them? Or did being around all the bitches at the diner change her?

The third option was a knife in his gut: *the nigger*.

They were fucking, and conspiring to clear Nick from the picture so he could swoop in and play daddy to McKenna.

"No fucking way!"

"What?" Gary said.

"I'm not letting them take McKenna!"

"Dude, just chill out, and sit down. Vinnie will be here

soon, and we'll figure things out. Right now, you're just annoying the shit out of me."

Nick's mind was a beehive. His heart was racing, sweat painting his face and body, the world closing its shutters around him. He needed another bump of meth *now*.

Nick reached into his pocket. The envelope was empty, though he'd been sure there was enough for a couple more bumps.

"What the fuck?" Nick dug through his pockets, fingers feeling around in case some had fallen out.

Nothing.

"Fuck! I'm out. You got any?"

Gary laughed. Of course he didn't. Gary did a line or two of coke from time to time, but he was *too good* for meth.

"I've gotta go."

"Go where?"

"I need to score."

"Shit man, you can't fucking wait?"

"No, I can't."

"Just smoke some of this." Gary offered Nick his joint.

"No! Give me your keys."

Gary laughed. "I am *not* giving you my keys."

"Then you're driving me."

"Driving you where?"

"Cappy's place."

"Oh, fuck that shit. I am *not* going to Cappy's place. Besides, Vinnie's on his way. Just wait. We can swing by your dealer on the way to getting you the fuck out of town, if you want."

"I'm not waiting, asshole! Give me your fucking keys."

Gary looked at Nick like he was trying to decide if this fight was worth having. While Gary might have been bigger and stronger than Nick, he wasn't nearly as vicious or willing to get down in the mud and fight like an animal. No way Gary

12

would win in a fight. And scrawny-ass Ron wouldn't do shit, especially baked as fuck-all.

Gary, seeming to size up the situation and realizing he wouldn't win, rolled his eyes. "Fine," he threw his key ring at Nick, "but you better get your ass back here the minute you score. And do not smoke that crap in my car! I don't need you stinking it up with that toxic shit."

Nick wasn't sure if he could wait that long, but he said okay and left, eager to settle his mind and feel human again.

FORTY-SEVEN

Dima Kosta

DIMA SAT ON THE TOILET, sneaking a few minutes away from work, staring at the wall of texts from Alicia that had piled on his phone in the past few hours. He hadn't dared pull it out on the way home, otherwise his mom might have thought to take his phone as punishment. He turned off the ringer, and buzzer, and bided his time until he could sneak off to the bathroom.

Now he saw how worried Alicia was since she last saw him getting dragged off to the dean's office.

WHAT HAPPENED to you and Tim?
I can't believe he freaked out like that.
I feel sooooo horrible!
Fuck. This sucks.
Hello? Are you okay?
Text me back. I'm worried.
Okay. School's out, and I can't find you. Someone said they saw you leave with your mom. So I guess you're suspended?
Text me back.

. . .

12

Dima was touched to see Alicia so worried. He felt awful that she'd been left in the dark for so long.

He texted back.

I'm suspended. Five days.

She responded fifteen seconds later. So she *was* waiting by the phone.

Alicia — *That sucks. Sorry. What about Tim?*

Was she really asking about Tim? That freak had started the fight. Hell, he probably did it to get sympathy from Alicia, his stupid way of trying to win her over. Tim was clueless when it came to girls. He thought they wanted to see someone like them, emotional, and sensitive. Tim didn't realize that girls didn't want someone like them. They saw *emotionally available* and *sensitive* as weak and needy. They wanted strength. Anything less, and they couldn't respect you. And if a girl couldn't respect you, she'd never let you in her pants.

Dima had been just as stupid as Tim last year, but that was the difference between them. Dima knew when to grow some balls and own his life. Tim was a whiny fucker who would never amount to anything because he lived his life with a victim's mentality.

He wrote back: *I don't know about Tim. His dad picked him up. I'm guessing he's fucked.*

. . .

ALICIA: *awww.*

Dima: *Hey, fuck Tim. He started this shit. He gets what he deserves. Maybe his dad will knock some sense into him.*

Alicia: *Really?*

Dima: *Yeah, really.*

Alicia: *You don't feel bad for him at all?*

Dima: *Don't tell me you're buying into his act. He wants you to feel bad for him.*

Alicia: *Whatever happened between you two? You used to be best friends.*

Dima: *I grew up. He refuses to.*

THERE WAS NO RESPONSE, and for a moment, Dima felt like his bluntness might push Alicia away. Maybe he was playing into Tim's plans, and Dima would be the asshole in all of this. No way he'd let that happen.

DIMA: *I get it, you feel bad for him. But Tim isn't the angel you think he is. He's just as hateful as the "bullies" he whines about. He just whispers shit behind people's backs like a sneaky two-faced fucker. Don't think he's so innocent.*

ALICIA WROTE NOTHING. Dima wasn't sure if she was mad, or maybe upset and crying. She and Tim had been good friends, so maybe Alicia was still on Team Tim, even after this little incident.

The Old Dima would've begged for her understanding and tried to convince her he was right. But Old Dima was no better than Current Tim — spineless, afraid to stand his ground.

He wouldn't beg. Either she'd get what he was saying, or not. He couldn't let himself worry like a little bitch.

12

He texted back: *Gotta get back to work. Seeya.*

DIMA DIDN'T WAIT for a reply. He returned the phone to his pants pocket, out of sight, even if not yet out of mind then stood and opened the stall door.

I'm not gonna be anyone's bitch.

Jeff walked in. "Whachya doin', jackin' off?" He laughed, punching Dima in the shoulder, hard but playful.

Dima wouldn't let him know it hurt. That was a bitch move. Instead, he sparred with words, like he'd learned to do over the summer.

"Yeah, your mom sent me tit pics, again."

"Yeah, you sure you don't mean my dad sent you dick pics, you fag?" Jeff said, pissing into the urinal.

"Wait, your dad is sending an underage boy dick pics, and somehow *I'm* the fag? Do you even think before you say shit? Man, I think you've had a few too many concussions. Maybe you should find a sport a bit more your speed, like bowling. I hear the Special Olympics is holding trials."

"Only thing I'm bowling is your bitch." Jeff zipped up and turned, holding three fingers as if inserting them into a ball. "*Ooh, Alicia.* Your holes are so tight."

"Fuck you," Dima said, playfully. He pushed Jeff back instead of punching him, sure his punch was weak-ass enough to earn him ridicule.

Dima washed up. Jeff just stood next to the door, laughing. "So, you hittin' that?"

"I'm not saying shit," Dima said. "Hey, Jeff, aren't you gonna wash your filthy-ass hands?"

"Nah, let the fuckers choke on my ball sweat."

"Wow, stay classy, my friend," Dima said then pushed his way out of the restroom and headed to the window to pick up Table Six's food.

Dima passed his mother, chatting it up with anyone who

would listen at the counter, annoying people with her stupid stories and donkey-like laugh. In a lot of ways, her behavior made him as uncomfortable as Tim's. Neither of them seemed to have a clue how people perceived them.

Doesn't she see that people don't like her overbearing presence? People want to come in and eat without the awkward entertainment. She's not Grandpa, and she should damned well stop trying to be.

Dima brought Table Six their food and noticed Jeff at Table Three, handing the family four baskets of fries, his germy fingers over the edge of one of the baskets, all over the food. The asshole was grinning. Dima couldn't help but hear Tim's voice in his head, echoes of a conversation they'd had when Dima first started talking to Jeff.

Don't people realize what a dick he is? It's like he's got the whole world fooled into thinking he's this awesome, cool, dude-bro, but in fact, he's just a shitty human being.

Dima had argued that Tim didn't give anyone who wasn't like him a chance. Dima felt proud that he was above Tim's judgmental ways and could see Jeff for who he was, a decent guy with a few issues who sometimes took things too far. But as Jeff winked at Dima, holding up his three fingers again, as if fingering Alicia, Dima wondered if perhaps Tim was right. Maybe Jeff *was* a shitty human. Sure, he was fun to hang out with, and could be funny as hell, but God help you if you were the butt of his jokes or the target of his wrath.

Dima shook his head, trying to bar Tim's negativity from his brain.

No, that's whiny Tim thinking. I don't need my friends to be perfect. Jeff is who he is. Holding him to any other standard or whining because he made fun of my girlfriend is stupid bitch-ass thinking.

Dima hated when he found himself thinking like Tim. Those thoughts were an infection, and when he let them inside, Dima could feel Tim dragging him down, making him feel more like Old Dima than New and Improved Dima. And Old Dima was still a rung higher on the social ladder than

Whiny Ass Tim — there was no way Dima would allow himself to be a social outcast, never again.

Fuck anyone who tried holding him back, including Alicia.

Tim whined that Dima had changed, that he was different. But why was that wrong? Especially if you hated the person you used to be?

Dima was tired of his old life. Tired of caring what everyone thought of him, of trying to please his mother (*impossible!*), and of being such a pussy. It wasn't until he started hanging around his father and sharing in a few enlightening, late-night discussions that Dima finally saw a different path.

For most of his life, Dima's mother had made his dad out to be an asshole. A selfish man who left his family for a younger woman and turned a blind eye to his responsibilities. Dima had resented him for years, believing his mother's version of history. In many ways, Dima was living like a victim, blaming his father for everything that sucked in his life. It was probably one of the reasons that he and Tim had been so close, bonded over a mutual hate of their fathers.

But during the past summer, Dima had spent more time with his dad and saw that the real story was vastly different from his mother's now obvious fiction.

It wasn't that his father had been selfish and left her for another woman. It was that he couldn't take her constant mood swings, her bitchiness, her jealous insecurity. She'd been afraid enough of her husband's infidelity to shove him out of her life with constant accusations.

Finally, he gave up fighting and decided that life was too short to devote to trying to make a miserable person happy. He decided to live for himself rather than under her thumb. And while it had been damned hard to not be there for Dima, it was far better than staying put and subjecting his son to their constant arguments.

Dima finally realized that his mother was doing a lot of the same things to him. No, she wasn't accusing her son of cheating on her, but she was possessive and always undermining him with guilt trips and slight insults. His life was lived with eggshells underfoot. Dima would never be happy until he learned to stand up for himself, and that meant crushing some of those shells to powder.

He couldn't cut his mother out of his life, but he could stop living to please her and snip the other most destructive force from his life — perhaps the most insidious of all, because it pretended to be his friend: Tim.

Dima wasn't happy with how things had gone down, and didn't really like being friends with the asshole, Jeff, but he wasn't about to go back to his old life as a weak-kneed, limp-wristed boy trying to please the world.

He went to Table Eight, grabbed the patrons' cups to refill them, and wondered if Alicia had texted him back.

FORTY-EIGHT

Corrine Walker

CORRINE SAT OUTSIDE THE DINER, wondering whether she should go in, or turn around and leave.

Ever since the meeting with Tim and his father, she'd been unable to shake the notion that her student was in trouble. From his eyes haunted by an obvious terror, likely scared of his father's response, to his dad's bizarre almost robotic reaction upon his arrival, Corrine felt scared for Tim's welfare.

She'd briefly discussed her fears with Dean Keller, but he said it "wasn't their problem."

If the principal wasn't already looking for a reason to get rid of her, Corrine would have gone to her directly. She briefly considered calling the police but only had her gut to go on. You didn't make an accusation like abuse lightly. If she was wrong, there was a damned good chance that Tim's father would make her regret it — with a complaint, a lawsuit, or both. And Principal Kern would have every excuse to let her go.

Corrine had considered taking the dean's advice, yet here she was in Goldman's parking lot, certain she was about to make a big mistake. But how could she, in good conscience, ignore the signs?

She couldn't.

Corrine got out of the car.

Get back in, and go home. You'll lose your job if you don't.

She closed the door and looked at the diner.

Dima might not be working. Go home, have a drink, relax before tonight's meeting.

Corrine ignored the voice and quickly walked toward the diner's entrance.

She opened the door and inhaled the scent of burgers, fries, baking pies, and any number of foods that wanted to demolish her diet. Her stomach growled.

The hostess greeted Corrine with a smile. "Hi, welcome to Goldman's. Are you dining in?"

"Is Dima working?"

"Yes."

"Can I sit in his section?"

"Sure thing." The hostess led her to a mirrored wall spanning the length of the building's west side then gestured at an empty booth.

Corrine sat, and the hostess handed her a menu.

Corrine held up her hand. "No, thanks. I know the menu."

She didn't know it, and had only been to the diner a couple of times, but Corrine didn't need the temptation. She'd keep things simple. A turkey sandwich and maybe some fries. Or better yet, a salad, no dressing.

"Okay." The hostess took the menu and retreated to her station.

Corrine fished the phone from her purse to check her messages and look busy to bury the oddity of sitting in her student's section.

Unfortunately, she saw Jeff before Dima.

12

Jeff approached, wearing his big stupid smile. "Hey, Ms. W, how's it going?"

"I'm good, Jeff. And how are you?"

"Awesome," he said with no trace of remorse. Corrine didn't think kids like him were capable of that emotion, alongside a host of other feelings separating humans from the future psychopaths cultivated in high school's toxic social experimentation lab.

They stared at one another awkwardly, or rather Jeff stared at her, grinning his asshole's smile while she tried not to steal a glance at her phone and let him win whatever game he was playing.

She maintained her gaze, wondering if he could tell how vile she thought he was. Part of her didn't care. If he could be bold enough to routinely terrorize the geeks, freaks, and other misfits he saw as helpless prey, then screw it — let him see her disgust.

He flinched first, looking down, then quickly looked back up with his smile repasted. "Okay, gotta get back to work."

"Very well," she said, feeling like some ancient disapproving schoolmarm.

Jeff slinked away. Corrine couldn't help but smile.

Dima appeared moments later, eyes wide, not meeting her gaze. This was how Jeff should have approached, with acknowledgement, if not guilt, of what he'd done earlier.

"Hi, Ms. Walker. Surprised to see you here."

She smiled. "Teachers have to eat, too."

"Yeah." He looked down at her table, clearly confused. "Do you need a menu?"

"No." Corrine had intended to get a turkey sandwich on rye with mustard, but now she thought about lunch and the burger and fries she didn't get to have. It felt stupid to deny her craving after such an awful day. Besides, a burger and fries weren't awful on their own, so long as she didn't eat too many fries or load a bunch of crap on the burger.

"I'll have a burger, well done, no fixings other than Swiss cheese."

"Okay, and a side?" Dima scribbled furiously — or nervously — on his pad.

"I think I'll have fries."

"And to drink?"

"Diet Coke, please."

"Okay," he said then left to leave her order with the kitchen.

She looked back down at the phone and saw a new text from Phil.

Still on for tonight?

She wrote back: *Yes.*

After a moment, she added: *I'm about to do something stupid.*

Phil: *WHAT?*

Corrine: *I'm going to ask a student if he knows if another student is being abused at home.*

Phil: *Which students?*

Corrine: *I'm going to ask Dima Kosta if Tim Hewitt is being abused.*

Phil: *What makes you think Tim is being abused?*

Corrine: *A bad vibe I got when his dad came into the dean's office. Tim looked terrified. Ghostly pale. Plus some stuff I overheard Tim saying to another student.*

Phil: *I might be concerned too given what he did today.*

Corrine: *It wasn't Tim's fault. He's being bullied. He snapped, but he's not a bad kid.*

Phil: *OK. Well, be careful. Call me if you need to talk or meet earlier.*

Corrine: *OK. Thanks. XOXO.*

Dima returned with a tall red plastic cup overflowing with Diet Coke, enough to spill some on the table.

"I'm sorry," he said, nervously, grabbing napkins from his apron pocket and wiping the mess.

"It's okay," she said.

12

Dima wiped down the side of the cup and met her eyes. Corrine could tell he was wondering why she was there, at his station no less.

Corrine thought she'd have a hard time working up the courage to ask him, delaying until her meal was nearly over, unsure how to surface the topic. But as their eyes met and the awkward moment stretched, words flew from her mouth.

"Can I ask you something?" She kept her voice low, in case Jeff was lurking in earshot.

"Yeah, what is it?" Dima leaned closer, looking eager to help if he could.

"It's about Tim."

"Oh." Dima straightened his posture, no longer leaning in or looking friendly.

"I'm not going to talk about earlier," she said, hyper aware that saying you weren't going to talk about a subject wasn't really all that different from bringing it up. "I want to ask you about his dad."

"Oh," Dima said, relaxing. "Yeah, what do you wanna know?"

"Do you know if his father ever … " she wasn't sure what to say. Hit him? Abused him? Turns out she didn't have to say either.

"Hit him?" Dima offered.

"Yeah."

"Oh, yeah. A lot."

"Oh, God," she said. "Like, bad? I mean, what kind of hitting? Spanking, or … "

"That, but also worse. He beats the hell out of him. A lot."

Corrine looked down, swallowing, fighting the welling tears as she imagined the hell he must be enduring.

"Did he tell you this, or did you see it?"

"He told me. I never saw it. His dad didn't really let me hang around. Seems I was a *bad influence* on Tim or something.

But I *have* heard his dad yell at him while we're on the phone. And he said some pretty horrible things."

"Do you know if Tim has ever told anyone else? An adult?"

"I don't think so. I think he's afraid."

"Okay, thank you, Dima."

"No problem," he said then left to take care of another table.

Corrine sat there shaking, not sure what to do. School policy was to report suspected abuse to the dean, but the dean had already said it wasn't their problem. That was insanity, but if Corrine came back now, he'd likely question why she went to investigate something she'd more or less been ordered to leave alone.

She needed Phil. He would know what to do.

She texted him back.

Can we meet earlier?

Phil: *I can meet you at 6:30. Where do you wanna meet?*

Corrine: *How about I swing by and pick you up for the meeting? That work? We can talk on the way?*

Phil: *Works for me. Anything you wanna talk about now?*

Corrine: *No. Better in person.*

Phil: *OK. Seeya then.*

When Dima returned with Corrine's burger and fries, his eyes met hers again. It seemed like he wanted to say something, but wasn't sure how to bring it up.

"What is it?"

"Before, when you asked about Tim's dad?"

"Yeah?"

"What made you ask?"

Corrine wasn't sure how to respond. First, there was the

privacy issue. You didn't share those details with other students. But then there was the potential blowback that could result from whatever Corrine did — or didn't do — next. The last thing she wanted to do was make things worse, or involve anyone she didn't need to.

"Just curious." She looked back down at her food a bit too quickly. If Dima was at all perceptive, he'd understand her discomfort and why she was holding back.

"Oh, okay." Dima left the table so fast that Corrine wasn't sure if she'd offended him or if he'd spotted another table in need of attention.

But then Corrine glanced up and saw that it wasn't either. It was the person who'd come through Goldman's front door: *Alicia.*

FORTY-NINE

Clarence Dumont

PATRICK SLAMMED Gary against the wall. "Where the hell is he?"

The apartment's only illumination, barely seeping through a crack in thick, filthy curtains, cast a gloomy light on the dark clutter alongside a paused game of *Call of Duty* glowing from the fifty-five-inch screen.

"I said I don't fucking know!" Gary's arms were cuffed behind him, eyes wide, neck veins taut like cables under his tight black tee.

Clarence turned to look at Vinnie and Ronald Dempsey, both sitting on the couch, clearly nervous as hell, not yet cuffed. Dempsey was a spent loser, arrested by Clarence and Patrick no less than a dozen times for crimes ranging from possession to petty theft. How the guy managed to stay out of jail long enough to keep landing jobs and places to live was beyond him. Either he was more connected than Clarence believed, or people genuinely liked the happy-go-lucky stoner.

Patrick, still holding Gary's face against the wall, turned and asked, "Hey, Dumont, do you believe this guy? That he don't know nuthin'?"

"No, I do not."

"Yeah, me neither. And that's a real problem for you, Gary. We thought you'd like to work with us like your pal, Vinnie. See, your buddy's smart. You," he said, thwacking Gary in the head with his index finger, "not so much."

"I told you I don't know shit. He was here, and said he needed to borrow my car."

"And you didn't ask him why or where he was going? Boy, maybe you *are* stupid as fuck. Did your momma drop you on your head when you were a baby, Gary?" Patrick ran his hands roughly over Gary's head. "I don't feel any indents, but ya never know."

Gary turned, practically frothing at the mouth, glaring at Patrick, barely able to mask his swelling rage. Clarence had seen that look before. A tough guy getting his ass handed to him by a cop. He was embarrassed, emasculated, and very likely imagining a scenario where Patrick wasn't a cop and they'd met in a back alley or bar. Gary was also likely picturing himself handing Patrick his ass.

But that would never happen, because unlike the musclebound pretty boy, Gary, Patrick was an authentic badass. A guy who didn't need to show off or strike a pose. He was big, awkward looking, and overweight, but beneath all that heft churned the heart of a bitter man with brewing anger at the injustices of the world perpetrated by assholes like Gary. And as much as Gary might wish that they'd met under other circumstances, without the law on Patrick's side, the officer yearned for it more — a scenario where he wasn't limited by his duty to the law.

Clarence looked down at Vinnie and Ronald then back at Patrick. "Screw it. Let's arrest them all. If Gary doesn't wanna talk, we'll book 'em all as accessories."

"No!" Vinnie said. "Say something, Gary! Tell them what they wanna know. Stop protecting that loser."

Through clenched teeth, Gary said, "Shut up!"

"All right, your choice, gentlemen." Clarence walked

toward the couch and made a show of pulling out two pairs of handcuffs.

Ronald broke. "He went to score meth!"

"Shut the fuck up!" Gary screamed, struggling to free himself from Patrick's hold.

"No, *you* shut the fuck up, Gary!" Patrick pulled on the man's ponytail, then shoved his face forward into the wall. Blood flooded Gary's mouth, coating his teeth, making him look even more like a trapped, desperate animal.

Patrick turned to Ronald, smiling, "Go on."

"He went to Cappy's, looking to score."

Nobody needed to ask who Cappy was, or where he could be found. He was a low-level dealer, an *associate* of Raul Luna, that the officers had their eye on, though the DEA had ordered them to lay off, as they were working on getting the bigger fish, Raul.

They couldn't just go to Cappy's, kick down his door, and arrest Nick. They'd have to work this through their superiors, and possibly the DEA, a prospect allowing for too many things to go wrong.

Clarence nodded for Patrick to initiate a private conversation.

"Have a seat on the couch with your boys." Patrick led Gary to the couch by his ponytail to further emasculate him then shoved him backward so he fell right between Vinnie and Ronald. None of them looked pleased by the seating arrangement.

Clarence met Patrick by the front door and whispered, "How do you want to handle this? You know if we run this up the chain, they're gonna tell us to stand down. Or worse, they'll take us off the case altogether, and suddenly this asshole, Nick, is being given protected status to help build a case against Raul."

"No, that isn't the way we wanna go."

"So?"

12

"I think we wait. We'll move the car and sit tight on the house, wait for our boy, Nick, to come home with his meth."

Clarence nodded. A big part of him wanted to go pick Nick up now, while they knew where he was, before he could do anymore stupid shit. But this was their best play. It seemed unlikely that Nick would return to the diner or his apartment, as there were cops sitting on both locations. Nick was probably in escape mode, not looking to fuck up more shit. And getting more people involved increased the odds that something would go wrong and they'd lose Nick.

Clarence didn't want to lose him.

He'd seen too many situations like this go south, and he had to protect Maggie and McKenna. That meant putting Nick behind bars with the best possible charge: the shit that went down at Goldman's.

Both the drug unit and the DEA introduced too many variables that Clarence couldn't account for. Too many ways a slippery fuck like Nick could wiggle free.

This wasn't just their best play. It was, sadly, perhaps their only one. Still, Clarence felt an uneasiness about not moving immediately.

Patrick, as if reading his thoughts, said, "We'll be patient and let him come to us. Cool?"

"Cool," Clarence said, even if he'd be feeling anything but cool until Nick was in custody.

FIFTY

Nick Kent

NICK FINALLY FELT HUMAN AGAIN.

After leaving Cappy's, he got back in the car, baggie in his pocket, eager to get somewhere he could grind it up and do a few bumps.

While smoking it might have been quicker at the moment, it didn't have nearly the same immediacy for him as snorting the crystals. Plus, snorting didn't stink up Gary's precious car as much.

He drove a few minutes, pulled into a Walmart parking lot, swung into a spot at the back, and got down to business.

This is more like it.

Like cocaine, it was impossible to recapture the intensity of Nick's first hit, no matter how hard he pursued it. But still, there was nothing quite like meth, especially after a period of abstinence, even a few days.

It felt like an antidote to poison. Once you ingested the chemicals into your body, you were back to feeling alive, like a video game power-up one bar from death.

Now he was ready for Ron's. Finally less anxious.

His hand on the knob, about to reverse and head back to Ron's, Nick had an epiphany.

12

All of the day's bullshit, from the accusations that he'd flattened Maggie's tires to the scene at Goldman's, none of it would've happened if he hadn't let her kick him out of their apartment.

How was I ever so damned stupid and weak to let her control me like that?

Didn't the marital vows say *in sickness and in health, 'til death do you part?* Wasn't an addict sick? He sure as fuck wasn't dead.

So how in the hell are we apart?

Again, he felt like pieces of some puzzle were sliding into place. For the first time, with a bit of chemical assistance, Nick was finally seeing the puzzle from above, and how everything fit.

Maggie had been planning shit for months, maybe a year.

She and her cop lover.

Suddenly, all those sideways glances that the staffers, and even some of the other patrons, had given Nick when he worked at the diner were starting to make sense. Everybody knew she was fucking the cop. And they were all laughing behind his back.

Ha, ha, poor white trash can't even keep his bitch from running off with a nigger.

Fucking cunt!

Nick pounded his fists into the steering wheel, feeling as if all those glances were born only yesterday. The pain, the embarrassment of being cuckolded by Maggie and the coon.

It felt fresh, and cut deep.

How dare that monkey swoop in and take my woman? Take my daughter?

It wasn't enough that the blacks, and the fucking illegals, were already stealing any job worth a damn while honest, hardworking white men couldn't keep a shit gig at a fucking diner. Now they were after the white man's family.

No fucking way.

Not a chance in Hell.

Not on my goddamned watch.

Nick flashed back to one of the arguments he and Maggie had before she kicked him out.

He'd come home from killing time with Gary and the boys, and McKenna was sitting at the table, playing with this nigger doll.

"Where'd ya get that?" He certainly didn't remember her ever having a nigger doll before.

"Uncle Clarence got it for me!" McKenna beamed with a big, innocent smile.

"Uncle Clarence?" He'd eyed Maggie to show his disapproval without getting preachy in front of the child. Though some liberal types would accuse Nick of being a racist, he didn't consider himself one at all. He didn't think blacks should have to ride in the back of the bus, use separate water fountains, or go to different schools and shit. *That was racism!* His father had thought like that, for sure. Nick was more culturally sensitive. He even had a few black friends. Not many, just the right amount. So he never tried to preach to McKenna, telling her who she could be friends with and stuff. He didn't want to pass the hate he inherited from his father on to her. If she could get along with the spooks, all the better. She'd probably be able to at least keep a job in the new America.

But he did draw the line at subtle things, like the nigger doll and TV shows. It was a subtle indoctrination of race mixing, the way he saw it. And it wasn't just that. It was the fact that these niggers were trying to make white people feel guilty — guilty for shit they hadn't even done.

Nick never had any slaves. He never lynched anyone.

But you give a nigger a foothold into your home, and they will try and turn your kids against you. Make your kids feel guilty for being white!

Nick hadn't said shit about the doll to McKenna. But

when she went to sleep, he went into her room, took the doll, and threw it in the garbage where it belonged.

Maggie had taken it out of the trash. "You can't throw her toy away!" the bitch said. "She'll know it's gone. What am I supposed to tell her?"

"I dunno. Tell her a nigger broke in and took it."

He'd thought that was pretty funny. But Maggie got all pissy and threw a fit. Asking him when the fuck he'd become such a racist.

"Is it racist to like your own race? It's funny that you call me a racist, yet those niggers can have all sorts of organizations, their own United Nigger College Fund, and yet *they're* not racist. What the fuck?"

Maggie exploded. Said he'd changed, and asked if he was back to using coke. He had been, of course, but he lied. Couldn't give her the benefit of being right.

Goddamn, she's so smug when she thinks she's right!

"I don't want you around our child like this," she said. "I don't want this for our child. I don't want her growing up in a house where she can't have a black doll or watch TV shows with black characters. This isn't healthy." Maggie burst into tears and short-circuited his anger.

Surprisingly, Nick felt guilty. Maybe she was right, and the drugs were making him an asshole. A racist asshole, at that. So he'd agreed to leave for a bit and get his shit together.

But now, as he remembered their argument, he couldn't help but see everything through this new filter, now that he knew how the pieces all fit.

She hadn't *really* been devastated that he was being mean, or racist, bad for McKenna to be around.

No, she was working to clear him from the picture, so her lover could swoop in and steal his bitch and baby girl.

"Fuck! How the fuck was I so stupid?"

He flashed back to the diner, how everyone had looked at him like white trash.

Like a fucking loser.

Laughing behind his back.

Who the fuck do they think they are?

Who are they to laugh at me?

They don't fucking know me, know the shit I've put up with.

He thought of Sebastian charging him with murder in his eyes.

The big Spic was probably fucking Maggie, too.

Or wanted to.

Nick had always thought Sebastian looked at Maggie like he wanted to stick his hard parts in her soft ones. And looked at Nick, wondering how *he* had got so damned lucky.

Nick had never thought much about it because Sebastian was too trailer trash — more so than Nick — for Maggie's tastes.

No, Maggie liked her men with a bit more money.

Golddigging cunt.

Nick would never give her the pleasure of suing for alimony. Or even child support, because she'd use the money for herself like every other lying cunt looking to bleed their man dry.

He'd rather be homeless than pay her each month.

Does she think I'm fucking stupid, Imma let her bleed me dry?

Take my girl, and my money, while she's fucking that pig?

No fucking way.

Nick squeezed his fists tight, wishing she was in front of him now. He'd only ever hit her once — and kinda by accident. But if Maggie were here in front of him now, he'd punch her right in the face. Punch her over and over, knock her goddamned teeth down her throat.

No, fuck that, I'd run the bitch over.

I'm drivin' a loaded weapon!

Nick laughed as he imagined Maggie under Gary's car. Tires crushing her skull, popping it like a melon, her eyes rolling out of their sockets onto the pavement.

12

He'd get out of the car and piss on her corpse, maybe fuck her skull.

Cunt!

Something clicked in his head. He thought back to the car as a loaded weapon then remembered.

The trunk.

His eyes widened. He could feel a smile spread across his face as a seed sprouted like Jack's fucking beanstalk in his mind.

Did Gary leave 'em in there?

He laughed, uncontrollably, feeling like he'd won the lottery.

He killed the engine, hopped out of the car, happy enough to shake on his way to the trunk.

He pressed the key ring button, and the hood lifted with a hiss.

Nick leaned down and pulled the black carpet out of the way, revealing the bounty Gary had left in the trunk from last weekend when they'd gone out in the woods to fuck around.

Two AR-15s with scopes and extended mags, a duffel full of ammo, and a Walther P22.

Fuck the car as a weapon. I got weapons as weapons!

Ain't nobody gonna be laughing now.

5 p.m. - 6 p.m.

FIFTY-ONE

Dima Kosta

DIMA ASKED Jeff if he would mind taking his tables so he could use his fifteen-minute break to hang with Alicia.

After Jeff said yes, likely eager to keep the tips for himself, Dima headed over to Alicia's booth. She had her backpack sitting on the seat beside her and seemed lost drawing in her journal. Dima wasn't sure if she was truly absorbed in the drawing of a long-haired boy, maybe a girl, riding some kind of dolphin in the sky, or if the page was a prop to ignore him. Alicia wasn't a drama queen like so many other girls in school, but Dima could see her coming to his job and ignoring him just to prove some kinda point. She was still a girl, after all.

"Hey." Dima sat on the other side of her booth.

"Hey," Alicia said, glancing up at Dima then returning her eyes to the drawing.

What the hell?

Why even come here?

It certainly wasn't for the food; she'd hardly touched the basket of fries or her drink, and Maggie had delivered both about five minutes ago. That annoyed him: Why didn't Alicia ask to sit in his section like she had in the past when they'd been just friends. Was she *that* pissed about Tim?

12

Dima watched her draw, like he had a hundred times, if not more. He'd never been quite as entranced by her artistic process as Tim had been, but he could certainly appreciate her talents. Sometimes, she got in the zone and tuned everyone out. But coming here today and ignoring *him?* It was impossible not to see that as her version of the silent treatment.

"So, are you mad at me?"

"Yes," she said, without looking up.

Great!

"Why?" he asked, sounding whinier than he'd like.

I sound like Tim.

Jeff walked by and made the sound of a cracking whip.

Dima couldn't even look at him, knowing the dumb jock was waiting to dig in. *Ooh, Dima's girlfriend is mad at him. Someone's not getting laid. Maybe I can slide my fingers in her.*

"Your friend is *real funny*," Alicia said, still not looking up, shading her background with tiny black lines.

"Ignore him."

"Is that what you tell Tim? Ignore the bullies?"

Dima sighed. Of course this was about Tim.

"As a matter of fact, yes, I did tell him that. Not that he ever listened to anything resembling good advice."

"Tell me, Dima." Alicia looked into his eyes. "Did *you* ever stick up for him?"

"What do you mean?"

"When those assholes you call your friends made fun of Tim, did you ever once stand up for him? Did you ever say, 'Hey, stop, Tim's my friend'?"

"I dunno. I'm sure I did."

"Hmph."

"What? You think I'm lying? Do you know how hard it is to be Tim's friend? He's embarrassing to be around and practically begs these guys to fuck with him. I tried to help him. I tried to get him in with the guys, but he refused. He acts like he's too good for them."

"Maybe he is."

"Yeah, but he doesn't have to act it. He could be cool like you. You get along with everyone. But Tim, he, he's just an asshole."

"He's awkward, yeah, but he's not an asshole. Not like your friend, Whipmaster General over there."

"Yeah, well if you like Tim so much, why don't you go to the dance with *him*?"

"Because I already said yes to this jerk named Dima." Alicia finally smiled to indicate that she wasn't *totally* mad. He felt like a raft in her churning sea.

"Besides," she added, "I don't like Tim like that. He's just a friend."

"Fair enough," Dima said, not sure where to take the conversation.

"I want you to make up with him."

"What? For real?"

"Yes, *for real*."

"How am I supposed to do that? Dude hates me. He thinks I'm a sellout and that I stole his girl. You really think *he* wants to make up with *me*? Did you not see the look in his eyes at lunch? He looked like a rabid dog."

"You can try."

"Why? What does it matter?"

"It matters to me."

"But why?"

"Because he's my friend, and that's not going to change. And he's a good kid with nobody else. Do you know how much life sucks when you don't have any friends?"

"How do you know? People have always liked you because you're pretty and kinda weird, and you fit in with everyone. But if you remember, just last year, I wasn't a helluva lot better off than Tim."

12

"No, I don't know personally, but a girl I knew online last year was bullied all the time, just horrendous shit, the kind of things nobody should ever do to anyone. The kind of shit *your buddies* do to Tim. Anyway, she couldn't take it anymore and killed herself."

"Damn," Dima said. "Why didn't you ever say anything?"

"Because you didn't know her. And besides, would you have cared? She was just another loser."

"I'm not like those guys."

"Prove it."

"How? What am I gonna do, make my new friends like Tim? Even if I could, Tim would still have a problem with them. He'd hate them for being jocks, being popular, doing drugs, whatever. Tim is a picky motherfucker for someone without any friends."

"I dunno, Dima. You're a smart guy. I'm sure you'll think of something."

Again, he sighed then looked at Alicia's fries. "Can I have one?"

"Sure." She laughed.

"What?"

"You're cute when you're defeated."

"You didn't *defeat* me," he said, laughing back. "And besides, I'm telling you, I can do whatever you want about Tim, but it ain't gonna change *him*."

"Maybe I can work on him."

"Good luck with that."

Jeff appeared at her table. "Hey, this guy bothering you? I can have him kicked out if you like."

"No, I think I can handle him," Alicia said with a killer smile that made Dima laugh harder. Jeff had no idea how much Alicia — and Dima — were laughing at him on the inside.

"Ah, well, he is rather small, and easy to handle, I hear," Jeff said.

Alicia responded with razor-sharp timing: "Yeah, your mom tell you that?"

"Oh, she nailed you!" Dima laughed loud enough to draw unwanted attention from patrons.

Alicia stared at Jeff with a killer's icy smile, but either Jeff was too dumb to notice she didn't like him or too full of himself to acknowledge it. He laughed along with them.

"Good one. I think Dima should hold onto you," Jeff said, retreating before she eviscerated him again.

Dima heard his mother's loud voice. "Ooooh, hello, Alicia. I heard you're going to the dance with my little boy. I always suspected you had a thing for him when you used to come by all the time."

"*Really*, Mom?" Dima felt his face burning bright red.

"Hello, Mrs. Goldman, and yes, we are going to the dance together," Alicia said, red faced as well.

Jeff, meanwhile, passed behind Dima's mom, holding a tray of food, smiling at his friend's embarrassment.

Dima looked up at the wall clock above the front register. "Okay. I've gotta get to work."

"You do that. Give us girls some time to talk."

"Really, Mom? I'm sure Alicia has to get going."

"No, I'm fine." Alicia smiled, seeming to enjoy his pain as much as Jeff.

Dima rolled his eyes, vented a frustrated sigh, and returned to work.

FIFTY-TWO

Tim Hewitt

EVEN THOUGH TIM'S tiny frame swam in his large black jacket, the gun bulged like a cannon. *Someone* would spot him as he walked drunkenly down the street on a mission to kill his bully.

But to Tim's surprise, none of the joggers, bicyclists, or homeless people he passed between his house and the diner seemed to notice him, let alone the gun in his pocket.

The world swarmed with its usual business, and like always, Tim was invisible.

Not for long.

He found a spot, a sheltered bus stop in front of the shopping plaza where Goldman's loomed a few dozen yards off, far enough to stand and spy without drawing attention.

Jeff was, in fact, working. So was Dima.

Tim smiled, thinking maybe he could get himself a twofer.

A skinny black guy in his midtwenties approached, wearing large orange headphones, a tangerine-colored backpack, and sneakers that matched them both. His jeans and shirt were both dark blue.

Tim felt his heart speed up with the man's approach, afraid he'd take a seat at the bus stop and notice Tim's odd behavior. Maybe he'd see the bulge in his jacket and call the cops. Or hell, take matters into his own hands. Most anyone could easily take Tim down.

Please keep walking.

Please keep walking.

The guy got closer, looked up at Tim, and nodded.

"Hey," Tim said as nonchalantly as possible.

The guy passed Tim then sat at the bus stop.

Shit. Just don't talk to me.

Fortunately, the guy seemed to be immersed in his music, staring at his iPad while waiting for the bus.

Tim returned his gaze to the diner's large windows, watching Jeff and Dima wait on customers, smiling as if they weren't assholes.

He'd already decided to kill Jeff; the question was whether he'd leave Dima alive. He *had been* his best friend. Could Tim really kill him because they'd had a fight and he'd stolen Alicia?

Tim flashed back to all the many times he'd spent hanging out with Dima, playing video games, shooting the shit, watching shows on TV that Tim's parents would never let him see. Dima's mom passed by the window, chatting with someone just out of sight. Tim swallowed. She'd always been kind to him, treated him like her own child: made him food, gave him money for the movies, and vowed to keep it secret that he was watching shows that he wasn't allowed to. Though Dima never seemed to appreciate her, his mother was pretty damned cool.

She was also pretty, with long dark hair and large breasts. Tim remembered one night in middle school that he'd slept over at Dima's house and they'd made a tent in the living room. He'd a hard time sleeping, tossing and turning through most of the night. Dima's mom had come out of her bedroom to get a drink sometime long after midnight, wearing black lingerie which was practically see through. He'd spied a fair glimpse of her breasts, nipples and all, through the sheer fabric. The first tits he'd seen in real life, and fuel for many jerk-off sessions to follow.

He'd thought of telling Dima a few times, just to mess with him and make his friend uncomfortable, but was afraid Dima would think he was some kinda freak. "Eww, my mom?"

And worse, Dima might tell his mom, which would be way too embarrassing to live down.

Tim watched Dima's mom pop back into view before heading into the back of the diner and felt a swell of guilt.

No, he couldn't kill Dima.

Despite everything, his ex-friend wasn't the enemy.

Jeff was.

Tim watched Jeff go from table to table with his stupid fucking grin. He couldn't wait to put a bullet in the asshole's face.

While Dima was *technically* innocent of Crimes Against Tim, Jeff was not. He'd verbally abused him for years and had finally become physical. Not just an ass whooping, but getting in his face and threatening to kill him.

If Jeff could kill him and get away with it, there was no doubt in Tim's mind that the dumb jock would.

He was a wretched person, a smear on the planet that needed to be cleaned. Someone had to do it, and it might as well be Tim before he went away — possibly for life — for killing his father.

Tim wondered if his mother was home. If not, she would be any minute, meaning the police would be looking for him soon. His picture would appear on TV. At first, he might be considered a possible kidnapping victim of whoever murdered his father. Someone had broken into the house, killed his dad, threw a bunch of cake at the body, then accosted Tim at gunpoint.

But any detective worth half a damn would quickly figure

it out. They'd have forensic analysts on scene, piecing together what happened. They'd know: *the son did it.*

Tim was more intelligent than roughly 95 percent of the people in his school. That didn't mean he was smart enough to outfox the cops. At least not without months of planning.

But today, he'd snapped without a thought.

And now, the clock to his crime's discovery was ticking.

Suddenly, Tim noticed that Dima wasn't working now but rather sitting at a booth. And he wasn't alone. He was talking to someone just out of sight. Tim couldn't quite see from his angle.

He moved to get a better look, walking away from the bus stop's shelter, and out into the middle of the sidewalk where, if anyone in the diner happened to look out the window, they'd easily see him.

Who is he talking to? Why isn't he working?

The other person came into view: *Alicia.*

Tim froze.

Why is she here?

His head hurt, confused. His walk to the diner had taken almost half an hour. The entire time he'd been imagining walking into Goldman's and blowing Jeff away roughly a hundred times in fifty different ways. But none of the scenarios had accounted for Alicia.

Suddenly, Tim realized someone was yelling at him.

"Hey, hey, man!"

He turned, surprised to see the black guy standing in the open door of the bus.

"You gettin' on?"

Part of Tim wanted to say yes, leave, and go wherever the bus took him: the other side of town, the end of the line in another city, wherever the busses ended their runs. Just get the hell as far away from his past as he could. Maybe start over.

But reality was quick to set in. He had maybe two hundred bucks in cash — not exactly enough to start over.

"Yo, you comin' or what?"

"No," Tim said, shaking his head. "Sorry."

The guy turned, and the bus door hissed closed behind him. It drove away, leaving Tim standing alone, staring at the diner, at Dima and Alicia talking and laughing.

How can they laugh after what happened today? Don't either of them give a shit about what happened to me?

He wondered if they were laughing at him.

Alicia would say, "Can you believe that Tim asked me out? Like he thought he stood a chance with *me*? As if."

"What a loser," Dima would laugh.

Then Jeff would come by, "Hey, guys, what are you laughing about? Oh, Tim? That faggot?"

They'd sit there having a grand time making fun of the loser.

No, Alicia wouldn't do that. She'd never do that.

But then Tim wondered how well he really knew her. Sure, they'd been friends since first grade, but so had he and Dima. Just that morning, he'd believed that Alicia maybe had feelings for him, too. There were so many hints: the way she sometimes looked at him and smiled, how she hugged him all the time, the way she would occasionally lean on him like he saw girls do with their boyfriends.

Why would she be so nice and do those things if she didn't like him at least a little? He never saw her act that way with other guys, not even Dima.

While he'd always thought Alicia would probably say no, simply because it was too good of a dream to ever come true, Tim didn't think she'd say no, just to go out with Dima! He didn't know her nearly as well as Tim did. Nor had he put in the time, caring for her, being there for her whenever she was down.

Yet here Dima was, doing none of the work that goes into a relationship and being rewarded nonetheless.

Tim felt sick to his stomach.

Dima had also become a raging dick not much better than Jeff. Alicia was friends with some questionable people, but she'd never been shy about telling an asshole that he was being an asshole.

Speaking of assholes, Jeff appeared at their table, grinning his idiot's smile.

Tim glared through the window, wishing he'd taken his father's rifle instead, not that he was practiced enough to pull off a shot from this far away.

He stared, his fingers caressing the pistol in his pocket. It no longer felt heavy and obvious, now warm and waiting to be used as his instrument.

Tim saw something he never thought he'd see — Dima *and Alicia,* laughing — *with Jeff.*

They are *laughing at me.*

Tears welled in Tim's eyes. His throat started closing.

He swallowed, wiped the tears with his left hand, and closed his eyes, preparing himself for what he needed to do.

After a couple of minutes, Tim headed toward the diner's entrance, hand in his pocket, finger on the trigger.

It's time.

Maybe I'll just kill 'em all.

FIFTY-THREE

Sebastian Ruiz

MOST DAYS, it seemed the rail was only there to mock you.

The more you needed to step away — whether you had to shit, were starving for a bite to eat, or had to make a phone call to find out if the mobster you were conspiring with had delivered on his promise to save your sister — the more tickets seemed to pile high.

Sebastian raced through ten tickets, getting meals to the window as fast as he could, watching the number dwindle when Bob started lining another six tickets from the servers.

Together, they cleared through the worst of the early bird rush. With the rail at a manageable level, Sebastian said, "I need to take care of something. You got this?"

"Yeah." Bob looked over as if he wanted to ask Sebastian if something was wrong. Bob took enough breaks to support his pack-a-day habit, so he probably wasn't annoyed, especially since Sebastian rarely took more than a few. But Bob could definitely tell something was going on. Fortunately, Sebastian had never let any of his coworkers get too close, particularly kitchen workers under his charge, so Bob didn't start asking questions.

Sebastian headed outside again, phoned Gino, and waited on a return call from Gino's secure line.

Seconds turned to minutes; Sebastian paced.

What's taking so long?

Sebastian went over to the dumpster in case Loretta came out for a smoke. He couldn't stomach small talk while waiting for Gino.

He paced behind the dumpster.

Come on, come on.

Six minutes had passed. He didn't have much longer before someone would miss him or the rail would get backed up again. Bob could handle small rushes, but if the diner got slammed, he'd fuck shit up and set Loretta on the warpath, wondering why Sebastian had left Bob alone.

None of this would be an issue if Loretta had let *him* do the kitchen hiring and paid enough to land more decent cooks. But like most shit jobs, management paid the pennies they had to and relied on a few loyal, good-hearted workers to carry the underfunded load.

In Sebastian's dream restaurant, he'd pay top dollar to secure the best servers and staff. He'd also pay top dollar for fresh ingredients rather than relying on the shit Loretta was willing to settle for. His costs would run higher, sure, but Sebastian figured customers would appreciate what he was doing and support him with their wallets.

He wasn't sure why the hell he was considering his future at a moment like this. Even if Gino's uncle came through, Sebastian now had a debt. He'd have to pull a job, likely high risk, to repay what was owed. And with people like Petr, one job was never enough. He'd get sucked back into the life he'd fought so hard to steer clear of.

How could he dream of a legit future while working for the Russian mob? In what reality could he do *one job* and be done?

12

In that moment, Sebastian was back to hating his sister and felt guilty for his twisted wish.

Sometimes, I wish she'd just die. Life would be so much easier if I didn't have to constantly look after her.

Sebastian shook his head, trying to clear the horrible darkness from his mind, lest he tempt the Devil into granting his horrible wish.

No, I didn't mean it.
I love Ana. I'd do anything for her.

The phone rang.

An ice pick stabbed his heart; the Devil himself might be calling. "So, I heard you had a wish. Consider it granted."

He looked down at the caller ID. Unknown name and number.

"Hello?"

Gino: "Hey, Sebastian. Bad news."

Oh no.

"What?" Sebastian braced himself.

"Shit went south. Big time."

"What happened?" Sebastian shouted into the phone.

"Uncle thought it would be a good idea to go grab Raul's sister. You know, make an exchange."

"He *what?*"

"Yeah, and things didn't work out too good."

Sebastian sank to the ground, ass slamming the rocky pavement.

"What happened?"

"We lost three guys."

"Oh fuck. Does Raul know who was behind it?"

"We don't know what he knows. My uncle hires guys that know how to keep their mouths shut. And I doubt he would've told them why they were targeting the sister anyway. So I'm not sure if there's any way this comes back on you. But there's a damned good chance he knows Uncle's behind it, and this could get ugly."

"What the fuck was he thinking? I knew he should've just paid the fucking ransom! Fuck, Gino!"

"I dunno what to say, man. You know Uncle didn't want to hand money to Raul."

"So, now what? I mean, you think there's any way that your uncle, or any of his men, would meet Raul and pay to get Ana back?"

"I don't think so."

"Can you lend me the money directly? Let me meet with Raul like I'd planned?"

"I wish I could help you, man."

"You *can* help me, Gino. Please, don't make me beg."

"There's not enough time to get my hands on that kind of cash."

Sebastian looked at his watch: 5:10 P.M. He cycled through his mind, trying to find some way to get the money before the hour elapsed. Robbing the safe was out of the question now.

Maybe he could ask Loretta to borrow the money then repay her tomorrow, assuming Gino could get him the money by then.

"How soon *could you* get the money?"

"I dunno … maybe tomorrow. You said you need it by six tonight, though, right?"

"Maybe I could borrow from my boss and pay her back tomorrow. Could you swing that? Please, Gino. I'll owe you. I can still do a job for your Uncle. But please, help me save my sister."

"Okay. I'll come up with something. You'll have the money mañana. I'll call you later tonight, we can work out the rest."

Sebastian sighed, wondering if he should inquire more about the dead men, killed while acting on behalf of Sebastian. But his concern would feel hollow. He hadn't asked the men to pull such a stupid-ass stunt. Maybe Raul would go after someone's family, but Sebastian liked to think he was above that. You didn't target innocents, even if it meant protecting Ana.

Instead, Sebastian said, "Thanks, Brother."

"Talk to you later."

Sebastian hung up then wondered if he should call Raul to check in, quickly nixing the idea after figuring Raul would likely get suspicious and link Sebastian to the attempt on his sister.

He'll probably make the connection: On the day he takes my sister hostage, his own sister's a target? One plus one equals Sebastian.

Fuck. Shit. Fuck.

Well, maybe he won't connect me to Petr Romanov.

No.

Bullshit.

He knows I was Gino's cellmate. He can connect the dots. He'll assume I'm behind this whole damned thing.

Sebastian pulled out Raul's cell. He checked the display to make sure he hadn't missed any calls or texts, and that the battery was still charged.

No calls. No texts. Battery at 80 percent.

He brought up Raul's number, his finger shaking over the call button.

No, I can't call him.

I've gotta play it dumb, or he'll kill Ana.

Just play dumb, wait for him to call, then say I've got the money.

But Sebastian didn't have the money — yet.

He stood, shoved Raul's phone back into his pocket, then headed back into the diner.

First things first. Gotta get the money.

Sebastian walked toward the diner's rear exit, wondering how he could ever convince his notoriously cheap boss to hand him seven grand.

He stepped through the door, and his eyes fell on the kitchen clock.

It was 5:15 p.m. — and time *was running out.*

SEBASTIAN KNOCKED on Loretta's closed office door.

No answer.

Maybe she'd gone home, or to the bar at the end of the plaza like she sometimes did during her shift. If so, maybe he could just take the money.

"Who is it?" she said, snuffing his hopes.

"Sebastian."

The door opened to Loretta, her nose red and eyes redder. Her office lights were off, save for the faint glow coming from the closed circuit monitor.

"You okay?" Sebastian stepped inside.

"Just a rough day."

She'd been laughing and joking a few minutes ago; Loretta's moods shifted like the wind.

"Anything you wanna talk about?" He closed the door behind him.

"I dunno, you got advice on how not to make your son hate you?"

"Dima doesn't hate you."

"We had a tough day today. He got in a fight at school with one of his best friends, well, former best friends. Then on the way here, he pretty much told me I suck as a mother. That I'm too hard on him."

"He's a kid. Kids say those sorts of things. Didn't you ever go through a phase where your parents couldn't do anything right?"

"I guess. It just feels like I'm losing him to his father."

The land felt full of mines, and no response could possibly resolve his pressing problem. Still, he said, "In my experience, things only get ugly when we stop talking. As long as you two are communicating, even if he's saying things you don't like, you still have a chance. Once one of you closes the door, *that's* when you worry."

12

Loretta sat back at her desk, grabbed a handful of tissues, wiped the tears from her eyes, and blew her nose.

"Thanks, Sebastian. That makes a lot of sense. You're pretty good at this."

"Yeah, well, I'm not so good at other stuff."

"What do you mean?"

"I need a huge favor. I mean a huge, gigantic favor that I have absolutely no right to ask."

"Sit down." Loretta pointed to a chair on the other side of her desk.

Sebastian sat, and told her everything, except for the part where he was planning to rob her.

"I can get the money tomorrow, I swear."

Loretta looked at him for a long moment of silence, her eyes still wet with tears, maybe for her son still, or maybe for his situation.

"Of course I'll help you."

Sebastian started to cry.

FIFTY-FOUR

Tim Hewitt

TIM PUSHED THROUGH THE DOOR, clanging the bell against the glass.

His breathing was more rapid.

His heart was pounding.

His skin tingled with the sensation that everyone was looking at him, as if they could see the gun in his jacket.

The hostess greeted Tim with a smile. "Welcome to Goldman's. Will you be dining alone, or are you waiting for someone?"

"Alone." He scanned the diner for his target but saw neither Jeff nor Dima. Just Alicia sitting alone at a booth along the windowed front, drawing, not yet noticing him.

The hostess grabbed a menu, led Tim down the row of tables, past Alicia, who still hadn't seen him, and sat him down in the booth directly behind her.

His stomach roiled, feeling like he was manning the wheel of a rickety old wooden ship fighting to stay afloat in a violent sea. It was all Tim could do to keep his hands from slipping off the wheel, let alone attempt to wrestle control, warring to keep whatever was left in his stomach after hurling cake and alcohol on his walk to the diner.

12

He stared at the back of her head moving ever so slightly while she focused on her drawing. He'd watched Alicia get lost in her art so many times over the years. To think that he might never see her do it again, or even see *her* for that matter, burned like hellfire. He wondered if she was drawing more of *Project Riding Hood*, or if she abandoned the story after his freakout. Who would want to work with someone so emotionally unstable?

As angry as Tim had been watching from afar outside as she and Dima laughed with Jeff, he couldn't maintain his anger toward her now just a few feet away.

Instead, he felt an overwhelming love. A need to get up, go to her table, and explain his side of things in hopes that she wouldn't hate him before he did what he did and got locked up for life.

When Alicia had first told Tim she didn't feel the same way about him, he wanted to be far, far away. If he couldn't have her love, he didn't *want* her friendship. But now, so close to her, he'd gladly settle for any speck of attention she was willing to give.

If you truly love someone, you want them to be happy, even if it isn't with you. Or maybe that was wimpy Friend Zone thinking, used to justify a loser's inability to find someone to love them. Tim didn't care: it was what he felt.

A waitress approached Tim's table, a pretty woman in her early thirties with long brown hair and big blue-green eyes. Her name tag read, *Maggie*.

"Hi. Can I start you off with a drink?"

Tim wasn't particularly thirsty, or hungry, but he *did* want to rinse the tang of vomit from his mouth.

"Yeah, I'll have a Coke, please."

"Sure thing." She smiled. "Do you need a few minutes to look over the menu, or do you know what you want?"

"I'll need a few minutes, I think."

"Okay, I'll be back in a jiffy with your Coke."

The waitress left. Alicia turned around.

"Tim?" A wide smile lit her face. She popped out of her booth, leaving her book bag and drawing supplies behind, and came over to his booth and pulled him into a hug.

She squeezed him tight. He clamped his mouth shut, worried that she'd smell the vomit on his breath while blinking back his tears, relieved she didn't hate him.

"How did you even get out of the house? I thought for sure your dad would've killed you."

Tim smiled at the irony.

Part of him wanted to tell her that he killed his father. But she'd freak out if he did. Any closeness between them would vanish, and she'd likely be frightened.

"I sneaked out."

"Holy shit! Way to go, Timmy Boy!" Alicia raised her hand for a high-five.

Tim slapped it, wishing as their skin touched that he could hold her hand and never let go.

"Okay, you have to tell me everything that happened!" Alicia went to her booth and moved everything — her bag, art supplies, basket of fries, and drink — to his table.

After moving everything, Alicia paused to meet his eyes.

"Oh, I'm sorry. I didn't ask. Do you mind if I sit with you?"

"If you don't mind sitting with me."

She smiled, slugging him on the arm, then sat. "I know things might be a bit weird, but Tim, you're like a brother to me. You're my best friend! I'm hoping what happened won't change that. Because I'm not sure I could stand not having you around."

The words *brother* and *best friend* felt sweet as they stung. He wasn't sure how to respond, so Tim said nothing, smiling nervously as he tended to do when uncomfortable. He was thankful that Alicia hadn't greeted him with an awkward silence like a lot of other people might have — hell, like Dima would. Just one more thing he loved about Alicia: she was never afraid to say what was on her mind.

Maggie returned with Tim's Coke. He felt thankful for the distraction.

"Oh, are you sitting here now?" Maggie asked Alicia.

"Yeah. And can you put Tim's food on my check?"

"You don't have to," he said.

"It's cool." Alicia held up her hand. "Your dad doesn't give you much money, and my parents practically pay me to relieve their guilt."

"Sure thing, single check," Maggie said. "Did you have a chance to look at the menu?"

"No, ma'am."

"Okay, I'll give you a few more minutes," she said then left.

Alicia looked at Tim as if he'd said something awful.

"Oh, wow, you just ma'am'd her."

"Huh?"

"You called her ma'am. Women hate that."

"They do?"

"Oh yeah, it's like calling them old."

"No!"

"Oh, yeah." Alicia dipped a fry into a tin cup of ketchup and popped it into her mouth.

"You're making that up."

"No."

"Nobody ever told me that."

"Tim, honey, there's lots nobody told you."

Tim laughed, feeling as if the day's tragedies existed in some other world. This Tim, in the diner with Alicia, was in another reality — one where no corpse rotted at home. The thought of his father's body creeped in, threatening to unravel his moment of normality, of happiness.

He denied his reality. "So, what were you drawing?"

"No, you first. What happened with your dad?"

Again he thought of his father's corpse, covered in cake, shit staining his pants. His mom had to be home by now. What was she thinking? Had she called the police? Were they already out looking for him?

The realization that he was living on borrowed time reminded Tim why he'd come to the diner.

Then his reason approached their booth, grinning like an asshole.

"Well, well, well, if it isn't my *pal*, Tim." Jeff stood where Maggie had been standing a few minutes earlier, as if he were going to be their waiter.

"Go away," Alicia said, meeting his eyes.

"Sorry, honey, in case you didn't realize, I work here. What's the big deal, I'm just dropping by to say hi to my pal, Tim."

His smile was pleasant, but his eyes burned with hate.

"We already have a server," Alicia said.

Dima came to the table. He looked down at Tim, then Alicia, and finally at Jeff.

"What's going on?"

"Just sayin' hi to my pal." Jeff grinned his asshole's smile.

The way he said *pal* made Tim want to pull out the gun and wipe the stupid fucking grin from Jeff's stupid fucking face.

His hand found the gun in his pocket, drawing comfort from the smooth handle at his fingers.

He wondered if Jeff had any idea how close he was to dying. No, of course not. Bullies like him never thought someone would end their tyranny, because most people rarely stood their ground.

Tim would never be *most people* ever again. He'd crossed the line from victim to sinner, and there was nothing stopping him from finishing what he started.

"Just go," Dima said, not hiding his annoyance.

Jeff backed away, eyes glued to Tim the entire time, then

turned back to Dima and Alicia, running a finger across his throat in a promise of what was to come.

If only he knew.

Dima turned to Tim. "What are you doing here?"

"A guy can't go out to eat?"

Dima shook his head, like he was about to argue with Tim, but turned to Alicia instead. "Is he bothering you?"

"No," Alicia said with a look that dared Dima to make an issue.

Tim realized that they'd had an argument about him. Apparently, he'd created a rift between the lovers. Part of him felt happy.

Fuck Dima.

Dima met Tim's eyes as if trying to suss him out. Dima knew him better than anyone. If anyone could guess why he was at the diner, the horrible thing he'd done, and the horrible thing he still planned to do, it was his former best friend.

Dima knew, even if he didn't yet know what he knew.

"Why are you here, Tim? How are you even allowed out?"

"He sneaked out," Alicia said.

"Really?" Dima asked, eyebrows arched.

"Yeah."

"So, um, how bad was it at home, with your dad?"

"Pretty bad," Tim said.

Dima leaned closer and whispered, "I dunno why, but Ms. Walker's here, and she was asking about you and your dad."

"Asking what?"

"I dunno. I think she wanted to know if your dad abused you."

"What did you say?"

"That he was a real dickhead. But I didn't know what I should say."

Tim looked around then saw Ms. Walker sitting in a booth against a mirrored wall. He nodded and waved. She waved back but didn't seem like she was about to get up and come over.

"I've gotta get back to work," Dima said.

"Ahem ... " Alicia looked at Dima.

"What?"

"You were going to say something to Tim?"

Dima looked down at the table then up to Tim. "I'm sorry about what happened earlier."

Tim wasn't sure if he meant the apology, or if Alicia was forcing it out of him, but Tim wasn't going to be a dick. "I'm sorry, too."

"Okay, I need to ... " Dima looked back at the kitchen then left.

Tim looked out the diner window, staring at nothing in particular, not sure what to say as an awkward silence settled over the booth.

"So," Alicia said, "what are you going to eat?"

"I dunno. I'm not really hungry."

"Order something good. Your dad might not let you out for months!"

"Yeah, I don't think I need to worry about him anymore."

Alicia's eyes met Tim's; he'd inadvertently begun his confession.

"What are you talking about?"

Tim swallowed and chewed on his lip, stalling as he tried to decide if he was going to tell her.

She'll know soon enough. Everyone will.

Her obvious concern made him want to confess everything, as if only Alicia could promise absolution.

"What are you talking about, Tim?"

"I killed him."

FIFTY-FIVE

Joe Harcourt

WHENEVER MAGGIE CAME to his table, Joe tried forcing himself to hand her the letter. But courage failed him every time. The envelope stayed facedown in front of him, hiding her name.

After she took his empty dinner plate, Maggie returned and asked if he wanted dessert.

He wasn't hungry, or ready to leave. Plus, he still had the uneaten cookie. If he left now, he'd never return, or give her the letter. She'd never know who her parents were.

"I'll have an ice cream sundae, please."

"Sure thing!" Maggie smiled.

Joe ran his fingers over the thick envelope. In addition to the letter, there were photos of Grace, and the two of them together, even a few with Grace's distended belly — the closest there would ever be to a family photo.

Joe thought of the photo, which he'd stared at at least a hundred times if not a thousand, mourning the life that could have been had he not allowed his jealousy, insecurity, and anger at Grace's affair to destroy everything.

He wondered how different their lives would've been. Most of their marriage had been happier than he had any right to expect. But without kids, their family had never truly felt like a *real family* to Grace.

They had tried countless times before she got pregnant from her affair. And again several times after. But apparently, Joe's plumbing was at fault. At the time, that had only served to make him more resentful of her lover, Bill Tamberlain, and more certain that he'd made the right choice in forcing Grace to give Maggie up for adoption.

Now, in hindsight's infinite wisdom, Joe saw that it was his fault that they never had a family.

His fault that Maggie lived with less than she deserved.

His fault that he'd never get to have a daughter or granddaughter. Maggie and McKenna (assuming Maggie had still married her husband) would've been Joe's by title, if not blood. And while that hadn't felt like enough back then, he would have gladly traded his last years of aching loneliness to have that family by his side. Blood was irrelevant.

Instead, he had a dog, an envelope with photos, and memories that would soon disappear.

Again, Joe found himself trying to remember the song Grace had sung to him so many times.

Dammit!

He balled his fists in frustration.

Again, he saw her by his bedside, looking at him with her big, blue eyes, singing while touching his face. Joe tried reading her lips in the memory, as if they were somehow perfect in recall and he could make something from nothing.

"Here's your ice cream!" McKenna's squeaky voice said as she carried the bowl carefully with two hands to his table.

Maggie stood behind her, with a second bowl, chocolate, covered in colorful sprinkles.

McKenna set the ice cream in front of Joe. "I'm back!"

"Do you mind if she sits with you again? She's better now."

Joe couldn't remember why the girl had gone away in the

12

first place. He vaguely recalled her crying, and hoped it wasn't something he'd said.

But dammit if he could remember.

"Sure, you can sit with me!"

Maggie left to wait on another table, Joe decided to stop grieving over a never-lived life long enough to enjoy McKenna's company. Because in the end, all anyone had was the present.

Nothing else was guaranteed.

FIFTY-SIX

Sheryl Dumont

"So, what are you going to do? Come on, Sheryl, we have to talk about it." Chloe had been on repeat for twenty long minutes.

At first, Sheryl had said nothing.

She'd changed the subject then flat out said she didn't want to discuss it. She needed time to absorb the truth that she was pregnant.

The news felt like both blessing and curse.

A blessing in that it could bring Clarence and her closer. Early in their marriage, he'd wanted children, many, in fact. But after years of trying, and the doctors telling her she probably couldn't have any, he'd let go of the dream.

But their broken marriage made it a curse, and having children never made marriage easier. If he *were* having an affair, then there was no way she could stay with him. Sheryl had too much self-respect to stay with an unfaithful man. She'd seen too many women try and make things work with men who swore it was just one time, and that they'd never do it again. But it was never just once. People cheat because they're unsatisfied. Getting caught didn't cure what led to the cheating — the crack in the relationship. She still wasn't sure

12

whether Chloe's husband was really faithful to her, or if Chloe was closing her eyes to the truth that he might cheat again.

While this fissure between them felt recent, Sheryl knew better. It had happened slowly: years of little things left unsaid, petty grievances clung to instead of worked out, and then suddenly, before either of them realized, they were standing on opposite ends of a gulf.

Even if Clarence *was* cheating, Sheryl couldn't blame this waitress. You can't steal a heart that's already taken.

It was on Clarence and Sheryl to either work things out or walk away before the baby came.

As Maggie approached, Sheryl stared at her, trying to see if she could tell she was guilty just by looking at her.

Is she the kind of woman who'd steal someone's man?

She was young, pretty, and had a perky smile. What wasn't to like? Maybe Clarence was able to talk to her in ways he couldn't talk to Sheryl. Maybe they had more in common. They both liked music, whereas Sheryl saw it as a hobby at best, and a useless distraction at worse.

"So, can I get you anything else?" Maggie asked.

Before Sheryl could stop herself, the words left her mouth.

"Are you fucking my husband?"

FIFTY-SEVEN

Maggie Kent

MAGGIE STARED AT THE WOMAN, speechless.

She could only manage to stammer. "W-w-what?"

"Are you sleeping with my husband, Clarence Dumont?"

"Clarence? *The cop?*" Maggie could barely believe the accusation.

Maggie thought the woman had been looking at her oddly since she came over but wasn't sure if it was just her imagination. She'd also felt a catty vibe from the woman and her friend, giving her the runaround, whispering behind her back. It hadn't made sense, until now.

They were sizing her up, trying to figure out if Maggie was sleeping with Clarence.

"Yeah, Clarence the cop. Are you sleeping with him?" Her eyes burned into Maggie. She was afraid that the woman was seconds from standing to slap her.

"God, no! I'm married. Married to an insane asshole, but married. The last thing I need in my life is another guy complicating things."

"Then why did you give him a CD of your music?"

"Because he's a friendly regular. He told me he wanted to be a musician but could never work up the courage. I told him

12

how I was putting my music on YouTube and thought he might be interested. He said he didn't really watch YouTube, so I made him a CD. That's all it was, I swear. There's nothing going on between me and your husband."

The woman stared for what felt like eternity. Maggie could usually read people well, but she wasn't sure what was happening behind the woman's fiery eyes. Anger, yes, but something else. Confusion? Sorrow? Maybe regret from asking the question?

The second woman's stare was equally odd. They seemed like they were both intent on coming into the diner to hate Maggie, but now had to consider that they might have been wrong. They didn't seem ready to let that anger go just yet.

"Why does my husband talk about you so damned much then?"

"I don't know." Maggie looked around, feeling the diner's eyes upon them. She lowered her voice. "I swear, I don't know. I get the feeling he has a hard time making friends, though. That he's kinda on the quiet side, and most of the other cops, at least the ones that come in here, aren't. He doesn't seem like he has many people he can talk to. I think he likes having someone who will listen to him talk about music and stuff."

Maggie realized how damning her words were, after they left her mouth.

"He has *me*," the woman said. "That's all he needs."

"I'm sorry. I didn't mean to imply anything. Listen, I don't know what you want me to say, or how I can prove I'm not sleeping with your husband, or am not even interested in him for that matter. Sure, Clarence is a nice guy, and he's helping me deal with my shitty husband who came in here earlier and sent one of our servers to the hospital. So maybe he talks about me because he's worried about me, I don't know. But I swear, there's nothing going on. The only thing that means anything to me is that little girl right over there, my daughter, McKenna. I don't have time for anyone, or anything, else."

The woman looked over at McKenna, eating ice cream with Joe, then back at Maggie, her eyes suddenly welling with tears.

"I'm so sorry," she said then stood and hugged Maggie.

Maggie felt everyone watching them, regulars, staffers, her boss, and even McKenna — everyone probably wondering what was happening.

"It's okay," Maggie said, awkwardly patting the woman on the back, just wanting to get back to work.

"It's just that I found out I'm pregnant, and I don't know what to do, or if Clarence even loves me anymore."

Her surprising confession made Maggie feel even more awkward.

"Do you think he loves me?" the woman — whose name Maggie didn't know — asked through sobs.

"Yes," Maggie said. "He talks about you all the time. I know he loves you."

"Really?" She pulled away and met Maggie's eyes.

"Really," Maggie said, hating to lie, but also feeling that this woman needed to hear these words, honest or not.

FIFTY-EIGHT

Nick Kent

NICK SAW the pig sitting in an unmarked car in front of the diner, so he wasn't about to go through the front doors.

He decided to head around back and parked behind a broken-down-looking van to get a good look at the diner's rear.

From his brief time at Goldman's, Nick was always surprised that no one ever locked the diner's back door during the day. Anyone could walk right into the kitchen and hell, into Loretta's office. Nick had even told Loretta, "Hey, you oughta lock this door." But she always gave him the kind of look you give a kid when he suggested something stupid.

The fact that nobody had robbed Goldman's before now was sheer dumb fucking luck.

Their luck just ran the fuck out.

He snorted another bump of crystal and closed his eyes as the jolt rushed through his body.

The meth made him feel like he had pure energy coursing through his veins, through his brain,

He felt like a god.

Nick stared at the back door, thinking of every indignity

he'd suffered in that diner. Sideways glances, snarky comments, whispers and giggling, countless lies from Maggie.

"No, they *do* like you. You just come off strong sometimes."

Bullshit.

He thought of Maggie.

You think you can fuck me over?
Steal my daughter from me?
Think I'll sit back and let you destroy me?
No, bitch.
No fucking way.

The back door opened, and Sebastian stepped out.

Nick grabbed the rifle.

FIFTY-NINE

Sebastian Ruiz

SEBASTIAN DIALED Raul on the burner, eager to tell him the good news — he had the money to make the deal. Bring Ana to the diner, and they could put this whole nasty mess behind them.

He paced behind the diner, waiting for Raul to answer.

After four rings and nothing, Sebastian was worried.

What if Raul connected the dots? What if he blames me for what happened?

Sebastian felt sick to his stomach.

Come on, pick up!

His heart raced faster. He hung up, dialed again, and returned the cell to his ear.

Answer the fucking phone!

Raul picked up.

"Why you calling me?" Raul asked.

"I've got the money."

"Too late."

"What do you mean *too late?* You said six o' clock!"

"That was before you sent those fucking Russians after my sister!"

Sebastian considered lying, saying he had no idea what

Raul was talking about, but if he played his cards wrong, Raul would shoot Ana on principle alone.

"I didn't ask for that. I swear! I called Gino to ask him to borrow money. I swear, that's all I asked for."

"He went after my fucking sister!"

Sebastian didn't bother to argue that Raul was doing the same thing by holding Ana hostage. Instead, he said, "I didn't know. I swear, Raul. Please, just come, get the money. I got it, and it's yours. Please, let Ana go."

"You know I can't do that, Sebastian. What kinda message will it send if I don't hold you responsible?"

"I didn't do it!" Sebastian yelled, not giving a fuck who in the diner might hear.

"Say goodbye to Ana."

"No!" Sebastian yelled.

Seconds later, Ana's voice was on the other line.

"Seb?"

"Ana!"

"Please, give him what he wants."

"I'm trying. Put him back on the phone."

Ana said, "He wants to talk to you."

A loud boom crackled in the phone, followed by the sound of a dropping phone.

"Ana!"

Silence.

"Ana!"

"Goodbye, Sebastian," Raul said.

"I'm going to kill you, you motherfucker!" Sebastian screamed into the phone. "Raul!"

The line was dead.

Sebastian stared at the phone in disbelief.

Ana was gone.

Just like that.

He wanted to cry.

He wanted to scream.

12

He wanted to murder Raul with his bare hands.

But Sebastian could only stare at the phone.

Something caught his eye — movement coming toward him.

He was confused at first then recognized Nick, a split second before he registered the rifle aimed right at his head.

Sebastian turned, both to dodge the line of fire and to warn everyone in Goldman's.

He didn't make it three steps before his back exploded in pain.

Sebastian fell to the ground, desperately trying to crawl toward the back door.

Nick pulled the trigger again and ended his struggle.

SIXTY

Maggie Kent

MAGGIE WAS STANDING on the other side of the window, loading Table One's food onto a tray, when all hell broke loose.

First, gunshots outside. The sound of automatic fire. The kind of thing you only hear in video games or movies.

Here, in their shopping plaza.

Close.

Very close.

She tried to tell herself that no, it was fireworks or something.

Then she heard the back door in the kitchen burst open, hitting the wall.

Oh, God, they're coming inside!

McKenna!

She turned from the window, scanning the diner for her daughter. McKenna was still sitting with Joe, both of them looking over at her, confused.

More gunshots, inside the kitchen.

Sebastian? Bob?

Screams erupted throughout the diner with the sudden realization that Death was coming.

And all at once, it felt like nearly everyone was racing toward the front door to escape.

No, no, no!

In the confusion, people were falling, and too many people were trying to get out the door at once, creating a logjam of screaming, crying, panicked people.

It felt like the jaws of Death were closing in on them and the diner was a trap.

She had to do something other than just standing there stunned. Paralyzed.

Maggie couldn't see through the crowd to the rear of the diner where McKenna was sitting with Joe, but she started to make her way back, not sure what to do other than try and get out of the diner with her little girl.

She would push, pull, claw, and bite to cut through the crowd if she had to.

She'd made it just a few steps when a familiar voice screamed her name from behind.

"Maggie!"

Oh, God, it's Nick!

She turned around and saw him in the kitchen doorway.

"Everybody stand still with your arms up!" he screamed.

People were still trying to flee through the front door. Maggie wasn't sure if they didn't hear him over their panicked cries, or if they were ignoring him, hoping to get the hell out.

Nick fired shots into the crowd.

Maggie turned, horrified, watching as Clarence's wife hit the floor. Her friend screamed just before bullets ripped through her chest. She fell beside her friend, in a quickly spreading crimson pool.

Three others were shot as well, two writhing in pain, the other, a short, old bald man, slumped against the front door with only two-thirds of his head left on his shoulders.

More screaming.

Maggie looked around for McKenna but couldn't see her.

Too many people between her and Joe's table, now obeying, hands in the air, many crying.

Maggie turned to Nick, mouth agape, unable to say anything.

Her heart pounded, her stomach churned in disgust, her mind raced, trying to figure out where McKenna was without alerting Nick to his daughter's presence.

She'd seen too many murder-suicides on the news. Parents who killed their spouse, and their children, no matter how young, before turning the gun on themselves.

She'd never understood how someone could kill their own child. Killing a spouse, sure. People get angry at one another. Rage bred violence. But what the hell did the children ever do to deserve such a fate?

"What are you doing, Nick? *Why?*"

"I got nothin', Maggie. You saw to that. You took my home. You took my daughter. You left me with nothing!"

"You don't have to do this."

"She's right." Loretta stepped forward. Jeff and Dima both cowered behind her. "We can work this out."

"Oh, we can? I should trust you? Ha! You fired me for no fucking reason! I blame you as much as I blame Maggie for this!"

"Please, Nick. We can help you."

"I don't need your fucking help." He fired several shots at Loretta.

Maggie stared in disbelief.

Dima screamed, falling to the floor beside his mother.

Loretta stared up at the ceiling, eyes rolling back in their sockets, blood gurgling from her mouth.

Jeff screamed, "You fucker!" and raced toward Nick, arms out like he was going to sack him.

Nick didn't flinch.

He fired straight into the kid's face and sent him to the floor.

12

"Anyone else got something to say?"

Maggie could do nothing but stare at the bodies, knowing she'd soon be among them.

Please, God, don't let McKenna die. Please.

SIXTY-ONE

Tim Hewitt

TIM HAD CONFESSED his awful truth to Alicia.

She sat beside him, holding him as he shuddered, the realization of what he'd done finally settling into his bones.

He'd killed his father.

He was going to jail for a long time.

His mother would never understand why Tim had done what he did. Why he couldn't just hang in there another few years until high school was behind him. If she did come to understand, she might blame herself for not doing something to stop her husband's brutality sooner.

She might even kill herself.

Tim wished he could take it all back.

Wished he could go back in time and take this whole fucking day back.

"It's going to be okay," Alicia said, hugging him, stroking his hair. "Everything will be fine. You need to call the police and tell them what happened. I can vouch for you, tell the police the things your father did to you. Dima can vouch for you, too."

"You think he would?"

"Of course he would. You guys are best friends."

12

"Were."

"No, *are*. This bullshit between you stops now. Friends come together in times of crises. I promise you that Dima will do the right thing."

For some reason, Tim felt some sense of hope, allowing himself to believe Alicia.

"Are you okay?"

Tim looked up, wiping tears from his cheeks to see Ms. Walker standing at their booth, concern in her eyes.

Tim looked at Alicia then Ms. Walker. "I did something bad."

"What?"

"I killed my father."

"Oh my God," Ms. Walker said.

"He didn't mean to," Alicia said. "His father was abusing him. He snapped."

"Did you call the police?"

"No," Tim said.

"You have to call the police," Ms. Walker said.

"I'm scared," Tim said, his body shaking.

"Do you want me to call?"

Tim stared at Ms. Walker, uncertain. This was all happening too fast. He'd come here to kill Jeff, not confess to murder.

But in the light of compassion from two of the few people in this world who seemed to care for him, his anger faded like a ghost.

Tim nodded.

Ms. Walker stepped away from their booth to make the call.

He stared at the back of her head. She was turned away, and he had to wonder what she was saying.

Any moment now and everything would be over.

The cops would be here, and he'd be led away in cuffs, never to see Alicia again.

He cried harder, feeling like an idiot.

Dima came over. "What's wrong?"

Alicia looked up to tell him, but she didn't get far before being interrupted by gunfire from outside.

Everyone in the diner turned toward the back of Goldman's.

The gunfire was closer — in the kitchen, joined by screams.

The diner went nuts.

People ran toward the door, screaming.

Dima and his mother rushed to the aid of an old woman thrown to the floor, helping her up and shielding her from injury.

Even if Tim wanted to get up, there was no way he could make it through the crowd.

He, and maybe five other diners, stayed put in their seats.

The gunman entered from the back, holding an assault rifle, shooting at diners rushing for the door.

Tim was glad that he and Alicia had stayed put.

The man's eyes were wide, crazy, and dark.

His hair was sweaty and disheveled. His clothes looked like they'd been on him for weeks.

Who the hell is he?

The waitress, Maggie, started talking to him; Tim realized he was her ex-lover or husband.

"Let's just stay put," Tim whispered to Alicia. "He's here for her, let's not give him a reason to notice us."

Then Loretta did exactly that, trying to reason with the madman.

The madman shot her dead.

Tim gasped, unable to believe what was happening.

He'd shot his father, but this felt different. Somehow more real.

Someone he knew, and liked a lot, had been murdered in front of him.

12

Dima cried out and fell beside his mom, probably trying to think of something, anything, that might save her.

Jeff, meanwhile, went full-on nuts, racing toward the gunman.

And then Jeff went down.

Tim was horrified again.

It was one thing for Tim to shoot Jeff. He'd earned the right. But this stranger came into the diner killing whomever the hell he wanted, and for what?

Nick, as Maggie had called him, turned and asked if anyone else had something to say.

"Hey, you!" Nick yelled, pointing his rifle, into one of the huddles standing along the aisle, "What are you doing?"

Tim turned to see who he was talking to.

Ms. Walker.

"Nothing," she said.

"I said hands up!"

She lifted her hands. One was holding the phone — the phone she was using to call the police. Maybe the police would get here before Nick could kill anyone else.

"Are you calling the fucking cops?"

"No," Ms. Walker said.

"Bring me your phone."

Tim's heart raced as he watched his teacher slowly approach the gunman, visibly shaking.

He had to do something.

He *could* do something.

Tim reached into his jacket pocket and grabbed the gun.

He was far, maybe twenty-five feet from where the gunman stood. A long shot for him, with a pistol, and Tim was only about 20 percent sure he could make the shot in the best of conditions, let alone in a showdown with a crazed gunman.

And so many lives on the line.

But if he didn't do something, Nick would kill Ms. Walker.

Tim pulled the gun from his pocket and felt Alicia's hand stop him.

"No," she whispered. "Don't. He'll kill us."

She was right. If he missed, Nick would fire back. And even a shit round of shots from an assault rifle would likely hit Tim and Alicia, plus countless others nearby. Nobody else would be dumb enough to rush him now that Jeff was dead and Dima was sobbing over his mother's body.

"Give me your phone," Nick instructed Ms. Walker.

She handed it to him.

He looked down at the screen.

Please, don't kill her. Please don't.

"You lying cunt! You called the fucking cops!"

"I—" she tried to say something, but Nick cut her down.

More screams.

SIXTY-TWO

Joe Harcourt

WHEN ALL HELL BROKE LOOSE, Joe knew he'd never make it out the door. He was too slow. Too frail. Nor would McKenna escape. They were both as likely to die by trampling as they were to be caught in a hail of gunfire.

So Joe did the only thing he could think to do — he hid, taking McKenna with him under the table. They were along the mirrored wall. Nick was standing at the front of the diner, near the counter, but didn't have a good angle to see under the tables, unless he started walking the aisle.

McKenna cried, "I want my mommy."

Joe covered her mouth, as best he could, whispering in her ear, "You've got to be quiet, or he'll hurt you and your mommy."

Nick shot more people; Maggie cried for him to stop; McKenna tried to wiggle free.

"Let me go," she cried, though he was able to muffle most of it.

"Please," he begged, "we have to be quiet."

Nick was yelling at Maggie again. "You did this! You thought you could take her from me? You thought I wouldn't stop you? That I'd let you just steal my daughter?"

McKenna managed to twist her mouth out from his grip. "Daddy!" she cried.

Joe's heart raced, wondering how far the girl's voice had carried. He froze, waiting for Nick to say something, or march down the aisle.

Would he shoot his own daughter?

Of course he would.

Men like Nick, so consumed with themselves above all others, had little regard for lives that didn't serve them.

Nick would kill McKenna and Maggie then like a coward he'd turn the gun on himself to avoid living with the guilt of what he'd done. Joe had seen this story play out on the evening news many times before.

McKenna tried to wriggle free, but Joe kept his grip tight around her, and on her mouth. "Please," he whispered, afraid he'd be heard.

Joe craned his neck to look across the aisle. There was a boy and girl sitting in the booth together, high schoolers it seemed, terrified, cowering like himself, hoping not to die.

Then Joe saw something which gave him a glimmer of hope and a palpable sense of dread.

The boy had a gun, just out of sight, under the table.

Did Nick only tell the people standing to raise their hands? Or is he just not noticing these two?

Would the boy play hero?

And if so, would he save the day or make things worse?

Joe hoped the boy wouldn't draw attention to the diner's rear. If Nick came back, there was no way he wouldn't find his daughter, and the old man keeping her under the table.

Joe had never felt closer to death. Even in 'Nam when he came face to face with that scared kid in a rice patty aiming an AK-47 at his face, Joe had never felt Death's shadow until after the fact. He'd been too scared and surprised to feel Death's breath on his skin.

12

But now, it felt alive, its dark tendrils slithering around the diner in search of victims.

He thought of the only other time he thought he might die, while in the hospital with pneumonia.

When Grace had sung him that song.

The song he couldn't remember.

If only she were here now, to sing and make everything better.

McKenna kicked, crying, "Please, let me out."

Joe saw Grace sitting beside his hospital bed, holding his hand, singing to him. But this time, he could hear her, too.

"Amazing Grace! How sweet the sound … "

I remember!

Tears streamed down his cheeks.

"Amazing Grace," of course! How could I forget that?

More gunshots.

These sounded different.

Are the cops outside, or is he using another gun?

McKenna cried, trying to break free again. If only he could keep her calm, keep Nick from finding her.

Then it hit him.

He put his mouth next to her ear and whispered:

"Amazing grace! How sweet the sound."

McKenna stopped fighting, listening to Joe, or perhaps comforted by a familiar song.

"You want a piece of me?" Nick shouted. "You fucking want a piece of me? Come and fucking get me!"

He had to be talking to cops outside, unless he'd lost his marbles and was fighting with a mirage.

Nothing would surprise Joe.

Maggie begged, "Please, Nick, stop before it's too late."

"It's already too late, bitch! Get over here."

"I once was lost, but now am found."

Nick screamed, "You shoot me, you shoot her!"

Joe imagined that Nick had ditched the rifle and was holding a pistol to Maggie's head.

That might have been a positive development for the diner's customers overall, but it wasn't for Maggie.

A gun to the head was a personal commitment, and easy to follow through with. Probably harder *not* to shoot her.

"'Twas grace that taught my heart to fear."

McKenna was still squirming but not enough to break free. She had quieted a bit, too. The song's effect made Joe feel like Grace was somehow reaching out from beyond the grave to soothe her granddaughter through him.

"And grace my fears relieved."

Joe wondered why he wasn't hearing any officers over a megaphone, trying to negotiate the situation. Perhaps the hostage team was still on its way.

He hoped they'd last long enough for the team's arrival.

"Please, Nick, let us go." Maggie cried. "You don't have to do this."

"Shut up!" Nick screamed.

There was a sound, him probably hitting her with the gun, and Maggie screamed in pain.

McKenna heard her mom and cried out, "Stop it!"

Joe's heart froze.

He turned and saw the boy and girl across from him looking down at them; they'd heard McKenna.

Nick must have, too.

"Babydoll, is that you?"

"Yes, Daddy!" she yelled before Joe could muffle her reply.

"Where are you?" Nick sounded somewhere between frightened and angry.

Joe held her mouth shut.

She kicked and squirmed, trying to break free.

If he let her go, she was dead. Along with her mother.

"Where are you?" Nick yelled, voice coming closer.

Too close.

12

"Don't come out!" Maggie shouted, her voice also closer. He must've been marching her down the aisle at gunpoint.

"Shut up!" Nick screamed.

Joe turned, seeing Maggie's and Nick's legs to his right.

"Let my daughter out," Nick growled.

Joe didn't dare look out. He turned his back to the man, holding McKenna tighter.

"No," Joe said.

"Excuse me? I said let my daughter go, you old fuck!"

"No!" Joe yelled.

Joe heard movement behind him. He barely had time to suss out what was happening before Nick was dragging him out from under the table with one hand, a gun against his head with the other.

Joe held up his hands. "Okay, okay, I'm coming!"

Joe stood, hands in the air, next to Maggie, helpless to do anything but wait and hope that Maggie, or maybe McKenna, could convince Nick not to kill them.

Was there anything resembling a heart left in the killer?

"Come out, baby girl." Nick bent down and scooped up McKenna, holding her with one hand under her bottom as his other hand aimed the pistol at her mother and Joe.

"Why are you doing this, Daddy?"

"Because your mother was very mean to Daddy. She tried to take you away from me. But we're not gonna let that happen, are we?"

McKenna said nothing, tears streaming down her red cheeks.

"I asked you a question," Nick said, his face inches from McKenna's. "Are we?"

"Are we what?" McKenna asked, confused.

"Who do you want to live with, Mommy or Daddy?"

She shook her head, either not wanting to answer or afraid that the answer would lead to more bloodshed.

"Who do you want to live with?"

McKenna pointed at her mother.

Nick glared at Maggie.

"You poisoned her against me."

"No, I didn't."

"Stop fucking lying!" Nick fired two shots at Maggie.

Joe screamed as Maggie fell down.

McKenna screamed.

Nick turned the gun on Joe, firing once, hitting him in the chest.

Joe fell back, pain exploding through his upper body.

He looked over at Maggie, also shot in the chest, lying on the floor, hands clutching her gushing wound, eyes wide in shock.

McKenna screamed, pummeling Nick with both her tiny fists, demanding he let her down.

Finally, he dropped her.

Time slowed to a crawl. Several things happened at once.

Nick glared at McKenna with the same poisonous gaze he'd given her mother.

McKenna ignored him, turning and dropping beside Maggie, crying for her to get up.

Nick raised the gun, aiming at the back of McKenna's head.

Joe tried to get up, move forward to stop what was about to happen. But the pain was too great, and he fell to his knees instead.

The high school boy at the other table, the one with the gun, stood and yelled, "Hey, you!"

Nick, seemingly surprised to realize the boy had been sitting at the adjacent table the entire time, turned to look at the boy.

The boy fired — emptying his gun into Nick.

McKenna screamed as she watched her father fall. Then she turned back to Maggie, burying her face against her mother's shoulder, wailing.

12

Joe's eyes welled up, thankful that the boy had finally ended the madness.

McKenna was okay, though in torment at the moment. But she wasn't shot.

Maggie was hurt bad though, maybe dead.

Joe reached up to grab a hold of the table to pull himself up, so he could go to Maggie and offer help, even if he wasn't sure what he could do.

His hand found the table, his head swam, his vision blurred at the edges.

He looked down to see what looked like a gallon of blood gone from his body and fell into darkness.

For a long moment, Joe felt nothing, saw nothing, heard only the sound of voices around them, concerned, calling for help. For him, for Maggie, for all of Goldman's.

He heard cops rushing in, radios squawking.

Joe wanted to open his eyes to see if Maggie was okay.

He needed to know.

But then he heard a sound in the distance: Grace, singing.

Amazing grace! How sweet the sound ...

He followed her voice, eager to join her after too many years.

Epilogue

CLARENCE DUMONT

CLARENCE STEPPED INTO THE DINER, over broken glass and a blood-spattered floor, his stomach churning, careful not to disturb the crime scene, or get in the way of the forensics team gathering evidence and photographing the scene.

He'd barely made it into Goldman's before seeing a corpse he recognized: Sheryl's friend, Chloe.

Her dead eyes stared up at the diner's ceiling tiles.

Clarence had to turn away from her face.

He looked down, among the bodies, searching for Maggie. His heart stopped when he saw something that shouldn't be there.

Clarence leaned down, not caring about rules of evidence, and picked up the purse.

"Hey," one of the forensics guys said, "what are you doing?"

Clarence ignored him, opening the purse and fumbling through it until he found the familiar wallet.

No, no, no.

12

He opened it, already knowing what he'd see — his wife's driver's license.

Clarence dropped the purse, looking around among the other bodies, and down the aisle at the crowd of paramedics tending to patrons. "Sheryl! Sheryl!"

He couldn't find her.

"What's going on?" Patrick asked.

Clarence ran back outside, screaming, "Sheryl!"

There were too many people.

Too much chaos.

Too many lights blinding Clarence as he looked around, his heart racing, his breath short.

Sheryl was here with Chloe.

Where the hell is she?

She wasn't on the floor, among the bodies, which meant she was either being questioned by the cops, or …

Clarence looked over to the chopper, where three paramedics were rushing two wheeled stretchers.

He ran after them.

"Wait!"

The paramedics either didn't hear Clarence, or were ignoring him to get the patients aboard the trauma copter.

Clarence attempted to get a glimpse of the patients, but couldn't see a thing from his angle. The paramedics reached the chopper and were met by another paramedic waiting at the open helicopter door.

The third paramedic, a young black woman, turned as the others started to load the stretchers onto the chopper.

"Who are the patients?" Clarence asked, not giving her a chance to speak.

"I don't know their names. Two women, gunshot wounds, in critical condition."

"What do they look like?"

"One in her late twenties, white, brown hair, blue eyes, a waitress uniform."

Maggie.

"And the other?"

"Thirty something black woman, gunshot wounds to her stomach."

Clarence pushed past the woman, despite her pleas to wait, and made it to the chopper in time to see Sheryl being secured. Her eyes were closed; a paramedic was working to save her.

"Oh God, Sheryl!"

~

Four hours later...

CLARENCE DUMONT

Clarence sat, head in hands, praying for his wife to get out of surgery. The waiting room was mercifully empty save for McKenna lying on a pair of chairs he'd pushed together side-by-side. He'd covered her with his jacket while she waited for her mom to wake from surgery.

Maggie's surgeon had said things were looking good, but it was too early to know for certain. Social Services was going to take McKenna, but Clarence said that she'd stay with him until they had news on her mom.

She'd been through enough already. McKenna needed a familiar face, and in a way, Clarence needed someone to be there with him, someone to be strong for, even as he felt his world crumble around him.

The surgeons didn't say much, but given how long they'd been operating on Sheryl, he was preparing for the worst.

Clarence couldn't stop wondering why she'd been at the diner. Sheryl had always made fun of him for eating at "that trashy dive," so why would she go? He definitely didn't picture Chloe being a fan of Goldman's.

A TV on the wall had been broadcasting from the diner all night, showing pictures of Nick Kent, photos of his gun, pictures of the kid, Tim Hewitt, who was being called both a hero and a murderer for having killed his father earlier.

The death toll was nine and counting, including: Chloe; Loretta; the cook, Sebastian; the server, Jeff; a teacher, Corrine Walker; and an old man Clarence had seen at the diner many times, named Joe Harcourt. There were others, though none whose names or faces seemed familiar to Clarence.

He hoped to God that Sheryl's and Maggie's names wouldn't be added to the tally.

If only we'd nabbed Nick sooner.

Clarence was pissed that he allowed red tape to keep him from going after Nick when they heard he was at Cappy's. They could've had him then. But no, Patrick had convinced him it wasn't an option with the DEA having an undercover agent in place and building a case against the drug lord, Raul Luna.

But Clarence couldn't blame Patrick; he was following the rules. Though what good were rules when they protected a scumbag like Nick and a fucking drug lord while nine innocents died in a diner?

Because of rules, he might lose Sheryl, and McKenna might lose her mother.

Again, he wondered why Sheryl had been there.

Her purse was on the floor beside him. Patrick had handed it to him before heading back to the station for a week's worth of paperwork. Clarence looked at the purse, as if it might hold some answers. He reached down, careful not to wake McKenna, and grabbed it.

He opened his wife's purse, feeling like an intruder.

It was so weird holding something of Sheryl's when she was fighting for life in a nearby room.

He'd been to enough crime scenes, to appreciate the surreal feeling of combing through dead people's belongings.

She's not dead.

Stop it.

McKenna let out a sound, which might have been crying, and turned a bit in the chairs.

Clarence looked over, waiting to see if she'd wake and need consoling. He watched her eyes rolling beneath their lids, her mouth twitching. He hoped she wasn't having nightmares of what she'd seen.

He imagined she'd have a lifetime of nightmares, particularly if Maggie didn't pull through.

It was all he could do not to cry for McKenna. If he allowed himself to break down, he wasn't doing anyone any good, not her, not Sheryl, not Maggie, and not himself.

He had to stay strong, for just a while longer.

Thankfully, McKenna fell back asleep.

Clarence looked back down into Sheryl's open purse and saw all the usual stuff — makeup, cell phone, gum, pads, a small spiral notebook, about a dozen different pens, and something that wasn't usually in her purse: a Walgreen's bag with something inside.

He pulled it out and saw the box: a pregnancy test.

Oh, God.

Clarence reached inside with trembling fingers, pulled out the test, and saw the result.

Oh, God.

～

Twelve months later...
 Los Angeles, California

MAGGIE KENT

12

. . .

MAGGIE WOKE TO GUNSHOTS.

She bolted upright in bed, terrified until she realized that the gunshots were only in her nightmares.

Everything was all right.

The clock read 7:01 a.m. Morning light spilled through her sheer white curtains.

McKenna was lying beside her. She must've come into her room late last night to sleep.

McKenna was doing well more days than not but didn't like sleeping alone. Maggie didn't mind.

Hoss whined at the foot of her bed.

"Need to pee?"

The German shepherd wagged his tail.

"Come on," Maggie whispered, getting up and leaving the room.

Joe's letter for Maggie had answered many of her life's biggest questions, and left her a sizable sum to start her life over, along with his dog.

Hoss was a sweetheart, and McKenna loved him.

She slipped on her sneakers and took the dog into the backyard. Having a yard was great. Between her record deal and Joe's money, Maggie didn't have to worry about money for the first time in her life. She didn't have to work at a dead end job, or choose between work and time with her family.

Still, Maggie had been through too much in her life to ever feel totally secure. It was impossible to relax and assume she'd made it, so Maggie was taking online college courses in business administration, in case the music thing turned out to be a temporary stroke of luck.

Hoss was taking forever to find a spot. She thought about Joe's letter, which had warned her that he might be finicky, especially if it was the slightest bit cold.

She missed Joe. He'd died protecting her and McKenna,

and any anger Maggie might have felt for his role in her life couldn't stay aflame when weighed against his sacrifice.

She often thought of Joe during breakfast, wishing she could've talked to him and learned more about her mother.

Following his death, Joe's estate had sent Maggie a treasure trove of photos, documents, old vinyl records, books, and even Grace's wedding dress, not that she'd ever rush into marriage again.

For the first time in Maggie's life, she felt relatively secure, and relatively whole. She no longer felt like someone discarded by her parents. She knew why, and it wasn't that she wasn't loved.

Just knowing that her mother had loved her, as had Joe, made Maggie's future brighter.

~

TIM HEWITT

IT WAS VISITING day at East Florida Treatment Facility. Tim sat in the rec room, wondering if his mother would come.

He was surrounded by crazies, some quiet like him. Others were prone to violence. A few talked to themselves or people they imagined beside them.

Despite the court's opinion, as well as that of several doctors that Tim had seen since his arrest, he wasn't crazy, and didn't belong here.

He hated how alone he felt and hated it more when his mother didn't show up on visiting day.

It had been two weeks since her last visit. A part of him wondered if she hated him for ruining her life.

Dr. Martinez claimed that her behavior was normal, and that she was simply dealing with her own process, even a year after the murder.

12

"Nothing will ever be the same, and the best we can do is move forward, slowly and patiently."

Easy for him to say. The doctor wasn't sentenced to ten years in a psychiatric hospital.

But, as Dr. Martinez pointed out during one of Tim's more depressing spells, he was lucky to have stayed out of prison, or worse.

Tim's nurse, Tina, approached.

"You have a visitor."

"I do?" he said, perking up a bit.

Tim followed Tina to one of the visitation rooms, surprised to find that it wasn't his mother waiting.

"Hi, Tim." Alicia smiled and waved, as if unsure whether she could hug him.

Or scared of the crazy person.

Tim waved back, tears filling his eyes. He hadn't seen or heard from Alicia since the diner incident. He thought she hated him. Maybe blamed him for not saving Dima's mother. Dima surely held him responsible.

Tina slipped out and closed the doors, leaving them alone in the small room with the couch and TV.

Tim sat on the couch, nervous, wondering why Alicia was here but grateful to see her.

She sat next to him.

On the ground, he saw her backpack, same one she'd had that day in the diner.

"How's it going?"

"You're looking at it," Tim said, twirling a hand in the air. "Lots and lots of this."

"Well, at least you have TV. Do you have games or books?"

"They do have a game area in the rec room, but I don't play much. Mom brings me books every now and then, but not nearly enough."

"Well, you'll be happy." Alicia reached into her bag and

started pulling out hardcovers from some of his favorite authors: Stephen King, Clive Barker, Neil Gaiman, Brent Sanderson, the newest George R.R. Martin book in the *Song of Ice and Fire* series.

"Oh wow!" Tim picked each one up, inspecting the jackets. "These must've cost a fortune!"

Alicia waved her hand. "Nothing's too much for my best friend."

He met her eyes and smiled, glad she still considered him her best friend. Her eyes were filling with tears, too.

"Thank you," he said. "This is so awesome of you!"

"I would've brought them sooner, but, well, I wasn't sure you wanted to see me."

"Why wouldn't I want to see you?"

"I don't know. Maybe you hated me because of Dima and me being an item."

While Tim didn't know for certain that Alicia and Dima were together, he figured they were and had been jealous. But he wasn't about to make her feel bad.

"How is he?"

"He's OK. Was tough for a while, but he's living with his dad and coping."

"And how are you two?"

"Sometimes good, sometimes bad, but I don't want to bother you with my love life."

"It's okay. I don't mind. It's not like I have anything else going on. There's only a few people here I like talking to. Everyone else is kinda scary or weird."

"I bet," she said. "But still, I've got something better to talk about."

"Yeah? What's that?"

"Well, you kinda started this thing and left me hanging."

"What's that?" he asked, confused.

Alicia reached back into her bag, retrieved a red hardbound journal, and handed it to Tim.

He opened it and saw an unlined journal filled with writing and drawings. The front page showed an intricately drawn forest with branches twisted around a dark circle of black ink.

In that ink, written in white space were the words:

Project Riding Hood
by Tim Hewitt & Alicia Bailey.

Tim smiled, turning pages to see that she'd started writing the story, but had petered off around chapter 4.

"I'm hoping you can help me finish."

Tim closed the book and held it close to his heart, "Thank you. I'd love nothing more."

~

CLARENCE DUMONT

The last thing Clarence wanted to do on his birthday was meet his old partner, Patrick. Even if lunch was at his favorite restaurant, the Steak House.

Clarence had been working as an insurance investigator for Lloyd's firm for eleven months. Yet every time he met Patrick, lunch still eventually fell into a conversation about when Clarence would be ready to come back.

Why couldn't he understand that Clarence was never going back? He'd spent nearly a decade tilting at windmills, and what good had he really done? Sure, he'd solved a few crimes, locked up some bad guys, and made the streets a bit safer, but when it came to cleaning the streets, politics and red tape kept them from doing the job they needed to do.

Clarence was tired of fighting.

"Working for the man" was the best decision he'd ever made. He only wished he'd taken Sheryl's advice sooner.

He parked his car then went inside and was greeted by the hostess.

"Clarence Dumont. I'm meeting a friend. Patrick Allan?"

She looked down at the chart on her hostess station and found where she'd seated Patrick. "Right this way, sir."

She led him past the bar toward the restaurant's rear.

Man, they must be busy if they opened the back room.

But the back room wasn't open.

The hostess opened the door and led Clarence inside to a room packed with around forty people, all standing around.

He was confused for a moment, wondering why people from his new job were hanging out with people from his old one. It hit him when they all said, "Surprise!" in a chorus.

As they began to sing "Happy Birthday" to him, Sheryl approached holding their baby, Ava, and gave him a big kiss.

"What?" The singing stopped, and the room applauded. Clarence was still surprised to see so many people he knew all in one room.

"I wanted to do something special for my special man," Sheryl said. "Patrick helped me put it all together."

Clarence looked up to see Patrick standing in the corner with his girlfriend, Mona. Patrick lifted his beer, winking.

"Thank you." Laughing, Clarence kissed Sheryl then moved his lips to Ava's head. His baby girl gave her daddy the precious smile that always melted his heart.

Clarence stood surrounded by a room packed with people who cared about him. Old friends he hadn't spoken to in forever had come to celebrate his birthday.

To think how he'd nearly lost everything a year ago. He'd been close to losing his marriage, close to losing his wife, and close to never having a child.

But something happened in the hospital that night when

12

he was sitting with McKenna. She'd woken up when the doctor came in and said that Maggie was awake. Just like that, her sadness had faded. McKenna had lost her father and witnessed brutalities that might scar her for life, but in that moment, she didn't seem to care. Her mother was alive, and that was all that mattered.

When the doctors came in and said that Sheryl was okay, Clarence had an epiphany. She'd been right. He'd spent a lifetime trying to change the immutable past, and in doing so, neglected his present. He'd almost lost it all.

But then, inspired by a child who had come close to losing everything, Clarence realized how much he had. And in that realization, he stopped fighting the past, and started fighting for his present.

THE END

What to read next

Where her law ends, his justice is only beginning …

Detective Mallory Black's world shattered when her daughter was murdered. Jasper Parish is a vigilante who hunts killers that escape traditional justice. They failed to save Ashley Black. But the man who killed her is back, and another child will die unless Mallory and Jasper can save her.

Get the complete No Justice Box Set

Author's Note

We're all going to die.

Unless there's some remarkable leap in science in your lifetime which allows you to attain immortality, your days are numbered.

As are those of everyone we know.

I think I first became obsessed with death when I was a child and my grandfather died. Prior to that, death was something that happened on TV shows, in comic books (though comic book deaths were rarely permanent), and in the movies. But not in real life.

My grandfather's death hurt.

But it didn't shake me nearly as much as the next death.

In high school I had a close friend, whom I'll call J. She was a bit younger than me, and infinitely more carefree. We hung out all the time, riding our bicycles (before either of us had access to a car) and we'd find places to hang out where we shouldn't be — closed down restaurants, fenced off areas, a park that was under construction where we'd hang out on a dock. And we'd have these great conversations. We'd talk about the weirdest most fantastical stuff — aliens, ghosts, what we'd do if we could go back (or forward) in time — the

Author's Note

sorts of things I'd always thought on my own but never talked about with friends, particularly girls.

She was weird and geeky in all the same ways I was.

And I loved her. She might be the first girl I truly felt like I loved. Like the painful way you want to be with this person so much that when you're not, you feel empty sorta way.

Of course I was too damned chicken to tell her. I was a fat kid with a pizza face, and my few awkward attempts at something more were met with rejection.

So I settled for her being one of my best friends.

The thing I remember most about her, though, is something she told me in secret. Something she told me she'd never told anyone before.

She knew that something bad was going to happen to her.

And while she was prone to saying things to get attention or to endear herself to someone, there was a look in her eyes when she told me this that shook me to my core.

She was so convinced that she even made up a secret code that she'd tell me if she were ever in trouble. How she'd get this code to me, I have no idea. But at the time, I don't think either of us thought it out that thoroughly. And neither of us really thought how paranoid that notion was.

Over the years, she started changing. She was being accepted by a cooler crowd (kids with cars, too) and she suddenly had no time for me. In a lot of ways, I felt like she'd "broken up" with me. It hurt like hell.

While I was an insecure kid, I had enough sense (and a bit of self-confidence) not to beg someone to be my friend.

Flash forward a few years. I'm out of school, am a bit more confident, and have a lot more friends. Well, for me, anyway.

One night I had this weird moment. I thought of J and her code word for her being in trouble. I don't know if it was my OCD or some unexplainable phenomena (the kind she

Author's Note

and I would talk about a lot), but I was suddenly convinced that she was in trouble.

I decided to call her.

I felt totally stupid doing so. She had pulled away, not me. Yet, if she was in genuine trouble, I would have been there for her. She still meant a lot to me. I still treasured our time together even if I no longer loved her in the same way.

No answer.

This was before cell phones. And I don't remember if her family had an answering machine so I can't remember if I left a message or if I just hung up before I could.

In any event, I didn't attempt to call her again.

I felt stupid for even trying to repair something that was probably better left broken. I felt weak, like I had been when she knew me.

That was Old Dave.

Besides, I had a feeling that someday we'd be friends again. A friendship as strong as ours had been could recover from anything, right?

Flash forward a short while later.

I'm hanging out with my future roommate at her father's house when I hear about a shooting on TV. A news reporter is live on the scene where an estranged boyfriend has killed his girlfriend.

Happens all the time.

Except this time, the name is one I know.

J.

And I just stared at the TV.

No.

Not her.

It can't be.

Can it?

It was.

I felt as if someone had blown a hole in my world.

Flash forward again, another year.

Author's Note

I'd been thinking about J a lot. I know if I'd tried harder to reconnect that maybe I could've prevented her death. I don't know how. Hell, maybe her boyfriend would've shot both of us, I don't know.

All I do know is that there's this hole in me where she used to be. And I feel horrible for her, her family, and for the young child she left behind.

And I can't stop thinking about how she knew something horrible was going to happen to her. Some part of me feels like the only reason I thought of her was because somehow, some way, she was reaching out to me.

And I didn't answer the call.

At this time, I'm working graveyards at a gas station. I've become friends with a cop (who is also friends with my now roommate), and we're shooting the shit one night.

I asked him what's the worst call he ever got.

He started to tell me about this shooting he responded to a year or so ago.

As he was talking, too many things seemed familiar.

I asked the victim's name.

It's J.

He was there when she died.

I needed to know more. Every detail.

He then got behind me, putting himself in the shooter's role, holding me, just as the shooter was holding J.

It was all I could do not to break down right there.

Flash forward a few more years.

I'm working graveyard shifts at yet another gas station. Hey, this writing career took years of toiling away and honing my craft at gas stations!

When I wasn't writing or drawing my comics, I was reading up to four newspapers a night.

I couldn't help but notice a pattern of stories about mass shootings. Every time it felt like the same story, just a few

Author's Note

details changed. Following each shooting, the papers would explore every facet of the shooter's life.

Who was he?

Why did he do it?

What could've been done to prevent it?

Didn't anyone know this guy was gonna snap?

Always the same story, with the shooter becoming something of a celebrity while the victims' lives faded into the background, mere footnotes to the story the media wanted to tell.

The death of J, along with these stories, inspired me. I wanted to write something about a mass shooting which delved more into the lives of the people involved. Not just the shooter's.

I wanted to write about fate, destiny, and paths not taken, and how the smallest event can turn into something horrible.

12 is my attempt to find catharsis from something you can never really come back from.

12 is also about how we're all going to die, and what we do with the hours we have left.

Thank you for reading,
    Dave (and Nolon)

A quick favor...

Thanks for reading *12*.

If you enjoyed this book, please leave a review on your favorite bookselling site so others can enjoy it too. Just a couple of sentences would be great.

Thanks!
Nolon & Dave

Special Thanks

Thank you to Jason Whited, Steve, Mike, Christine, and Terry Boen for your invaluable experience and knowledge. You helped us get into the heads of these characters and flesh out the story in a way we couldn't have done without you. Thanks to Garrett Robinson for proofreading, even if the story was too dark for you.

About the Authors

Nolon King writes fast-paced psychological thrillers set in the glitzy world of entertainment's power players with a bold, insightful voice. He's not afraid to explore the darker side of human nature through stories featuring families torn apart by secrets and lies.

Nolon loves to write about big questions and moral quandaries. How far would you go to cover up an honest mistake? Would you destroy your career to protect your family? How much of your soul would you sell to get the life of your dreams? Would you cheat on your husband to keep your children safe? Would you give in to a stalker's demands to save your marriage?

∼

David W. Wright is the co-author of edge-of-your-seat thrillers including the best-selling post-apocalyptic series *Yesterday's Gone*, the paranoid sci-fi *WhiteSpace* series, and the vigilante series, *No Justice*, as well as standalone thrillers *12*, and *Crash* which was recently optioned for a movie.

David is an accomplished, though intermittent, cartoonist who lives in [LOCATION REDACTED] with his wife and son [NAMES REDACTED.]

He is not at all paranoid.

He is "the grumpy one" on *The Story Studio Podcast* with

fellow Sterling and Stone founders, Sean Platt and Johnny B. Truant.

You can email him at david@sterlingandstone.net

We swear, he almost never bites. Unless you feed him after midnight.

Also By Nolon King

Cold Justice

Cold Justice

Cold Reckoning

Hidden Justice

Hidden Justice

Hidden Honor

Hidden Shame

Hidden Virtue

No Justice

No Justice

No Escape

No Hope

No Return

No Stopping

No Fear

Once Upon A Crime

Once Upon A Crime

Twice Upon A Lie

Three Times a Murder

Dead For Good

Dead For Good

Left For Dead
Dead Of Night
Wake The Dead
Dead For Life

Stand Alone Novels

Pretty Killer

12

Blown

Miserable Lies

The Target

Secrets We Keep

Close To Home

Heat To Obsession

A Simple Kill

Tell Me No Lies

Red Carpet Black

Fade To Black

Victim

Also By David W. Wright

Cold Justice

Cold Justice

Cold Reckoning

Hidden Justice

Hidden Justice

Hidden Honor

Hidden Shame

Hidden Virtue

No Justice

No Justice

No Escape

No Hope

No Return

No Stopping

No Fear

Karma Police

Jumper

Karma Police

The Collectors

Deviant

The Fall

Homecoming

Yesterday's Gone

October's Gone
Yesterday's Gone Season One
Yesterday's Gone Season Two
Yesterday's Gone Season Three
Yesterday's Gone Season Four
Yesterday's Gone Season Five
Yesterday's Gone Season Six

Tomorrow's Gone

Tomorrow's Gone Season One
Tomorrow's Gone Season Two
Tomorrow's Gone Season Three

Available Darkness

Darkness Itself
Available Darkness Book One
Available Darkness Book Two
Available Darkness Book Three

WhiteSpace

WhiteSpace Season One
WhiteSpace Season Two
WhiteSpace Season Three

Stand Alone Novels

12
Crash
Emily's List

Threshold

The Secret Within

www.ingramcontent.com/pod-product-compliance
Lightning Source LLC
LaVergne TN
LVHW031535060526
838200LV00056B/4499